I0763492

THE RISE AND FALL OF THE FOURTH REICH

Published by: Owens Publishing LLC

www.owenspublishing.com

Facebook: neal.owens.733

Instagram: owenspublishing

Introduction

At the downfall of the Third Reich, high-ranking and wealthy members of the Nazi party fled to the autocratic regime in Spain to plan the Fourth Reich. The leader of these former SS, Gestapo, and Nazi intelligence officers was a man named Heinrich Dorfmeister. He was the intellectual leader of the SS think tank and had a backdoor business partnership with Joseph Stalin.

At the end of World War II, the Soviet Union had stretched its grip across Eastern Europe, and Communism replaced Nazism as the biggest threat to the United States of America.

To combat the threat, the CIA recruited the Nazis in Spain to work as spies and consultants because of their expertise on Soviet Union affairs. In return, the Nazis received asylum in the USA and increased wealth.

Those war criminals found kinship in the America First Coalition, whose ideology was ultranationalism, and used their wealth and influence to help certain political candidates get elected to Congress and the White House.

With Fascism disguised under democracy, these far-right-wing members of the Elephant party planned the rising of the Fourth Reich in America.

Chapter 1

On the Nuevos Ministerios highest floor, a beautiful fräulein's accented voice came over the office intercom, "Herr Dorfmeister, an American man is here to see you."

Dorfmeister paused with his eyes narrowed and lips tight. "Is he alone?" he said in German.

"*Ja.*"

"Let him in."

The gray-haired American entered wearing a brown fedora and a brown three-piece business suit with a long matching coat draped over his left arm. His right hand gripped a brown leather briefcase.

As if he had been told, the American stopped behind the gold-accentuated, black-leather barrel chair that faced the artfully arranged executive desk. Dorfmeister sat behind it with a fearless expression on his Errol Flynn semblance. He leaned forward with his hands clasped on top of the desk. "Have a seat."

The American sat with his hat on top of the folded coat. The briefcase lay at the side of the chair.

After seconds of staring at the American's unreadable expression, Dorfmeister said, "Are you going to tell me why you're here, or do I have to guess?"

"My name is Evan Scott. I'm with the CIA, here on official U.S. business. We have a proposition for you."

Dorfmeister's brows lifted over tight-lidded eyes. "What does the CIA want from me? I don't know where Eichmann is."

"We know where he is. It's only a matter of time before the Israelis track him down."

"Israelis? Are the Allies giving those vermin their own state?"

"Soon."

"Soon! Jews aren't humans. They are lower than animals. They don't have the right to exist!"

The American didn't seem fazed by those words and said, "I'm not here to talk about them. I'm here to leave with you as a friend."

"A friend?"

"Yes, a friend."

"I don't have any American friends."

"You do now, and in very high places."

For a few seconds, the only sound in the room was the voice of Kurt Weill singing "Speak Low" from the desk radio.

"Mr. Dorfmeister, we are both enemies of Communism. That is enough to start a friendship."

With eyes seemingly in deep thought, Dorfmeister unclasped his hands, leaned back, and said, "What do you want from me?"

"Now that the war is over, we need to remove the threat of Communism from spreading around the world and believe you and some of your associates can help."

"How?"

"By spying and working as consultants."

Dorfmeister's lips pressed upward before he said, "Spying? Why would I spy for the Americans?"

"Because we have mutual interest?"

"Mutual interest?" Dorfmeister stood in his tailored black-striped, double-breasted silk suit, white silk tie, and a white silk handkerchief in the breast pocket. He stared at the American before sauntering to the open-pane window and gazing at the snowfall in downtown Madrid.

He turned and faced the American. "I thought you were here to arrest me for war crimes."

"Why arrest you? The Third Reich has fallen, 1946 is less than a month away, and you're one of the Party leaders whose face isn't known to the world. That's very beneficial to us."

"Beneficial?"

"Yes. While most of the powerful persons in your Party stepped out from the shadows when Hitler paraded through Paris, you, among a few others, were smart enough to stay out of the light. No one is looking for you but us—and you can help us in our fight against Communism."

"How did you find out about me?"

"We are the CIA."

Dorfmeister held the wry smile. "Do you know why I'm wearing this Hugo Boss suit?"

The American sat in silence with eyes seemingly reflecting the search in his mind for an answer.

Dorfmeister stepped closer and said, “He was a member of the Nazi party and designed the SS uniform. That is where my loyalty lies. My honor is loyalty.”

“Under a different name, we share your loyalty. We also share your blood and soil.”

Dorfmeister seemed surprised by those words. And with a deep-thought expression said, “What makes you think that I can help you?”

“You were in the room with Stalin when the German–Soviet Frontier Treaty was signed and began a business partnership with him that day. You told Hitler not to betray the Soviets, and Stalin knows it. That is why he is continuing to do business with you here in Spain. He knows you hate Communism, but democracy more. Consequently, he will not consider that you or your associates are working with the Americans.”

“You want me to spy? What do you want my associates to do?”

“You and your associates are experts on Soviet affairs. We need your expertise against the Soviet Union.”

“If I help you, what becomes of my wife and children?”

“A home in America, with new names and a prosperous business. The house will accommodate your lifestyle, and the business will thrive while working for us.”

“I already have a prosperous business.”

“We can make it more prosperous. Germany and other parts of Europe are going to be rebuilt. Your trading company is currently operating in Spain, South America, and the Soviet Union. We will expand it throughout Europe, Australia, and America.”

“Am I to come to America?”

“Not initially. We need you here in Spain. When your work is done, you will join your family.”

“And when will my work be done?”

“A man of your talents and connections... shouldn’t be more than three years.”

Dorfmeister chuckled slightly. "You want me to be away from my family for three years?"

"No. You can visit them twice a year for a week. Christmas and Easter."

"Twice a year? What do I tell my wife and children when they ask why I'm always away?"

"Of course you need to tell your wife the truth. The children will believe whatever you tell them."

"What is my name in America?"

"Henry Smith, born in Gillette, Wyoming, in 1903."

Dorfmeister laughed. "With this accent, who will believe I was born in America?"

"Our records show your American father married an immigrant from Switzerland. He died the year you were born. The following year your mother returned to her Germanic community in Switzerland, where you finished your schooling and met your fiancée. In 1933 your fiancée received a visa, and you returned to America and married her."

"What happened to my mother?"

"She died in Switzerland."

"What about pictures of my mother and father, and my wedding pictures? Where are those?"

"There was a fire that destroyed your house in Gillette—and everything in it." He lifted the briefcase. "Everything is in here."

Dorfmeister's brows and eyelids lifted. "The Americans have a Germanic community in Switzerland that can vouch for me and my mother living there? And also knowing my wife? And who are the people that will say I've been living in Wyoming since 1933?"

"Mr. Dorfmeister, we have communities and people that work for us all over the world."

With attentive eyes Dorfmeister slid his index finger across his chevron mustache. "What are the names of my wife and children?"

"Your wife's name is Margaret. Your children are Shawn, Leigh, April, and Summer. The child in the womb is Theodore, if a boy, and Julia, if a girl. Everything you and your family need to know is in this briefcase."

"May I see it?"

"Of course." The American stood, opened the briefcase, and handed him the folder inside.

After scanning a few of the pages, Dorfmeister glared at the American. "My family and I are safe in Spain. No one, not even the U.S., can touch me here. I'm not interested in working for you because I don't want to live in a democracy when I don't have to. I don't need your money. I'm already a billionaire."

The American grinned, back-stepped, and sat. "One-point-two billion to be exact," he said. "I'm sure you heard my country won't be a democracy much longer. We have common interests and the same goals. The Reich would've stretched across the Atlantic if Hitler hadn't betrayed us. Now instead of flowing east to west, it will flow west to east. And your wealth will grow another ten billion when you complete the mission."

Dorfmeister couldn't hide his smile and said, "When do I start?"

"Now."

"Now?"

"Yes, now."

"Three of my children are old enough to question their new names. And how can I remove their accent to appear American born?"

"As for why they are given new names, you and your wife will have to figure that out. Regarding their accents, the children will be placed in one of our exclusive private schools under the daily tutelage of expert speech therapists."

"You Americans are smarter than we thought. I have one more question."

"I'm listening."

"Where is Himmler?"

"Do you mean where is he buried?"

Dorfmeister grinned and said, "Are we friends?"

"If you accept our offer."

Dorfmeister sat on the front of the desk, gripped his knees, and locked eyes with the American. "Friends don't lie to each other. Himmler told me that he had an agreement with the Allies. You think that fake picture of his death could fool a Nazi? And telling the world that his body was buried in an unmarked grave at an unknown location? If you want our friendship to last, don't insult my intelligence. It was Himmler who told you about me, right?"

The American seemed surprised and said, "I don't know where he is. But he is alive."

Dorfmeister smiled. "Thank you. Will I meet the General?"

"When he's president."

"Himmler told me that he didn't know if he should greet the General with the Nazi salute or shake his hand. I look forward to doing both."

* * *

Six years later, Dorfmeister was released from his obligation to the CIA and became Henry Smith full-time. He was an active member of the Elephant party and one of the leaders who persuaded the General to select Senator Milhouse as his running mate. And in 1952, the General won the presidency by a landslide.

During the General's second term, Henry Smith attended an American Nationalism conference in Las Vegas. In the swanky hotel's presidential suite were his twenty-seven-year-old son Shawn, fourteen-year-old son Theodore, and ten colleagues from the Third Reich who were also given refuge by the CIA.

Mr. Smith said to the group, "It's 1960. We can't look back. Thanks to the CIA, our wealth has grown, and we have friends in high places. The Fourth Reich will rise in America."

Mr. Halston, formerly Herr Offenmier, bellowed, "I'm happy the America First Committee that Lindbergh started is alive and well. I was present when Goering, on behalf of the Führer, awarded him the German Eagle Service Cross. Despite the critics and pressure to return it, he didn't. That is why I accepted the CIA offer and registered as a member of Lindbergh's party. I wasn't sure his political stance would last, but it has. We are standing on the verge of political power that will raise the Reich for a thousand years."

The group stood, applauded, and saluted the American flag. Moments later, the phone rang. When Mr. Smith answered, his eyes closed and head slumped. "Thank you," he solemnly said and slowly hung up the phone. He faced the group. "The Mossad kidnapped Eichmann."

Mr. Halston yelled, "Fucking Jew-ass bastards!"

Silence held the room a few seconds before Mr. Smith said, "We are safe here. We don't have to hide because no one knows our faces. We've been planning the Fourth Reich since our days in Spain. The only change is the country where it will stand. We will finish what Hitler started!" He stood in the Nazi salute and said, "*Sieg Heil!*"

The others stood with the same salute.

And when Mr. Smith sat, they all sat.

Mr. Gatez, formerly Herr Feldhander, said, "It's more urgent now that we get our man elected president. But can we? Fitzgerald is very likable."

"That he is," Mr. Smith said. "He's very charismatic. That pretentious charm might be the edge he needs to win."

Shawn interjected, "If he wins, aren't we are strong enough to kill him?"

Mr. Covington, formerly Herr Guttenberg, bellowed, "A president? We can't kill a president!"

"We can't kill a president? Why not?" Shawn bellowed. "It's been done before in this country. We can blame it on the Russians."

"There will be a congressional investigation, that's why. This country is still a democracy."

Shawn shouted, "*Na und*! The chief justice is a friend. The Coalition has the power to ensure he oversees the investigative committee. He will make the final report favorable regardless of the evidence."

Mr. Wells, formerly Herr Schroeder, said, "We need to have several heads onboard to kill a president."

Mr. Smith interjected, "Thanks to the General, we have them. But they aren't willing to make that happen until it's necessary. If he wins, with the help of the Russians, we'll make it necessary."

Mr. Covington said, "Aren't we moving too fast? The American people aren't stupid."

With the wry smile Mr. Smith said, "They are the same as those who brought our party to power in Germany. The loyalists in Congress will pave the way into the White House."

Chapter 2

On the grounds of his fifteen-hundred-acre estate, Mr. Smith, his wife, and two sons were watching the presidential election results. Bottles of the most expensive champagne were waiting to be opened. But as the evening grew, the race tightened, and disappointment replaced optimism.

Shawn yelled, "They stole the election! I told you we should've killed him!"

Without his eyes turning from the television, his father calmly said, "We're not yet the owners of this Party, but your children and the children of our friends will be. Until then, keep climbing."

"How tall is the ladder, Father?"

"It's not how tall, but how many steps are left. There are only a few."

* * *

The day after the election, the America First Coalition met via a secure conference call. The Chairman, a former senator of the Donkey party, said, "That middle-aged preppy has gotten in our way. He has to be removed ASAP, or he will be a two-term president."

Silence held the phone a few seconds before Mr. Smith said, "We should've removed him before the election as I suggested. We can't concern ourselves with what the people might think. We need to remove him and have a fall guy at the ready. I spoke to Milhouse last night and again this morning. He is very distraught; he believes we let him down. He doesn't want to wait another four years, let alone eight."

The Chairman said, "We haven't let him down, and we won't. We are going to challenge the results in several states."

"In a democracy, that won't go anywhere," Mr. Smith said.

"We are going to try. If unsuccessful, we will remove him another way. But if we do, Milhouse will have to wait until '68."

Disconcerted, Mr. Smith said, "Sixty-eight? Why? Fitzgerald might as well stay president if we have to wait eight years?"

"We have to wait because we will have to pay a debt to get the necessary people in the boat."

Mr. Chase interjected, "If it's money, why wait?"

"It's not money, but power," the Chairman replied. "Fitzgerald's vice president wants the Oval Office until '68. He has agreed to stay out of our way if Milhouse doesn't run against him in '64."

Mr. Cromwell said, "Are we supporting the Democrats in '64?"

"No," the Chairman said. "We will stay on the sideline in the presidential race. Our focus is on the down-ballot candidates. We need loyalists in charge of the House, Senate, and State legislatures. That will build up Milhouse in '68."

Mr. Smith shouted, "Milhouse won't be happy! You're telling him that he has to wait eight fucking years!"

"I know he won't be happy. But if we don't do it this way, he will never become president."

"I don't trust the vice president," Mr. Smith said. "He's a cowboy without a hat."

"We have to trust him. We need him to make it happen."

After a few seconds of silence, Mr. Smith said, "Okay. I will convince Milhouse to stay patient if we agree to remove any threat to his presidency during or after the '68 primaries."

The people on the call unanimously agreed.

The Chairman said, "We will ensure that happens," and ended the call.

* * *

In the first year of Fitzgerald's presidency, the threat of Communism intensified with the construction of the Berlin Wall. As if the Russians had sensed weakness in the American president, their aggression grew, and nuclear weapons were placed on the island ninety miles from the U.S. shore. That momentous confrontation between the two superpowers ended when Fitzgerald agreed not to invade the Communist island. That decision by Fitzgerald to back down made America weak in the eyes of the Donkey party leaders, and they held a secret meeting that included the vice president.

The organizer of the meeting said, "The threat of Communism has increased with this president. He has a back channel with the Russian leader and is committing infidelity with Communist spies. Only God knows what information he is giving to those Communist whores. He is unworthy to be president because he is a major threat to national security! If we allow him to continue, the Russians will take over our country!"

* * *

A year later, President Fitzgerald was assassinated and the killing linked to the Russians.

Two days later, in Harrisburg, Pennsylvania, nine-year-old William Walker, his eleven-year-old brother Devin, and their mother were watching the evening news when William said, "Ma, he the man that killed the good president?"

His mother replied, "He's the one they said did it."

"Where they taking him?"

"To another jail."

"Why?"

"For his safety."

The handcuffed suspect, in a supposedly secure location with law enforcement attached to his sides, said to the authorized reporters and cameramen, "I didn't shoot the president."

Then, from out of the crowd of reporters, a man stepped forward and shot the suspect.

William's mother screamed, "Oh my God!"

Devin's eyes widened.

William yelled, "Ma, they shot him!"

"What the hell is going on?" his mother said. "How could he get shot with all that security around him? Russia ain't got nothing to do with this unless they have taken over the country."

William stared at his mother, seemingly pondering her words. And as the days passed, instead of watching *Batman*, William watched Walter Cronkite.

* * *

In the aftermath of the president's assassination, the investigative committee appointed by the new president concluded a lone gunman killed the former president—and that the man who killed the assassin also acted alone.

Two days before the report was made public, the Coalition met. The chairman said, "Though the report is firm in its conclusions, it will not silence the conspiracy theories, nor the investigative reporters. The next time, we need to use one gunman and have him captured on the scene."

Mr. Halston said, "If there is a next time, use one of those desert men. They are the future threat. Don't we have some of them programmed in the stable?"

"We do, and I agree," the chairman replied. "All in favor?"

Everyone said, "Yes."

* * *

At the 1967 two-day Coalition conference, Mr. Smith shouted, "I told you that son of a bitch couldn't be trusted! He's running for another term!"

"He'll drop out," the chairman said. "He's hardheaded, but his party will give him the boot."

"That's not the point. It's a matter of trust. For the record, I'm not concerned about that clown from the jackass party. What are we going to do about Senator Roberts? He's polling way ahead of Milhouse."

"We will handle as agreed."

"We better!"

"Is that a threat?"

"A fact!" Mr. Smith shouted. "I came to this country and joined this party because the leaders had the vision of an authoritarian and nationalistic right-wing system of government and social organization. I'm here to rid

Communism and democracy. Milhouse is the reason I'm still here. If he can't be the president, then I'm leaving."

"Be patient," the Chairman said. "Change cannot move as fast as you like, but it will come."

"I've run out of patience. Where I came from change moved quickly because we controlled the change. If we allow the people to make the changes, the change we want won't come."

"Trust me. The change we want will come."

* * *

William was watching the *Green Hornet* when Breaking News interrupted, "*Senator Roberts has been shot. Details of his condition are unknown at this time. The suspect, described as a Middle Easterner, has been taken into custody at the scene.*"

"Ma, they shot the brother!"

His mother hurried into the room. "Oh my God!"

William's young mind was thinking as his eyes shifted back and forth from the television.

Teary-eyed, his mother said, "What the hell is going on in this country?"

William kept his eyes locked on the screen, seemingly oblivious to the voices around him. In that moment, the mind of a teen became the thoughts of a man, and he said, "Ma, there are people more powerful than the president."

His mother gazed into his troubled eyes but didn't say a word.

* * *

With the path cleared, the "far-right authoritarian ultranationalist political ideology" won the presidency.

At the first-stop inaugural ball, secret donors and high-powered allies were led into the private room. The Elephant party chairman held a full glass of whisky and slurred, "Gentlemen, we have waited eight years, but we now control the White House, both chambers of Congress, and the Supreme Court. Nothing can stop us now."

Out from the applause and cheers, one yelled, "It's time to bring back the Bellamy salute!" The room joined the recital of the Pledge of Allegiance with the Bellamy salute.

After, the chairman of the America First Coalition said, "I share the enthusiasm in this room. But it's not time to bring back the salute outside of this room. This country is still a democracy." He gestured to his aides and said to the group, "I have a gift for you."

With an intoxicated breath, the chair of the Elephant party said, "What is it?"

The Coalition chairman lifted an African blackwood case out of one of the black matte shopping bags in the hands of his aides. "I was going to wait until our new Führer enters, but I'm too excited." He opened the case and raised a golden goblet engraved with a portrait of George Washington in front of the American flag with a swastika at his left and right. Two Aryan postermen handed each person one of the goblets.

Shortly thereafter, the president, a six-foot big-nose man with a receding hairline entered with both hands in the two-finger salute. Beside him was a towering, physically fit, iron-faced retired general with brows that resembled the devil.

The Coalition chairman handed the president and the retired general a goblet. The president said, "This is beautiful. This is who we are."

"Yes. And it has now come to fruition," the chairman said.

The room applauded.

The chairman signaled his aides, and blindfolded servants with chilled bottles of champagne were led into the room and guided to fill the goblets. When all the goblets were filled, the servants were led from the room, and the president toasted the America First Coalition.

With the retired general at his side, the president approached Mr. Smith, and shook his hand.

Bright-eyed, with a wide smile, Mr. Smith said, "Congratulations!"

"Congratulations to us," the president said. "I have a seat for you in the White House."

"Thank you, Mr. President, but you know I prefer to be among the unknown."

The president whispered, "*Das Vierte Reich ist auferstanden.*"

Mr. Smith said, "*Seit tausend Jahren.*"

The retired general said, "A thousand years it shall be."

When the president left the room, Mr. Smith rode the private elevator to the penthouse. When he entered the room, Shawn was fucking a porn star on the marble floor, and Theodore was on the sofa with his cock up the ass of another. Two scantily clad natural blondes sitting on the balcony followed Mr. Smith into the master bedroom for his customary weekly threesome.

When the fornication ended and the women were sent away, in German Mr. Smith said to his sons, "They can kill the man, but they can't kill the ideology. We have eternal life in our ideology. Remember that."

* * *

Despite the nationwide protests against the president's policies, Fascism under democracy was popular because of the strong economy. The president rode that wave to win forty-nine of the fifty states in his reelection, even though the White House was embroiled in the failed attempt to spy on the Donkey party. But the evidence that continued to mount against the president made way in the midterm elections for the Donkey party to regain the majority in the House and Senate.

Under intense pressure from the members of Congress for the president to resign, the Coalition met in person. At that meeting, Mr. Smith said, "This scandal will surely bring a halt to our plans. Someone in the FBI is leaking confidential files to investigative reporters."

Mr. Musgrove, formerly Herr Kiplinger, said, "Some good men will fall like the vice president fell."

Mr. Weathers interjected, "But the chief of staff, secretary of state, and national security advisor will be unscathed for use later."

Mr. Smith interjected, "For use later? The president wants to go down swinging."

Mr. Hilton said, "We can't let him do that. There is too much in the public eye already. An impeachment trial will only bring more. Can you convince him to resign?"

Mr. Hilton's eyes shifted to the chairman. "Can you make sure his successor has the last name of an American? The reporters are snooping into backgrounds, questioning the last names of the president's men."

Mr. Tinkler, formerly Herr Oslo, worryingly said, "How secure are our backgrounds?"

The chairman replied, "Untouchable. Thanks to the CIA."

Mr. Halston locked eyes with the chairman. "You should've removed the entire FBI leadership when the Director died. Now there is a turncoat inside the White House. We are going to lose some great men from their seats, ending with the Führer, because you didn't have his back."

The chairman glared back at Mr. Halston. "You need to watch your tone! You are only here because of me. You're free because of us. Don't ever forget that."

The chairman swung his eyes to Mr. Smith. "Keep your people in check!"

"My people are in check. Everyone in this room told you what needed to be done. Milhouse shouldn't resign. The retired general will call in the Army to control the streets if needed. We haven't come this close to throw it all away because of what the people might think. There is no crime if the president does it."

The chairman sarcastically said, "Can you convince the American people of that?"

Mr. Smith stood. "The American people don't care about that scandal. The president's name was in it before the election, and he still won by a landslide. Why are we asking him to resign? Because of that blue wave in the midterms? Because Senator Leadwater and others on Capitol Hill are afraid they will be voted out? Let the House impeach him, and if the Senate convicts, we will keep Milhouse in the Oval Office by military force."

The chairman held the repudiated expression and stood. "As chair, the decision is made. This country is not Nazi Germany yet. Milhouse must resign. Meeting adjourned."

* * *

The year was 1974, William and two other budding journalists for the college newspaper were discussing the current political climate.

William said, "Something is going on in this country more important than inflation, recession, the energy crisis, and the country's financial stability."

"What's that?" asked one of the budding journalists.

"The threat of losing democracy."

"Democracy? Democracy isn't under threat."

William emphatically said, "Of course it is. What do you think that scandal was about? The president was trying to remove the rival political party."

The second budding journalist interjected, "I think you're overanalyzing. Democracy in this country isn't under threat. We the people decide our leaders with open and fair elections."

"For now," William said. "But the country is changing."

"Changing how?" asked the first budding journalist. "The president did the honorable thing—he resigned. At the next election, the people will select the president. This is America. The greatest democracy the earth has ever seen."

William sarcastically smiled and said, "I hope you are alive when democracy ends. Those burglars were former CIA. Haven't you asked yourself, why did Milhouse's men have German names?"

The second budding journalist said, "Just a coincidence. We are a country of immigrants."

"Yes, we are. But I'm concerned when powerful men in the White House have German names."

"Do you honestly think our country is run by Nazis?"

William paused before he said, "Why did President Roosevelt refuse to allow a ship of Jews fleeing Nazi Germany to enter the country? Why didn't America join the war when our allies France and England were attacked by Hitler? And isn't it strange that the Bellamy salute instituted in 1892 is similar to the Nazi salute and was the standard procedure for schoolchildren in pledging allegiance to the American flag until 1942—one year after the Pearl Harbor attack? Something isn't right."

Consideration was on the faces of the two budding journalists, but they changed the topic.

* * *

Marred by the scandal that led to President Milhouse's resignation and the imprisonment of several of his men, the right wing lost control of the White House.

The Coalition met in person, and Mr. Halston said, "Mr. Smith told us to back the actor, and he was right. We were so close, and now we are set back years because of the poor decisions in leadership."

The chairman contemptuously exhaled. "This is the second time you have questioned my leadership. Who do you think you are?"

"As a member of this Coalition, I took an oath to speak truth to power. You advised the Führer on that botched burglary, and you overruled the majority of members when we told you to replace everyone in the FBI leadership."

"Yes, I advised the president after I learned about the burglary. And I overruled the decision to back the actor because he is an incompetent puppet. He would've thought that he really was the president. The puppet I selected knows better. He would've gladly returned to his role as VP."

"Yes, but your puppet was a stiff board without the personality for a nationwide election in this political climate. We voted not to back him because of that. We chose the actor because he is a puppet with personality. We only needed him to win the election. We would've quickly removed him."

The chairman exhaled.

Mr. Halston continued, "Your last two decisions have been poor and costly. You forced the Führer to resign, and he committed suicide because of his depression. And you overruled the majority decision to back the actor. That's two strikes! We cannot take the chance of a third. I make the motion that we vote for a new chairman."

Mr. Bumgardner, who served in the 1939 president's cabinet, said, "I second the motion."

The chairman said, "Any oppose?"

Silence held the room for a few seconds before the chairman said, "Motion carried. Any nominations?"

Mr. Halston forcefully said, "I nominate Henry Smith, formerly Heinrich Dorfmeister."

The chairman tried to hide his contemptuous expression. And after a few seconds of silence said, "Mr. Smith, do you accept the nomination?"

"I do."

The chairman paused, seemingly surprised, before he said, "Any other nominations?"

Silence held the room until the chairman said, "I'm nominating myself. We will reconvene in a week to vote."

Chapter 3

Mr. Smith phoned Coalition members to secure votes but met personally with seventy-nine-year-old Thomas Hancock, the oldest and most influential member. At Mr. Hancock's oceanfront home in Palm Beach, they sat on cushioned stone chairs at the round, matching patio table.

"Thank you for making the time to meet with me," Mr. Smith said.

In his ageing, but strong, voice, Mr. Hancock said, "I'm glad you asked to meet in person. Now I know how much you respect me."

"How can I not?"

"Believe me, many have. Tell me, what is your vision if elected chairman of the Coalition?"

"We all have the same vision. The better question is what's my plan to bring it into existence."

Mr. Hancock grinned. "You have passed the first test. Now, tell me, what is your plan to bring our vision into existence?"

"The plan begins with what we have already learned. Milhouse had a thick cloud of criminal conduct hanging over him, yet he won forty-nine states in his reelection. That told us the American people love our policies and didn't care if the president was involved in a criminal coverup."

"So, you think democracy will eventually bring our vision into existence?"

"Of course not. But like in Germany, we will use democracy to gain power and then remove it."

"And how will you remove it?"

"Milhouse, like Hitler, was very persuasive and one of us. He knew what to do and how to do it. He would've been president for life if some in our party hadn't bowed to political pressure."

"You're looking for another Milhouse?"

"There isn't another Milhouse like there isn't another Hitler. One like them might not come again for a hundred years. We can't afford to wait that long. America is in decline. The Jews control the banks, media, and everything in this society. Blacks and non-Aryan immigrants are poisoning our blood. We need a puppet that we can quickly remove and put our man in that seat."

"Puppet? Why a puppet? Why not use a loyalist?"

"Because no one in our circle has the personality to win the presidential election. We need a person the voters will believe in, a personality they will trust."

"Who do you have in mind?"

"The actor turned politician. We should've backed him as the nominee of our party four years ago."

"And who will be the vice president when we remove him?"

"Someone who will take the backseat?"

"And who is that?"

"The beer man."

"Who do you have in mind for the front seat?"

"The retired general."

"Milhouse's chief of staff?"

"Yes."

"Why not let him run as the VP? It'll be easier if he's the VP."

"It would, but he isn't tactful. He will scare voters away. I suggest we make him the secretary of state."

"Secretary of state? That's fourth in succession?"

Mr. Smith leaned forward with acute eyes and said, "Democracy ends when the puppet is removed. We are the puppeteers. When our puppet is elected, we will appoint the people that matter—the Directors of Defense, Justice, the FBI, and the Joint Chiefs. The administration will be comprised solely of loyalists. Immediately after the puppet is removed, the Constitution will be terminated, and the New World Order will begin."

With enlightened eyes staring at him, Mr. Smith leaned back.

"You have an excellent plan, Mr. Smith."

"Thank you."

"I have a question. How will you enact the New World Order?"

"That's a question you already know."

"I want to know if you see the whole picture as I do."

"You wouldn't've accepted my request to meet if you felt that I didn't. To appease you, my friend, the Coalition money is spread into elections worldwide. We have risen strong populist and far-right-wing candidates for the leaderships in Europe, which are on the brink of successful coups. In Canada and South America, our money has raised authoritarian leaders. In Mexico, our partnership with the Cartel controls that country. We only need an authoritarian leader here to complete the World Order."

"What about Russia and China?"

"The retired general has a back channel with the leaders of Russia and China. When he sits at the Resolute Desk, he will formalize the partnership. They will have what they want, and we will head the New World Order."

Mr. Hancock smiled. "Now that our business is over, our pleasure begins." He lifted the air horn off the patio table and pressed the button. Seconds later, four naked Aryan women in heels walked across the capacious lawn. Two escorted Mr. Smith inside the enclosed canopy at the side of the Playboy mansion-style swimming pool. The other two led Mr. Hancock into an enclosed white tent next to the sauna.

An hour or so later, Mr. Hancock and Mr. Smith were in the ten-person Jacuzzi connected to the pool. Two of the four women were with them. In German, Mr. Hancock said, "My bloodline was on the Mayflower. I always knew this was the country that would raise the thousand-year Reich. That's why America is called the New World."

In German Mr. Smith said, "It has all the trimmings of the Holy Roman Empire. America is the Promised Land for Aryans."

* * *

At the Coalition meeting, Henry Smith was voted the new chair. In his acceptance speech, he said, "Gentlemen, I assure you this left-wing president will be a one-term president. In the interim, we need to focus on the midterms. We need control of the House and Senate when the puppet is elected.

And he will be elected! If not, I will resign. And this is how we will get him elected..."

* * *

Two years before the presidential election, Henry Smith died from a cardiac arrest during his weekly threesome, and Mr. Halston was voted the new chair. He added Mr. Smith's son, Shawn, to the group. In that meeting, Mr. Halston said, "We are not changing the plan laid out by Shawn's father, who remains with us in spirit. The international crisis he put in motion with help from our friends at the CIA is on course. The plan to remove the puppet when he becomes president is on schedule."

Mr. Chase said, "And if the plan fails?"

Mr. Halston acutely stared. "If any part of the plan fails, I. Will. Resign."

* * *

Heinrich Dorfmeister's funeral was a private Protestant service in Gillette. On the morning before the funeral when his wife Margaret was alone, she placed the Waffen SS National Emblem over his heart and closed the casket. The iron-faced retired general draped the American flag over the coffin. Dorfmeister's children, Shawn, Leigh, April, Summer, and Theodore gave remarks at the funeral. A full ensemble orchestra played tunes by Richard Wagner and Beethoven.

Mr. Halston spoke the eulogy that ended with these words: "His dream was for this country to reach ultra-nationalism. He said that ideology will spread the eagle's wings forever. He said ultranationalism will make America great again. I say to him as he sleeps before us, 'My dear friend, when you awake, you will find the dream fulfilled. Rest in peace, my *Parteigenosse*.' "

Summer was sitting in-between Shawn and her mother, and whispered to her mother, "Is that a German word?"

"Yes. It means *party member*."

"Why did he say that in German?"

Shawn interjected, "He is recognizing our father's German side. He's telling everyone there are good Germans in the world."

* * *

Several months after the funeral, Summer was approached by a man during the lunch break at a medical conference. With a pleasant smile, the man extended his hand and said, "Hi, my name is Saul."

She smiled and shook his hand. "Hi, nice to meet you. My name is Summer."

"Nice name. Can I sit with you?"

Her smile extended. "Sure."

"I saw you eating alone, and you don't have a ring on your finger, so I saw this as an opportunity to meet you."

She blushed. "Are you here for the conference?"

"I am."

"Are you a doctor?"

"I am."

"How long have you been practicing?"

"Eight years. And you?"

"I'm in my last year of residency."

"I remember my last year. It went very slow."

She giggled. "Ah-huh. The same here. What's your practice?"

"I am a general practitioner. What about you?"

"I'm specializing in gynecology."

"Ah. Do you live here?"

"I live in Boston. Are you from here?"

"No, I live in Syracuse. Are you going back to Boston this evening?"

"My flight leaves tomorrow."

"Would you care to have dinner with me?"

"When? Tonight?"

"If you like."

"Sure. I would like that."

"Are you staying at this hotel?"

"Yes."

"Me too. We can meet in the hotel restaurant. Is seven a good time?"

"Okay."

"I'll make the reservation under my name: Saul Goldberg."

"Okay."

With a smile in his eyes, Saul stood and said, "See you at seven. It was nice meeting you, Summer."

"Nice meeting you too."

She watched as he walked away, and with a tight-lipped smile said within, "I like him."

* * *

Summer arrived at the restaurant five minutes early and was seated by the maître d'.

Saul arrived six minutes late. "I'm sorry. I had an emergency call from a patient."

"Is everything okay?"

"It is now."

She half-smiled and said, "I was getting ready to leave."

"I'm sorry."

"You're here now. Let's eat."

"You look like I disappointed you."

"You did. But now that I know the reason why you were late, it's all good."

"Thanks for understanding."

After they had ordered their drinks and meal, Summer said, "Why are you staring at me?"

"I don't mean to. It's just that you look like a short-haired Farrah Fawcett."

"I've never heard that before."

"It's true."

She blushed.

Saul smiled and said, "You weren't born in Boston because you don't have the accent. Where were you born?"

"Gillette, Wyoming, in 1945. Have you heard of Gillette?"

"No."

"You're not alone. Most people haven't."

Saul grinned.

Summer smiled. "Where were you born?"

"Copenhagen, Denmark, in 1936. I'm a holocaust survivor. My parents were killed in the Holocaust."

Sadness replaced her joyful expression.

"Are you okay?"

"How could people be so evil?"

"Because they aren't people. They're devils."

"I'm sorry your parents were killed, but all Germans aren't bad. There are some good Germans. My grandmother was an immigrant from a German community in Switzerland. She married my American-born grandfather, who died the year my father was born. She was lonely in America without him and moved back to Switzerland where my father met my mother, and they moved back to Gillette. I'm not ashamed of my German bloodline because the Germans who lived in that Switzerland community are good Germans."

"They are. I heard about them. I didn't mean to imply all Germans are devils. Only the Nazi party."

"I agree." She gleefully said, "Do you have any siblings?"

"No, I was the only child."

"How did you get to America?"

"After the war, an American family adopted me."

"That was God's blessing."

"It was."

"Are they still alive?"

"No, they were elderly and died years ago."

"Are you alone now? I mean, do you have family on the adopted side?"

"I do, but we aren't very close. I miss my birth parents. I've spent most of my adult life searching Copenhagen for family members, but I think they were all killed. I will never forget what the Nazis did to my parents and people."

Summer stared at his bald head and round face as if she didn't know what to say.

Saul broke the silence. "Did you know some of those bastards sneaked into this country?"

"Here? I heard they went to South America."

"Some went there—some to Spain and other places—but some are in this country too."

"Well, they all should be old or dead by now."

"I'm sure their children are alive. Eichmann had his wife and children with him in Argentina. Like we found him, we'll find the bastards that are hiding in this country."

"Can we talk about something else?"

"I'm sorry, I'm boring you?"

"N-no. I-I just want to think about happy times."

Saul turned the conversation to smiles and laughter.

After dinner, in the warmness of the night, while strolling on the hotel grounds, Saul said, "Do you have any brothers or sisters?"

"Two brothers and two sisters. I'm next to the youngest."

"And the prettiest, I'm sure."

She blushed.

Saul led her to one of the iron benches along the walkway. They sat, and he said, "Tell me about your family?"

"My father died last year. My mother still lives in Wyoming. My brother Shawn replaced our father as the CEO of the family business. The youngest, Theodore, is the company's VP. Leigh, the second oldest, is a corporate lawyer in San Francisco. April, the third oldest, is a bank executive in Minnesota."

"Impressive. What is the family business?"

"A worldwide trading company. I'm not involved, so I don't know much about it. Since I left Wyoming and attended UMass, I don't see or talk to my family often."

"Living in Boston, I understand why you don't see them often, but why is it that you don't communicate?"

"Because I'm busy, and they're busy. But mostly because I'm a private person. I'm not one to share my private life with others, even with family. They ask, but I keep my personal life to myself. I think they believe I'm a lesbian because I don't mention a boyfriend, and they haven't seen me with a guy since the high school prom.

"The last time I saw my family was at my father's funeral. I usually attend the Thanksgiving and Christmas family gatherings if I'm not working, and I always visit my mother on her birthday."

Saul felt the moment and kissed her. "Excuse me. I should've asked if you had a boyfriend before I kissed you."

"If I did, I wouldn't be here with you."

He kissed her again, and she returned the passion. He tried to hit a home run that night but had to settle for second base.

* * *

On Christmas day 1979, Summer introduced Saul to her family.

Shawn, six foot three, with short dark hair and the perfect body for a Hugo Boss model, said "Hi" but didn't shake Saul's hand. Theodore, a thin six foot five with a childlike face, did the same. Their mother, a natural blonde, blue-eyed woman that resembled Lilli Palmer when younger, shook his hand but didn't say a word to him.

Leigh, a tall, slender Ava Gardner look-alike, and her husband Ken who resembled Cary Grant, graciously welcomed Saul.

April, whose similarity was to Adele Mara, and her husband Brian, who had a rugby player-type body, politely welcomed Saul.

Bright-eyed, Leigh said, "Finally, we get to meet your boyfriend. We were thinking you were a lesbian."

Her sisters and their husbands chuckled.

Saul smiled and said, "Why did you think that?"

"Because she was always alone when she came to the family gatherings and never mentioned a guy."

Saul extended his smile and said, "Maybe she was waiting for me to walk into her life."

Leigh's smile widened. "Must've been. You're here."

April turned her attention to Saul. "You have a Jewish name. Are you Jewish?"

"I am."

"Is it okay for a Jew to celebrate with us on Christmas day?"

"I don't celebrate the day, but I'm here because Summer asked me to come."

Brian said, "Well, we're glad you came. Would you like a cup of eggnog?"

"Sure."

Saul took the cup, sipped, and said, "Would you happen to have some Jack Daniel's?"

Ken enthusiastically said, "Yes we do!" He opened the fully stocked liquor cabinet and grabbed a fifth. "You want it on the rocks?"

"Please."

After he handed Saul the drink, Ken said, "Let's toast to Summer and Saul's relationship. May it last forever!"

Everyone toasted except Shawn, Theodore, and the mother.

While Saul was engaged with the sisters and their husbands, Shawn whispered in Summer's ear, "I need to speak with you alone."

"When?"

"Now. Follow me."

He led her toward the front door.

"We're going outside?"

"Yeah."

"Wait, I need to get my coat."

"You don't need it. You can handle the cold. You always won when we played as kids to see who could stay outside in the cold the longest without a coat. We're just going to the first guesthouse."

"I'm not a kid anymore. That's a long walk in the cold without a coat."

"It's not that long. Come on. Do it for me." He wrapped his arm around her shoulder and pulled her body beside him as they swiftly walked fifty yards to the guesthouse.

When they entered the cream-stone-layered villa, Shawn pointed at the living room. "Have a seat."

With her mind wondering what was on his, she sat on the sofa that faced the unlit fireplace.

Shawn lit the fireplace and stood in front of her. "Why are you with him?"

"I love him."

"You're embarrassing your mother and stomping on your father's grave."

"What are you talking about? What's wrong with Saul?"

"He's a Jew!"

Her voice raised with furrowed brows, "What's wrong with a Jew? I love him. We are getting married, and I am going to convert to his religion."

With his brows squeezed together, eyelids tight and straight, he yelled, "Are you crazy? He's a Jew! The scum of the earth! Those people aren't human! They're vermin! I rather see you with a nigger than a Jew! I forbid you to marry him!"

"What? You forbid? You're not my father!"

"I'm the head of this family now. That Jew is only interested in stealing the thirty million dollars you inherited from Father."

"He doesn't know about my inheritance because I haven't told him."

"He knows. Jews can smell the money they are going to steal a mile away."

Summer's eyes watered. "When did you become antisemitic?"

"When I was conceived."

"When you were conceived? Our mother and father aren't antisemitic."

"You didn't know your father, and you don't know your mother."

With a blank stare, she said, "What are you saying?"

"He's a Jew."

"I never heard our parents speak against Jews."

"That's because one was never brought into our house."

"I'm leaving! I don't want to be around here another second!" she said and headed toward the door.

Shawn glared and shouted in German, "Blood and soil! Don't contaminate it."

Did he speak German? She didn't look back and ran to the mansion. She wet her fingers and wiped away the frozen tears before she entered. But when she saw Saul, tears leaked again.

He quickly embraced her and worryingly said, "What happened?"

She didn't answer.

Her sisters and their husbands concerningly approached. "Summer, what's wrong?"

She ignored the questions, locked eyes with her mother, and removed herself from Saul's embrace.

She kneeled in front of her mother's blank expression and lovingly held the palms of her hands. "Ma, I have to go."

Her mother nodded with eyes that seemed to know the reason.

Leigh said, "You're not staying for dinner?"

Summer stood and faced her. "No. Saul and I are leaving."

Ken said, "Why? What happened? What did Shawn do?"

With tears leaking, Summer turned and faced her mother and said, "Goodbye, Mom," and kissed her on the cheek.

Her mother's mouth didn't open, and her expression didn't change.

Summer hugged her sisters and their husbands, kissed their children, grabbed her and Saul's coats, and left the house.

As they walked to the car, Saul was questioning her, but she remained silent.

When they entered the car, he frustratingly repeated, "What happened? Did he hit you?"

"No!"

"Then why are we leaving?"

"I don't want to be here any longer."

"Why?"

She tearfully shouted, "Stop asking! Just drive!"

"Drive where?"

"To the airport."

"You're leaving your gifts?"

"I don't celebrate Christmas anymore."

Saul paused in a thought that reflected in his eyes, and with eyes on the road, said, "When are you going to tell me what happened?"

She shifted teary eyes to the side of his face. "My brother is a racist."

Saul's eyes left the road to face her, then quickly went back to the road. "I know he's antisemitic. Both of your brothers are. I saw their expressions when you told them my name. There are a lot of antisemitic Americans. I discovered that growing up."

With her voice cracking, she said, "I'm sorry I brought you here. I don't believe Theodore is racist—he's just following Shawn. I don't know where Shawn got those evil thoughts. He even implied my father and mother are antisemitic, but I know they aren't."

Saul pulled the car to the side of the road and turned off the engine. He faced her and said, "It's okay," and kissed her. "Do you still love me?"

"Of course, I love you."

"That's all that matters. I don't care if your brothers don't like me."

She kissed him and said, "I love you."

"And I love you."

"Let's go home."

As the vehicle continued to the airport, Summer's head lay with jumbled thoughts on Saul's lap.

Chapter 4

The year was 1980. William was a beat reporter for his hometown newspaper in search of a story that would make him famous and followed the conspiracy theory he held since childhood. As usual, he debated with his mother.

"Ma, who do you think will win between that B-movie actor and the groundnut farmer?"

"Don't call him a groundnut farmer."

"Why not? Doesn't he harvest groundnuts?"

"'Cause it's offensive. He's a good man. I hope he gets reelected."

"He won't."

"Why not? He's done a good job."

"He's weak. He tries to hide his weakness with a smile, but the jig is up. He's a one-timer."

"He's not weak?"

"Oh yes, he is."

"What makes him weak?"

"American diplomats are hostages in a foreign country."

"That's not his fault. There was a revolution in that country. You can't blame him for that."

"Why not? He's the president. The buck stops with him. It's been months. A strong president would've freed the diplomats by now."

"He tried to rescue them."

"Yeah, and that was a fiasco. That's why he will lose. The American people see him as weak and incompetent. They won't vote for him again."

"Who's the better choice?"

"It's not who is better; it's who appears better."

"What makes you believe that former actor will win his party's nomination?"

"Did you watch the debate? He's an actor who has read the script. He will win because he's humorous and appears to be strong. He even makes me enjoyably laugh."

His mother chuckled. "He is funny sometimes, but I don't trust his party."

"You know I don't."

"Is this why you sounded so pressed to speak with me? To talk about who will win the election?"

"No. I need a big favor."

"What is it?"

"I need a loan?"

"A loan? How much?"

"A hundred thousand dollars."

"What! Boy, you crazy. You know I ain't got no hundred thousand dollars."

"You will if you take out a home equity loan."

"A home equity loan?"

"Yeah. This house is paid in full and worth more than $100,000. I'll pay you back."

"Why do you need the money? What's going on?"

"I'm working on a story that will make me famous. But I have to quit my job and move to Washington, DC."

"Quit your job! Why do you have to quit your job?"

"To finish this story, I have to go undercover."

"Undercover? What you are planning sounds stupid and dangerous. Are you trying to get some dirt on a politician?"

"I'm trying to find the truth about the Elephant heads."

"And how are you going to do that?"

"Follow the big money?"

"I told you before. The big money in political circles is dark money."

"You're right. But it can be seen if the light of truth shines on it."

"William, you're a kid playing with fire. Those dark-money people are very powerful, and you don't even have the backing of your small newspaper."

"Ma, I'm not a kid. I'm twenty-seven."

"Then act like it. You should know you are way over your head if you think you can shine light on dark money. That money is in the hands of people more powerful than the president. You know that."

"Do you remember when you told me there is a reason for everything that happens? The challenge is finding the reason. I'm taking that challenge, and I need your help."

"You want me to gamble my house for something famous investigative reporters haven't discovered?"

"It's not gambling. It's an investment in me. I want you to believe in me. I can do this. The reason why is because of you."

She lowered her eyes, seemingly in thought, with the silence between them. A few seconds later, she lifted her eyes and stared at him. "I hope you come back alive."

"Ma, if the story comes back, I came back, whether I'm alive or not."

Her eyes watered. "William, you're gonna get yourself killed."

"I won't—but if I do, you are the beneficiary of my life insurance. That's a $300,000 policy. That will pay back the loan and leave you with extra."

She cried. "I don't give a damn about your life insurance. I don't want to bury a son. I want my sons to bury me."

He embraced her. "Ma, I'm not going to die. I can do this. Trust me."

* * *

When William left his mother's house, he went directly to his brother's home.

"Hi, William," Devin's wife said.

"Wassup, sis." He hugged her. "Where's Devin?"

"He's in the man cave."

William scooted into the basement.

"Wad up, bruh?" Devin said.

"You, big bruh."

They dapped.

"What's happening?"

William smiled and said, "I'm quitting my job and moving to DC."

"What?"

"I'm quitting my job and moving to DC."

"For what?"

"To work on a story that can make me rich and expose the truth."

"What kind of story?"

"You know I believe the heads of the Elephant are Neo-Nazis. I'm going to DC to get that evidence from the new administration."

"The new administration? So, you gambling they will win the presidency?"

"I believe it's a sure thing."

"A sure thing? You should know better. Even if they win, what are you gonna be when you get there? One of their trunks?"

"Nah, you should know me better than that. I'm gonna find a girl with Elephant ears inside the room."

"What you gonna do with Sandra?"

"I have to end the relationship. I can't tell her where I'm going or what I'm doing. Only you and Ma can know, so don't tell your wife."

"How you gonna live if you're not planning to work for them?"

"Mama's loaning me $100,000."

"A $100,000? Where did she get that money from?"

"She's taking out a home equity loan, and I will pay it off when I sell the story."

"What? Man, that's irresponsible! You're putting her in a bind. What happens if your story flops?"

"It won't. Anything about the inside of the White House sells."

"Yeah, but you're not inside the White House."

"I will be when I hook up with one of the staff."

"Man, that's one in a million. And most of those girls are white."

"White girls love black men. We're the most popular man in the world. Remember what we saw when we went to Europe? Pretty white girls' arm-in-arm with Africans who were far from the handsome side."

"Yeah, but they're not racists."

"All Elephant women aren't racists."

Devin paused, seemingly searching his brother's eyes. "You serious?"

"Very."

"How long will you be gone?"

"A year. Maybe less if I get lucky."

"Ah-huh. Why do I feel you need something from me?"

"I don't need anything from you. I just want you to know what I'm doing."

"I don't know what you're doing. Are you sure you know what you're doing?"

"I have a plan."

"What I heard so far sounds spotty."

"It's not spotty. My cover is mostly true. I'm William Walker, twenty-seven, born in Harrisburg, Pennsylvania. I grew up with my mother and brother, and graduated from Harrisburg U. All true. I need to give enough true information so I don't get caught in a lie."

"What's your job?"

"After graduating from college, I worked as a ghostwriter. After a couple of the books became bestsellers, I decided to write one with my name on it and moved to DC because it's Chocolate City."

"Isn't saying you moved to DC because it's Chocolate City gonna make you look like a radical in their eyes?"

"No, because I'm playing the role of a young conservative looking to make more blacks a part of the conservative party."

"What are you going to say when they ask, 'Why are you a Republican?' "

"Abraham Lincoln was a Republican and he freed the slaves. That's enough reason for me to be a Republican."

"What if you are asked about the books you wrote as a ghostwriter?"

"I can't divulge that information because of my contract with the authors."

"What if you are asked about the book you're working on?"

"I have seventy-three pages of a sci-fi that I wrote in high school. If questioned about what I'm working on, I will share that."

"So, you gonna live in southeast DC?"

"Nah, I need to live like a Republican, so I have to live among the middle class. I'm going to rent a furnished apartment in the Palisades neighborhood."

"How much is it?"

"Two thousand a month includes utilities. If I stay a year, that's twenty-four thousand of the hundred thousand."

"You taking your car?"

"Nah, it makes me look poor, so I'm selling it. I don't need a car. I'll use public transportation."

"You got everything but the girl. And she's the most important."

"And I will get her for sure."

"What if she's ugly?"

"She won't be. I'm targeting an assistant to someone in the know—like the assistant to the chief of staff. She is always young, attractive, and single. If she has a boyfriend, he won't be coming to DC with her, so that is perfect for me. Even better if she doesn't have a boyfriend."

"How do you plan on meeting her?"

"I'm going to use some of the money to make a large donation to the campaign when the general election starts."

"How much?"

"Fifty thousand."

"Fifty thousand?"

"That will get me noticed and a VIP ticket to the main inaugural ball where I will be introduced to the campaign manager, cabinet members, and party heads. One of their assistants is the one I need to get started."

"You make it sound easy, but it's not."

"I know it's not. But all I need is a foot in the door—and a VIP invitation to the inaugural ball is that foot."

"Yeah, but that foot might get cut off."

"Not before the work is done."

Devin held his silence with wary eyes.

William smiled. "I can do this."

Devin nodded and hugged his brother.

* * *

William was in his car outside Devin's home, peering at the sneakers draped over the high wire that stretched across the undivided street, thinking about the children the shoes memorialized and how he would tell Sandra that he was leaving.

As he drove to her apartment, he felt a snag in his plan for the first time. Everything that seemed so easy wasn't anymore. *If I leave, she will find another nigga. How am I going to stop that from happening?*

He was wrestling with indecision when he arrived at her apartment.

She kissed him and gleefully led him into the bedroom. After their climax, she said, "That was intense. It was like you were making love to me for the first time. Mmm, I loved it."

As their heads lay on the double pillows with the soothing voice of Minnie Riperton across their ears, William's eyes were on the ceiling, his mind searching for a way to tell her.

"Babe, I got to tell you something."

Happy feelings turned her body on the side to face him. "What is it, babe?"

His body hesitantly turned to face her. *How am I going to say it?*

His expression dampened her smile, and she said, "What's wrong?"

Damn. He slid his tongue across the top and bottom lips of his closed mouth.

"What's wrong, babe? You know you can tell me."

After pausing a few seconds, he said, "I'm quitting my job and going away."

"Going away? Where you going?"

"I'm going away for a while."

Her puzzled expression turned angry. She raised up. "You going away for a while? What that mean?"

"I need to go away for a while, and I can't tell you where I'm going. I hope you still love me when I come back."

"When is that?"

"I'm not sure."

"What's going on? Where you going, William? You been cheating on me?"

"Cheating on you? How can I cheat on you? We're not married, and we're not shacking. I hate it when women say their boyfriends cheated on them when they aren't living together. I told you before that I'm not going to live like a married man when I'm not."

She raised her voice. "Oh, so what you saying? I can fuck another nigga and you won't think that I cheated on you?"

"I won't because we're not married, and we aren't living together."

"So you gonna go and fuck other bitches and expect me to wait for you to come back? Nigga please, you got the wrong girl for that." She rose from the bed and yelled, "So this was your farewell fuck? Nigga, get out!"

William leaned up. "I don't want it to end like this?"

"Oh, you don't? How do you want it to end? You want me to say, I'll wait for you? Nigga, I ain't waiting for no man unless he is locked up or fighting a war. Are you gonna be locked up or fighting a war?"

"It's not that."

"Then get the fuck out!"

She was whimpering as she hastily put on her panties and bra.

William rose from the bed and tried to embrace her.

She pushed him away. "Nigga, get out! And don't come back!"

"Sandra, I have to do this."

"Do what? You can't tell me what it is? Why?"

"Coz, I have to be incognito to do it."

"Do what? You ain't no secret agent or undercover cop. What the fuck is up?"

"I just need you to trust me."

"Nah, you need me to be stupid. You are quitting your job, moving away, don't know when you coming back, and want me to wait for you. Nigga, your dick ain't that good."

She left the room in tears while he was putting on his clothes.

Shit. I need to reconsider this move. I love her more than I realized. Damn. But I have to do this.

When William left the bedroom, Sandra was sitting on the sofa with her pain-stricken eyes on him.

He stepped to her and said, "Sandra, I love you. Trust me. I need to do something that I can't tell you."

"What you gotta do that you can't tell me? If you love me, you can tell me. You can trust me. Stop asking me to trust you when you don't trust me."

He lowered his forehead and slowly rubbed his fingers across it, seemingly searching for words to say. *I really love her.* He lifted his head in the silence between them, and with endearing eyes, said, "I love you, Sandra. I trust you, but I know you won't be cool with what I have to do. Please trust me. I need to do this. It's only temporary."

Her wanting eyes turned abhorrent. "You got that right! I'm not cool with you fuckin' some bitch and then coming back to me when you get tired of the hoe. Get the fuck out!"

With uncertain eyes, he backed away and headed toward the front door, hoping she would stop him, but she didn't. He held that hope until he heard the door slam behind him. He turned with the thought of knocking. *Shit. I can't turn back now. I have to do this.* He slowly backed away with eyes on the door as if he was trying to will her to open it.

She didn't.

In a desolate state of mind, he slowly headed down the stairs, looking back with each step, but she wasn't there.

Inside the car, he was wrestling with conflicting thoughts and feelings for several minutes before he left the complex. "I have to do this," he repeatedly said as he drove into the next chapter of his life.

Chapter 5

An idyllic feeling held Summer as she watched the sun setting over the lake from her bedroom window. With a happiness she hadn't felt in her life, she phoned her mother. "Hi, Ma, I miss you." She felt her mother smile and said, "I'm getting married."

"Married? When?"

"In July."

"July? So soon?"

"Yes. Are you coming to the wedding?"

"Yes! What makes you think I wouldn't?"

"Because you didn't seem to like Saul."

"I shook his hand."

"But you didn't speak to him."

"I didn't want him to hear my accent."

"What's wrong with your accent? You came from the good Germans."

Guilt kept her mother silent.

"Ma, do you think Theodore will stand in for Father at my wedding? I can't ask Shawn because he's racist. I don't believe Theodore is a racist—he's just following Shawn. Do you think Theodore will do it?"

As if she didn't know, her mother said, "He might. Ask him."

"I called his office and left a message. I've even paged him, but no reply."

"He must be very busy. I haven't seen or talked to him since Christmas. If I speak to him, I will tell him to call you."

"Thanks."

"When are you coming to see me again?"

"Ma, I just saw you last month. I know you miss Father. I'll visit as soon as I can. I'm living in Syracuse now with Saul, working at the University hospital."

"You should've waited until you were married before you moved in with him."

"Ma, this is 1980. Things have changed."

"Some things shouldn't change. Are you still coming to my birthday party?"

"Of course I am. Why would you ask that?"

"Because you're getting married in July, and my party is in August."

"Nothing is going to keep me from celebrating your seventy-fifth birthday with you."

"Are you bringing Saul?"

"Do you want me to bring him?"

"Y-yes. He's the first Jew that I met in my life. I like him. He's a good man. Nothing like I expected."

"What did you expect?"

"I heard they didn't have morals. But I could see he does. I was listening to his conversation with your sisters and their husbands. He's very respectful—and makes you happy."

"He does, Ma. He makes me very happy."

"Why are you getting married so soon?"

"Because I love him, and I know I will always love him, so why wait?"

"I have an idea. Why don't you and Saul stay a week after my party?"

"We can't. We're leaving for our honeymoon the day after your party."

"Where are you going?"

"To Israel."

"How long will you be in Israel?"

"Ten days."

"Ah, I'll be alone. I don't like living alone. I've been very lonely since your father died."

"Isn't Shawn and Theodore living there?"

"Sometimes. Mostly it's only me and the servants."

"Do you want to live with Saul and me?"

She meekly said, "Shawn won't let me."

"Ma, don't let Shawn control your life. He isn't your husband."

"He's the head of the family now. Your father told me to trust him."

"Father didn't know Shawn was antisemitic."

Her mother's silence hung over the phone again.

"Ma, what's wrong?"

Her mother didn't say a word.

"Ma, let's talk later. I need to cook dinner. I love you."

With watery eyes that her daughter couldn't see, she said, "I love you."

* * *

Valentine's Day, 1980, Summer left the hospital after a sixteen-hour workday that started at four a.m. When she arrived home, a crystal vase held twelve long-stemmed roses on the small round table in the foyer. A card in an envelope leaned on the vase.

She lifted the vase, inhaled the roses' freshness, and after reading the card, happy tears warmed her cheeks with the energy that replaced the weariness, and she phoned Saul at his office.

"Hi, honey! The roses are beautiful, and I love the card! You surprised me. I thought you forgot about Valentine's Day."

"To forget Valentine's Day is to forget how much I love you," he said.

"Aw, you're so sweet. I have a surprise for you."

"What is it?"

"I'll show you when you get home."

"Hmm."

"I have another surprise."

"Can you tell me this one?"

"Yes. On my lunch break, I went and found the perfect wedding gown."

"Oh. Can I see it when I get home?"

"You can't see it before the wedding."

"Why not?"

"Because it's bad luck."

"Hmm... okay." He chuckled. "I hope you don't outgrow it before the wedding."

She giggled. "Is that your way of saying I'm getting fat?"

He chuckled. "You were a size four when we met."

"I'm still a size four!"

"I know. I'm just teasing."

"Good. What time are you coming home?"

“I’ll be leaving in a few minutes. I’m just finishing up on some paperwork.”

“I don’t like it when you come home late. You know I get jealous. Especially on Valentine’s Day.”

“You have no reason to be jealous. I love you, and only you. I told you I had to make special arrangements to accommodate a new patient.”

“He must be a VIP for you to accept him after eight p.m.”

“He’s the friend of a friend.”

“The patient was a man, right?”

“Yes, a very elderly man.”

“Okay, hurry home. I’m sure everyone has left the building by now. It’s after nine o’clock.”

“I’m getting ready to leave the office now. You want me to bring anything home?”

She soothed, “Just you, and don’t be tired.”

“Mmm, I won’t be. I love you. See you soon.” He closed the folder on his desk and quickly put on his suit jacket and coat, grabbed his briefcase, and headed toward the elevator.

Saul seemed surprised when two women boarded the elevator two floors down. He smiled and said, “I thought I was the only one still in the building.”

The two women smiled and quickly turned their backs to him. One of them pressed P2.

They aren’t very friendly.

When the elevator opened on P2, the two women hurried out.

“Have a good evening,” Saul said.

Both women politely said, “Goodnight,” without looking back.

Saul stepped out of the elevator on P1 and headed toward his car in the nearly empty and well-lit parking garage. He was feeling his love for Summer when he saw the back of a man tussling with a woman for her purse outside the back of a car.

The woman’s frightened eyes saw Saul and she screamed, “Help!”

Saul ran toward the woman as she fell on her back with the purse in hand. “Hey, fella, leave her alone!”

The man turned, and Saul saw the pale red face of a mature man and shouted, "Get away from her!"

The woman scrambled to her feet and sped toward the exit, screaming for help.

The man reached into his coat pocket and pointed a gun at Saul.

Saul stood still and said, "Just leave. You don't want a murder charge. If you need money, you can have my wallet."

The man grinned and fired two shots into Saul's chest.

The two women that had exited on P2 heard the commotion and gunshots. They were the first to notify the police.

Saul lay bleeding, trying to get words out of his mouth as the assassin looked down at him.

When the police arrived, he was dead, and the woman was found trembling a block away. One of the uniformed officers escorted her back to the garage exit and placed her beside one of the squad cars.

A seasoned detective approached. "Miss, my name is Detective Mallory. Are you okay?"

The woman shuddered. "Yes."

"What is your name?"

"Kate."

"And your last name?"

"Bauer."

With a sympathetic voice, the detective said, "Kate, can you tell me what happened?"

"I-I w-was w-walking t-to m-my c-car, and a man grabbed me from behind. I screamed, and that's when I saw someone trying to help me. I was scared and ran away. I heard shots, but I didn't know who was shooting or if the shots were directed at me. I didn't look back."

"How many shots did you hear?"

"I think two or three. I'm not sure."

"Why were you in the parking garage?"

"To get my car."

"Do you work inside the building?"

"No. I was at the bar across the street."

"Were you alone at the bar?"

"Yes."

"Did you have a conversation with anyone at the bar?"

"Several men approached me, but I wasn't looking for a valentine."

The detective held the stare of thinking eyes. "How did you know it was a man that grabbed you? Did you see his face?"

"He had on a mask, but he was black."

"How do you know he was black?"

"I could tell by his voice."

"What did he say?"

"He told me to give him my purse. I thought he was going to rape me."

"Did he have an accent?"

"No."

"Did he sound young or old?"

"Young, like a teen."

"Can you tell me what he was wearing?"

"I only remember the dark mask."

"Could you see his eyes?"

"No. The mask covered his eyes."

"What type of mask was it?"

"A ski mask, I think."

"You couldn't see the eyes or mouth?"

"No. Everything was dark."

"How tall was he?"

"About your height."

"Is there anything else you can remember about him? His shoes, et cetera."

"No. Can I go home now?"

"Did he take anything from you?"

"He tried to take my purse?"

"Thank you, Ms. Bauer. You can go home. I'll be in touch if I have any more questions."

The detective spoke to everyone who notified the police, and those who stated they had seen or heard something. But no one saw the described person leave the garage.

The police did a thorough sweep of the building and the three-level parking garage but didn't find the suspect.

Detective Mallory said to another detective on the scene, "I'm going to the victim's home."

* * *

Summer had fallen asleep on the living room sofa when the doorbell awakened her. *Saul must've forgotten his key again.* She hurried to the door, and without asking, opened it.

Her excitement disappeared at the sight of a man holding a badge and a uniformed officer beside him.

"Sorry to bother you so late. My name is Detective Mallory, and this is Officer Bennett. Is this the home of Saul Goldberg?"

The anxiety that had taken hold of Summer said, "Where is he?"

"Can we come in?"

She allowed them to enter.

"Can we sit?"

"No. I want to know why you are here?"

"What is your relationship to Mr. Goldberg."

"I'm his fiancée. Where is he?"

"I'm sorry to inform you that he was killed tonight."

She screeched, "What?" Rapid tears followed—and her body matched the shock in her mind. She cried, "Wh-what h-happened?"

"Can we sit?"

With jumbled thoughts and tears like a little girl whose hope was gone, she led them to the green linen semicircular sofa.

The detective was patient as she mourned.

With puffed red eyes that dripped tears into her mouth, she said, "How did he die?"

"He died a hero. He tried to save a person's life."

"H-how d-did th-that h-happen? He said he was on his way home."

The detective shared the story as he knew it.

Summer wailed, "How could that happen?" Her face lowered into the palms of her trembling hands.

"I can assure you that I will find the murderer. I won't rest until I do."

Summer lifted her head. "He's dead. The killer doesn't matter. Finding him won't bring back the love of my life."

"But it will bring justice. And I'm sure your fiancé wants that."

"I'd like to be alone now. Thanks for letting me know what happened."

When the detective and officer left, Summer felt the need to call her mother but didn't because it was past eleven p.m. in Wyoming. Instead, she slowly went upstairs to the bedroom and held memories as she looked at pictures and recalled moments.

She cried on the bed in those thoughts until she fell asleep, which was short-lived. The conscious heartache continued with her eyes wide open in the darkness of early morning.

* * *

When the light of day rose, Summer didn't eat, she didn't watch television, and she didn't answer the phone or door. She entered solitude, ignoring the responsibility to inform the hospital that she wasn't coming to work.

In the silence that surrounded the home, she lay in bed, periodically crying at the memories, and the future that wouldn't be.

On the second day of solitude, she phoned her mother and cried, "Ma, Saul was killed."

She couldn't see the water in her mother's eyes but felt it.

Her mother shockingly said, "Wh-what happened?"

"He tried to stop a man from robbing a woman and got shot."

"Oh my God! Summer! I'm so sorry. When did it happen?"

Her voice cracked as she said, "On Valentine's Day."

"Valentine's Day? Why are you just now calling? Are you okay?"

"I'm okay, Ma. I just needed time alone."

"Come home, Summer. Come live with me."

She paused in the thought and said, "I will after the funeral."

* * *

On the day of the funeral, her mother, sisters, and their husbands and children attended. But no one from Saul's side of the family was there.

A few days later, Summer paid the mortgage balance and enshrined the home. Two months later, she moved to live with her mother on the Gillette estate and resided in the guest-house fifty yards from the mansion. There, she also opened her private practice.

* * *

A day didn't pass without Saul in Summer's thoughts. But she was happy living on the estate and with her private practice.

In her second month on the estate, Summer was upstairs in the residence area of the house when she heard a knock on the door. *That must be Theodore. He said he was coming by.* She hurried downstairs and opened the door. Shawn stood in front of her.

"What do you want?" she irritably asked.

"Can I come in?"

She turned her back and walked away with the door open.

Shawn entered, closed the door, and followed her into the private office.

She faced him. "Why are you here?"

"I came to see my little sister."

"Why? What do you want?"

"I have a friend who would like to meet you."

"I'm not interested in any of your friends."

"Why do you have an attitude?"

"You're my brother, but I don't like you."

"Why? Because I don't like Jews?"

"Because you're racist."

"I'm the man that Father made me to be."

"Father wasn't a racist!"

"I'm not here to talk about that again. You're my sister, and I want you to be happy."

"I was happy. It was a Jew who made me happy. And the evil in the world killed him because he cared about the safety of others more than himself."

Shawn didn't try to hide the contempt in his eyes and said, "Are Jewish women among your patients?"

"Why?"

He turned and headed toward the front door.

She stared. *What happened to him?*

He paused when he opened the door, and with thoughts seemingly on his mind, turned and faced her. "They won't be around much longer," he said in German, and left.

Chapter 6

At her mother's seventy-fifth birthday party, Summer avoided Shawn and his friends.

When Theodore arrived, she hugged him. "How have you been? You never called me back. You don't like me anymore?"

He smiled and said, "You know I will always love you," and kissed her on the cheek.

"I wanted you to stand in for Father at my wedding."

"I know. Mother told me."

"Why didn't you reply to my messages?"

"I was busy. This hostage matter is making the company lose money."

"How?"

"Too much detail to get into it right now. How have you been since the death of your friend?"

"He was more than my friend. He was my fiancé. We had planned to get married last month. Were you going to stand in for Father?"

"I will at the next wedding. I'm glad you're living here. We will see each other more often."

"Where are you living now?"

"I'm in Cheyenne during the week, and Idaho on weekends."

"I need to come and visit you."

"Sure. That would be nice. When?"

"You the busy one. You tell me when."

"Soon. Let's chat about it later."

He kissed her on the cheek again, and she embraced him.

"I love you," he said, and went to April.

Summer sat beside her mother for the reminder of the party. Afterward, she escorted her mother to the private elevator that carried them directly to her mother's bedroom.

"I have something that I need to give you," her mother said.

"What is it, Ma?"

Her mother opened the top bedside-table drawer and took out a sealed letter and key and handed both to Summer.

"What is this?"

"Promise me that you won't open the letter or use the key until after my funeral."

"Your funeral? Ma, you aren't dying yet."

"Promise me."

"Ma, why? What is this? What does this key open?"

"Promise me."

"Ma, you will outlive me."

"Promise me."

"Okay, I promise. Now tell me about this letter and key?"

With watery eyes, she lay the palm of her hands on Summer's cheeks and kissed her forehead. "I'm sorry."

"Sorry for what?"

She lowered her hands with a smile as if she was looking at her daughter for the first time. "I love you. Don't tell anyone that I gave you a letter and key. That includes your sisters. After my funeral, read the letter when you're alone."

"Ma, it will be a long time before you die."

"Promise me you will read it when you are alone. When none of your sisters or brothers are in the same city."

Summer held the thinking expression.

"Promise me."

"Okay. I promise. I won't mention it, and I won't read it until I'm alone."

Her mother smiled and said, "I love you. I will always love you."

"Ma, you are scaring me. Stop talking about dying."

"I'm tired." She removed her slippers and climbed under the sheets fully clothed.

"Ma, you're not going to undress?"

"I will later. Goodnight. I love you."

Summer kissed her mother again and said, "Goodnight. You want me to turn off the light?"

"No, leave it on."

* * *

The next morning, Mr. Jeffries, the butler, tried to wake Summer's mother but couldn't. She was dead. He quickly notified Shawn, who had spent the night in the house. Shawn informed his brother and sisters, who had also spent the night on the estate.

The coroner informed them the death was by suicide. He said their mother had taken a cyanide pill.

While her brothers and sisters had bewildered faces, Summer said, "What! Why would my Ma kill herself? She went to bed happy."

Shawn said, "She wanted to be with Father, so she went to be with him."

The others seemingly agreed. But Summer said, "This has something to do with that..."

"That what? Something to do with what?" Shawn asked.

I'm sorry, Ma. I almost slipped. "Nothing."

Shawn suspiciously said, "You were going to say something. What is it?"

Summer paused with eyes that felt like she had been put on the spot. *I have to say something, or they will keep pressing.* "Ma told me about a TV evangelist who was preaching about life after death. I guess you're right, Shawn. She wanted to be with Father."

Shawn seemingly accepted her answer and eyed Leigh and April. "I don't want you to miss your flights. It's nothing else you can do here. I'll make the funeral arrangements. I think we all need to be alone right now."

Summer went to her residence, relieved she hadn't mentioned the letter. As the seconds passed, she grew restless and curious about the letter and key and opened her safe. She lifted the envelope with wanting eyes, but at the forefront of her mind was the guilt of breaking her promise.

I can't read it yet. I promised. She put the letter and key back in the safe and locked it.

* * *

Her mother's repast was held on the estate. And when family and friends left to return to their homes, Summer ambled in the twilight, her feet headed toward her residence but her mind was in other places.

She was numb when she entered her home and fell asleep on the waiting room sofa. In the darkness of 11:19, her eyes opened, and the letter was the first thing that came to mind. She hurried upstairs, opened the safe, lifted the envelope, and read the letter.

My precious daughter. I pray after reading this letter, your love for me and your father remain. You were too young to remember your true name. Greta is the name you were given at birth. I was not among the good Germans in Switzerland. I was born in Germany and married your father in Berlin. He was a member of the Nazi party and one of the Holocaust architects.

We came to America at the end of the war under the protection of the U.S. government because the CIA recruited your father to work for them. Shawn, Leigh, and April were old enough to remember their names. I told them their names were changed for their protection because your father was fighting against the Communists who were trying to overthrow this country.

The key unlocks a door in the guesthouse that you were forbidden to enter. There you will find the family history.

I hadn't met a Jew until I met Saul. I hated the Jews because your father hated Jews. I was told they were the reason for the country's poverty and why we lost World War I. I believed everything your father said about them until I met Saul. He wasn't what I had been told. I felt ashamed for thinking that way about them. I didn't realize the charity they were doing for people in need. I'm sorry that I celebrated their deaths. I ask God for forgiveness. I ask you for forgiveness. I'm sorry. I hope Shawn isn't the reason for Saul's death. I pray that Theodore doesn't become like him. I love you, Summer. But I will always remember you as Greta.

Tears flowed, and in the darkness of early morning, curiosity led Summer to the estate's third guesthouse. The key didn't open the front door. She walked around to the back door but it didn't work. She went back to her residence and phoned Mr. Jeffries.

As if he wasn't asleep, he said, "Good morning, madam. What can I do for you?"

"Who has the key to open the third guesthouse?"

"Only Mr. Smith."

"My brother Shawn?"

"Yes, and your brother Theodore."

"You can't open it?"

"No, madam. I don't have the key."

"The cleaning lady doesn't have a key?"

"No, madam. Mr. Smith leaves the door unlocked when he wants it cleaned and has given strict orders to lock the door when finished."

"Have you been inside that house?"

"Yes, madam, to serve special guests."

"Is there a room inside the house that is kept locked?"

"Yes, madam. If you like I can inform Mr. Smith that you would like to enter the house."

"No, don't do that. I will speak to him myself. I'm sorry I called so early in the morning."

"Quite alright, madam. I'm here to serve you day and night."

Troubled by the letter, she phoned Leigh.

Her husband answered with the voice of one untimely wakened.

"Hi, Ken. Can I speak to Leigh?"

"She's asleep."

"Can you wake her? It's important."

"Okay, hold on."

Leigh's groggy voice said, "Hello."

"Leigh, is Ken beside you?"

"Yeah."

"I need you to move so we can speak privately."

"Why?"

"Trust me."

"Okay, I'll call you back."

Leigh paused, seemingly in thought as to what might be so urgent.

Ken said, "Is everything alright?"

"Yeah, she just had a bad dream. I'm going to make some coffee and talk to her in the kitchen."

Leigh went downstairs, prepared coffee, and phoned Summer. "What's so important?"

"Ma gave me a letter before she died. She made me promise not to read it until after her funeral, and when I was alone."

"A letter? What does it say?"

"My birth name was Greta."

"I remember that. Mine was Elsa. April was Matilda. Shawn was Maximillian. We had to change our names because Father was fighting the Communists in this country who wanted to kill us if they learned our true names."

"Did you know Father was a Nazi?"

"Who told you that?"

"It's in the letter."

"Let me read that letter."

"The next time you come to Wyoming, you can."

"Why don't you bring it to California?"

"My calendar is full of patients for the month. I don't want to fly to San Francisco and come back the next day. I'll wait until you can come here."

"Okay. Does anyone else know about the letter?"

"No. And please don't tell anyone until I see you—not even your husband."

"Okay."

* * *

Leigh was anxious to read the letter and flew to Wyoming that weekend.

Summer met her at the airport and drove to a secluded restaurant a few miles from the estate.

As soon as they sat in the private booth, Leigh said, "Let me see the letter."

Stages of shock were seen on Leigh's face while reading. "They lied to us! Why did Ma wait until she died to tell us? And why did she say she hoped Shawn didn't have anything to do with Saul's death? Saul was killed by a mugger."

"I don't know what to think," Summer said. "But I know Shawn is a Nazi."

"Theodore's not."

"I know. He's not like Shawn."

"We need to get inside that house and use the key. Something is in that room to support this letter."

Summer seemed to be floating in thoughts.

Leigh said, "Let's break a window and climb inside."

"I thought of that, but it will trigger the alarm."

"So how do we get in?"

"Mr. Jeffries told me a special guest will arrive next month and stay a few days. We can enter then. Shawn doesn't know I have a key to the room."

"I don't want to wait that long. I want to know what's in that room now."

"Me too. But I don't want Shawn to know we're trying to get into that house. If an opportunity comes up before then, I will take it. But for now, we must be patient. Please keep the letter a secret. Don't tell anyone about it. When we find out what's in that room, we can decide if we want the family to know."

"I won't say anything. You can trust me."

* * *

The speculation of things that might be inside that room weighed heavily on Summer's mind, and the knowledge that her father was a Nazi raised guilt every time her Jewish patients brought up the Holocaust as the conversation during their exams. She tried to discreetly change the topic, but it always ended with their anger and hatred for the Nazis.

Rhoda Nirnberg, whose parents were teens that survived occupied France because they were hidden during the war and later married in 1950, was her best friend and patient. Because of the guilt, Summer made excuses to avoid seeing and speaking to her as often as Rhoda wanted but attended the Labor Day cookout at the home of Rhoda's parents.

In conversation with one of the guests, Summer was asked, "Did they find your fiancé's killer?"

"Not yet. But hopefully soon."

"Rhoda told me he was Jewish."

"Yes. But he wasn't killed because he was Jewish."

"Jews aren't liked around here. My family is leaving Wyoming."

"Why?"

"Because antisemitism is growing."

"It is? I haven't noticed."

"That's because you're not Jewish. Our synagogue was spray-painted twice."

"Twice? Rhoda told me about one that happened a month ago."

"The second one happened Friday during Kabbalat Shabbat. I don't feel safe here anymore."

"What state are you moving to?"

"We're moving to another country."

"Another country? Why?"

"The Republicans scare me."

"Why? I'm a Republican."

"I was a Republican. I voted for Milhouse and he surrounded himself with Germans—that was very scary. But I felt safe in the country when he was forced to resign and his goons were sent to prison. I voted for the Democrat in the next presidential election, but he pissed me off when he commuted one of the goons' twenty-year sentence. Can you believe that? A man who tried to spy on his party was released from prison after serving only fifty-four months of a twenty-year sentence. Do you know the first thing that man said when he was released from prison?"

"I don't."

"Outside the prison gate, he spoke in German to the American media."

"What did he say?"

"I don't know. The news anchor didn't know but confirmed his words were German. I no longer trust the presidents of either party. I'm not voting for either of them. This country is changing in the worst way. It's best my family move to Israel."

"The Republican nominee seems like a good man."

"He does. I like him. But members of his party in Congress want to cut Social Security and Medicare. There are a lot of people in this country that depend on Social Security and

Medicare to survive. It's cruel to even think about removing it. I believe in cutting spending but not there. Cut that pork barrel spending."

Seemingly to defend, Summer said, "The members of his party aren't him. He said he won't touch any of the safety nets, and I believe him. He can veto anything from Congress that he doesn't like. I believe he will veto any cuts to Social Security and Medicare if Congress tries to make it law."

"I must admit I find him believable. I'm thinking about voting for him because he might restore the Republican party to moderation. I joined the party when I was eighteen because I'm a conservative, but Milhouse changed the party. I felt like he was trying to bring Nazi Germany here. But this nominee seems like he will bring the party back to its roots."

"I believe he will."

"I'm glad we chatted. I'm going to vote for him. If he wins, my family will stay."

Summer smiled. "I hope he wins. I want you and your family to stay."

They hugged.

Summer said, "What's your name?"

"Rebekah Silverstein."

"I'm Summer Smith."

"I know your name. Everyone in the Jewish community knows your name because you have a lot of Jewish patients who only say good things about you."

Summer smiled. "I'm happy to hear that. Thank you."

"You're welcome. Let's hope the Republican wins. He'll be a great president—and what this country needs."

"I agree."

* * *

Summer was examining a patient when Mr. Jeffries entered the office and left a note with Aponi, the Native American receptionist. When Summer received the note, she said within, "The guest has arrived!" While waiting for the next appointment, she phoned Mr. Jeffries from the receptionist's desk.

"Hello, madam."

"Mr. Jeffries, is Shawn and the guest still at the house?"

"They are, madam. But they will be leaving soon."

"How soon?"

"Within the hour."

"Call me when they leave?"

"I will, madam."

Summer hung up the phone and eyed the receptionist. "Notify me when he calls back."

"I will, Ms. Smith."

Summer was in consultation with a patient when the receptionist entered the examination room. "Excuse me, Ms. Smith, you have an important phone call."

Summer quickly said to the patient, "Excuse me, I'll be right back," and hurried to the phone.

"Hello."

"Madam, your brother and his guest have left the grounds. They should be away for a few hours."

"Thank you."

The thought of canceling her remaining appointments lingered, but she didn't. And at the close of business, she quickly phoned Mr. Jeffries. "Has Shawn or the guest returned?"

"No, madam."

With the car key in hand, she sprinted toward her car. *Wait, I can't drive there. They might come back and see my car*. She decided to walk the hundred and fifty yards, nervous at each step, and paranoid in her thoughts.

When she arrived, the front door was locked. She hurried to the backdoor and it was locked. Other options also became dead ends. She disappointingly hustled back to her residence and phoned Leigh at work.

When Leigh answered, Summer spurted, "The guest is here."

"Is it a man or woman?"

"I don't know. Mr. Jeffries told me Shawn and the guest left the grounds, so I went to the house, but the doors were locked and curtains closed."

"What are you going to do?"

"Get inside that house."
"How?"
"I will figure something out."

* * *

An hour later there was a knock on Summer's door. She opened and Shawn was standing with a young woman clothed in designer attire from head-to-toe.

Shawn said, "I have a friend staying at the guesthouse for a few days, would you like to have dinner with us tonight?"

"Where?"

"At the guesthouse."

"Which one?"

"The one that Father kept off limits."

"Um, okay. What time?"

"Seven. By the way, this is Kimberly."

Summer smiled and said, "Hi."

Kimberly sophisticatedly said, "Hello."

"Will you be joining us for dinner?" Summer asked.

Kimberly's eyes shifted to Shawn, and he said, "Yes, she will."

"I'll see you both at seven."

* * *

In preparation for the dinner, Summer was contemplating how to get inside that room without being noticed.

When she arrived at the guesthouse, Shawn introduced her to Ronald Rudolph, an attractive forty-something. She flirted with eye contact. He flirted back by placing his free hand on top of their handshake.

They sat for dinner prepared in the house kitchen by one of the estate cooks, and during the meal, Ronald said, "Summer, what are you looking for?"

She shieldingly said, "Looking for?"

"I noticed your eyes roving every few seconds."

"That's because I've never been in this house."

Shawn interjected, "Father restricted this house to my mother, brother, and special guests only."

"Ah, I see."

Summer said, "Ronald, what are your aspirations as a lawyer?"

He held the closed-mouth smile before he said, "Head of the Justice Department. I want to rid the streets of crime and remove the dirty politicians."

Kimberly said, "I know you will make a great attorney general."

Shawn said, "When we win the presidency next month, he will be nominated and confirmed by the Senate."

With unsure eyes, Summer said, "I like your confidence."

Shawn looked at her side-eyed. "Are you voting for the Democrat?"

"No. I'm a Republican like you. I'm just not as confident. The polls have a close race."

Shawn sarcastically smiled. "It won't be."

After dinner, the four entered a room lit by the fireplace and distant candles. Each held a long-stemmed glass of sherry as they sat on the tan leather sofa that faced the fireplace.

After a half an hour or so of casual conversation between the four, Shawn said to Ronald, "I will see you in the morning," and led Kimberly from the house.

Ronald eyed Summer and said, "You look uncomfortable. You can leave if you like. I'll be disappointed, but I rather be disappointed than to be in the company of an uncomfortable guest."

"I'm not uncomfortable. My brother has been trying to be a matchmaker since my fiancé died. I'm just not ready for a sexual relationship."

"I'm not asking for one. I think you're beautiful and would be honored to see you again. For now, I only want to know the woman you are."

Summer slid back on the sofa and shifted her body to face him. "First, I'd like to know who you are."

He smiled. "Okay. What do you want to know?"

"How long have you known my brother?"

"Sixteen years. Our fathers were friends."

"Are you here for business or pleasure?"

"No matter how much time for business is needed, there is always room for pleasure. I find pleasure in having a conversation with you. Would you like some more sherry?"

Summer extended her glass.

He lifted the bottle off the fused-silica glass coffee table that was in front of the sofa, and with the smiling face said, "Half empty or half full?"

"You decide."

He poured, keeping his eyes locked on hers.

"That's enough," she said, and sipped.

"Half full. I'm surprised. I thought you wanted half-empty."

She sipped again without losing eye contact and said, "How long will you be here?"

"Only for one more night."

"Ah."

"You sound disappointed."

"Let's just say I'm enjoying the company."

"Happy to hear that."

"What are your plans for tomorrow?"

"Your brother and I are flying to Wisconsin. We want the people to know Republicans are the true patriots. The Democrats are socialist and Marxist. They want sanctuary cities for illegal immigrants and rampant crime."

"Let's not talk about politics."

"You are a Republican, right?"

"I am. But I'm more on the moderate side. It's getting late. I have an early patient tomorrow."

"I hope it wasn't something that I said."

"It wasn't. I'm just tired. Maybe a little too much sherry. What time are you coming back tomorrow?"

"Um, we should be back by six."

"I'm sure you will be hungry when you get back."

"Are you offering to take me to dinner?"

"Better. I'll cook dinner for you."

A huge smile lit his face. "Your place or mine?"

"Let's eat here. I'll have dinner ready when you arrive."

"I wasn't expecting you to say that. You must like me."

"I'd like to know you better."

"It's mutual."

"How can I get in to cook? I don't have a key."

"I will leave the door unlocked."

She smiled and slowly headed for the door. *I hope he doesn't try to kiss me.*

He said within, "I think I should wait until tomorrow to kiss her. The odds of going all the way will be better." He accelerated his steps to open the front door for her. He eyed her and extended his hand. "It was nice meeting you, Summer."

She looked him in the eye and shook his hand. "Nice meeting you too. Goodnight."

"Goodnight."

Whew. I got out of there without him trying to kiss me.

The short drive back to her residence held multiple and various thoughts as she walked into the house. She hurried upstairs and phoned Leigh.

"I can get into the room tomorrow."

"How?"

"I had dinner with the guest tonight. I'm cooking dinner for him tomorrow."

"How are you going to get into the room with him there?"

"He won't be. He's going to Wisconsin tomorrow. I told him that I would have dinner ready when he returned."

"What time is he leaving for Wisconsin?"

"Sometime in the morning I guess."

"Okay. Be careful."

"I will. I'll call you after."

* * *

The next morning, Summer was anxious, and struggled to keep her focus on the patients. When her lunch break finally came, she sped to the guesthouse. Surprisingly, the maid was there when she entered.

"Hi, Ms. Smith."

"Hello, Keisha."

"I'm sorry. I didn't know anyone was coming so soon. I'll hurry up."

"Don't mind me. Take your time." Summer started checking the downstairs doors and found one that was locked. She tried the key and the door opened. She turned the knob and slowly entered the room's darkness. She stopped, with her hand searching for the light switch. She found it and saw a room without windows, a Nazi flag pinned to the center wall, and on each side of the flag was a mannequin in full SS uniform.

She closed the door and was marveling as she slowly walked around the spacious room, looking at family pictures from Germany: a picture of her father and Himmler in street clothes outside the Wannsee House; a picture of her father and Shawn in the SS uniform outside Dachau; a picture of her father, Eichmann, and Mengele inside the Hadamar Euthanasia Center; and a picture of her father and Hitler with Shawn in a Nazi youth uniform.

Tears leaked when she saw the pictures of men that looked like walking skeletons and sobbed when she played a VHS tape that showed the aftermath of the gas chamber.

On the top shelf with her parents' wedding pictures was a copy of *Mein Kampf*. She opened the book and saw that it was autographed by Adolf Hitler. In a mind that didn't want to believe what her eyes saw, she hurried from the room without turning off the light and locking the door.

Keisha heard Summer weeping as she headed toward the front door. "Ms. Smith, are you alright?"

Summer didn't answer. She rushed into her car and quickly drove away.

Keisha watched, then looked back, and informed Mr. Jeffries.

When Summer arrived back at her residence, she hid her tears and said to Aponi, "Cancel my remaining appointments for the day."

"Okay. Are you alright?"

"I have a headache. Tell Mrs. Lyons and Ms. Loveland that I'm sick and will reschedule when I'm feeling better."

"Okay, Ms. Smith."

"After, you can leave for the day."

"Thank you, Ms. Smith."

She ran upstairs to her bedroom and phoned Leigh.

In tears, Summer said, "I went into the room. It's horrible. Our father was a murderer."

"What? What did you see?"

"I don't want anyone else to see what I saw. I can't stay here any longer. I'm leaving!"

"Where are you going? What about your patients? You just can't leave."

"I can't stay here. Our father raised Shawn to be a Nazi. For all I know he is the one that had Saul killed."

"You know Shawn wouldn't do that. He's an asshole sometimes but not a murderer."

"I saw a VHS tape that showed dead bodies from the gas chamber. Father wasn't alive when VHS tapes were invented. Someone put that old video on a VHS tape. Only three people had a key to that room after Father's death. It wasn't Ma. I know it wasn't Theodore, so it had to be Shawn."

"Can you wait until I come before you leave?"

"When is that?"

"This weekend."

Leigh could feel her thinking and said, "P-pleassee."

"Okay. I'll wait."

* * *

Mr. Jeffries phoned Summer's residence several times, but each time the line was busy, so he went to the residence.

She answered the residence doorbell with signs of fallen tears.

"Are you okay, madam?"

"Everything is okay. I'm fine, Mr. Jeffries."

"Something in that house upset you. What was it?"

"Nothing. I was just thinking about my fiancé. I need to be alone right now."

"Of course, madam." He backstepped and turned away.

She closed the door and stood. *Maybe I should tell him.* But she went back upstairs.

Mr. Jeffries took the long walk to the mysterious guesthouse, believing the answers to the questions he had about the family were in that room.

When he arrived, Keisha said, "Is Ms. Summer alright."

"She said she is, but she's not. Don't mention this to anyone."

"I won't."

"Are you finished here?"

"I am."

"I'll lock up."

"Thank you."

When Keisha left, Mr. Jeffries went to the room that was always kept locked. He turned the knob and didn't expect the door to open but it did, and he entered the lit room. On the television screen were the mutilated bodies of men, women, and children. He saw lampshades made from human skin. "This is why hell exists," he said within, and turned off the television, light, and locked the door as he left the room.

In an angry mind, he somberly headed toward the mansion where he saw Summer leaving her residence.

She stopped and rolled down the driver's window. "Mr. Jeffries."

He stopped and faced her with emotionless eyes.

She hesitated before she said, "Please notify Shawn's guest that I had to leave for an emergency."

He lifelessly replied, "I will, madam," and continued walking.

The sound of his words gave her pause. "He saw the room," she said within and contemplated if she should ask him as she watched him amble toward the mansion, seemingly waiting to see if he would look back. When he didn't, she left the estate.

* * *

In a weltering state of mind, Summer drove to Rhoda's home in Carlile. With the evidence that tears had removed her mascara, she knocked on the door.

"What happened? What's wrong?" Rhoda supportively asked.

With the back of her fingers, Summer wiped the new tears that leaked, and said, "Nothing. I just miss Saul."

"Have you eaten?"

"I'm not hungry."

"Something's wrong. You know you can tell me."

"I'll be okay. I just need to be with a friend."

Rhoda embraced her. "I love you. I will always be there for you."

Summer cried, "I can't go back home. Can I stay here until the weekend?"

"Of course. You know you didn't have to ask."

"Thank you."

For the first two days, Summer's body was with Rhoda, but her mind was everywhere. On the third day, she said, "I'm not going back to my mother's estate."

"Are you moving back to Syracuse?"

"No. I will miss you too much. I'm going to transfer my practice to this county. That way Aponi won't lose her job."

"It would be selfish of me to celebrate that news without asking why you're leaving your mother's estate."

"I'm leaving because my brother doesn't like Jews. I don't want to be around someone who doesn't like Jews just because they are Jews."

Rhoda was speechless at the information received—and surprised—but didn't ask the question in her mind.

Summer said, "There are available office suites in Crook and Laramie counties. I'm thinking about opening an office two days a week in Crook County and two days a week in Laramie County. I can keep my existing patients and have new ones."

"That's a great idea! I told you to expand your service to more populous areas. I'm glad you decided to make that move."

"I have. Thank you!"

They hugged, and during her stay Rhoda didn't ask Summer for the details surrounding her decision to abruptly leave the estate.

* * *

On Saturday afternoon, Summer met Leigh at the Gillette airport, and they drove along the Bighorn Scenic Byway, stopping along the side of the road a few times to cry, exhale, and smile. They spent the entire weekend combing the state of Wyoming.

Leigh asked, "Are you still going to vote for the Republican nominee?"

"Yes. I believe he will return the party to sanity."

"I do too. But Shawn is a major donor to his campaign. You think Shawn will have influence over him?"

"I think Shawn will try, but he doesn't believe what Shawn believes. Shawn is supporting him because he doesn't want a Democrat to be president."

"Maybe we should vote for the Democrat."

"No. I don't trust him because your Aunt Rebekah told me he commuted the sentence of a Neo-Nazi."

Leigh chuckled and said, "Shawn should be giving his money to him."

"He won't. You know Father raised us to be Republicans for life. But I'm not voting for a Republican because he or she is a Republican. I'm voting for the person that believes in democracy as it is. But Shawn will vote for anyone who is a Republican."

"Have you told anyone about the room?"

"No."

"Let's take a vow not to tell anyone about that room, not even April. I don't want her to know the truth about our father, and I don't want my husband and children to know their grandfather was a murderer."

With solemn eyes, Summer said, "Agreed."

Chapter 7

On election day, William was living in the Palisades neighborhood in Washington, DC, listening to commercial-free WHFS while waiting for the polls to close. As he predicted, the former actor won the presidency.

He phoned his brother to gloat.

Devin said, "I didn't vote for him."

"I didn't vote for him either," William said.

"But you gave money to his campaign. You said he's only a puppet, and I agree. Sooo, the money you gave was to the man behind the curtain. Who is that?"

William smirked. "The beast. We can't prevent the beast from rising."

"No we can't. But I'm not going to be found guilty of helping the beast rise. You helped the beast. Whatever happens, good or bad, you are part of the reason. If his administration is what you believe it is, then you are guilty of every bad thing they do. You didn't look at it like that did you?"

William was silent in the truth that pierced his heart.

Devin felt his brother's mood and said, "Maybe God chose you to tell the story. If he did, your sin will be forgiven."

William stayed silent in his thoughts. He felt his brother was right in every word.

"You can't turn back now," Devin said. "Maybe what you're planning will help in the end."

With a doubtful voice, William said, "How?"

"I heard a wise man say, the end justifies the means if the end is righteous. Maybe the end of your work will make things righteous."

William paused on the thought, and said, "Thanks. I needed to hear that."

* * *

On the morning of the inauguration, William lay in bed with eyes and ears on the television. His brows lifted when Breaking News announced, "The American hostages are preparing to be released." *Wow!* The news coverage continued with a split screen of the plane waiting for the hostages to board and the president waiting to be sworn in.

William's analytical mind went to work throughout the coverage. *This isn't a coincidence! Hostages are taken for ransom, leverage to escape, or swapping prisoners. The hostage takers are in their own country with the protection of their government and don't have any prisoners in this country. That means they got paid to release the hostages. That's why the plane didn't depart until after the president was sworn in. The Elephant heads staged it to make the incoming president appear strong and feared. Wow! I'm definitely on the right track.*

* * *

As expected, William received an invitation to the main inaugural ball, and when he arrived, several women were eyeing him, some with husbands at their side. In his pretentious posture, he was approached by a short, porky, middle-aged, pale-red-skinned woman.

"Hello," she said. "My name is Beth."

"Ah, Beth. Nice to meet you. I'm William Walker."

Her eyes seem to sparkle. "Mr. Walker. I wasn't expecting someone as young as you. So glad you were able to make it." She poshly extended her hand.

He shook her hand and said, "Thanks for the invitation."

"Thank you for the generous donation. Your contribution made tonight possible."

He paused in the guilt of his brother's words.

Beth said, "What is your work, if you don't mind me asking?"

"I'm an author."

"You must be a very successful author. What are the names of your books?"

"My books have sold over a million copies. But as the ghostwriter, I cannot share the names of the books. That will violate my contract."

"I see."

"But I've given up ghostwriting. I'm currently writing a book with my name on it."

"What genre?"

"Science fiction/fantasy."

"Interesting. Maybe you can tell me more about it later."

He smiled and nodded.

"Let me introduce you to some of the guests."

She flirtingly locked arms and escorted William around the enormous ballroom, introducing him to familiar and unfamiliar politicians in search of six-figure donors.

Afterward she said, "Enjoy. We will talk later."

William was strolling around, listening to music that bored him, when a middle-aged woman in four-inch heels and a red dress that revealed every part of her silicone breasts except the nipples approached. She lifted the martini glass to her overly fat-injected lips and sipped with eyes staring. "H-helloo," she said.

William smiled. "Hello." *She definitely isn't the one I'm looking for. Too whorish and old.*

Her horny voice said, "I love your smile."

He politely extended the smile. "Thank you."

"Are you alone?"

"I am for now."

Her head tilted with light brown eyes looking up at him.

"What are you trying to see?"

She grinned. "I like chocolate. I'm always on the lookout for chocolate. Deep chocolate is my favorite."

"I can see it in your eyes."

She slid her tongue across the bright red lipstick, took a step closer, and coquettishly said, "What else can you see?"

William grinned. "Excuse me. I see a friend over there."

He walked away and joined a group that included two men that Beth had introduced earlier.

She watched as he inserted himself into their conversation, then turned her eyes away in search of someone to satisfy her apparent heat.

The party was a bore for William until the orchestra played *"Hail to the Chief."* The attention of all eyes shifted to the entrance, and William joined the applause for the President and First Lady.

After the president and his wife danced the waltz, William watched Beth direct a group of men into a side room. Then she escorted the president and his secret service entourage into that room.

"That's the dark money," William said within and periodically kept his eyes on the room.

When the president came out, he and the First Lady exited the ballroom. William approached Beth and said, "Where's the afterparty?"

A smile stretched across her face. "Where do you want it to be?"

"My place."

"Give me a minute."

He watched Beth walk over to a woman and lean her mouth into the woman's ear. When Beth returned, she said, "Let's go."

They rode in her car and kept the conversation away from politics. When they entered his apartment, they quickly engaged in raw sex and fell asleep in bed.

The morning sun through the eleventh-floor open window awakened William. As Beth lay asleep, he turned on the news at a low volume.

Seconds later, Beth woke and smilingly said, "Good morning."

William returned the smile. "Good morning. Are you hungry?"

"Depends on what you have?"

"I think I got what you want."

She grinned. "What's that?"

He lowered the sheet and showed an erection, and Beth quickly gave it the ten-minute workout.

Afterward she said, "You know I'm married."

"I see the ring. Where's your husband?"

"Home."

"Where's home?"

"Topeka, Kansas. He'll be here in two days."

"Why is he coming to DC?"

"There is a social on Friday night for the White House staff. It's a time for everyone to meet and get to know each other."

"People like the chief of staff, presidential advisors, and their assistants?"

"Exactly."

"Are donors allowed?"

"None is expected. You wanna go?"

"I would like to go, but your husband will be there."

"It's okay. I know how to stay professional. Besides, you'll blend in with the staff because of your age."

They kissed, and he slowly went down on her.

* * *

William wore a debonair black suit with an open-collar white shirt to the social, and curious eyes from women and men followed his steps.

Beth smilingly approached and introduced him to her husband, Nils, a bald, stocky man who looked twenty years older than her.

"My wife told me that you made a generous donation to the campaign. Where does your money come from?"

William smiled. *I bet he doesn't ask those young white donors where their money comes from.* "I was a ghostwriter for a couple of bestsellers. Instead of having a small slice of the pie, I decided to have the whole pie and write a book with my name on it."

"I'm an avid reader. Maybe I read one of the books you wrote. What are the names?"

"I can't share that information. I will violate my contract. But I can tell you the books were literary fiction."

"Is that the genre you're currently writing?"

"No. I'm writing a sci-fi thriller. I need a beta reader. Are you interested?"

Nils smirked and said, "I only read non-fiction."

"I don't write non-fiction."

Beth interjected, "Thanks, William, enjoy yourself," and led her husband away.

William smiled. *That man is suspicious of me. I have to be very careful around him.*

Nodding to "Dreaming" by Blondie, he approached a group of five men—three white, one black, and one Hispanic. With a drink in hand, he introduced himself and joined their debate.

One of the white men said, "You're not born anything except male or female."

The black guy and the two other white men agreed.

The Hispanic guy didn't comment.

William said, "I disagree."

The man who made the statement locked eyes with him and said, "You can't be born anything other than male or female. Everything else is learned behavior. You can't be born evil, gay, or a liar."

"I disagree," William said. "If you believe in the Bible, it's written, 'The wicked are estranged from the womb: they go astray as soon as they be born, speaking lies.' " (Psalm 58:3 – AKJV)

The five were silent with their eyes on William, seemingly marveling.

He added, "And wasn't Jesus born the Christ?"

The Hispanic guy marked himself with the cross while the others sipped their drinks without comment.

William changed the subject and said, "There are a lot of hot women in here."

The Hispanic guy said, "The hottest is Laura."

"Who is Laura?" William asked.

"The assistant to the press secretary." He pointed at her.

The black guy said, "Naw, it's Ramona with that Brazilian ass and plump lips."

One of the white guys said, "You're both wrong. It's Valarie."

The other two white guys agreed.

The black guy said, "Valarie is hot."

"Who's Valarie?" William asked.

The white guy replied, "She's the assistant to the chief of staff."

William enthusiastically asked, "Where is she?"

The black guy said, "She's not here. I heard she went home for the weekend to see her boyfriend."

"The lucky bastard," said one of the white guys.

The black guy said, "She's coming to my birthday party next month."

William's eyes gleamed.

One of the white guys said, "How did you get her to come to your party?"

"I invited her, Ramona, and Laura during the orientation."

The Hispanic guy said, "I know I'm coming to your party now."

William said, "Am I invited?"

The black guy broadened his smile. "Sure."

William eyed him. "I'm sorry, what's your name again?"

"Steve."

William shook his hefty hand.

The black guy said, "What's your name again?"

"William."

"I look forward to seeing you at my party."

"I will definitely be there with a bottle of Hennessy."

The six men shared backgrounds and contact information. Then in conversation, William said, "There are seven types of a woman's ass."

One of the white guys said, "What are the seven?"

The black guy interjected, "Flat is one," and laughed.

William said, "Flat is one. The others are almost flat, baseball, softball, volleyball, basketball, and beach ball."

One of the white guys pointed at the rear of a woman in jeans and said, "What ass is that?"

William said, "A beach ball in need of air."

They all laughed.

The night ended with William as their new friend.

* * *

William and Beth had a daily conversation.

One evening after their phone sex, she said, "Wow, I needed that! It's been a stressful day."

"Why?"

"One of the donors is a real pain in the ass."

"Why?"

"He's too damn demanding."

"Let your assistant cater to him."

"He's too important."

"Oh, he's a big donor."

"Seven figures."

"Word, that's big. What's his name?"

"Shawn Smith."

"Never heard of him. What's his business?"

"He owns a worldwide trading company. That's all I know."

"Is he the dude that looks like a male model?"

"Yeah! How did you know?"

"I saw him at the inaugural ball. He carried himself like he was the most important man in the room. Even more important than the president. I saw you escort him and others into a room, and then you escorted the president. I said, 'That room must be for the big donors.' "

"They are. Mr. Smith is the biggest."

"Don't let him stress you out."

She exhaled. "I'll be glad when Valarie takes over."

"Who's Valarie?"

"The chief of staff's assistant. She'll be the one scheduling the meetings with him and her boss."

Bingo. "Good! Let her take on that headache."

"Gladly. I'll be back in DC next month. I want to see you."

She couldn't see William's lips curve downward but felt the vibe.

William said, "That would be nice, but we need to slow down. You're married, and I need to focus on my book. I've been neglecting my work since I met you."

"Are you saying I'm not good for you?"

"No. I just need to concentrate on my book. I came to DC to get away from distractions. It's not good for you to get too close to me."

"How do you know what's good for me?"

"Okay. It's not good for me. I need to be in insolation for a few months to concentrate."

Beth felt the relationship she didn't want to end had ended, and said, "You're tired of me already?"

"Let's be real. I like you. I like talking to you, and I enjoy the sex. But you're older and I'm younger. You're married and I'm single. You're living your life and I have a life to live. We'll still be friends with fond memories. Keep your head up. You're a beautiful person."

She forced a smile he couldn't see.

"Take care until we talk again. Goodnight."

She hesitantly said, "Goodnight."

* * *

Steve's birthday party was on Capitol Hill where he and two co-workers rented a three-story house. The place was packed when William arrived. He immediately went looking for Steve and found him in conversation with the guys he met at the social. They greeted him, and William handed Steve the bottle of Hennessy.

Steve said, "You are a man of your word. Pull up a seat."

William sat, and one of the white guys said in conversation, "Why is there evil? I believe in nature. If you have righteous thoughts, you are a righteous person."

William interjected, "A righteous person can have unrighteous thoughts because we naturally know good and evil. It's not the thoughts, but the actions of your thoughts, and you control your actions."

With a subtle frown, the white guy said, "What if you can't control your actions? Does that make you evil or just weak?"

William felt the friction and calmly said, "Every thought brings the feeling, and every feeling brings the thought. Those are our impulses. As human beings, we must learn how to control our thoughts and feelings. If we don't, our thoughts and feelings will control us. A person becomes an addict because the feeling of desire has become the feeling of need in their mind. The same for a mass murderer."

"So evil is a choice?" the white guy said.

"It is," William replied.

Another of the white guys interjected, "So why do we have that choice? Why did God allow us to have the choice to choose good or evil? Why didn't he just give us the choice of good only?"

William said, "Because we are beings of nature, and nature has an opposite. There is male and female, light and darkness, good and evil, life and death."

The first white guy asked, "Where did you get your understanding?"

William held his closed-mouth smile a few seconds before he said, "I learned the nature of myself. The laws of nature are within us."

The men were silent in the thoughts that reflected on their faces.

Steve ended the silence. "Enough debating. Let's party."

"I'll drink to that," the Hispanic guy said, and opened the cognac.

William said, "I've never been to a party with so many fine-ass women around. Where did they all come from?"

Steve said, "We work in the West Wing. Beautiful women love to be around men with power."

The Hispanic guy pointed and said, "There's Ramona."

A desirous expression took hold of William's face as he eyed her wearing the white long-sleeve above-the-knee romper with the V-shaped top that covered only the nipples of her succulent, round breasts.

"She's very hot," William said. He shifted his eyes to the Hispanic guy. "Why don't you make your move? She's alone."

He didn't answer.

William looked back at Romana and said, "Is Valarie here?"

Steve said, "She's here somewhere."

"Is her boyfriend here?"

"Nah, she came alone. I'll point her out when I see her."

"I'm gonna walk around. What is she wearing?"

One of the white guys said, "Look for a long-haired brunette with an off-the-shoulder blue dress and silver neck bracelet with Elizabeth Taylor's eyes."

"Wow," William said, smiling.

Steve said, "You're wasting your time. She's locked down."

"Does she have a ring on it?"

"Not yet."

"Then I'm not wasting my time. I'll see y'all later."

William stepped into the flow of guests. Some were dancing to music by the Gap Band; some were in conversations; and others were standing around with roving eyes.

She's not down here. He went to the second floor where people were lounging to doo-wop songs and scanned the space for the woman described. She was sitting on the black velvet sofa that faced an unlit fireplace, seemingly in a joyous conversation with another woman.

He stared, contemplating between approach and patience, and chose patience.

When she stood and walked away, he abruptly slithered around a mixed group and gently took hold of her arm. "Hi. Do you have a minute?"

With violet like eyes, she smiled and said, "I'm getting ready to leave."

"Can you give me a minute?"

Her high cheeks puckered. "How 'bout thirty seconds?"

"I'll take it. My name is William. When I saw you, I had to introduce myself before you left."

"Hi. I'm Valarie."

"The assistant to the chief of staff?"

"How did you know?"

"Steve and a few of his friends told me about you. They said you're the hottest in the West Wing."

She blushed.

"Can we chat?"

She politely smiled. "Um, I have a boyfriend. You will have more fun chatting with someone else."

"Now that I've seen you, I'm not interested in chatting with someone else. I want to know you."

Her polite smile widened.

William lifted his cheeks and said, "At least give me until the song ends."

"Hmm, okay. I'll be back. I have to go to the ladies' room."

"The song will be over when you get back."

She chuckled and said, "We can start with the song that is playing when I come back."

William's smile dented. "Are you coming back? I hope you don't leave me hanging."

"I wouldn't do that to you."

He locked eyes on her rear as she walked away. *She got everything but the ass. Is she going to come back? How can I keep her here if she does? What should I say? What if she doesn't come back? If she's in love and has locked the door, how can I get her to open it?*

Valarie was smiling, with both hands cradling her purse, when she returned.

"Would you like a drink?"

"No. I'm leaving after the next song, remember?"

William smiled. *She's given me a little more time.* "Since I don't have much time, I'm not going to tell you about my background or ask about yours. But I'd like to know your age, and how long you've been with your boyfriend?"

She warmly said, "I'm twenty-four. I've been with my boyfriend for almost two years."

"Two years? If I were your boyfriend, I would have a ring on your finger by now."

"How do you know I want a ring?"

"Because you were straight up. You told me from the jump that you have a boyfriend and not to waste my time. That means you love him enough to accept his ring if he gives it."

"And why would you give me a ring if you were my boyfriend?"

"Because I know my needs and desires, and the woman that fits those needs and desires is my soulmate. It doesn't take two years to realize that."

"You haven't known me for two minutes and you think I'm your soulmate? I think you're full of it."

"I'm not full of it. The Bible tells us that God delivers all things. I recognize the gifts from God because I spiritually discern the people I meet, the places I go, and the things I see. I can see you are a gift from God. I'm not saying you are my soulmate. I'm saying I see some of my needs and desires in you. That's why I want to know you."

"And what are those needs and desires?"

"Honesty and loyalty—and a woman who loves a man because of the things inside the man."

Her right brow arched with a smile in her eyes. And with a thought on her face, she said, "The man inside?"

"Word. The man inside. There is a difference between loving someone and being in love. Love is care and concern, so it's the beginning of a relationship and the desire to be with that man. But being in love is with the heart and mind of that man. That is what you feel when you look at him—you see the man inside. He should be greater than the man outside."

Her eyes twinkled.

William continued. "When the heart and mind match yours, you have found your soulmate. A soulmate doesn't have to be a lover. He or she can be a friend only."

Valarie paused with eyes seemingly searching for his soul.

William said, "The body is only a desire. The need is in the heart and mind, and when you find that need, it doesn't matter if the person becomes paralyzed or disfigured. You will still be in love because you're not in love with the body but the heart and mind."

The next song ended, but she didn't leave.

"Why are you staring at me?" she asked.

"I'm not staring. I'm marveling."

"At what?"

"The woman behind the eyes."

"But I'm already taken."

"Today you are. But all relationships aren't meant to enter marriage. What will happen if you break up with your boyfriend?"

"I don't think that will happen?"

"Maybe not. But what if it does?"

"I just won't date for a while."

"But in time, you will. Let me ask you a hypothetical question. Would you be interested in me if you didn't have a boyfriend?"

"Maybe."

"So why can't we take this opportunity to get to know each other, just in case we might see each other again when you might not have a boyfriend?"

"You're very persistent."

"With things I want."

"I think you want me to say you had me."

"No. I want you so I can say I have you."

Her right brow arched again. The red lipstick across her full lips twisted. "Okay. Tell me about yourself?"

"Can we sit?"

"Lead the way."

He turned with a hidden smile and headed toward an area he had previously spotted. "I'm the One Who Knows" by Brenton Wood was the music in their steps. He stopped at the self-service bar. "Would you like a drink?"

"I'll have a glass of white wine."

He lifted the classiest bottle and half-filled a clear twelve-ounce plastic cup and handed it to her with a napkin, then filled a cup of beer from the keg and led her to the vacant love seat facing the picture window.

When they sat, she said, "Why did you choose the love seat?"

"I chose the view."

With a thought written on her face, she slid her eyes to the picture window. In the seeming ambiance of the view, she sipped her wine before turning thoughtful eyes to William.

He read her expression and said, "I'm from Harrisburg, Pennsylvania. I was the ghostwriter for a few bestsellers and decided to write a book under my name. I moved to DC to work on it."

"Why DC?"

"I like the city, and it's away from distractions."

"What's the book about?"

"It's a sci-fi thriller."

"Were the other books sci-fi?"

"Sorry, I can't tell you the genre. I will violate my contract."

"Ah."

"Enough about me. Where are you from?"

"Nebraska."

"What college did you attend?"

"Liberty."

"Never heard of that school. Are there any blacks there?"

She giggled. "Of course."

"Well, it must be a great school 'cause you got a great job to be so young."

"I was lucky."

"I believe we make our own luck through effort."

Her eyes sparkled as if the words had touched her heart. She quickly finished her wine. "I have to go. It was nice meeting you."

"Can we have lunch?"

"I have a boyfriend, remember?"

"I can't forget that. But I have a question. Does he act like a boyfriend or a father?"

Her eyes narrowed with her lips twisted upward. "What do you mean?"

"Does he ask you what you want to do or where you want to go, or does he tell you where you should go and what you should do?"

She seemed in thought.

"I'm the kinda guy that likes to listen. I want to know you as a woman. Your thoughts. Your feelings. Your dreams. I want to feel the passion in your mind. I want to go where you want to go. I want to be where you want to be."

Curious eyes circled his face in the silence between them. A few seconds later, she said, "No man has ever said those words to me."

"Why am I the first?"

"I don't know."

"Maybe it's meant for us to have lunch."

She paused with her eyes locked on his. "I'll think about it. Give me your number."

"Are you gonna call me?"

"Maybe."

She opened her purse and handed him a pen.

He wrote his number on the napkin and said, "I hope you call."

She stood. “Goodnight. It was nice meeting you, William.”

He stood and extended his hand. “Nice meeting you, Valarie. I hope I’m blessed to see you again.”

She shook his hand and left without commenting.

He watched with attentive eyes as she headed toward the stairs, hoping she would look back, but she didn’t.

Chapter 8

In the second month of his presidency, the puppet was leaving a speaking engagement at a downtown hotel. He stopped and waved at the cheering crowd when gunshots replaced the joyous mood. One of the bullets had struck the president, and he was raced to the nearest hospital.

Breaking News covered the airwaves, with the condition of the president unknown.

Valarie hysterically ran into her boss's office and screamed, "The president was shot!"

The secretary of state calmly said, "Is he dead?"

"I don't know?" she said in a state of shock.

The chief of staff eyed Valarie with the blank expression and said, "Thanks."

With bulging eyes, she stood frozen-like, seemingly confused by their demeanor.

"Keep us updated," the chief of staff said.

With concern stamped across her face, she returned to her desk. *They act like they don't care.*

* * *

The media had camps set up at the hospital, White House, and Capitol in search of updates on the President's condition and the whereabouts of the vice president and Speaker of the House.

The chief of staff's private phone rang, and the caller said, "The president is dead."

The chief of staff cracked a smile and eyed the secretary of state, then said to the caller, "Don't announce his death. We will make the announcement in the press room."

"His wife is here," the caller said.

"Keep her in the dark. Tell her he's still in surgery. We are getting ready to enter the press room for the briefing."

When the chief of staff and secretary of state entered the press room, they were bombarded with questions. "What is the condition of the president?" was the question yelled by all the reporters.

The secretary of state calmly stood at the podium and said, "Only one question at a time," and pointed at the reporter that had shouted the loudest. "Can you tell the American people the condition of the president?"

"The president didn't survive his wounds. He passed away just before we entered the room."

The sounds in the crowded room were sighs and cries.

After a few seconds, one of the reporters asked, "Where is the vice president? And where is the Speaker of the House? Who's in charge?"

The secretary of state said, "I'm in charge!"

The room went silent as if the reporters were unsure of what they had heard. Then another reporter said, "You are in charge?"

"Yes, I'm in control here?"

Commotion was in the voices and on the faces of the reporters, and one yelled, "Where is the vice president?"

The secretary of state shouted, "I am in charge!"

The reporter replied, "The vice president should be in charge, followed by the Speaker of the House. Where are they?"

"We are in a state of emergency," the secretary of state said. "I am declaring martial law. Effective immediately, no one can enter or leave the country, or a state. All flights to this country have been diverted, and all flights out of the country have been canceled. All roads entering and leaving a state are blocked. All airports in Hawaii and Alaska are closed.

"Effective at seven p.m. Eastern Standard Time, a twenty-four-hour curfew is in effect. Any unauthorized persons found on the streets will be arrested."

A black female reporter yelled. "Sir, can you tell us where the vice president is?"

"I do not know where he is, or the Speaker of the House, or the Senate pro tempore. In accordance with the Constitution, in their absence, I have all the authority of the presidency. I will address the nation tonight at nine p.m. to provide further updates. This briefing is over."

The secretary of state and the chief of staff abruptly left the room in a bevy of questions they didn't answer.

* * *

After the White House briefing, William phoned Beth. "What's going on?"

"I don't know."

"Where is the vice president?"

"I heard he was in the air."

"Over this country?"

"Yes."

"He can't assume the presidency in the air? And where is the Speaker of the House? He's not out of town nor is the pro tempore of the Senate. Something's not right here. Everyone has disappeared at the exact moment the president is shot. The secretary of state is a crazy man. He can't be left in charge."

"I'm sure the vice president will be seen soon."

"He should've been seen or heard from by now if he's on the plane because there are reporters on the plane. This feels like a coup."

"I'm sure it's not a coup."

"What makes you sure? The president is assassinated, the vice president has disappeared, the Speaker of the House and the pro tempore of the Senate can't be found. This isn't a coincidence."

"I'm sure everything will be okay soon."

William abruptly ended the call and ran to the neighborhood grocery store. The shelves in the overcrowded store were empty of bread, milk, water, eggs, and meats. He took what he could find and left as customers fought for the last cans and stood in lines that were six rows deep.

With the new reality at hand, he went back to his apartment and phoned his mother and brother but couldn't reach either.

He turned on the news and phoned Steve.

"I don't know what's happening," Steve said. "It's crazy here. Valarie said her boss acted like he doesn't care about the president or the missing vice president."

"Something isn't right, bruh. I think it's a coup."

"I hope not, but it feels like it."

"I'll be home. Keep me updated."
"Will do."

* * *

Reporters were cornering every member of Congress they could find. The few members of the Elephant party that were found all said, "No comment." The members of the Donkey party made themselves readily available and lashed out against the comments made by the secretary of state. Mr. Jefferson, the minority leader in the House said, "Somebody needs to find the vice president and the Speaker of the House. Have they been kidnapped?"

Mr. Schumacher, the minority leader in the Senate said, "I have been unable to contact the pro tempore of the Senate. That is the line of succession after the vice president and Speaker of the House. The secretary of state is not in charge!"

The reporters continued to scramble for clarity on who's in charge of the government and the whereabouts of the vice president, Speaker of the House, and Senate pro tempore. That scramble continued into the late night without any new information because the secretary of state canceled the nine p.m. address.

DAY 2

At nine a.m., the White House press secretary, a young thin blonde-haired woman, met with reporters and said, "The president will address the nation this evening at nine p.m."

A reporter shouted, "Will that be the vice president?"

She replied, "Until the vice president, Speaker of the House, or the pro tempore of the Senate is found, the secretary of state is the president."

Another reporter shouted, "Where is the vice president?"

"We do not know his location, or the Speaker of the House, or the pro tempore of the Senate. Hopefully, when the president addresses the nation tonight, he will have an answer for the question."

She turned and left the room with an earful of questions yelled at her.

* * *

The Donkey party was up in arms in both chambers of Congress and went to the floor. The majority leader in the Senate released a statement but hid from the cameras.

But the second ranking Republican leader in the House spoke to the media, "The assassination of the president was a tragedy. The disappearance of the vice president, House speaker, and pro tempore concerns me. The interim president did the right thing by imposing martial law. We have enemies within our gates, and by God, we will find them!"

He walked away, ignoring the questions asked.

The minority leader in the House met with his members behind closed doors and said, "We are experiencing a coup! We need to shore up the safeguards of our institutions. We start by telling the American people we are facing a coup."

One of the members said, "We shouldn't jump to conclusions. Maybe it's not a coup."

"The best way to defeat a coup is to stop it before it gains momentum. The vice president can't be found. The Speaker of the House can't be found. The pro tempore of the Senate can't be found. The secretary of state, the former chief of staff for President Milhouse, who wanted to call in the Army to prevent Milhouse from resigning has claimed the presidency. This is a coup! Call it what it is! We need to get on top of it now!"

One of the female members said, "How? The secretary of state has the Constitution supporting him. His voice is on the side of legitimacy, and the heads of the institutions are his loyalists. This was well planned."

"That doesn't mean it can't be defeated. Their loyalists are the heads, but if the staff refuse to carry out their orders, the work won't get done. Right now, he has the Constitution working for him, but that will only last as long as he keeps the Constitution, which won't last long because he is the head of the coup. We need to start calling this what it is."

Another female member said, "I agree with the leader. We need to go before the media and speak to the American people before the secretary of state addresses the nation tonight. A coup can begin with the Constitution but cannot continue with the Constitution. We need to get ahead of his speech by the telling the American people those exact words. A coup can begin with the Constitution but cannot continue with the Constitution. Those words should be repeated every day by everyone in this room and among the members in the Senate because the secretary of state is going to change the Constitution. If he doesn't, the coup attempt will fail."

The room was silent with all eyes on her. She added, "I suggest we go before the press as soon as we leave this room, just in case there is a spy among us."

* * *

When the members came from behind closed doors, the minority leader and his officers went before the press and said, "The assassination of the president and disappearance of the vice president, Speaker of the House, and pro tempore of the Senate is a coup attempt."

One of the reporters said, "In their demise or absence, the secretary of state rightfully holds the duties of the president according to the Constitution. How is he conducting a coup if the Constitution gives him the authority?"

The minority leader replied, "A coup can begin with the Constitution but cannot continue with the Constitution. If the secretary of state deviates from the Constitution, let it be known that he is attempting a coup."

* * *

Inside the Oval Office, the secretary of state, chief of staff, and the heads of Justice, Defense, the FBI, and the CIA watched the House minority leader's press conference. And when it ended, the chief of staff said to the secretary of state, "You can't give that speech tonight."

"I'm not going to pause what we have started," the secretary of state said. "We the People is voided, whether I say it tonight or tomorrow. Why wait? We have waited long enough. The Fourth Reich has risen! And the world will know it tonight! I don't give a damn what the people think! We control them."

Ronald Rudolph, the head of Justice, said, "I agree with the president. We have waited long enough. But we should slow down."

"We can't slow down," the secretary of state said. "We have a ninety-day plan to fulfill."

"And we will fulfill it. But we need to do the things the Constitution will allow first. We need to show legitimacy. Then unveil the New World Order. Wait a few days before announcing the Fourth Reich. I'm sure Shawn will agree with me."

The president seemed to fear Shawn, and said, "I won't announce the Fourth Reich."

* * *

At nine p.m., all television and radio channels in America aired the secretary of state's address to the nation.

"My fellow Americans and patriots, as we grieve the president's untimely death and search for the vice president, Speaker, and Senate pro tempore, I am bound by the Constitution to assume the role of president. Based on the intelligence report received today, because I quickly stepped into the role of president, we were able to block the Russians' attempt to start World War III.

"Our intelligence agencies also confirmed the leaders of the left-wing party in the House and Senate are spies for Russia and conspired to assassinate the president, kidnap the vice president, Speaker, and Senate pro tempore.

"I know this is shocking to you because it was to me. I have therefore ordered the immediate arrest of every left-wing member in the House and Senate. Those arrests are underway as I speak. The attorney general and FBI director will provide additional information tomorrow.

"Because we are in a state of emergency, martial law is extended until further notice. Only authorized individuals are allowed on the streets. To avoid major disruptions to your daily life, in the next couple of days the twenty-four-hour curfew will be enforced from seven p.m. to five a.m. Those who work during the curfew hours are considered authorized individuals and can move about if they have the proper identification. If any unauthorized persons are found on the streets during curfew hours, they will be arrested. Anyone resisting arrest will be shot.

"Until the state of emergency ends, I will address the nation every night at nine p.m. Goodnight, and God bless America."

* * *

The accusation about the left-wing conspiring with the Russians to assassinate the president and kidnap the vice president, speaker, and Senate pro tempore—along with the arrests in the House and Senate—had the press rooms in a frenzy. Vigorous discussions were heard every minute on every news channel and radio station.

A prominent left-wing political strategist debating a right-wing political strategist on the worldwide syndicated news channel said, "Make no mistake about it, this is a right-wing coup! It doesn't make any sense for our party to conspire with the Russians to assassinate the president and kidnap the vice president, Speaker of the House, and the Senate pro tempore. What gain is there for us when the next in line is the secretary of state? Why would we conspire with the Russians to keep the same administration we oppose? Doesn't make any sense when you think about it. The guilty ones here are the secretary of state and his enablers in Congress."

The right-wing political strategist replied, "Their plan wasn't to capture the presidency but to cause disruption in the country so the Russians could mobilize their troops to attack a NATO country. The left-wing are Socialists! Their plan was to bring down the American economy and weaken our defenses against Russia, which is treason! We have to stop the Marxists and radical left from stealing our country."

* * *

DAY 3

Court filings, lawsuits, and people protesting in the streets continued.

The daily White House briefing in the press room was canceled, and emails to the press secretary weren't answered.

The lack of information given to the press heightened the turmoil in America and forced the heads of Justice and the FBI to hold a press conference.

With the FBI Director at his side, Mr. Rudolph stood at the podium and said, "We have concrete evidence to support the arrests of every left-wing member in the House and Senate. We currently have 239 members in custody. The remaining warrants include Mr. Jefferson, the minority leader in the House of Representatives, and Mr. Schumacher, the minority leader in the Senate. Those two individuals are the ring leaders of a conspiracy to overthrow the government. Their plan included an insurrection that was foiled by the FBI. When Mr. Jefferson and Mr. Schumacher are arrested, we will release additional information."

The two headed for the exit without taking any questions, which caused an uproar among the many reporters from around the world, who repeatedly yelled, "This was supposed to be a question-and-answer session!"

"Fuck them," Mr. Rudolph whispered to the FBI director. "They won't be around much longer."

* * *

Mr. Rudolph and the FBI director went directly to the White House and joined the president's meeting in the Situation Room with the chief of staff, Joint Chiefs of Staff, Secretary of Defense, and the Director of the CIA.

"We cannot allow these people to continue violating the curfew," the president said. "I ordered a twenty-four-hour curfew, and people were on the street twenty-four hours with only a few arrests. If more aren't arrested today, the protesters will grow and become emboldened, and I will look weak in the eyes of those who put me in this seat and in the eyes of the world's authoritarians. I will not allow that to happen!"

The president eyed the chairman of the Joint Chiefs. "If the troops do not start arresting and shooting every curfew violator, I will send my own army to patrol the streets."

The chairman said, "There are too many white women and children on the frontline. We cannot arrest or shoot them."

"Why not? They are insurrectionists!"

"Mr. President, if we start shooting and arresting white women and children, we will lose our country and never get it back."

"Something has to be done, quickly!"

Mr. Rudolph interjected, "I was hoping we could appease the public for a few days, but those college students have gathered a large following, and the press is demanding evidence we don't have.

"This calls for strategic thinking. If we start shooting the protesters, things will just get worse. For now, arrest and shoot the non-whites. That should be enough to discourage others from joining.

"I agree with you, Mr. President. But we don't need to give any more red meat to the press. The left has people believing the truth. We need people to believe the lies. Let's keep talking about the Communists' plan to take over the country. That will increase patriotism, and then those who oppose us will be seen as traitors, even those white women and children. That will make it easier to shoot them."

The president smiled. "Shawn was right about you. You are smarter than most."

The vice-chair of the Joint Chiefs said, "Mr. President, I agree with Mr. Rudolph. But there is one thing we can implement right away that will increase patriotism on our side, and that is the Bellamy salute. I know it's in the ninety-day plan, but we can implement it now. We need to turn the people away from the premise of a coup and make them see our actions as patriotism.

"To make our country great again is not only bringing back George Washington, but the Bellamy salute as well because it was the norm in this country from 1892 through 1942. Those who were children then remember it, and those who were born after need to be reminded of it.

"The Fourth Reich has risen, and we need to show the world that we are first in the New World Order. The curfew is needed, but to be reminded of the things that made this country great is more effective because we can manipulate the people with the idea of patriotism.

"When you decide to lift the twenty-four-hour curfew, I suggest we reinstitute the Bellamy salute at the start of each school day for grades K to 12. I yearn to see every child reciting the Pledge of Allegiance with the Bellamy salute like I did as a child.

"And before the National Anthem is sung at sporting events, everyone in attendance should recite the Pledge of Allegiance with the Bellamy salute. And at the start of the workday in every federal building, every employee should recite the Pledge of Allegiance with the Bellamy salute. At every concert, and before every Broadway play, the Pledge of Allegiance should be recited with the Bellamy salute."

"Awesome," the president interjected. "Excellent suggestion, my friend. I'm ready to lift the curfew now."

* * *

At the nine p.m. address in the Oval Office, the president said, "Good evening my fellow American patriots. Despite extensive efforts to locate the vice president, the House speaker, and the Senate pro tempore, we have been unsuccessful. Our efforts to do so are hampered by the civil unrest from the curfew violators, who are causing us to divert resources. I am therefore calling for volunteers to be deputized into the militia. If you are interested in joining the America First militia, please register at the nearest police station. We need patriots to help in our war against the enemies within our gates. We need patriots to help guard our borders and protect our cities.

"At six a.m., the twenty-four-hour curfew is lifted. The new curfew takes effect from seven p.m. to five a.m. All schools will open, and public transportation that includes trains and planes will resume tomorrow from six a.m. to six p.m. All stores are authorized to open until one hour before the curfew begins. All sporting events and entertainment venues will remain suspended until further notice.

"Citizens wanting to register for the militia can register between the hours of six a.m. to six p.m. I am encouraging every adult American to register as a member of the militia to join our troops on the front line of protecting our borders from illegal crossings and assisting with the arrest and deportation of all undocumented immigrants in this country.

"Effective immediately, all sanctuary cities are null and void. The National Guard and the militia have authorization with the police to arrest all illegal immigrants, those suspected of being illegal, and those suspected of committing a crime.

"There are enemies within our gates disguised as loyal Americans but are not. You will know them because they are not law-abiding Americans. They are violators of the curfew, printers of false information against the government, and followers of a debunked conspiracy theory. To quell their efforts to steal our country, I have temporarily shut down the internet and all lines of communication except for authorized personnel that includes the Department of Transportation. The quicker we discover these people and remove them, the quicker we can go back to our normal lives.

"I want to freely go to church every Sunday, shopping, the theatre, sporting events, and just hanging out socially. The militia and National Guard will help us get back to doing those things.

"Again, the twenty-four-hour curfew will end at six a.m. tomorrow. The new curfew will take effect from seven p.m. to five a.m. until further notice. After seven p.m., any unauthorized persons found on the streets will be arrested. Those resisting arrest, destroying property, and looting will be shot. This will be strictly enforced by the militia and National Guard. We will not tolerate criminal behavior in our streets. Goodnight, and God bless America."

* * *

DAY 4

One minute before six a.m., William was headed to rent a car. The streets and highways were lined with angry but peaceful protesters marching to the White House. He joined the massive crowd that held signs and chanted, "Keep Democracy Alive!"

The sight around him was unlike anything he had seen before. People of all ages and races were in the crowd, even those in wheelchairs and needing crutches.

When the crowd of seemingly forty thousand arrived at the White House, there were tanks inside the gates and soldiers circling the grounds, but that didn't seem to frighten the protesters. They yanked on the gate, more in defiance than trying to enter.

After an hour or so outside the White House gates, William walked across the bridge, rented a car, and returned to the apartment to gather his belongings.

He drove for two hours and thirty minutes to Harrisburg, concerned about the state of the country and what would happen next.

His mother was noticeably nervous when he arrived. "Ma, everything will be okay. We're not undocumented immigrants."

"Are we supposed to feel safe because we're not? It ain't right! That's the point! We should be out there protesting too. The soldiers won't shoot peaceful protesters."

"The militia will. On the way here I was listening to public radio and there are reports of militiamen shooting women and children at the border. We need to stay inside and wait. The courts have blocked the president's decrees."

"I know you don't believe that?"

"What? That the courts blocked the decrees?"

"No! That he will accept the court rulings. Nothing can stop that man but a bullet."

"We will know in five days. If they start arresting people in the sanctuary cities, I'm gonna buy a gun."

"Why are you acting so surprised? You're the one that said this would happen."

"I didn't think they would kill the president before he had finished sixty days on the job. I thought they were planning to use him as the front while they did their dirt at the back. But they aren't trying to be subtle."

With worry in her eyes, she said, “You know they’re coming for us next.”

“They’re not coming for us next. The Jews are next—then us.”

“That’s why we need to join the protesters. We the people can stop this if we stay united.”

“Ma, have you spoken to Devin?”

“Not since the phone lines were cut.”

“I stopped and purchased groceries. I’m going bring the bags in.”

“I’ll help you. I need some fresh air.”

After they had brought inside the house ten bags of groceries and two cases of water, William said, “Stay in the house and keep the doors locked. I’m going to Devin’s.”

“I’m going with you.”

“It’s safer if you stay here.”

“I’m not staying here. I’m going with you.”

“Devin might be on his way here. If he comes here and you’re not here, he’s gonna freak out. Ma, stay here.”

“Okay.”

“I’ll be back before curfew.”

“You better.”

* * *

At one p.m. Eastern Standard Time, nearly four million people consisting of men and women ages eighteen to eighty-four had registered nationwide for the militia.

At 1:36 p.m., the White House press secretary entered the press room. On the podium were six enlarged pictures of American children reciting the Pledge of Allegiance with the Bellamy salute. The press secretary said, “Behind me are pictures of American children reciting the Pledge of Allegiance with the Bellamy salute. That was a time in our history when America was great. The president has sent a request to Congress to reinstate the Bellamy salute. Are there any questions about that?”

Hands raised and she pointed to one of the reporters in the front row. The female reporter stood and said, "Is that the only question you are answering today?"

"Yes."

The reporter sat.

The press secretary pointed to a reporter at the back of the room, and he said, "With all that is happening in the country right now, the assassination of the president, disappearance of the vice president, Speaker of the House, and Senate pro tempore, why does the president want to bring back the Bellamy salute? Congress removed it in 1942 because it was similar to the Nazi salute."

The press secretary replied, "Before there was a Nazi salute, the Bellamy salute was the national stance for Americans in reciting the Pledge of Allegiance. A brief history lesson—the Bellamy salute originated in 1892 and wasn't removed until December 1942, a year after Pearl Harbor. The president believes we should bring back the things that symbolized our country's greatness. What we need more than anything is patriotism. I'm happy to say that as of one p.m. today, four million patriots have joined the president's militia, and there is still another five hours of registration left."

She pointed to a reporter in the middle of the room. He stood and said, "How long will there be only one party in Congress?"

"What does that question have to do with the Bellamy salute?"

"You said the president is sending the request to Congress, but there are only members of his party in Congress. That isn't a fair representation of the American people."

"When all the fugitives are captured, the nation will hold special elections for Congress. Until then, Congress will operate as it is."

The press secretary abruptly ended the briefing.

* * *

Ten minutes after William left his mother's house, Devin arrived with his wife and two kids.

His mother said, "William is on his way to your house."

"He should've known I would be coming here. I would've been here earlier, but the grocery stores are crowded, and the shelves are empty in a lot of them. We had to travel to several to get these groceries."

He carried three bags into the kitchen. "Oh, good, William got you some groceries."

"Yeah, he got a lot. Are you going to join the protesters?"

"No. I'm going to meet with some people. Candace and the kids will stay here with you until I get back."

"I want to go to the protest."

"Ma, we can go another time. Right now, I have other things to do."

"Like what?"

"Like, I can't tell you." He kissed her and his wife and kids, and he left.

A half hour or so later, William returned, happy to see Candace and the kids. "Where is Devin?" he said.

"He'll be back later," Candace replied. "He has to meet with some people."

William nodded and said, "Ma, I'm hungry."

* * *

At nine p.m., the president sat at the Resolute Desk and addressed the nation, "Good evening, my fellow American patriots. Tomorrow at five a.m., the internet will be restored to homes, phone lines operable, roads open to leave the country, and flights out of the country will resume. Congress voted today to reinstate the Bellamy salute, and I signed the bill into law this evening."

He stood and faced the American flag at his right side, and with the Bellamy salute said, "I pledge allegiance to the flag of the United States of America, and to the republic for which it stands, one nation under God, indivisible, with liberty and justice for all." He sat and said, "Effective tomorrow and every school day thereafter, grades K to twelve will recite the Pledge of Allegiance with the Bellamy salute before classes begin. Any child reporting to school after the Pledge of Allegiance will not be allowed to attend school for the day. Any child that refuses to participate in the Pledge of Allegiance with the Bellamy salute will be sent to reform school and the parents arrested for being unpatriotic.

"All federal employees are required to recite the Pledge of Allegiance with the Bellamy salute every day when they report to work. Any employee that refuses will be terminated for being unpatriotic.

"When the sporting events resume, all in attendance are required to recite the Pledge of Allegiance with the Bellamy salute prior to the National Anthem. Anyone who refuses, including the coaches and athletes, will be arrested. We are going to remove all unpatriotic Americans from this country. And in doing such, we will make our country great again!"

The president ignored the teleprompter and said, "Anyone who opposes the Bellamy salute is not a patriotic American. The Bellamy salute is American history—and American history begins with the Holy Roman Empire, the greatest empire the earth had seen until this day.

"God has resurrected the Holy Roman Empire in America to reign for a thousand years. The Bellamy salute is not a Nazi salute but the ancient Romans' salute. And the ancient Romans are our ancestors. That is why the eagle is the symbol of this country. The temple of Jupiter in ancient Rome is where the senators of Rome gathered. That temple stood on Capitoline Hill. We call it Capitol Hill today. It's time for us to embrace our history—and in our history there is an emperor who reigns until his death. I am your emperor—and my kingdom is the Fourth Reich. And the Fourth Reich shall rule the earth for a thousand years.

"As emperor I make this decree: the freedom of the press is banned. After this address, only one news outlet is sanctioned in this country, and that is the State media. All others are outlawed.

"As emperor I make this decree." He lifted a copy of the Constitution and burned it. "We the people are no more. We are I, and I am the people. And I am taking our country back to where it began—the love for our Lord and Savior Jesus

Christ, who would've lived among us in flesh unto this day if it were not for the Jews.

"Therefore, I am rescinding the citizenship of every Jew. Beginning at midnight, all Jews in this country have twenty-six days to leave the country or face arrest and deportation to an undisclosed location. There are no exceptions!

"America was built as a Christian nation. Jesus Christ is our Lord and Savior, and he said, whosoever deny me before men, he will deny to his Father which is in heaven. Jews deny Jesus Christ! No one who denies Jesus Christ belongs in this country! Send them back to their own country! America is the Promised Land for Christians. We will not allow non-Christians to contaminate our country, to influence our children, and curse the name of our God! All Jews in this country must leave, or face arrest and deportation.

"Goodnight. And God bless America."

* * *

Summer and Rhoda were together during the president's address, and after, Rhoda said, "I can't believe this. Is it a joke? I have twenty-six days to leave the country?"

Summer seemed mystified and said, "That can't be. The courts won't allow it, and Congress won't allow it."

"That man controls Congress, and he doesn't respect the courts. He called himself the emperor. His decisions are the only ones that matter in his mind."

"He can give the orders, but he needs people to enforce those orders. I don't believe he can find the people to enforce those orders."

"He wouldn't've said it if he didn't believe he had the people to follow his orders."

"Congress will impeach him if he tries to remove Jews from the country."

"Summer, are you hearing yourself? There is only one party in Congress, and those men and women are his enablers. I need to figure out what I'm going to do. Where I'm going to go. Oh God, I'm glad my parents are out of the country. I need to leave too."

"You don't have to leave."

Rhoda eyed her and said, "You're not a Jew."

"But I'm a human being. That means I live by humanity. I'm not going to let anything happen to you or any Jew. I will protect you with my last breath."

"How? What can you do when they come looking for me?"

"They have to find you first. I'm not going to let them find you."

"Summer, it's best that I leave the country. Thank God I can afford to leave."

"No. You can't leave the country. I will hide you if necessary."

"You can't hide me. They know we are best friends. If they don't find me here, they will look for me where you are."

"How do they know we are best friends? All they know is that you are a patient of mine."

"Summer, people are scared for their lives. When people are scared, they talk. Someone who knows about our friendship will tell them. You should know that."

"I do. That's why I'm not going to hide you with me."

"Where are you hiding me?"

"I don't know yet. I have twenty-six days to figure that out."

* * *

One of the major Elephant party donors contacted Beth, barking, "What the hell is going on? No one is returning my calls!"

"I don't know what is going on, Mr. Rosenberg. I only know what the president said last night, and I can't believe it."

"I demand to speak to someone in the know. Get me someone in the know right now!"

"Mr. Rosenberg, I've been trying to reach the chairman since last night. No one is answering or returning my calls."

Perturbed, Mr. Rosenberg hung up the phone and sought advocacy with the opposition.

* * *

Prominent Republican strategist and community activists who were advocating for the president's impeachment mysteriously went missing. Members of Congress that advocated for the president's impeachment also mysteriously disappeared.

The relentless phone calls from Israel's prime minister and every head of NATO were unanswered. And the American reporters who tried to get their questions answered were arrested.

Chapter 9

DAY 6

Inside the daily morning Situation Room meeting, the president said, "We have to crush the protests."

"There are too many women and children among them to start shooting," Mr. Rudolph said.

The president lifted his voice, "If we don't stop them now, they will stop us!"

The chief of staff said, "We need to stick to the plan. Mr. Reaves is the second ranking member in the House. The people know him and trust him."

"I don't trust him," the president said. "He called me the interim president."

The chief of staff said, "We can use that to our benefit. The Democrats trust him. In all respect, Mr. President, you shouldn't've banned the left-wing and independent news outlets. The plan called for Mr. Reaves to be exposed to that audience so they would think he is neutral. Right now, they only see a dictator with no way out other than strong-arming the protesters. That wasn't the plan. The plan was to test Mr. Reaves before removing the freedom of the press. I suggest we stick to the plan."

The president seemed ruffled. "You want me to go back on my words?"

"I want you to stick to the plan. If he passes the test, let him announce that he has convinced you to restore the freedom of the press. The opposition will believe he is on their side, which will give us the time to maneuver our next steps. Then he will no longer be needed."

* * *

After the morning meeting of House members, one of them whispered in Mr. Reaves ear, "Can we speak privately?"

He nodded and said, "When?"

"Now."

"Where?"

"Outside the Capitol."

"Why?"

"The rooms and hallways are bugged."

He followed the member out of the Capitol and down the steps into the walkway surrounded by greenery. The member said, "We must do something to save our republic. The president burned the Constitution on live TV. We need to create a wall of resistance. There are other members who feel the same way."

"What makes you think I will join you and them?"

"Because we know you love this country and its democracy. There are more moderates in the House and Senate than extremists. We believe you can organize us to fight against the president's decrees."

"I'll think about it and get back to you."

* * *

"Yes, Valarie."

"Sir, Mr. Reaves is on the line."

"Put him through."

"Hello, Mr. Reaves, what can I do for you?"

"Sir, I was approached this morning by one of the House members who tried to recruit me into their resistance against the president."

"Who was it?"

"Marvin Hinkle."

"Thank you, Harvey. I appreciate your loyalty to the Reich."

"Of course, sir."

"As the second ranking member, you have a lot of influence in the House and among the American people. We need a cleanup on the aisle—and the president wants you to make the announcement that the freedom of the press is restored."

"When, sir?"

"When we end this call, schedule a press conference."

"Yes, sir."

“By the way, Mr. Hinkle is one of us. He was testing you. You proved yourself worthy to join the morning meetings with the president. We see you as a valuable member of the team.”

“Thank you, sir.”

“See you tomorrow morning at eight.”

“I will be there, sir.”

When the call ended, the chief of staff phoned the president. “Mr. President, he passed and will clean up.”

“Good work.”

* * *

Devin and William were at their mother’s house discussing the decrees announced by the president.

Devin said, “I’m going to the State Street rally tonight?”

“You’re going downtown after the curfew? That’s suicide.”

“Suicide is being afraid to die for a cause. They’re hoping we are afraid to die. But the people aren’t. They showed it last night. Nobody got shot anywhere in the country. The protesters are winning. It’s time for us to join them.”

“Us? You mean you and me?”

“Word.”

“I think we should wait on the decision from the courts.”

“Man, you know that cracker won’t listen to the courts. He said he’s the emperor. That’s the be-all and end-all.” Devin’s expression turned unilateral with neutral positioned eyes. “What happened to you? Now that the shit has hit the fan, you’re punking out.”

“I’m not punking out. I just know how vicious these people are.”

“And I don’t? We are living in a coup. The only ones who can stop it are the people. And if the people stay quiet, the coup will succeed.”

Their mother yelled, “Hey y’all, come here!”

William and Devin hurried into the den.

Congressman Harvey Reaves was holding a press conference and said, “I’ve spoken with the president and informed him the members of Congress have voted to remove his decree to ban the freedom of the press. Effectively immediately, all news outlets will air on television and radio without restrictions.

"As for his decree to rescind the citizenship of Jews and remove them from this country, the members of Congress disagree and will wait for the court's final decision.

"I want the American people to know that Congress is working on their behalf to rectify our current situation. I spoke to the president and he has agreed to lift the curfew tonight. All transportation will operate on its normal schedule. I will take your questions now."

Energetic hands were waving, and Congressman Reaves pointed at the Jewish reporter.

"Thank you for taking my question. Last night, the president burned the Constitution and ordered all Jews to leave the country in twenty-six days. Is that not the actions of a coup in place? Why is he still the president?"

"There is evidence the public hasn't seen but the president has. Because of what the president has seen and been told by trusted advisors, he blames the Constitution and believes it should be redone to meet modern times. That is why he burned the Constitution. It was only to make that point. He has not abandoned the Constitution.

"As for the Jews being removed from the country, the president is a very religious man who loves the Lord and rightfully blames the Jews for killing Jesus Christ. He believes America should be a country of Christians only. That decision is currently in the hands of the courts. If the decision goes against the president, he has the right to take his case to the appellate court and then the Supreme Court for the final decision. The president has assured me that he will abide with the court's final decision."

A reporter interjected, "The president said children who refuse the Bellamy salute will be sent to reform school and the parents arrested for being unpatriotic. That is the actions of an authoritarian government like Russia and North Korea. It's un-American."

"It's un-American if you refuse to recite the Pledge of Allegiance. If you cannot pledge allegiance to this country, then you do not belong in this country. Children are the future of the country. If they grow up without discipline, without the patriotism that founded our republic, what will become of our country? The president rightfully so is trying to prevent that from happening." He pointed to another reporter.

"I have two questions. Does the administration have proof that the vice president, Speaker, and Senate pro tempore were kidnapped? Or are they assumed dead?"

"The attorney general has informed me that he has evidence that proves the left-wing committed treasonous actions financed by Jewish donors to the Democratic party. He believes the fugitives, Mr. Jefferson and Mr. Schumacher, know where the vice president, Speaker, and Senate pro tempore are."

"My second question: You said the president 'rightfully blames the Jews for killing Jesus Christ,' and believes America should be a country for Christians only. Does that mean he wants to evict everyone who isn't a Christian?"

"Because the president believes the country should be for Christians only doesn't mean he only wants Christians in the country. He wants Congress and the Supreme Court to decide."

"I have a follow-up. As the leader of the House Republicans, what is your position? Do you agree that America should be a country for Christians only?"

"I believe in our founding fathers, the pilgrims. I am asking every member of Congress to vote their own conscience." He quickly pointed at a woman reporter.

"Thank you for taking my question. The president said he is the emperor. It's hard to believe he will accept any decision he doesn't agree with. Why should the American people believe the president will accept the court rulings if the rulings are not in his favor?"

"Because Congress ruled against banning the freedom of the press and here you are. The president called himself an emperor because he was comparing the Roman empire to the United States of America. His words were taken out of context. He was actually saying that if we were in ancient Rome today, he would be an emperor. He didn't mean he is an emperor."

Congressman Reaves quickly pointed to the Latino reporter.

"I have two questions. The president said all illegal and undocumented immigrants will be deported. What is the difference between illegal and undocumented? And what will happen to the children born in this country whose parents are undocumented?"

"Thank you for the question. Illegal immigrants are those crossing the border illegally. Undocumented immigrants are those who overstayed their visa and those awaiting their hearing for asylum. The children born in this country by undocumented and illegal immigrants are citizens by law. Their parents will have the option of taking their children with them when deported or leaving them here to be adopted.

"That is another reason why the president believes the Constitution is outdated because an immigrant can illegally cross the border and give birth to a child, and the child will be an American citizen. That is happening more often than you know. Women near the end of their pregnancy are illegally crossing the border to give birth in America. The president believes we need to change that law, and I agree."

"I have a follow-up question. The president said sanctuary cities no longer exist and has ordered the National Guard and the police to arrest immigrants that are waiting for their asylum hearing. The courts have put a stay on that order, but the fact that he made such an order is alarming. When that order was made, there was only silence from the members of Congress, which includes you. Do you agree with the president's order, and if you don't, why haven't you spoken against it?"

Congressman Reaves hesitated as if it was a gotcha question, then said, "I agree that immigrants who overstayed their visa should be deported. I disagree that immigrants waiting for their asylum hearing should be deported. Congress hasn't addressed that order because it is in the courts and will eventually be heard by the Supreme Court. The members of Congress will address it after the Supreme Court has made the final decision."

Congressman Reaves pointed to a black reporter.

"Thank you for taking my question. When will the American people see the evidence that justifies the arrest of the left-wing members in the House and Senate? And why haven't they been released on their own recognizance or given bail?"

"The attorney general has brought those indictments, which are sealed. I can't speak to his schedule. But I can assure you the evidence will be presented when they are arraigned. It's my understanding that the Justice Department is waiting to capture Mr. Jefferson and Mr. Schumacher to arraign them and the others together."

"Last question," the congressman said, and pointed to the reporter from State TV.

"Thank you, sir, for taking my question. Will the twenty-four-hour curfew be reimposed if the protesters become violent?"

"If the protesters remain peaceful tonight, a curfew will not be imposed. But the National Guard and militia will continue to guard the state capitals and other federal buildings. Both are ordered to engage only with violent protesters. If the protests turn violent, whereas property is damaged and businesses looted, for public safety those individuals will be arrested or shot, and the curfew will be reinstated. I am therefore asking all Americans to stay peaceful and trust the guardrails established to maintain our republic."

Congressman Reaves left the mics as reporters continued to ask questions.

* * *

The president and chief of staff watched the press conference in the White House dining room.

"He was great," the president said. "I love him. Give him an envelope?"

"How much?"

"A hundred K."

"Done."

"Do we have the instigators ready?"

"They will be among the protesters at nightfall."

"How will the militia know to ignore them?"

"They're wearing red hats."

"Good."

* * *

William was with his mother, Devin, Candace, and the children during the press conference and said at the end, "I don't trust a word that man said."

"We need to keep protesting," Devin said. He eyed William and said, "Are you coming with me?"

"For sure."

"I wanna go."

"Ma, you can't go out there. I would like to take Candace and the children but can't. The militia isn't shooting white women and children but will surely shoot black women and children."

His mother said, "But the curfew is over."

"Yeah, but the militia is still guarding the state capital. It only takes one person to act a fool and they will start shooting. You stay here. Candace has a gun and will protect you if the streets get out of hand." His eyes shifted to William. "You ready to go?"

"Yeah, but I need to call Sandra first." He phoned her house and left a message.

Devin said, "Knowing her, she's marching to the capital."

"Hopefully I'll see her there. C'mon, let's go."

When Devin headed toward the twelve-seat van, William said, "I know you're not trying to drive to State Street. Let's take the bus."

"The buses will be crowded going and coming back. We're going to park in Camp Hill and join the march across the bridge."

"That's a four-mile hike to the capital."

"Why you ailing? Most are marching from State & Linn Streets to North 7th. I know you ain't trying to take that walk. Get in the van."

"Why you driving your work vehicle?"

"Because I'm picking up some friends at the train station."

"The Transportation Center?"

"Word. When we cross the bridge we're going to 4th & Chestnut. I have some friends coming from Cleveland."

Devin drove to Interstate 81, parked in Camp Hill, and joined the march across the bridge.

When they arrived at the Transportation Center, they saw a group of young men depart the train.

William said, "What's up with those red hats? They some kinda gang?"

"Look like some thugs from Philly. I hope they not coming here to cause trouble."

They watched as the group headed toward Aberdeen Street with black backpacks. "Those bruthas gonna cause some trouble, I can feel it," William said.

Devin eyed them until they left his sight.

The train from Cleveland arrived a few minutes later and Devin introduced his friends to William. After, he led the group of nine to Market Street and saw the dudes in red hats smoking weed and giving joints and shot bottles of liquor to teens.

Devin said, "We don't need that out here," and turned right, then left onto North 5th , and right onto Walnut Street into the overflow crowd on North 7th, represented by every race with signs that read *Free Democracy Now!, Free the Left Wing!, We are Here to Stay!, Jews and Gentiles United!, Stop the Coup!, This Is America Not The Holy Roman Empire!,* and a picture of the Statue of Liberty that read *Give Me Your Tired, Your Poor, Your Huddled Masses Yearning To Breathe Free!* Those signs blocked the view ahead. But nothing was blocking the militia, who looked like mountain men and women, surrounding the state capital complex.

Devin was trying to see through the throng but couldn't.

"I see an opening on Commonwealth," William said and led the group to the avenue.

The massive crowd repeatedly shouting, "Stop the Coup!" intensified as darkness fell across the city and stars lit the sky.

The protesters were loud but peaceful until a commotion on Market Street hurried the reporters and their cameramen in that direction where smoke and flames were swirling and looters were in the hundreds.

William spotted a red hat throwing a Molotov cocktail into the grounds of the capital complex. "I told you those niggas was going to cause trouble."

Seconds later the militia leader repeated over the bullhorn, "The curfew is now in effect. Go home immediately, or face arrest."

An unprovoked anger infused many among the crowd, and people threw rocks and bottles toward the militia.

The militia leader yelled, "They're resisting arrest! Open fire!"

Ms. Walker and Candace watched the scene unfold on television.

"Oh my God, they're shooting people," Ms. Walker screamed.

Candace's mouth was closed with the worried expression, seemingly praying through her eyes.

As the minutes turned into hours, their anxiety and worry increased. "They're not home yet!" Ms. Walker stressfully said. "Dear God, please let them be safe."

Ms. Walker and Candace hadn't slept when William, Devin, and his friends entered the house. After relief hugs and kisses, Devin said, "The protest was peaceful until some youngins that looked like they came from Philly started some shit."

William interjected, "I think they were sent to disrupt. I saw them handing out weed and shot bottles to get people high and riled up."

Candace said to her husband, "Where did y'all go?"

"We ran across the Walnut Street bridge and stayed low until the chaos cleared. Then we crossed back over and went down Front Street to Highway 43, and into Camp Hill, where we parked."

"Thank God, y'all are safe," Candace said and kissed her husband again.

After Devin introduced his friends, his mother said, "I know y'all hungry. I'll cook breakfast."

"I'll help," Candace said and joined her mother-in-law in the kitchen.

The others went into the den to watch the twenty-four-hour independent news.

William took a moment to phone Sandra, and her groggy voice said, "Hello."

"Sandra! It's me."

She was silent as if the call was untimely.

William excitedly said, "I'm at my mother's."

She didn't say anything.

"What's wrong? You still there?"

Silence held her voice a few seconds more before she said, "I have to call you back."

He huffed, "Why? You got a nigga there?"

"Why you ask that? You the one that said it wouldn't bother you if I was with someone else. Why you trippin' now?"

"I'm not trippin'. I just miss you."

"I have to call you back, okay?"

"Why you gotta call me back?"

"I gotta call you back, bye."

With his mouth open to speak, she hung up the phone. *Damn, she rolling with another nigga.*

Heartbroken in a troubled mind, William lost his appetite and went upstairs to his childhood room where he eventually fell asleep after wrestling with thoughts and feelings.

Chapter 10

William woke that afternoon with Sandra on his mind. He wanted to call her again but found the strength not to. *I can't let her know I'm pressed.*

He went downstairs into the den, expecting to see Devin and his friends but didn't. He looked outside and Devin's van was gone. He went back into the den and turned on the local news.

The reporter said, "Five hundred and thirty-nine people were killed last night at the rally. Eight were members of the militia. There are reports that more than a hundred thousand people were killed nationwide. The president has reinstated the nationwide curfew from seven p.m. to six a.m."

Five hundred and thirty-nine people. A hundred thousand nationwide. They are trying to exterminate people.

Moments later the phone rang. *It's Sandra.* Before the second ring, he anxiously said, "Hello."

"It's not Sandra," Devin said.

"Man, what's up?"

"You heard about how many they killed last night?"

"Yeah. Can't believe it."

"That was just here. Tens of thousands more across the country. It was the militia. They kept reloading. It's all on camera."

"Damn. We were lucky."

"Check this out, I was watching NNC and saw bruthas with red hats marching with the protesters in Milwaukee and DC. One clip showed two red hats using a sledgehammer to break into a store and gesturing to the people to go inside. But they didn't go inside. They backed away as others started looting. The militia came seconds later and started shooting the people inside and outside the store but didn't shoot the two red hats that were standing right there with the sledgehammer."

"Where was that?"

"DC. Something's up."

"For sure. I'm going to try and get my job back. There's a story here."

"Did you talk to Sandra?"

"I think she's seeing someone else."

"Give it time. I'm sure she still loves you."

"I hope so."

* * *

The White House press secretary was bombarded with questions at the press briefing and said, "Public safety is the priority of this administration. We will not tolerate any kind of lawlessness. We are a law-and-order country. The destruction of property and looting are crimes. The American people have the right to peacefully protest, but when bottles and rocks are thrown, property destroyed, stores looted and burned, the National Guard and the militia will use deadly force.

"Let's not forget that policemen, national guardsmen, and members of the militia were also killed last night across the country. Twenty-seven members of the militia, eleven members of the National Guard, and thirteen police officers were gunned down during those so-called peaceful protests across the country. Some were struck down by sniper fire, others ambushed. Several police stations were set ablaze. The people who did that are not Americans!

"The left-wing has allowed people to get away with these actions too long. Those unruly people now believe they can commit crimes and only get a slap on the wrist. Those days are over. We are taking our country back from the criminals and all who engage in criminality. That is why the curfew has been reinstated nationwide from seven p.m. to six a.m. Anyone found on the streets without authorization between those hours is subject to be shot.

"The vice president, House speaker, and the pro tempore of the Senate are still missing! There are enemies within our gates, and we will root them out by any means necessary."

A reporter asked, "When will the president hold a press conference?"

"He will let you know."

Another reporter said, “The Supreme Court ruled this morning that children born in this country are rightful citizens. What is the president’s position on that ruling?”

“The Supreme Court also ruled that sanctuary cities are unconstitutional and undocumented immigrants are subject to deportation, which makes him extremely happy.” She continued, “Let me remind the American people of the multiple citizens that were killed, robbed, and raped in sanctuary cities this year by illegal immigrants. Among the victims was a twenty-three-year-old pregnant woman who was shot at the beach and a ten-year-old girl who was raped. Is this the America you want to live in? I don’t, and the president speaks for all of us who don’t.”

A reporter from State TV asked, “Is the press still exempt from the curfew?”

“Only State TV is exempt. All others are unauthorized and subject to arrest for violating the curfew.”

There was an uproar among the reporters. They all yelled follow-up questions that didn’t get answered because the press secretary left the room as if choreographed.

* * *

Rehired as a beat reporter for the local newspaper, William immediately began investigating the red hats. His first step was a trip to the Transportation Center. He went to the ticket counter and said to the young white man, “Hi, my name is William Walker. I’m a reporter. Can you tell me if the 5:40 p.m. from Cleveland on yesterday stopped in Philadelphia before arrival.”

He checked and said, “Yes.”

“Would you know the names of passengers that purchased tickets in Philadelphia?”

“I don’t have that information.”

“Thank you for your help.”

William drove two hours to the 30th Street station in Philadelphia, parked, and stood in line at the ticket counter. While waiting, he looked around for employees whose job encounters them with the passengers while boarding and departing the train and saw one of the ticket controllers. He stepped out of line and approached the bifocaled, bearded white man. “Excuse me, sir, I’m a reporter from Harrisburg. Were you working around this time yesterday?”

“I was.”

“Did you notice a group of young black guys, late teens or early twenties, wearing red hats with black backpacks.”

“Couldn’t miss them. They were very loud and disrespectful.”

“Did they board the 5:40 to Harrisburg?”

“They did.”

“How can I find their names?”

“Go to the ticket office.” He pointed.

William went to the ticket office. A middle-aged white woman was inside.

“My name is William Walker. I’m a reporter from Harrisburg working on a story. I’m trying to find the names of six black guys who purchased tickets to Harrisburg yesterday.”

“Do you know the departure time?”

“I don’t. But the arrival time in Harrisburg was 5:40 p.m.”

She checked the records and discovered six tickets purchased at the same time. She wrote down the names and handed him the paper.

“Thank you! Thank you very much!” He hurried back to the car and drove to City Hall. *I’m sure one of them has a criminal record.* In the office of public records, he searched the criminal records and found addresses that matched two of the names. He paused on the discovery, leaned back in thoughts with his left hand gripping the right and the back of that hand against his forehead. He stayed that way until his concentration was broken by an employee that announced the building was closing in ten minutes.

William headed back to Harrisburg, trying to arrive before the curfew, but was stopped at the city limits by two black national guardsmen.

“Where are you headed?” one asked while the other pointed his weapon.

“I’m a reporter. I’m headed home.”

"We have orders not to allow anyone in the city after curfew. But fuck those orders. You go ahead. But be careful. Those redneck militia are on the hunt."

"Thank you! I will."

William turned off the car's headlights to avoid easy detection and decided to go to Devin's because his house was closer.

He was traveling toward North 5th Street on Ridge Road when he heard gunshots. *Oh shit!* He quickly looked for a spot to pull off the road where the vehicle couldn't be easily seen and drove behind a row of trees at the side of a house that appeared vacant.

In the darkness, he turned off the engine and lowered his body where only his eyes could be seen. The moment at hand magnified the slightest sound.

Seconds later, the sound of gunshots was closer, and a white woman screaming for help came into view with the high beams from a pickup truck shining on her.

He watched as the truck sped past and turned to block her path. Four militiamen jumped out of the truck as the woman backed away, begging not to be hurt.

Each man took a turn in raping her. After, they executed the woman and left her like a dead animal on the road. As if it was an afterthought, they scanned area, seemingly to make sure there wasn't a witness.

When one of the men crossed the road with eyes on the seemingly vacant house, William lowered his body to the vehicle's floor, and felt the man's steps getting closer. *Please God, don't let him see me.*

A couple of seconds later, William heard a voice that sounded like it came from the other side of the road, "C'mon, Clarence, that house is vacant. We got to go."

William heard footsteps walking away, and seconds later the truck's tires squealing on the road. He eased his body up to see if they had left and only saw the woman. Unsure of the direction the militia took, he sat quietly, thinking of what to do, and decided to stay in that spot until the curfew was over.

While awake, he didn't take his eyes off the dead woman. *She's someone's daughter. Maybe a mother. Maybe a wife.*

Maybe someone's sister. For sure she was loved by others. He fell asleep wondering who she was.

When he woke, the curfew was over, and the body was still in the road. Cars were passing in both directions as if a human body wasn't there.

William was preparing to exit the vehicle with intentions to check if the woman was still alive, but thoughts came to mind. *What if someone thinks I killed her? Black man standing over a dead naked white woman who was raped.* He decided not to go and continued to Devin's house.

When he arrived, Candace had taken the kids to school, and Devin was preparing to leave for work. William told him about the things that had happened, and Devin said, "You were smart not to check the body. You would've been accused and probably killed before they arrested you.

"Forget about those red hats. Buy a gun and keep Mama safe. You're the one that's been saying Neo-Nazis have taken over the Elephant party, and now you're acting like you're surprised."

"I wasn't expecting it to happen so quick."

"This is what's up: Those redneck militia are the new Klansmen, and the president has given them authority over the streets. Who do you think they are coming for next? Buy as many guns and ammunition as you can. It's gonna get ugly. Have you talked to Sandra?"

"Naw. She hasn't called. She's moved on."

"Maybe. I think you should call her. Don't be a stalker, but let her know you miss her. Lock the door when you leave."

"For sure."

They dapped, and Devin left the house.

William phoned Sandra, but she didn't answer. He left a message, hoping for a moment to see her again.

I need to turn that rental car in. It's probably listed as stolen. He left Devin's house with the intention to drop off the rental car, but in his misery and loneliness decided to go downtown and report on the protest.

With his ID visible and notepad in hand, William moved around the crowd, randomly selecting people to ask them questions.

He asked an elderly black woman, who had her granddaughter with her, "Why are you here?"

She angrily said, "I'm here to save my country."

"Your granddaughter looks old enough to be in school. Why is she here?"

"It's more important for her to be here than in school. I want her to see what happens when democracy is taken away."

He went to a senior black couple and said, "Why are you here?"

The husband replied, "Why are you here?"

William seemed surprised by the question and paused in thought before he said, "I'm here to report why all ages, races, and religions feel it's more important to be in the streets protesting than at work, school, or home."

"Good. Now tell me why you think I'm here?"

"To save democracy."

"That's right! And I'm going to be here every day until democracy is restored."

William saw a multiracial group wearing Central Penn College shirts and approached. "What's up?" he said. "Why are you here?"

The Asian female student said, "To stamp out racism."

The Asian male student said, "Yeah! And to take back our country from the fascist."

The white male student said, "What are we supposed to do? Just accept the coup?"

The white female student said, "We're here to let the government know the people will not follow a rogue government. We're here to stop the coup with our voices."

Others among the group chimed in with the same words.

William said, "Are y'all staying out here past the curfew?"

One among them, who hadn't spoken, said, "We're not afraid to die. If they roll their tanks up in here, we will stand in front of them, daring them to roll over us. They can't kill all of us. What good is a coup if there are no people to hold power over?"

Another one that hadn't spoken added, "The people have the real power. If the people stop working for the coup, the coup will fail. That includes the soldiers and all civil workers.

We need to stop working, stop obeying the unlawful orders. Point your guns at those who started the coup and arrest them. They are the true enemies of the State."

* * *

William was among the protesters all day as if they were a refuge from his misery and loneliness.

At 6:30 p.m., a national guardsman said over the loudspeakers from across the capital complex, "Please begin dispersing. The curfew takes effect in thirty minutes. It's time to go home."

The crowd shouted, "We are home!"

Minutes later over the loudspeaker, the voice of a militia-man said, "It's 6:45 p.m. You have fifteen minutes to go home, or you will be arrested for violating the curfew. Anyone who resists arrest will be shot!"

The crowd yelled, "We are home! We're not leaving!"

William embedded himself in the crowd to defy the curfew as well. And at seven p.m., riot police, the militia, and national guardsmen moved forward with water cannons blasting from all sides of the capital complex.

William watched as the crowd in front of him didn't backtrack of their own free will. Those knocked down by the water cannons were arrested, and those pushed back didn't run but eventually were knocked down and arrested.

William backed away slowly as the crowd pushed forward with store-bought and homemade shields to block the water. He continued to backtrack with the other reporters who had braved to defy the curfew while most in the crowd tried to stand their ground.

To his surprise, the crowd refused to disperse, even when tanks were rolling forward. Expecting to hear gunshots, he didn't but witnessed the water cannons, riot police, militia, national guardsmen, and tanks back away like the ocean when it reaches the boundary.

One in the crowd of the peaceful protesters yelled in a bullhorn, "We are home! This is our home! We live in these streets! We are the people, and you should join us! Join us! Join us!" he repeatedly shouted.

The crowd repeatedly chanted in unison, "Join us!"

William moved forward to the front line and could see in some of the soldiers' eyes that they didn't want to be there.

He joined the chant, "Join us!" that continued for seemingly ten minutes.

When the clock neared midnight, the crowd dispersed as if they had won the battle.

With a story for the morning newspaper, William went directly to the office.

* * *

DAY 9

In the first seconds of a new day, the militia stormed every sanctuary city, arresting illegal and undocumented immigrants and their American-born children. Adult Latino citizens found among the illegal and undocumented immigrants were also transported to deportation centers, which outraged the Latino community led by prominent Cuban American members of the Elephant party. But their voices, along with the voices of some in Congress, and the court rulings that ordered the president to stop the arrests and mass deportations were ignored, because no one in power came forward to stop the president's unlawful actions.

The media begged the White House for comment, but the cancellations of the daily press briefings continued. Reporters frantically sought the leaders of the House and Senate, but they were in hiding, like every member of Congress that was enabling the president.

In the desperate effort to save their democracy, the American people in growing numbers of Democrats, Republicans, Independents, and the unregistered continued to march on the nation's capitals in defiance of the curfew despite the arrest and killings of many.

The world watched in horror as women and children peacefully protesting were arrested and shot in the streets of America. William was among the daily protesters, partly because of his job, partly because of the fight for democracy, and partly in the hope that he would see Sandra among them.

* * *

DAY 12

At the daily morning meeting in the Situation Room, the president in his frustration said, "These people won't quit. They shouldn't be this defiant when we are in power."

Mr. Rudolph said, "Sir, you're moving too fast. You give them hope, then you take it away the next day. The ninety-day plan is to expel all non-Aryans in ninety days. You started too soon."

The president's iron-face seemed to harden, if that was possible, and he said, "Those immigrants from Central and South American countries, Africa, and Asia are poisoning our blood every day with crime, diseases, homosexuality, and interracial relationships. We can't wait! The court of appeals this morning upheld the lower court ruling that blocked Jewish citizens from being forced to leave the country. Now we have to wait on the Supreme Court! I am the Führer. I shouldn't have to wait."

Mr. Rudolph said, "Mr. President, announce you respect the court's decision but have the right, like any citizen, to appeal to the Supreme Court, and that you will abide by their decision. We know what their decision will be, but it will give us a few days for the people to feel like democracy has returned, and they will relax. Let them feel like things are normal. They were shocked by the assassination, shocked by the disappearance of the vice president, House speaker, and Senate pro tempore, and shocked by your decrees no matter the justification. The people need what they know as normalcy."

Mr. Reaves added, "Mr. President, announce that special elections will be held for the vacant seats in the House and Senate. The people will become focused on the special elections. That's when you can dismantle the Supreme Court and begin the expulsion of Jews and all non-Aryan citizens."

"My God, Mr. Reaves," the president said. "I didn't know you had that in you." He turned to the chief of staff. "Give him another envelope."

* * *

That afternoon, the president took to the airwaves from the Resolute Desk and said, "As you already know, the court of appeals has ruled to uphold the lower court ruling regarding the Jews. While I respect their decision, I have the right to appeal to the Supreme Court, and I will today. If the Supreme Court upholds the decision, I will follow that decision. Our Constitution has three branches of government: the office of the presidency, the legislative branch, and the Supreme Court. I am beholden to all three.

"In accordance with maintaining our democracy, the freedom of the press is restored, the curfew is lifted, and special elections for the vacant seats in the House and Senate will be held in the next sixty days.

"It's time for healing. Americans should not be fighting Americans in the streets of our great country. I will take the blame for that, and I apologize. We have our differences, but we are a democracy and not a dictatorship.

"But we are a country of law and order and will not tolerate criminal behavior of any kind. We are patriots; and in this country it's a crime to be unpatriotic. There are still enemies within our gates, so stay alert as you go about in your daily lives, and report all unpatriotic actions. God bless America."

After listening to the president's speech, William said to his co-workers, "He left a whole lot of questions unanswered. Is democracy truly restored?"

One of his co-workers said, "Yes. He's holding special elections and will follow the Supreme Court decisions. That's democracy."

"Maybe."

* * *

DAY 15

The country had seemingly returned to normal. People were going to work and socializing, children were attending school, and all scheduled sporting events continued. Only at the schools and sporting events was the Pledge of Allegiance with the Bellamy salute mandatory.

In the schools, black children were told by their parents to secretly cross their fingers with their free hand during the Bellamy salute. Some of the white children did the same.

At the sporting events, the people who arrived after or during the Bellamy salute were unable to enter the facility. The people walking around the concourses during the Bellamy salute were arrested. The people inside the arenas and stadiums who refused to participate in the Bellamy salute were arrested, including the athletes.

To escape the Bellamy salute, the restrooms at the stadiums and arenas were overcrowded, and the venues were half full because many boycotted the sporting events.

The land of the free was no more because the party that preached freedom took it away.

* * *

DAY 17

The Supreme Court announced that it upheld the lower court ruling that revoking the Jews' citizenship was unconstitutional. The crowd outside the building, consisting of all races and religions, erupted in a celebration that carried across the country. People were hugging, kissing, dancing, and praying in the streets. And with their right hand on their heart, they recited the *Pledge of Allegiance*, followed by singing the *National Anthem*, then *God Bless America*. Those celebrations continued across the nation until the break of dawn.

* * *

Summer and Rhoda were together when the Supreme Court decision was announced. "Thank you, Jesus!" Summer yelled joyously.

Rhoda cried happy tears.

Summer embraced her. "We won. God is great."

Rhoda cried out in Hebrew, "Thank you, God!"

* * *

DAY 18

The White House press secretary stepped to the press room podium and said, "The president doesn't agree with the decision made yesterday by the Supreme Court but will abide accordingly. He has now turned his full attention to finding the left-wing fugitives. The FBI has placed a bounty of five million dollars on the heads of House Minority Leader Jefferson and Senate Minority Leader Schumacher. These men are dangerous and remain a threat to national security.

"The left-wing media and the radical left continue to criticize the president for not following the Constitution when the Constitution allows for freedom of speech. Because he's the president doesn't mean he doesn't have the freedom of speech. What he has said about the Jews and others is his opinion, and he has the authority to enact that opinion and allow the courts to decide, which he has done.

"The president is trying to save our country from the onslaught of immigrants illegally crossing our borders to commit crimes, infest us with incurable diseases, and rape and murder our women. That is what our country will become if we don't stop it now. The deportation of all illegal and undocumented immigrants will continue according to the law. To discourage our enemies abroad from taking advantage of the crisis at our southern borders, the president has replaced the military with the militia. The militia under General Weiskopf will patrol the borders of Texas, New Mexico, Arizona, and California. Anyone attempting to cross our borders illegally will be shot. There is a process for requesting entry into the country. Violators will be subject to American justice. Any questions?"

She pointed to one of the many with raised hands, and the reporter said, "What is American justice?"

"American justice is American law." She pointed at another reporter.

"Is the president considering holding a special election for president?"

"No, because he is the rightful president according to the Constitution." She pointed at another reporter.

"When will the Justice department release the evidence that justifies the arrest of the House and Senate Democrats?"

"The attorney general is waiting to capture the fugitives before he releases that information." She pointed at another reporter.

"There are reports of wealthy right-wing donors financing the travel of migrants from Central and South America to significantly increase the numbers at our border to help the president's rhetoric. Are those reports true?"

"Those reports are fake news." She quickly pointed at another reporter.

"I have two questions. Where is the location of the deportations? And when will those who were illegally deported return?"

"The deportation locations are undisclosed for national security reasons. And no one was deported illegally."

The reporter quickly said, "I have a follow-up question. There are reports of American-born children and adult citizens among the illegals arrested and deported. Those reports coincide with the disappearance of those adults and children. Is the president aware that children born in this country by undocumented immigrants are missing with Latin-Americans?"

"That reporting is more fake news. The children born in America have not been deported but are in an undisclosed location pending foster care. The government has not deported anyone that is an American citizen."

That reporter yelled, "Where are the missing adult citizens?"

The press secretary pointed at another reporter, and that reporter said, "I'd like an answer to my colleague's question.

Where are the adult citizens that were arrested with the illegals?"

"They were not deported but are being held at an undisclosed location pending trial for abetting and harboring fugitives."

The press secretary abruptly left the room with questions shouted at her.

* * *

Inside a Colorado mountain, the vice president, House speaker, and Senate pro tempore watched the press briefing.

The vice president said, "I hope we don't have to stay here longer than ninety days."

The Senate pro tempore replied, "If we must, we will. I can use another million dollars a day."

"I don't want to stay past ninety days," the House speaker said. "I miss my wife and children. Ninety million dollars is enough for me."

"I miss my children but not my wife," the Senate pro tempore said.

The vice president said, "I miss my life aboveground."

"Why?" the Senate pro tempore asked. "We have everything a man could want down here. Our choice of a woman or man every night, a personal chef, the wines and liquors we want, the music we want, the clothing we want, cable television. We can even golf when we want. I love it here. What better place for an old man like me?"

The vice president said, "I love this underground city. But I love my family more. I have friends up there. Fresh air is up there: the rain, the sun, the moon, the snow. All of life is up there."

"I'm confident we won't be here longer than ninety days," the House speaker said.

"I'm not going back," the Senate pro tempore said. "I prefer to live down here. This is my home now."

"That means we have to explain your death," the House speaker said.

"That's easy. Just say I died in captivity."

"How are we going to explain the missing body?"

"Old iron-face will think of something. I'm going to my room and finish counting my money."

"How much have you counted so far?" the House speaker asked.

"I opened all the bags but only counted two. Both have a million dollars in it."

The vice president interjected, "You can stop there. You have ninety bags, and if a million dollars is in each, that's your ninety million. I didn't even try to count mine. I opened the bags and saw money, and I have ninety bags. Made sense that a million was in each bag. We all have ninety bags, and we all have looked inside. No need to count it."

"I like counting," the Senate pro tempore said.

The vice president said, "I'm tired of looking at my bags of money. I want to spend some of it, but everything is free down here. That's another reason why I want to get out of here. This place is a nice vacation spot, but I don't want to live here. I can't experience the Fourth Reich down here. I don't want to see the New World Order on television. I want to live in it."

That night, the vice president, House speaker, and Senate pro tempore were executed as they slept. Their money was placed on an eighteen-wheeler and loaded on a military plane to Switzerland.

Chapter 11

Mr. Jefferson and Mr. Schumacher were hiding in the home of Ruby Thomas, a thirty-four-year-old mother of two teenage boys, who lived in the southwest public housing complex in Washington, DC. She and Mr. Jefferson had been in a secret relationship for nearly two years.

Mr. Schumacher said, "How long do we have to stay here? I need to let my wife know I'm alive."

"You haven't been caught, so she knows you're alive," Mr. Jefferson said. "Besides, they're watching her and your home. Your phones are tapped. They're waiting for you to call her."

"What about your family? Aren't you concerned about them?"

"Of course I am. But they know I can't contact them. If I haven't been caught, they know I'm okay. The longer it takes for them to catch me, the safer I am in their eyes."

After watching the press briefing, Mr. Schumacher said, "We have to leave."

"Why?"

"You heard it!"

Mr. Jefferson scowled and said, "Lower your voice."

With his voice lowered, Mr. Schumacher said, "There is a five-million-dollar bounty on our heads. Your friend or her sons are going to turn us in for that money."

"No, they won't."

"What makes you so confident they won't? Look at this place. A person living in a Park Avenue penthouse would turn us in for five million dollars. You think people living with rats won't?"

"No, they won't."

"Why?"

"Why is the reason I came here and brought you with me. I knew we would be safe. There may be other people in this building that would turn us in if they knew we were here, but not them."

"What makes you so confident? I hope it isn't because of your sexual relationship."

"It's because she knows if the coup is successful, after the Jews they will be coming for the African Americans. Her sons know that too.

"Here is some background on Ruby and her sons. She is from Monroe, North Carolina, and read the book authored by Robert F. Williams, who was the president of the Monroe North Carolina chapter of the NAACP. She educated her children in the teachings of Malcolm X and the Black Panther party. They are loyal to the cause. They know the derogatory things white people say about them is what those white people are themselves. Like the word *nigger*. The original meaning of the word is 'an ignorant person.' Racists are ignorant people.

"As a black man, I don't trust a person because they're black. I trust them when I know they see the world as it is. This family will lose their life to save ours—and I will lose my life to save theirs."

Mr. Schumacher stood shamefaced.

"It's okay," Mr. Jefferson said. "You weren't wrong for thinking that. I hope you understand now why I'm so confident. When Ruby and her sons come home, we'll talk about it."

* * *

Ruby's sons arrived home before her, and Mr. Schumacher looked at them with nervous eyes.

The eldest son said to him, "We heard about the bounty, but we're not betraying you."

Mr. Schumacher stayed silent with skepticism reflecting in his eyes.

The younger son said to him, "Have you read *Negroes with Guns* by Robert Franklin Williams?"

"No," Mr. Schumacher said.

"That book had intellectual influence on the Black Panther party. It told Negroes to fight back with guns against a racist society."

Mr. Schumacher looked stunned by the words that came out of the young teen's mouth.

Mr. Jefferson said, "The boys are letting you know they will die before helping a racist win. So relax."

* * *

At sunset, Ruby arrived home, and Mr. Jefferson shared Mr. Schumacher's concern.

Ruby said, "Calvin wouldn't've brought you here if you were an undercover racist. Because he brought you here, we know you're not. We knew this day was coming, and now that it's here, we are prepared. Have you thought why Calvin knew what to do so quickly?"

Mr. Schumacher shook his head.

"Ask him?"

He shifted his eyes to Mr. Jefferson and asked him with the expression.

Mr. Jefferson said, "President Milhouse's administration was the beginning of the far-right authoritarian ultranationalist political ideology. We were lucky that he resigned. When the right-wing came back into power and again put German names as heads of the administration, I knew a coup was on the horizon and began preparations.

"When the president was assassinated and those in the line of succession disappeared, I knew what time it was and left the Capitol, telling you a lie to get you to come with me because I knew you would've stayed, trusting the system guardrails. But the strongest guardrail is the people, and the people have slowed the coup. If you had stayed, you would be in jail with the others."

Mr. Schumacher seemed to be contemplating, then said, "What's the plan moving forward?"

"The vice president, speaker, and Senate pro tempore are most likely dead. I believe Congressman Reaves is on our side."

Mr. Schumacher held a befuddled expression and said, "What?"

"Keep your voice down. I know Congressman Reaves and I'm a good judge of character. He's not part of the coup."

"He sure talks like he is."

"That's because he's smart enough to work from the inside. We need people inside the coup to stop the coup."

"What makes you so confident about him? He's not black."

"We both know Harvey. He doesn't want to live under an authoritarian government. I believe he has positioned himself to be trusted so he can work against the coup from the inside."

"Maybe he changed."

"He hasn't changed. I have a way to get in touch with him."

"That's a big gamble I'm not willing to take. I don't trust him."

"Have I led you astray?"

"It's not you that I'm worried about."

"It is me if you're questioning my decisions. My life is on the line too. Trust me. We need to contact Harvey, Mr. Rosenberg, and other Republicans that are speaking out against the president's actions. They are in the resistance too."

"I agree that we should get a message to Mr. Rosenberg and others because we heard their opposition when interviewed. But Harvey has only defended the president. I don't trust him."

"I'm following my gut. If I was him, I would be doing the same thing. That is how you gain trust. Mr. Rosenberg can be helpful, but he isn't at the table with the coup enablers. Congressman Reaves is."

"Okay, against my better judgment, I'm going to trust you. What's your plan?"

"Ruby has a contact in the congressional cafeteria. Harvey often goes there in the morning for the continental breakfast. The woman who works there can slip him a note. As for Mr. Rosenberg, he lives in Montgomery County. Ruby knows the postman who knows the postman that works that route. We will send a message to him that way."

"How do you know the postman won't betray us?"

"There are a lot of things that are accurate about black people, but ignorant isn't one of them. We have our divisions, but we are united against the racists."

"Not all of you are."

"Yeah, there are some Negroes that are lapdogs, but we have learned to identify them quickly and make their names known among us so no one will trust them. We can trust the postal workers."

Mr. Schumacher was goggle-eyed with his mouth frozen open, then said, "You sound like a black revolutionist."

"I am. But not to take over the country but to keep the country free from racists taking over the country. That was the purpose of the Black Panther party."

Mr. Schumacher said, "I'm seeing a man I didn't know existed."

"If you see an intelligent black man, know that one like me is inside him."

Mr. Schumacher widened his legs and lay the palm of his hands on his thighs. "I'm sure someone at the post office is monitoring Rosenberg's mail."

"Our message isn't going through the mail but with the mail. There won't be a postal mark on it. No offense, but white people don't realize black people are the controlling civil servants in this country."

Mr. Schumacher paused, seemingly enlightened. Then said, "What will the messages say?"

"We will let Harvey know that we are safe and believe he is in the resistance, and that we are ready to help him in any way. The message will let him know the cafeteria worker is our line of communication. We will let Mr. Rosenberg know that we are safe and need financial backing."

"You're going to ask him for money?"

"Yes, the resistance needs money. It takes money to feed and clothe us and others in hiding, and to work the underground. When the FBI infiltrated the Black Panther party and dissolved it on the surface, they didn't kill the spirit. It continued to manifest underground. That spirit was kept alive in churches, songs, books, and child-rearing. While you were caught sleeping, we weren't. We knew the racist Democrats would eventually hijack the Republican party to try and do what they couldn't in the Civil War. We heard the dog whistles.

"Like the Jews say, 'Never Again!,' we say it louder. We will never again live in slavery, or under Jim Crow. We have organized to prevent that from happening, and we don't need the phone or internet to communicate. We speak in code. You call it slang, but it's much more than that."

Mr. Schumacher was speechless.

"Don't worry," Mr. Jefferson said. "Together, we will stop the coup."

* * *

DAY 19

The mailman pushed Mr. Rosenberg's doorbell, and a young white woman dressed like a maid opened the door.

"Special delivery for Mr. Rosenberg," the mailman said. "I need his signature for this letter."

"Wait," the woman said and closed the door.

Nearly a minute later, a tall slender middle-aged woman conservatively dressed in black with a lengthy silver pendant necklace, opened the door.

The mailman said, "I have a special delivery for Mr. Rosenberg that requires his signature."

"I'm authorized to sign for Mr. Rosenberg."

"I'm sorry Ms., but I have to witness Mr. Rosenberg sign it."

"I always sign for the mail that requires his signature." She turned up her nose. "I'm Mr. Rosenberg's personal assistant. Where do I sign?"

"I'm sorry Ms., but Mr. Rosenberg has to sign."

"Okay, give me the letter and I will take it to him."

"I'm sorry Ms., but I personally have to see him sign it."

She held a contempt expression.

"Ms., I'm just doing my job. Don't be angry at me. This letter is very important."

"Who sent it?"

"It's from one of the many fighting to keep democracy alive."

"Follow me." She led the mailman into a room larger than his entire house.

In a printed velvet smoking jacket, Mr. Rosenberg was sitting with his legs crossed in an oversized chair. The mailman's eyes were drawn to the line of smoke rising from the cigar on the ashtray table.

"You like cigars?" Mr. Rosenberg asked.

"I do. I was just admiring the ashtray. I have a letter that requires your signature."

"Who is it from?"

"Capitol Hill."

Mr. Rosenberg's brows lifted and eyes widened. "Hurry, bring it to me."

The mailman handed Mr. Rosenberg the letter, and the personal assistant led the mailman back down the long hallway.

Mr. Rosenberg was reading the letter when he yelled, "Bring that mailman back!"

The personal assistant led him back into the room.

Mr. Rosenberg uncrossed his legs and stood. "What is your name?"

"Daryl."

"Did Mr. Jefferson give you this letter?"

"A friend of Mr. Jefferson."

"Can I trust you with a million dollars in cash?"

"To be honest, I don't know."

"How old are you?"

"Thirty-nine."

"How much do you make a year?"

He hesitated before he said, "Thirty-three thousand."

"Because you were trusted to bring this letter, which was risking your life, which I believe is worth more than a million dollars, I can trust you with a million dollars. I need you to take a million dollars to the person who gave you this letter for them to give it to Mr. Jefferson."

"The person who gave me the letter is another postal worker that isn't directly connected to Mr. Jefferson. The person who gave him the letter is directly connected to Mr. Jefferson."

"I need you to take the money to him and tell him to give the money to the person directly connected to Mr. Jefferson. He is expecting this money, and I believe he is expecting to receive it the same way he sent this letter. That means he trusts every piece of the chain.

"Tell your friend that, starting tomorrow, I will give you $100,000 a day for him to send to Mr. Jefferson through his contact. And when it's all done, I have a lifetime job for you and him at $100,000 each."

"Doing what?"

"What you're doing now, but in a suit and tie with travel expenses. And when you turn sixty-five, you can collect Social Security and receive a half mil under the table."

"That all sounds good, but you might be dead when I turn sixty-five."

"I might be dead but my money won't. You can trust me. You will receive the money even if I'm dead. It's in the hands of a law firm that will be here when your great-great-grandchildren are dead and gone. And that's not all I'm going to give you."

The mailman stood anxious to hear.

"When I give you the first $100,000 tomorrow, I'm going to also give you a thousand shares of stock that is fifteen dollars a share today but in twenty years is estimated to be over $150 a share. It would be smart to buy extra shares with the extra salary you will earn when Mr. Jefferson receives the million dollars."

The mailman seemed overwhelmed and in a doubtful tone said, "You are going to do all that for me and my friend?"

"In risking your life, you are helping me to save mine. I've always been a philanthropist for charitable organizations, but when I find deserving individuals, I share my wealth with them too. I'm a Jew living in America, and this country has become like Nazi Germany. They're planning to kill all Jews no matter where we go. They aren't after you, but you're risking your life to help me. You don't know me. I'm not your friend. But you're helping a friend that is trying to help me. That says a lot about you. Thank you. I kept you long enough. You need to get back to your route."

The mailman said, "Thank you, sir."

And Mr. Rosenberg's assistant led him out of the house.

* * *

As the days passed, mass deportations continued, and all migrants requesting asylum at the southern borders were denied without a hearing. Those who crossed illegally were shot and left unburied. Among them were women and children in the hundreds.

* * *

DAY 24

Inside the morning Situation Room meeting, the president said, "Our partners in the New World Order are doubting we can raise the Fourth Reich fully."

"Why?" the chair of the Joint Chiefs asked. "They agreed to the ninety-day plan. We're only in day twenty-four."

"I told them I could finish the plan in sixty days."

"Sixty days?" Mr. Rudolph interjected. "That was a big mistake, Mr. President. We cannot complete it in sixty days. What moved you to think that we could?"

"I did, and we should be able to do it. Those who are with us today will be with us tomorrow. Those who are against us today will be against us tomorrow. So why wait? I'm not waiting anymore. I'm going to do this my way. I will address the nation tonight and announce that all Jews have six days to leave the country."

"Mr. President, that will throw the country into chaos," Congressman Reaves said. "I suggest you wait until tomorrow night to make that address. That will give us time to prepare for the fallout. May I ask, where will the seven million Jews in this country go?"

With a closed-mouth smile, the president said, "They have their own nation for now."

"But Israel is only the size of New Jersey?"

"Those vermin shouldn't even have that! Do you have sympathy for them?"

The congressman sharpened his expression and said, "Of course not! I just don't want a country to send them back."

"They aren't coming back when they go there, nor when they are stranded in the air and sea because no other country but their own will accept them. They will be forced to go to Israel to feel safe. But they won't be safe there for long when the desert men that surround them are released. And we will release them when the time is right."

Congressman Reaves stood and clapped, and the president leaned back and smiled at him.

* * *

After the meeting, the vice-chair of the Joint Chiefs approached Congressman Reaves outside the White House. "Can we talk privately?"

The congressman replied, "Where?"

"Where no eyes and ears are around. Have you been to Roy's?"

"The restaurant across the bridge?"

"Meet me there."

"When?"

"Now."

They entered their vehicles and drove directly to Roy's.

As they sat in one of the VIP booths, the vice-chairman said, "If I'm wrong about you, I'll be arrested. Will I be arrested?"

The congressman eyed him with multiple thoughts circling. *Is he another test?* He stared a few seconds before he said, "If you have something to say, say it."

The vice-chair paused with conflicting thoughts written in his eyes.

The congressman said, "Your instincts asked me here. Continue to trust your instincts."

The vice-chair stared for a moment and said, "I'm in the resistance."

Congressman Reaves leaned back with focused eyes and said, "You wouldn't've told me that if you believed I am one of the enablers. Why do you believe I'm not?"

"In your first statement to the press, you called the secretary of state an interim president. If you were part of the coup, you wouldn't've said *interim*. But when you spoke at the press conference, I thought they had successfully recruited you until I heard you this morning. You did a good job in covering up when the president questioned you, but I saw me in you. We both are looking for others to work against the coup from inside."

"Are there any others?"

"Yes. Another one at the table and more among the lower levels."

Congressman Reaves leaned forward with his hands cuffed. "Good. There are some in Congress too."

The vice-chair smiled.

"Why are you smiling?"

"Because now I know for sure that you are with me."

"And why is that?"

"Because you didn't ask who at the table is with me?"

"And you didn't ask who in Congress is with me."

They shook hands.

* * *

The next day at nine p.m., the president addressed the nation.

"My fellow American patriots, our intelligence agencies have discovered a broader Jewish-led plot to remove Christianity from the United States of America and replace it with Zionist states. The plan included assassinating me to free Mr. Abelman, the Secretary of the Treasury, the next person in the line of succession for the presidency, to complete their coup. Mr. Abelman was arrested this evening and his house thoroughly searched. A list of supporters was discovered on his personal computer. That list included every synagogue in this country.

"A state of emergency has reoccurred. By executive action I am overriding the Supreme Court decision and ordering every Jew to leave the US and its territories in six days from midnight. Failure to leave will result in arrest for deportation. Anyone aiding and abetting a Jew after the deadline will be treated as an enemy of the State. Anyone harboring a fugitive will be treated as an enemy of the State.

"Until further notice, a curfew is in effect from seven p.m. to six a.m. Only essential personnel, which includes hospital and sanitation workers, are exempt. Soldiers and the militia are under strict orders to shoot all curfew violators. No one is allowed to enter the country by land, air, or sea until the curfew is lifted.

"As your president, I will defend the Constitution against all enemies, foreign and domestic. I believe the vice president, House speaker, and the Senate pro tempore are dead, murdered in a plot funded by the Jews in collaboration with the Communist Democrats to remove Christianity as the official religion of this country.

"Jesus said, 'No man cometh unto the Father but by me.' All who deny Jesus Christ as Lord and Savior are enemies of God and worship Satan. There is no place for them in this Christian nation.

"Our courts and our democracy have fallen into the hands of Jews. Therefore, I have dismantled all courts, including the Supreme Court, and will begin rewriting the Constitution, effective immediately.

"I am outlawing the freedom of the press. Only State media can report the news or publish information about the government. All other news outlets are the enemy of the people.

"We are taking our country back from the Socialists, Marxists, and radical left. We are taking our country back from those that are trying to make us speak a foreign language in our own country.

"We are Americans—the Pilgrims' pride—Puritans. We are making our country great again, bringing back 1776 with a new declaration of independence that roots out all non-Aryans, and restores Western civilization. God bless America—and God bless every American patriot."

* * *

Immediately after the president's address, in Spokane, Washington, a Jewish woman phoned her neighbor and close friend of nineteen years. Inside the neighbor's home, the wife said, "That's Helena calling. I know it."

"Don't answer," the husband Roger said. "Let her call her Jewish friends for help."

"We told her that we will be there for her."

"Do you want to die? We will get killed if we help her."

The phone continued to ring as they listened, waiting for it to stop. When it did, they sighed, but the ringing quickly started again. "I should've connected the answering machine," Roger begrudgingly said. And they waited another minute for the ringing to stop.

"Why aren't they answering? I know they're home," Helena frustratingly said, and dialed again. Unanswered rings continued in her worried ear.

She slammed down the phone, hurried across the street, and angry knuckles sounded.

"Stay quiet," Roger whispered. Dottie whispered, "It's Helena." In the continued whisper, Roger said, "She will go away."

The knocks were more rapid and louder. "Dottie, it's me, Helena!"

Dottie's eyes watered with her silence.

The knocks turned to banging, and Roger irritably said, "I'm going to tell her to go away." He cracked the door to prevent her entrance and said, "Go back home. We can't help you."

"What! You and Dottie said y'all would help me if this happened. Where's Dottie?"

"Go away! We can't help you!"

"Oh my God! We've been neighbors and friends for almost twenty years! How can you do this to me?"

"I'm sorry, Helena, we can't help you."

"Where's Dottie?" She leaned forward and yelled in the crack, "Dottie, don't let your husband do this to me!"

Roger pushed her back, slammed the door, and double locked it.

Helena cried, "Dottie! Don't let him do this to me." She dropped to her knees, and with tears running down her face shrieked, "Dottie, please! If you can't help me, help my son and his family, p-pleassse."

Her pleas were unanswered, and she cried as she slowly walked back to her home, wondering what her future would bring.

Seemingly oblivious to the sound of sirens and gunshots nearby, she stood in front of her home for several minutes. The shock of her neighbor and close friend turning their backs led her to question everything she felt positive about in life. And after nearly an hour in that daze, she went inside her home and tried to phone the Rabbi, but his line stayed busy.

She phoned her son.

"Hello." The sound of tears trickled in his ear. "Ma, what's wrong? You need me to come there?"

"I-I'm o-okay," she muttered.

"I know the president's speech upset you, but we knew this might happen. Thank God Dottie is willing to help us until the coup is over."

Silence held the phone.

"Ma, you there?"

A teary low voice said, "Yes."

"I feel like you got something to tell me. What is it?"

She paused and said, "I love you."

"I love you too. Since we only have six days, I'm thinking about bringing the family tomorrow to stay with you until we go to Dottie's."

Helena didn't say anything.

"Ma, is everything okay?"

"Dottie said it's best that you stay home, and she will pick you up, because five people coming to her house at one time might be suspicious if the neighbors see us. Tell your neighbors that you are leaving the state. Hide your car and keep the lights off. Stay in that safe room you got until Dottie arrives."

"Ma, what's going on?"

"Nothing. It's just precautionary. If something happens to me, I want you to be safe."

"What do you mean if something happens to you?"

“Anything might happen in the next six days. This nightmare might be over. If not, just do what I said.”

“Ma, something’s wrong. I can feel it.”

“Nothing is wrong. Just do what I said.”

* * *

After the president’s address, there was an exodus of Jews fleeing the country by land, air, and sea, but they were only allowed in Israel. Some of the Jews believed their status as professional athletes and celebrities made them exempt and didn’t seek salvation out of the country. Others sold their possessions for passages that didn’t save them, and others went into hiding.

Mr. Rosenberg didn’t leave the country. He opened his home to family, friends, and Jews in need of a safe place and hired special op mercenaries to protect his home while he continued to support the Resistance.

In that hour of turmoil throughout the world, prominent religious leaders were standing on both sides, but the Pontiff was silent.

Chapter 12

Summer hid Rhoda and her family along with other Jews on the Indian Reservation where Aponi lived. "They will begin looking for all of you soon," Summer said. "You are safe here, but I can't stay in Wyoming."

"Where are you going?" Rhoda asked.

"I'm going back to Syracuse. Like you said, they know we are friends, so they believe I will hide you and your family with me. If I'm in Syracuse, they will think you are there too and won't look here."

"Are you flying?"

"No, I'm driving. If I fly, they will check the records and know you're not with me, so I'm driving."

"That's why I asked," Rhoda said and tried to hide her sadness behind the smile.

The reservation chief said, "You all with be safe here. This tunnel was built for us to hide from the white man. We have enough food and water stored for everyone."

Rhoda and the others graciously said, "Thank you."

"We're in this together," the chief said. "They're coming for us next."

* * *

DAY 31

At the stroke of midnight in every time zone, the militia, with files that listed the names and addresses of Jews, went hunting.

In Los Angeles, members of the militia targeted the homes of the rich and famous Jews, pillaging and murdering those who hadn't left their houses.

In Scottsdale, Arizona, the militia received a tip from the neighborhood that Jews were hiding inside a home. They went to that house and pounded on the front door.

Behind the locked door, a pale-red-skinned man shouted, "Who is it?"

"The militia! We need to check your home."

"For what?"

"For Jews!"

"There aren't any Jews here," a woman's voice replied.

"Open the door or we will break it open!"

The man opened the door, and the militia immediately began rummaging through the house. One of the militia said, "Are you Mr. and Mrs. Sinclair?"

"We are," the man answered.

"I need to see IDs."

The wife calmed herself and went to get their IDs.

One of the militiamen searching the back room looked at the wife with sultry eyes and grabbed her. She screamed, and when her husband ran toward her distress call, he lay dead from a shot in the back of his head.

Each of the five militiamen took turns raping the alluring twenty-six-year-old woman before continuing the search. The last one viciously beat her and said, "You should've let me be the first, you bitch!"

One of the militia entered the room and said, "There aren't any Jews here."

The one that had beaten the woman stood and emptied his rifle into the woman's body.

The elderly next-door neighbor held a happy face during the screams and gunshots and smiled as he watched the militia leave the house.

* * *

At the crack of dawn in Aurora, Illinois, a family was startled by the sound of intruders. The husband grabbed his gun and headed toward the sound. The wife grabbed the children from their rooms, hurried them into her bedroom, and locked the door.

With the pointed gun, the husband stood at the top of the stairs, unnerved in the darkness, and fired at the first person that came into view. The man fell with a grunt and landed on the bottom step. Return gunshots struck the husband, and he fell.

One of the men stood over his comrade and said, “Thank God for your body armor.”

“Yeah.”

He helped him to his feet and the three men proceeded up the stairs with pointed rifles, firing one shot into the husband as they passed.

After they had checked the open rooms, the three men stood outside the locked door. “This is the militia, open the door!”

Amid the children bellowing tears, the mother yelled, “We aren’t Jews!”

“Is this the home of Philip and Dorothy Simon?”

“No! We just moved into this house last week. Where is my husband?”

The militiaman kicked the door open and turned on the bedroom light. “Where is your ID?”

The children’s cries were louder, and the mother pointed at the purse on the dresser.

One of the militiamen removed the wallet from the purse and checked the ID. “Her name is Julia Newton.”

The militiaman who kicked open the door grabbed the ID, looked at it, then looked at the woman.

The pasty-faced boy among the two girls was struggling to breathe. “He needs his inhaler,” the mother frantically said. “Can I get his inhaler?”

The militiaman said, “No,” and shot the boy, then the two girls.

While the mother was weeping over the bodies of her dead children, the militiaman said, “You shouldn’t’ve bought a house that was owned by Jews,” and shot her.

They ransacked the house and set it on fire.

* * *

In Decatur, Georgia, a wife and husband were sitting at their kitchen table when five militiamen stormed their home. The wife screamed, followed by the sound of her breakfast plate crashing on the floor.

Her husband protectively jumped in front of her and said, "The mayor authorized another two weeks for us to leave."

The group's leader, a maniacal-looking man with a prison tattoo on his neck, said, "The mayor doesn't have the authority to grant an extension. All Jews had to leave the country like the president told you? Why didn't you leave?"

"We don't have the money?"

"Bullshit! All Jews have money."

"We don't. We're not rich. Do we look like we're rich?"

"Why didn't you go into hiding like the other vermin?"

"We don't have a place to hide. We can only pray."

"You see what praying has done for you? Nothing. God has turned his back on you because you killed our Lord." He spat in the husband's face. "Filthy ass Jews."

One of the militiamen entered the kitchen and said, "Look who I found."

The leader turned and a palish girl with a reddish pigtail hairstyle in a school uniform locked his eyes. She yanked her arm free from the militiaman's light grip and ran into her mother's arms.

With the eyes of a child molester, the leader stared.

The mother gritted her teeth, "Don't you touch her!"

The father beggingly said, "She's only eleven."

The leader seemingly wasn't listening. His eyes stayed locked on the girl. "What is your name?"

She didn't answer, and the mother tightened her embrace.

He smiled innocently and said, "Tell me your name. I won't hurt you. Please. Can I know your name?"

"Vivian," she hesitantly said.

"What a beautiful name for a beautiful girl. Vivian, would you like to play with me?"

As he stepped closer, the mother placed herself in between. "Take me! Please don't touch my daughter."

The father cried, "Please, don't hurt her. We will do anything."

His eyes swung to the father. "Anything?" He paused in thought, shifted his eyes back to the daughter, and extended his arm. "Give me your hand."

The mother pushed his arm away. He struck her with the barrel of his gun and grabbed the girl as she screamed.

The father aggressively reached toward the leader but one of the militiamen hit him on the back of his head with the rifle.

The child was screaming in horror as the leader dragged her up the stairs. The mother and father could only listen until her voice went silent. Their heads lowered in sobbing, seemingly believing their daughter was dead.

When the leader returned to the kitchen, the mother cried, "You bastard! You're going to burn in hell!"

The father whimpered, "Did you kill our daughter?"

The leader held a wry smile and said, "No, but I'm gonna kill you." He shot them both and left the house with the child bound.

* * *

In Corpus Christi, Texas, a Cuban American was spying on his neighbors to collect the $1,000 bounty for the arrest of an illegal immigrant and phoned the police about his suspicions of a neighbor.

The police sent the militia, and they invaded the home in the early morning hours. "Papers!" the militia leader shouted at the household that slept several on the floor.

Startled and frightened, they scrambled to show their papers, and every one of the fifteen people that included infants had citizenship or green cards. But the militia treated them as illegals and arrested everyone inside the house.

Later that morning, after the militia had left, the Spanish-speaking neighborhood stepped outside of their houses to discuss the arrests. One of the neighbors said to the Cuban American, "Why were they arrested?"

"I think because there were illegal immigrants living in the house."

"They weren't illegal. All of them were citizens or had a green card."

"I counted eleven people and four children taken from the home. That's a lot of people. All of them weren't citizens or had a green card."

"I know them personally. Everyone is a citizen or has a green card. They are from El Salvador and were living together temporarily."

"Well, they must've been doing something illegal because they were arrested."

"That's not right. Tomorrow they might arrest me and you just because we're not white."

"I doubt that. I'm a Republican. I'm on the right side."

The neighbor side-eyed him and went into the house without saying another word.

* * *

Through partially opened blinds, Roger and Dottie watched the militia take Helena from her home.

"She'll be okay," Roger said. "They will deport her to Israel. She will be able to come back when this is over."

Dottie was crying, and screeched, "We should've helped her!"

Roger faced his wife and firmly gripped her arms. "We couldn't help her! Do you want to go to prison? We couldn't stop them from looking for her, and if they hadn't found her, they would've asked people in the neighborhood if they knew where she went and who her friends are. What do you think our neighbors would've said?"

Dottie's head was pointing downward with tears her only sound.

Roger tightened his squeeze. "Look at me!"

With red stripes in the eyes of a shameful face, she looked up at him.

"They would've mentioned us. We would've been locked up with her. Is that what you want? It's over now. Only God can help her."

Dottie cried, "God wanted us to help her like we promised."

Roger rolled his eyes and went upstairs.

Dottie was floundering in regret and phoned Helena's son.

"Don't answer it," her son said.

His wife paused in the ringing, then said, "It might be Dottie."

"It also might be the authorities checking if we are home. Ma said Dottie wouldn't call. Just wait and pray for her to make it here."

The ringing phone went unanswered several times.

Hands of prayer covered Dottie's nose and mouth. *God, please forgive me! I'm sorry, Helena! Please forgive me! I won't forsake your son.*

She ran into the garage and entered her LTD, remotely opened the garage door, and drove toward Moscow, Idaho.

The militia stopped her at the border. A huge, bearded, pale-red man wearing camouflage and a cowboy hat, said, "I need to see your driver's license and car registration."

She handed him her license and the registration.

He took it into a tent that was set up off the road between the lanes in both directions, and checked if her name was on the list of Jews. When he returned, he said, "Why are you leaving the state?"

"I'm going to the farmers' market in Moscow."

"Step out of the car."

"Why?"

"Because I told you."

With the engine running, she got out of the car.

He readied his rifle and officiously said, "Open the trunk."

She opened the trunk.

He lowered his rifle and said, "You can go."

Dottie looked him in the eye and said, "I hate Jews too! I'm glad the president is kicking them out of the country. He should kick out everyone that is not white."

The militiaman had a smile that stretched into his eyes, and said, "Stay safe, my sister."

Dottie got back in the car, waved, and continued to Moscow.

When she arrived outside the home of Helena's son, the house appeared vacant. "Helena must've told them what I did, and they found another place to hide," she said within, and thought about leaving, but the spiritual voice told her to knock on the door and she did. There wasn't an answer, so she knocked harder and said, "Elias, it's Dottie."

With relief on her face, his wife opened the door, and they hugged.

Dottie said, "I'm glad you're here. I've come to take you to my house. Where's Elias?"

"He's upstairs with the kids."

"Pack what you need. I'm going to the farmers' market. Be ready to go when I get back."

"We're already packed."

"Okay. I'll back up into the carport so no one can see you get into the car."

Dottie went back to her car and turned it around to back up to the side door.

When she got out, she opened the trunk and said, "Theresa, where is the car?"

"Elias parked it in the backyard so people from the street would think we're not home."

Dottie put the two suitcases in the trunk and helped Theresa get inside. Elias came out with his two- and three-year-old daughters in his arms.

"Give them to me and get inside," Dottie said.

He handed her his daughters and climbed inside.

Dottie handed one to him and the other to his wife. "Keep quiet and pray," she said. "The militia has a roadblock at the border. I told one of the guys that I'm going to the farmers' market. I need to go there before I go back across the border. Hopefully, the same guy will be out there and he won't check my car again."

Dottie drove to the market and purchased two watermelons, baskets of peaches and apples and placed the items in her backseat. "Okay, we're headed to the border."

As she approached the roadblock, she said, "Roadblock. Make sure the kids stay quiet," and turned up the volume on the radio with her eyes in search of the man that stopped her. She didn't see him, and a young militiaman with a hairless face asked for her driver's license and car registration. He took it into the tent.

With her eyes continuously in search of that man, she lowered the radio and said, "Keep quiet and keep praying."

When the young militiaman exited the tent, Dottie turned up the volume. And when he came back to the car and handed her the license and registration, he said, "Can I have one of your peaches?"

"Sure." Dottie rolled down the back power window. "You can have a couple."

He reached in and took two. "Thanks."

Dottie rolled up the window and started to leave when the militiaman said, "Wait! I have to check your trunk."

Dottie stared straight ahead with doom written on her face. She was preparing to speed away but saw the man who had checked her vehicle earlier exiting the tent. She lowered her window and yelled, "Hey, I brought back some peaches for you!"

The man hustled across the road to her car.

Dottie got out of the car, lifted a basket of peaches from the backseat, and handed it to him.

"Thanks."

Dottie was getting back into the car when the young militiaman said, "Lady, I need to check the trunk."

The man said, "She's good. Let her go."

"Okay."

A sigh of relief ran through her body, and Dottie said within, "Thank you, Lord."

She drove away and lowered the radio volume to talk with Elias and his wife as she rode on the surprisingly empty US-195.

When she turned onto Interstate 90, protesters were standing in both directions with signs that read, *Honk if you support the Jews.* She honked, and the protesters opened a lane.

She said, "You should see how much support the Jews have. Protesters have blocked the highway in support of you. I'm going to change the radio to a news channel so you can hear what's happening around here."

Dottie struggled to find a news station that wasn't State media but found a public station and turned up the volume so

Elias and his wife could hear. The man on the radio was live on Boone Avenue and said, “This crowd looks like more than two hundred thousand people along Boone Avenue, here in Spokane. Every race and age are here. I’ve seen babies, grandmas, and grandads. I’m not sure how far this crowd is stretching, but I have talked to people who came from West Boone Avenue, and I am on the east side of Boone Avenue.”

She lowered the volume, “Did you hear that?”

Elias said, “Yes. We have hope. I can’t wait to see my mother. How far away are we?”

Dottie’s smile turned upside down. *How am I going to tell him that his mother was arrested?* “I have to detour because of the protesters. Stay quiet.”

Remorse held Dottie’s mind in the car’s silence that was broken only by the turn signals and ended with the closing of her house garage.

“We’re here,” she said and remotely opened the trunk.

“Thank you,” Theresa and Elias gratefully said.

Dottie helped them out of the trunk and led them into the house. She yelled, “Roger,” and was bemused when she discovered he wasn’t home.

“I don’t know where my husband is. I’m sure he will be back soon. C’mon, let me show you your room.” She led them upstairs to the guest bedroom and said, “Keep the blinds closed.”

Elias said, “Where is my mother?”

Dottie’s eyes watered.

Worry replaced Elias’s happy face, and he nervously said, “Where is she?”

“I’m sorry,” Dottie cried. “The militia took her.”

“When?”

“This morning.”

“How? She was supposed to be with you two days ago. What happened?”

Dottie sighed with uneasiness. “I can’t talk about it right now. I need to find out where my husband is, and I have to go to the store before curfew. I’ll tell you everything when I get back. Relax for now. This room has a full bath, and there are wash cloths and towels in the bathroom cabinet.”

Dottie left the room and closed the door. She leaned with her back against it and went downstairs in silent tears.

Where did Roger go? I can't leave until he comes home. The sound of the front door opening brought the moment she hadn't expected.

Roger angrily said, "Where did you go?"

Dottie took a deep breath. "I went to get Helena's son and his family."

"What!"

"Lower your voice, they're upstairs."

His eyes swung to the stairs as far as he could see. "Why did you bring them here? You will get us killed. Is that what you want?"

"I turned my back on Helena, and for that I am truly ashamed. You should be too. The Bible says there is no love greater than to lay down your life for a friend. I failed the Lord. I was afraid and that made me too weak to say no to you when Helena was begging at our door. The only way I can try to make amends is to die trying to save her son and his family."

"I forbid you to keep them here. Helena will be deported to Israel. Elias and his family will be deported to Israel. They will be safe. But we will be killed for hiding them. We cannot keep them here."

"We have to. I want them here. Do this for me. No one knows they are here. No one will find out that they're here."

"Someone might. They can't stay here!"

"I told you to keep your voice down. You're trying to make them hear that you don't want them here? If they have to leave, I'm leaving with them."

"Do you know what you're saying?"

"I know what I'm saying, and I mean it."

Roger paused in the angry eyes that stared at him.

"I mean it," Dottie emphasized.

Roger seemed to humble himself and said, "How long are you planning to keep them here?"

"Until democracy returns, which shouldn't be long. Have you seen how many people are protesting? This won't last."

Chapter 13

On the fourth day of hiding Elias and his family, Dottie returned to work. Roger came home early from work that day and went into the basement. He broke the backdoor window from the outside, went upstairs and knocked on the guest room door.

"Elias, it's me."

Elias opened the door. "Hi, Roger, you're home early."

"I came home early because we have a leak in our bathroom, and the plumber is coming. I need your family to go into the basement until he leaves."

"Okay." Elias gathered his family.

"You need to pack your belongings and take the suitcases to the basement with you. The plumber might need to come into this room. I don't trust anyone. People are spying everywhere."

Roger helped them pack the suitcases and led them into the basement. "The plumber shouldn't be here that long," he said.

He hurried back upstairs, locked the door, and phoned the police. "I think someone has broken into my house. I heard noise in the basement."

"What type of noise?" the dispatcher asked.

"Adult footsteps and a child crying. I think they're Jews."

"Go outside the house. A squad car is on the way."

Roger hurried outside without a second thought and stood on the sidewalk next to his car. The next-door neighbor stepped out of her house and said, "Is everything okay?"

"I'm waiting for the police. I think someone has broken into my house."

"Oh my God!"

The sound of sirens in the distance getting closer seemed to ease the woman's tension. "Thank God, the police are almost here."

Roger turned in the direction of the sirens, and when the two police cars with four officers arrived, he said, "I think Jews are hiding in my basement. I heard a child crying."

Two of them ran to the back of the house, and the other two followed Roger into the front of the house. The neighbors that were home were watching from their windows.

Roger led the two officers to the basement door, unlocked it, and stepped back.

One of the officers opened the door and yelled down, "This is the police. Come out with your hands up."

Fear took hold of Elias and Theresa. They grabbed their children and ran out the basement door but were apprehended by the two officers at the back of the house and placed in the backseat of the caged squad car.

When the police left, Roger stepped onto his front porch and looked around at the homes to see if anyone was watching. *Looks like no one is around. Good!* He knocked on the next-door neighbor's door. "It's Roger, Ms. Barksdale."

She opened the door. "Thank God, you found them. Was that man Helena's son? He looked just like him."

"He's not. He just favors him. I would appreciate it if you don't mention this to Dottie. It will keep her up at night, and that's not good for a schoolteacher."

"I understand. I won't say anything."

"Thank you, Ms. Barksdale."

A few hours later, Dottie arrived home and said, "You beat me home today."

"Only by a minute. I just arrived."

Dottie kissed him and as usual ran upstairs to the guest room. She yelled, "Honey, where is Elias and his family?"

"I don't know. They're not up there?"

"No." Dottie was panicking. "Their suitcases are gone."

Roger ran upstairs as if he was puzzled by the disappearance, and said, "Elias told me he was thinking about leaving."

"He never told me that. Leaving? Where would he go?"

"I don't know. They must've gone somewhere. If the militia had taken them, our house would've been ransacked. And if the police had taken them, we would've been arrested. They must've left on their own."

"Without telling us? They wouldn't just leave like that."

"They must've. They're not here."

"I'm going to go look for them."

"Look where? They probably left after we went to work. They're probably far away by now. Maybe they called a friend who came to pick them up."

"That doesn't make sense. Why would they just leave without saying anything or leaving a note?"

"Maybe they panicked. The militia might've knocked on our door."

"I'm going to see if I can find them." Dottie ran into the garage, hopped into her car, and sped down the street without a particular direction in mind. She rode around the community, asking strangers if they had seen a couple with two children. Her search drew a blank, and as the curfew neared, she headed back home.

She was driving slowly with her eyes shifting left and right. And when she turned onto her street, a neighbor flagged her down.

"Is Roger okay?" the neighbor asked.

Dottie seemed taken back a little by the question and said, "Yes, he's fine. Why did you ask?"

"I heard about what happened earlier."

"What happened?"

"You don't know?"

"No, I don't. I'm just going home now."

"Roger called the police because a Jewish family had broken into the house."

A state of shock mingled with anger covered Dottie's face. She sped up the street and into her open garage. *That bastard!* She yanked open the driver's door without closing it and ran into the house with her brows squeezed together, her eyelids tight and straight, and shouted, "Roggerrr!"

From the back room, she heard him lift his voice, "What happened? Did you find them?"

With disgust across her face, she ran into the back room. "How could you? You heartless bastard!"

"What are you talking about?"

"You know damn well what I'm talking about! You called the police and told them that Elias and his family had broken into the house!" She cried, "What kind of human are you? You're not the man I thought I had married."

"I'm trying to save our lives. We can't help those people. Let them go to Israel—that is where they belong. They'll be happier there. Have you watched the news? People caught hiding Jews are sent to prison. Is that where you want to be? Elias is going to join his mother in Israel. She will be happy to see him, and he will be happy to see her. I did the right thing! The police and militia are going house to house in search of Jews. It was only a matter of time before they came to our house, and then it would've been too late for us to escape. Elias and his family would be on a plane to Israel while you and me would be in prison for life. I'm not ashamed for saving our life!"

"I don't feel any love for you right now. I hate you, and I will never forgive you."

"You see how much of a hypocrite you are? Jesus said forgive seventy times seven."

"I've forgiven you seventy-one times seven. I don't have any more forgiveness for you in me." Dottie turned and walked away.

"Where are you going?"

She didn't answer. She went into the garage, stepped into her car, and drove away.

"She'll get over it," Roger said within and patiently waited for her return.

When she hadn't come home by midnight, he became concerned and was phoning her friends and family, but none of them had seen or heard from her, and his worry expanded.

Roger had fallen asleep in the living room waiting for Dottie when loud hard knocks on the front door woke him. *She must've forgotten her key. What time is it?* He looked at the digital clock that showed 4:16 a.m. *Where the fuck has she been all night.* Irritated he shouted, "I'm coming."

"Police, open up!"

Police? What do they want? He opened the door and two officers grabbed him. One handcuffed him while the other said, "You're under arrest."

"For what?"

"You have the right to remain silent. Anything you say can be used against you in a court of law."

A plainclothes officer entered and said, "Where is your wife?"

"She's not here. Does she have something to do with this? Why am I under arrest?"

"For aiding and abetting Jews."

"I didn't aid any Jews! They broke into my house! I did the right thing and called you. Why am I under arrest?"

"They told us that you and your wife brought them here, and that you were hiding them in the upstairs guest room for three days until you tricked them to go into the basement, to make it look like they broke into your house."

"That's a damn lie!"

"Tell it to the judge."

With red and blue lights circling in the street, the two officers escorted Roger to the patrol car as the neighbors watched from their porches and windows.

The other officers searched the house, but his wife wasn't there. An APB was put out for her.

* * *

Anger and guilt kept Dottie awake all night in a motel room. At daybreak she turned on the television and changed the channel to the news station. She didn't seem surprised when she saw a picture of her as wanted by the police and cracked a smile when she heard that her husband was arrested.

What are you going to do now? Where are you going to go? You can't stay here. She peeked out the window and noticed a truck stop across the street. A thought crossed her mind and she said, "I have to try." She grabbed her purse and ran to the truck stop, tapping on the windows of the parked eighteen wheelers but no one answered.

She was trying to hide without looking like she was hiding when she saw an obese black man walking toward one of the trucks with a cup of coffee in one hand and a box of donuts in the other and approached him.

"Hi, I'm not a prostitute. I need your help. The police are after me."

"For what?" the man said.

"For hiding Jews."

"Take my donuts and get in."

She grabbed the box of donuts and hurriedly climbed into the passenger seat.

When the man entered, he said, "Relax, let me finish my coffee."

Dottie was nervous with multiple thoughts of his intentions and kept her right hand at the ready in case she needed to open the door quickly.

"Pass me one of those donuts," the man said.

She opened the box with her left hand, and he grabbed a donut.

"You can take your hand away from the door. I'm not gonna hurt you."

She didn't say a word, and she didn't remove her hand.

"Let me see your ID?"

"It's in my purse."

"Open your purse and take it out."

"Why do you want my ID?"

"I want to know if you're telling the truth."

"Take my word for it."

"I'm sorry, lady, it doesn't work that way on this rig. You either show your ID or get out."

Dottie paused, seemingly in thought, and with her left hand handed him her purse.

He opened it, took out her wallet, looked at her ID, and turned on the CB radio.

Scared, Dottie said, "You gonna turn me in?"

He didn't respond. He held the microphone and said, "Breaker one-nine."

"Go head."

"What you got on a Dottie Hasbro?"

A few seconds later, the voice said, "ABP."

"Give me the open channel."

"Go head."

"Dottie Hasbro is headed south toward Mexico in one of those cracker rigs. Let's hope she make it."

"Ten-four."

"Why did you say that?"

"I opened the channel for the police and militia to hear. Now they're looking for you headed south toward Mexico in a rig driven by a white guy."

"That was smart."

"You sound surprised?"

"By what?"

"That I'm smarter than the police."

She didn't reply.

"I'm headed to Indiana with several stops along the way. There are roadblocks set up at most state crossings. You're not going to be able to ride in the passenger seat."

"I'm not getting back there. You might be a serial killer, or a rapist."

"Listen, lady, I'm not a serial killer, and if I was a rapist, no offense, but you're certainly not my type. Either you get back there or find another ride. I'm trying to help you."

"Why do you want to help me?"

"Didn't you interrupt my morning breakfast by asking for help? And just because the law said helping Jews to hide is a crime doesn't make it a crime in my eyes."

She looked at him with mixed thoughts.

"How did you get to this stop?" the man said.

"I spent the night at the motel across the street?"

"Did you walk to the motel?"

"I drove."

"Your car or a stolen car?"

"My car."

"Where is it now?"

"Outside the room at the motel."

"How long have the police been looking for you?"

"Since this morning."

He started the engine and eyed her. "What it's gonna be? You getting back there, or you getting out."

She paused, trying to look deeper into his eyes.

"You need to decide right now. I'm on a schedule."

Dottie climbed into the back as he drove toward the interstate.

"What's your name?" she asked.

"Reggie."

"Where are you from?"

"Gary, Indiana."

"How long you been driving a truck?"

"Listen, stop asking questions."

"I'm just trying to have some conversation while you're driving."

"You look like you need some sleep, so go to sleep. I'll wake you if needed."

"Why do you want me to go to sleep? You gonna rape me or kill me while I'm sleeping."

"Lady, you are starting to irritate me. You better go to sleep or keep quiet. I'm not in the mood for chitchat."

Dottie didn't sleep but kept her mouth shut.

An hour or so later, on the CB radio, the trucker said, "Breaker one-nine, do you read?"

A male voice replied, "Go head."

"The hens are hunting the fox, and the paperboy is leading them."

"Copy that. Tell that paperboy to finish his route."

"Copy, over and out."

Dottie said, "What's that about?"

"If you're still with me when I get to Indiana, I will tell you."

"Why can't you tell me now?"

"Because you haven't proven yourself worthy to know. But if you make it to Indiana, then you are worthy."

"Why wouldn't I make it to Indiana if you make it?"

"I'll tell you when the time comes."

"You're scaring me."

"I can't be any scarier than you being out there running from the police."

"At least I know if the police catch me, they won't kill me."

"You sure about that?"

"Yes, I'm sure."

"I'm sure you never thought you would see the day when democracy ended in America. But here it is."

Dottie was thinking about those words when the voice on the radio said, "Breaker one-four, Superman and Spiderman have left the building."

Reggie said, "Copy that."

"What does Superman and Spiderman mean?"

"Why are you always asking questions?"

"Because I want to know what I don't know."

"Some things aren't meant for you to know."

"I disagree. I'm a teacher. We should try to know everything."

"I saw your wedding ring. Where's your husband?"

"He was arrested."

"How did you escape?"

"I wasn't home."

"Where were you?"

"Now you're the one asking questions."

"You're the one who said we should try to know everything. So where were you when the police came?"

"At the motel."

"You were cheating on your husband?"

"Nooo. I left the house because he betrayed the Jews we were hiding."

"Why did he do that?"

"Because he's a heartless bastard. Now the police are after me. The good thing is that the family we were hiding will be deported to Israel where their mother was sent."

"The government isn't deporting Jews."

"What you mean?"

"They are sent to death camps."

"Death camps? That can't be true."

"It's true."

"How do you know?"

"I took a load to one of the camps. I thought I was transporting them for deportation, but it was a camp originally built to shelter captured illegal immigrants."

"Maybe it's being used as a temporary holding place until deportation."

"No, I saw the dead bodies."

Dottie shrieked, "Oh my God! What have I done?"

"What have you done? I thought your husband was the one that betrayed them."

"He was, but I turned my back on their mother."

"How?"

"When the president first announced the Jews had to leave the country, I told her that I would hide her, her son, and his wife and children at my house. My husband agreed. But we didn't think it would really happen, and when it did, I got scared and followed my husband, who went back on his word. I repented and went to get her son's family. I brought them to my house without my husband knowing. I figured once they were there it was nothing he could do because we would be accused of hiding Jews if he turned them in.

"But when I was at work one day, he called the police and told them that a family of Jews had broken into our house, and they came and arrested the family. He was too stupid to realize that they would tell the police we were hiding them. I can only pray this mess is over quickly. Can you believe what this country has become?"

"Yes, I can. Actually, I knew what this country would become. The black community has been preparing for this since the fifties. Today it's the Jews. Tomorrow will be the blacks. We would be fools not to prepare for tomorrow when we know what's coming."

"What are you doing to prepare?"

"It's not what I am doing, but what black people are doing. We won't be blindsided like the Jews. We know the announcement is coming, and when it does, we will already have our strategy in place. Do you think we are going to let them send us back to Africa? We were born in America. We helped build this country from its structure to the streetlights. We ain't going nowhere."

"I want to help. How can I help?"

Reggie kept his eyes on the road and said, "Stay quiet. I have to read the mail." He turned on the CB radio and was listening without saying anything. When he turned it off, Dottie said, "I couldn't understand a word that was said."

"That's because they were talking in code. I believe you're one of us. I don't have to wait until we get to Indiana. You see that satchel on the side where you are?"

"I see it."

"Open it."

"It's heavy." She opened it and took out one of the flyers. "What is this for?"

"All across this country there are black truck drivers carrying loads to shipping docks, warehouses, stores, manufacturing companies, and other places. In our travel, we distribute and collect information for the black communities.

"You see an advertisement flyer, but the points of contact see a message for the people, telling them what they should and should not do, and they share that information in the urban streets and with the ANCs."

"Who is the ANCs?"

"The Advisory Neighborhood Council in the inner cities. Who do you think is working in the government Xerox rooms? Who cleans their offices at night? Who delivers the office mail? Who is typing their memos? Who is serving them in the restaurants, listening to them when they think no one is?"

Dottie held an overwhelmed expression.

Reggie said, "We've always been smarter, even when we were slaves. You hear a song on the radio, but we hear the message. You see graffiti, but we see the message.

"You wanna help, write down the names and phone numbers of people that you know are willing to die to save this country from the coup. Don't write any names that you think might be, only those you are confident in by their actions since the coup started."

Dottie was thinking.

After a minute, Reggie said, "Don't rush yourself. We have a long ride."

* * *

Summer's brows lifted at the sound of knuckles on her front door. *Who's that this late?* She ambled to the door. "Who is it?"

"The militia."

She quickly opened the door, and a short, overly obese man said, "Are you, Summer Smith?"

"I am. How do you know my name?"

"You're listed as the owner of the house."

"This house is listed under my late fiancé's name. Who told you that I'm the owner?"

The man paused before he said, "I'm not at liberty to say."

"What are you at liberty to say?"

"My name is General Weiskopf, head of the militia sanctioned by the president of these United States."

"What do you want?"

"We are searching the neighborhood for illegals. Can we come in and search the premises?"

"Illegals. You mean Jewish citizens?"

"I mean illegals according to the president."

"Come in. I wouldn't want to do anything against the president's orders."

The general and six of his men entered and respectfully searched the house from top to bottom.

After the search, the general said, "Thank you, Ms. Smith, your home is very clean."

"What made you think it wouldn't be?"

"We are just checking every home in the neighborhood."

I don't believe that. With antagonistic eyes, she said, "Goodnight," and closed the door. *Shawn sent them. I hate him.*

The following morning, after she had filled her car's trunk with food, water, clothing, and medical supplies, she drove across the Onondaga Lake Parkway Bridge to a house nestled within a farmland owned by a prominent Republican member of Congress.

Workers on the property removed the items while she entered the house and opened a trapdoor that led into a fallout shelter. Inside were thirteen Jews who greeted her as if she was a rabbinate.

Summer said, "My God is your God too, and He will deliver you from the grasp of Satan."

After participating in the Amidah prayer, Summer returned to Syracuse to tend to her patients. One of them appeared nervous and said, "I think I can confide in you."

"Of course you can, Mrs. Young. But may I ask, what makes you feel that you can?"

"You told me that your fiancé was a Jew, and that you were planning to convert."

"Yes."

Mrs. Young paused, seemingly second-guessing her decision, but said, "I feel that I have some neighbors spying on me."

"Spying?"

"Yes. Some have never spoken to me before and now they have become very friendly, even inviting themselves to my home. I think they're looking to collect on the bounty for a Jew."

"You're not a Jew. Is anyone in your family a Jew?"

"No."

"Then ignore them."

She paused. "I can't."

"Why?"

She hesitated, then slowly said, "I'm hiding a Jewish family in my basement."

Summer seemed shocked in her silence.

"I'm afraid someone will find out, and they will arrest me and my husband."

After seconds had passed, Summer slowly said, "How many are in the family?"

"A wife, husband, and four-year-old."

"I-I can help you."

"How?" Mrs. Young anxiously said. "You have an address where I can take them?"

"I will take them."

Mrs. Young surprisingly said, "You're going to take them to live with you?"

"Yes."

"Oh, thank you!" With tears of joy, she embraced Summer. "Thank you so much! God bless you!"

Summer extended her arms and said, "My life is in your hands now. I can only hope that you won't betray me."

"How can I do that? If I betray you, I will betray myself because my husband and I were the first to hide them."

Summer smiled and said, "That's the answer I wanted to hear."

"When are you going to get them?"

"What time do you go to work in the morning?"

"I usually leave around eight."

"Do you have a garage?"

"Yes."

"Is it in the front, side, or back of the house?"

"In the front."

"You have seen my car. Will it fit in your garage?"

"Yes. My husband's car is bigger than yours, and he parks it in the garage."

"What time does your husband go to work?"

"At seven."

Summer was thinking, then said, "Tell him to leave his car at work this evening and catch a cab home. If any of the neighbors ask him about his car, tell them it's being serviced. At the start of the curfew call 911 and say you are having discomfort in your uterus.

"When the ambulance arrives, refuse to be transported. I'm exempt from the curfew so I can travel during curfew hours. Have your husband call me when the ambulance arrives, and I will drive to your house and park my car in the garage. Your neighbors will be nosey but won't come out because of the curfew. Those who have your number will call the house, and your husband can tell them that you refused to go to the hospital and that your doctor is coming. When I arrive, I will park in the garage."

"You're going to take them tonight?"

"No. That's too risky. Even though I am exempt from the curfew, the militia might stop me and check the vehicle. I'm going to spend the night at your house. And in the morning, your neighbors will see us talking before I drive off and you get into your car. The family will be in the trunk of my car, just in case one of the neighbors walks up to us."

"That is a great plan. How did you think of that?"

"I learned a lot from my fiancé."

* * *

As planned, Summer arrived shortly after the ambulance left and parked her vehicle in the garage. Feeling the neighbor's eyes on her, she knocked on the front door and Mr. Young opened.

Behind the closed blinds and drapes, Mrs. Young embraced her, and Mr. Young said, "Thank you!"

The following morning, after Mr. Young went to work via cab, the Jewish family was placed in the trunk of Summer's car. "I know it's a tight squeeze," she said to the family. "But the ride won't be long."

Mrs. Young and Summer walked out the front door and were chatting as planned when the nosey and retired next-door neighbor walked over. "Sallie, are you alright," the neighbor said. "I saw the ambulance last night."

"I'm feeling better. This is my doctor."

Summer smiled and said, "Hi."

The neighbor smiled and said, "Hello."

Summer hugged Mrs. Young and said, "I called in the prescription. You can pick it up after work. I'll call you this evening."

Mrs. Young said, "Thank you for everything," and remotely opened the garage.

Summer stepped into her car, and as she backed out, the neighbor swung her eyes to the backseat and watched until the vehicle entered the street.

Mrs. Young closed the garage and said to the neighbor, "Thank you for checking on me. I have to go to work," and headed toward her car without looking back.

* * *

After the eleven-mile drive, Summer parked in the side garage and quickly led the family upstairs to the hidden room. "My late fiancé had this room built. He was a Holocaust survivor, but his parents were killed. He believed if they had

had a hiding place in their home, the Germans wouldn't've captured them, so he had this room built for his family. You are our family now."

The wife cried and thanked her. The husband also cried with thanks. The child looked up at Summer with grateful eyes and hugged her waist.

Summer pointed at the light bulb on the wall over the refrigerator and said, "If that light starts blinking, it means someone that might be a threat has entered the house. Remove the sound from the television and radio, and anything that might be cooking on the stove. As you can see there are no windows, so the lights cannot be seen outside the room.

"Behind that door is a full bathroom. In the cabinets are towels, washcloths, and extra blankets. The twin beds can be pushed together if you like, and the sofa has a pull-out bed. Put your dirty clothes here and I will wash them every Sunday. I will notify you when I leave the house and when I return. Do not leave this room unless I am home and have given the OK."

The husband and wife nodded and said, "Thank you."

Summer said, "May God keep us safe."

Chapter 14

The prime minister of Israel was terrified because the American president didn't answer his relentless phone calls. He sought protection from Russia but was denied. With the walls closing in, he told his country to prepare for an invasion by their Arab enemies.

The presidents of France and Germany, and the prime minister of Great Britain, who were pretending to be against the American president's actions, revealed themselves as allies of the Fourth Reich and ordered all Jews to leave their country. That turned the protesters' anger toward the American president to the leadership in their countries. And the arrests and killings of peaceful protesters were in France, Germany, Great Britain, China, Russia, Australia, Canada, and South America.

Frustrated by the support for the Jews, the American president ordered the militia to plant bombs that exploded during the morning rush hour on lines five, six, and seven of the New York City subway and accused the Jews of the bombings. But most of the country trusted the banned news outlets that continued to broadcast and report from the underground. They quickly accused the president of the bombings, and people nationwide walked off their jobs.

In retaliation, the president reinstated the twenty-four-hour curfew and cut the phone lines, but the people continued to protest on the streets.

* * *

DAY 41

William was in Harrisburg at the closed Broad Street Market, interviewing folks who dared to violate the curfew like him. And when thousands of protesters en route to the state capital came into sight—some with blankets and pillows, sleeping bags, tents, picnic baskets, and coolers—he joined the march down North 6th Street and asked one of the many white protesters, "Why are you out here? Aren't you afraid of being shot?"

The protester sneered and said, "Why are you out here? Are you afraid of being shot?"

William sternly said, "I'm out here for democracy."

"We all are, and they can't kill us all," the protester said and continued his march.

When William arrived on Forster Street, the National Guard had blocked off access to the state capital complex. In front of the National Guard were riot police; behind the National Guard were the militia. The peaceful protesters had stretched from North 6th Street to North Front Street and were being entertained by African drummers and street performers. At nightfall, boom boxes added to the entertainment from different areas of the crowd, blasting rock, folk, jazz, and rap music.

William followed "Rapper's Delight" by the Sugarhill Gang, which led him to a circle of people sitting on the street at least ten rows deep. He sat at the back next to an Asian couple and said, "Do you believe a peaceful protest will bring the change you want?"

The man said, "I wouldn't be out here if I didn't."

"I'm hearing from a lot of people that say we should start a civil war. What do you think about that?"

The woman said, "I believe a peaceful protest will be more effective because it will influence those on the other side to join us."

"How?"

"If we are combative, they will become defensive and won't listen. But if we remain peaceful, even in their aggression, they will listen, and listening can change hearts—and hearts changes minds."

"Good point, and very well said."

William stayed among that group for nearly an hour, listening to the music and chatting with the people.

After, he made his way to the back of a crowd sitting on a grassy area singing gospel songs. He sat and listened as they passed around a bullhorn. After each song, the person with the bullhorn stood and gave testimony for Jesus Christ. Then another song was sung as the bullhorn was handed to the next person who wanted to testify.

While the crowd was singing, a national guardsman dropped his weapon and joined the crowd. The crowd roared, and the eyes of others among the protesters turned in search of the cause.

The national guardsman was given the bullhorn and said, "Forgive me, Father, for I have sinned." He broke down in tears, and everyone stood and embraced him.

The word that a national guardsman had laid down his weapon spread quickly among the hundreds of thousands of protesters that stretched to the Susquehanna River. The knowledge of that phenomenon produced an energy in the crowd that strengthened worldwide defiance.

* * *

DAY 42

At the daily morning meeting in the Situation Room, the president angrily said, "Find that national guardsman who joined the protesters and execute him and his family! We cannot allow others to feel free to do the same."

The secretary of defense said, "Mr. president, we have a bigger problem. The people aren't afraid to die. They're standing in front of tanks, and when a tank rolls over that person, another person jumps in front of the tank. We are arresting and shooting curfew violators nationwide, but they are continuing to ignore the curfew. They're even sleeping in the streets now."

The labor secretary said, "People have walked off their jobs, and others are refusing to report to work."

"Replace them!"

"That's easier said than done, Mr. President. Most of the jobs are skilled workers."

The FBI director said, "We have killed the known leaders. But now they have evolved into everyone as the leader. We have cut off their phones and blocked the television and radio signals, but they are still communicating with each other."

"How do you know that?" the president asked.

"Because they are doing the same thing nationwide. I don't know what to make of it. Interrogation and torture haven't revealed anything. It's like they are possessed by some type of alien force that doesn't fear death or worry about the basic needs to live. We need to discover how they are communicating and cut it off."

"Isn't that your job?" the president angrily said.

"It's the job of all the intelligence agencies."

"Then do it! How difficult can it be? You should've infiltrated them in every city by now."

"We have. That's the problem. We are still unable to learn how they communicate. We have ears on the underground radio, but they're speaking in some type of code."

"Code?" the president asked. "What are the words they're using?"

"Superman, Spiderman, the Hulk, and a bunch of gibberish."

The president said, "Superman, Spiderman, and the Hulk are heroes. Have you considered that is the code name for their leaders?"

"We have, but like I said earlier, everyone is a leader, so Superman, Spiderman, and the Hulk are not one person."

"Keep working on it."

The secretary of defense said, "Mr. President, what are we going to do about the curfew violators?"

"Keep arresting and shooting them."

"That's killing the morale among our troops."

"So put the militia on the frontline. They don't give a damn about morale. Most of them are born killers."

The vice-chair interjected, "Mr. President, I suggest you remove the curfew and restore the communication lines. We need to provide the people with a sense of normalcy. They are defying the curfew because there is a curfew. Let them have the freedom to protest peacefully, to go to the stores, parks, theaters, sporting events, and socialize. The more things they can do, the less they will think about the things they can't do. They are upset because their freedoms have been taken away. Give those freedoms back and fewer will be on the streets, and more will report to work. That includes the freedom of the press. Allowing it can't hurt us any more than it already is. They are still broadcasting and reporting. Putting a muzzle on them only makes them look more credible.

"Also, set a date for the special elections. Mentioning it isn't enough. Give them a date, and they will focus on the future instead of the present, which will allow us to finish the ninety-day plan."

The president smiled and said to the vice-chair, "Excellent suggestion!"

When the meeting ended, State media announced the lifting of the curfew, and Congressman Reaves announced the freedom of the press and the phone lines restored.

* * *

That evening, Congressman Reaves met with the vice-chair. "We have to put things in motion right now," the vice-chair said. "That one national guardsman has opened everything for us. The soldiers are looking for new orders, and the people aren't bowing down. We need to eliminate the chair."

"By eliminate, you mean kill?"

"Yes. There is no other way. The president will believe it's the opposition. You saw how he looked at me. He will appoint me as the new chair. I will give the troops new orders and arrest the president and his enablers. You will be appointed Speaker of the House and take the presidency to free the political prisoners and restore the Constitution."

"If all goes well—and it will if we can remove the chair. But that will be very difficult."

"Yes, it will. But I have a plan."

* * *

In the spring morning mist, Mr. Jeffries was chatting with the truck driver who was unloading supplies for the estate.

"Is Shawn trying to feed the whole city?"

"He's planning something," Mr. Jeffries said. "This is enough food to feed an army."

The driver chuckled as he loaded boxes on the hand cart.

Mr. Jeffries said, "Reggie, what's up on the hotline?"

"The last time I was out this way, I picked up a white woman in Washington state running from the law for hiding Jews."

"What did you do with her?"

"I dropped her off at my home, had my wife change her appearance, and now she's working with us, recruiting white people into the resistance."

"Is her name Dottie?"

"Word."

"I heard about her on the news. They are looking for her in Mexico."

"I made that happen."

Mr. Jeffries smiled.

Reggie said, "The Hulk lost one of his men last night."

"Oh, where?"

"He changed back to normal in Harrisburg. But there still isn't enough gravy for the mashed potatoes."

"I'll make some more gravy."

"We all are."

Both men smiled and dapped.

Then Reggie blurted, "I just saw a girl run into the bushes."

Mr. Jeffries turned around. "Was she black or white?"

"White."

"She must be a Jew on the run."

"Is Shawn or Theodore around?"

"They're not here."

"Good. You want me to get her? I can take her with me."

"No. She might be a hot escapee, and the militia might check your rig at the state border. I'll handle this."

"You got it. Let me know if you need my help."

"You better get going to your other routes. I'll handle this."

"Ten-four."

They shook hands. Reggie climbed into the eighteen-wheeler and left.

With succoring eyes, Mr. Jeffries walked toward the shrubbery and said, “Hello. Come out. I’m not going to hurt you.”

A young woman stood with fright in her light blue eyes, her blonde hair, and beige skin stained with mud.

“Why are you hiding?”

She didn’t answer.

“Are you a Jew?”

She didn’t answer.

“Are you hungry?”

She hesitantly nodded.

“Follow me.”

She slowly stepped out from the shrubbery and followed Mr. Jeffries to the back of the mansion.

Without them noticing, Keisha watched as they entered the basement.

Inside his basement residence, Mr. Jeffries handed the woman a loaf of French bread and a bowl of jambalaya.

“You’re very hungry. When was the last time you ate?”

She didn’t answer but continued to rush food into her mouth.

He handed her a glass of cold water and she quickly drank. He refilled the glass and said, “Can you tell me your name?”

The sound of sirens interrupted, and panic took hold of her body.

He quickly opened the closet and said, “Hide here.”

She ran inside the closet, trembling as if the ground beneath her feet was shaking.

“Stay quiet,” he said and ran upstairs. He opened the front door and stepped out.

The sheriff of Campbell County and two of his deputies exited their vehicles. The clean-shaven, potbellied, middle-aged sheriff said to his deputies, “Wait here,” as he proceeded toward Mr. Jeffries.

“We’re looking for a runaway Jew,” the sheriff said. “Have you seen anyone?”

“No. Only staff are here.”

“Is Shawn home?”

"No."

"Mind if we take a look around?"

"I don't if you stay outside. Mr. Smith doesn't like anyone inside the houses without his authorization."

The sheriff held the wry smile as he stepped closer. "I don't think Shawn would mind us looking for a runaway Jew inside the houses."

"I will. I'm sixty-three years old with no family. I've been working and living here for over thirty years. Where am I going to go if I lose this job? And I certainly will if I allow a Jew inside any of these houses, or if I disobey an order from Mr. Smith, no matter how miniscule."

The sheriff stared at Mr. Jeffries with the thought of searching inside the houses without permission but turned and directed his deputies to search the grounds. They didn't find anyone and left.

Mr. Jeffries stayed in front of the mansion until every car was out of sight. He then hurried back into the basement and opened the closet. "You can come out."

Frightened, she stepped out and sat at the table.

"What is your name?"

She shyly said, "Neri."

"My name is Mekhi. Where are you coming from?"

"C-Colorado. M-my p-parents were killed on our way here."

"Why were you coming here?"

"B-because w-we h-heard about a woman doctor that's helping Jews. Is-is sh-she here?"

She must be looking for Summer. "No, she isn't."

The hope in her eyes disappeared.

"I'm sorry, but you can't stay here. I can give you food and water, and a place to sleep for the night, but you must leave in the morning."

With her head lowered and appetite seemingly gone, she nodded.

"I'll be back. I'm going to try to find a change of clothes for you."

She kept her head down and mouth closed.

He left the mansion and went to Summer's residence in search of clues to where she might be and clothes that might fit Neri. He found clothes but didn't discover any clues.

When he returned to the basement residence, Neri was crying. "Everything will be okay," he said. "I will help you as much as I can. You can't stay here because the man who owns this estate hates Jews. Is there another place you can go? I will help you get there."

Her tears subsided, and with a hopeless expression she looked up at him and shook her head.

He sighed and said, "You need to take a bath. Here are some clean clothes. A washcloth and towel are in the bathroom." He took the clothes into the bathroom and turned on the water for a mildly hot bath.

She entered the room and began removing her clothes.

He stepped out of the room and closed the door, thinking of a way he could help her.

Fifteen minutes or so later, she came out of the bathroom wrapped in a white towel. Mr. Jeffries back was to her.

She softly said, "Sir."

He turned and held an unexpected and indecisive expression.

She opened the towel and it fell to the floor.

He didn't turn his eyes away from the nakedness, but said, "Please put on the clothes I gave you."

"You don't like? I'm ugly?"

"You're beautiful. You're not wearing any makeup and you are still very beautiful."

"Why don't you want me?"

"How old are you?"

"Twenty."

"I'm old enough to be your grandfather."

"But you're not my grandfather, and you don't look old enough to be my grandfather. I want to thank you for helping me. I want to make you happy."

"Please put on some clothes. That will make me happy."

She cried and shamefully ran into the bathroom. Two minutes later she came out fully clothed.

"I know you're scared and trying to survive, but offering sex to let you stay isn't what I want."

She pleaded, "What do you want? I will do anything you want?"

"I want to help you because you need help. Helping you is my reward. I don't want anything else."

A confused expression looked up at him. "Are you a homosexual?"

"No, I'm not."

"Then why you don't want me. Are you too old for sex?"

"I'm old, but my johnson hasn't expired. I desire you. What man in his right mind wouldn't? When all of this is over, if you still feel the way you do now, let me know. Until then, keep your clothes on."

She seemed to be marveling at the words when he said, "You need to rest. You can sleep in my bed. I'll sleep on the couch."

Neri slept from sunset to midmorning. When she woke, Mr. Jeffries had prepared breakfast and was listening to "If I Didn't Care," by The Ink Spots.

"I like that song."

"You heard that song before?"

"Yes. It's one of my parents' favorites."

"C'mon, let's eat."

While she ate, she said, "What time do I have to leave?"

"You don't have to leave until I can find a safe place for you to go. But stay out of sight. Don't leave this room for any reason, and keep the curtains closed and door locked. If you hear any sound from upstairs or outside, hide here." He pointed at an elongated hamper. "Cover yourself with the clothes."

With a happy face, she said, "Okay. Thank you!"

She tried to hug him.

He extended his arms. "Don't get too close. I'm still a man."

Chapter 15

DAY 46

In Dearborn, Michigan, a Jewish family was on the run from the militia. Desperate for a place to hide, the husband ran toward a mosque.

The wife, dragging the son, screamed, "We can't go there!"

The husband, holding the daughter in his arms said, "We have no other choice," and led them into the open doors of the mosque, interrupting the Imam's sermon at the Friday prayer.

With fear on their faces and the cry for help in their eyes, the Imam waved them forward as the faces of most frowned at the soiled shoes that ran across the room's prayer rug and up the steps to the minbar.

The Imam pointed to the mihrab. "Hide there."

Several of the worshippers spoke loudly against the Imam allowing Jews in the mihrab.

In Arabic, the Imam said, "Silence! Allah has spoken to me. There is an exception to every rule."

There was murmuring among the worshippers when the militia entered with guns pointed. The leader yelled, "We are looking for a Jewish family. Did they enter here?"

The Imam said, "If you were a Jew, would you enter a mosque?"

"I would fear us more, so yes I would."

"No Jew is here or has been here. You are interrupting the prayer service. Will you kindly leave?"

The leader ignored the Imam, and walked around the large room looking for a place where the family could be hiding and locked eyes on the mihrab.

The Imam said, "That is qibla wall, our holy of holies. Only Muslims are allowed to enter."

The leader's eyes shifted to the Imam with an expression that he was going to enter anyway. And the Imam said, "Cursed are those that enter without the purity of the Muslim faith."

The leader stared at him then shifted his eyes to the worshippers and said, "Are there any Jews hiding here? There is a five-thousand-dollar reward for every Jew."

The people were silent with facial expressions that appeared to detest him more than a Jew in the mihrab.

"I'm not your enemy," the leader said. "Jews are."

One of the worshippers said, "So what makes you think we would hide Jews here?"

The leader stared as if he wanted to shoot him but led his men out of the mosque.

"Allah is great!" the Imam said, and continued the sermon in Arabic, ending with a quote from the Quran:

"God does not forbid you from being good to those who have not fought you in the religion or driven you from your homes, or from being just toward them. God loves those who are just." (Surat al-Mumtahana, 8)

When the prayer service ended, the Imam led the Jewish family into a secret passage where they sat comfortably. "Are you hungry?" he asked.

The husband said, "Thank you for helping us. Those men should be gone by now. We will leave."

"And go where? Allah has brought you here to be cared for. What are your names?"

The husband told him their names and said, "May I ask your name?"

"Akir Abdullah. Allah has told me to serve you."

The husband and wife seemed stunned by those words and looked at each other with nonplussed eyes.

"Relax," the Imam said. "You are safe here. I will bring food and water."

When the Imam left, the wife said, "I've never met a Muslim like him. I didn't know there was a Muslim who didn't hate us."

The husband said, "When have we known any Muslims? When have we talked to one?"

The Imam returned with a loaf of halal bread, a large bowl of vegetables, and bottles of water. He blessed the food, and the family ate.

“No matter what faith or language, God is great,” the Imam said. And as if he had received the divine calling, he kept the family hidden and started an underground railroad to hide Jews in mosques across Michigan, Ohio, Wisconsin, Indiana, and Ontario.

* * *

DAY 49

Shawn and Theodore arrived at the estate unexpectedly with a group of militiamen.

In servitude, Mr. Jeffries said, “Good afternoon, Mr. Shawn and Mr. Theodore.”

“Has my sister returned?” Shawn asked.

“Ms. Summer?”

“Yes.”

“No sir.”

“The FBI told me that Jews are trying to find her because she’s helping them. Have you seen anyone on the property?”

“I haven’t sir.”

“The sheriff told me that you wouldn’t allow him to search the houses.”

“I was following your orders, sir. You told me not to allow anyone inside the houses without your authorization.”

“Why didn’t you call me?”

“Sir, I know you are a very busy man. If it was important, the sheriff would’ve called you.”

“He should’ve. These men are going to search the houses and grounds.”

“Yes, sir. Do you want me to escort them?”

“No. We will.”

Theodore led two of the militia into Summer’s residence.

Shawn led the other two into the mansion, and Mr. Jeffries followed.

“Sir, no one is in here.”

“We need to check. One of them might’ve snuck in when you weren’t around. Jews are like rats. They hide in attics, basements, and crawlspaces.” Shawn led the men upstairs to the attic, and said to Mr. Jeffries, “Come with us.”

While the militia were searching Summer's residence, Theodore was outside the house and saw Keisha. He waved and said, "Come here."

She hurried to him. "Hello, sir. What can I do for you?"

"Have you seen anyone on these grounds who shouldn't be?"

"No, sir."

"Have you heard any noise or seen anything moved out of place?"

"No, sir. It's been quiet here. Only me and Mr. Jeffries. Do I need to prepare one of the guesthouses?"

"No, we're not staying. You can go back now."

"Thank you, sir."

After searching the attic, upstairs and downstairs, Shawn led everyone into the enormous basement. He eyed Mr. Jeffries and said, "I apologize for having to check your residence, but we're hunting human rats. They might've found a home in one of the crawlspaces."

Unlike the other rooms in the house, the militia wasn't respectful when they searched Mr. Jeffries' residence and violently turned over the bed and couch. They yanked the refrigerator from the wall and didn't return it. When one of them opened the hamper, Mr. Jeffries politely said, "Please don't throw my filthy clothes on the floor." The militiaman said within, "I don't want to touch a nigger's dirty clothes," and closed the hamper.

Mr. Jeffries walked with them as they left the room.

"Thank you, Mekhi," Shawn said. "You have done an excellent job in keeping the rats away."

As they headed toward leaving the basement, Mr. Jeffries said, "Sir, aren't you going to search the bunker?"

"Not even a rat can get down there. And only Theodore and I have the key."

Mr. Jeffries waited outside his room until he heard them leave and then quickly went inside and opened the hamper. "Neri, you can come out now."

She quickly raised and frighteningly said, "I thought they had caught me."

"Thank God, they didn't. They would've killed you and me." He turned his bed and couch back over. "They haven't left the grounds. Get under the bed."

"Why? The hamper is safer."

"If they come back, they might check the hamper because it's the only thing they didn't completely check. I can tell they believe someone is hiding on the estate. They might come back."

She crawled under the bed and lay quiet in prayer. Seconds were like minutes in her thoughts.

Her body shivered when she heard loud footsteps on the basement stairs, and her silent prayer turned intense.

"Stay quiet," Mr. Jeffries whispered and sat on the bed with his eyes on the door.

The knob turned and the door opened. It was Keisha.

"I know you're hiding that Jew girl," she said. "I saw you bring her into the basement."

Mr. Jeffries stood. "Did they ask you if you had seen someone?"

"They did, and I lied."

"Why?"

"Because we're next."

Mr. Jeffries hugged her and said, "We are next. But that will be the mistake that will bring them down. Have they left the estate?"

"Yes. Where is the girl?"

"Neri, come out."

She crawled from under the bed and stood.

"Neri, this is Keisha."

Keisha smiled and said, "Hi."

"Hi."

She took Neri by the hand and led her to the sofa. While they were chatting, Mr. Jeffries played Marvin Gaye's *What's Going On* album at a low volume.

* * *

The sheriff of Campbell County with a caravan of militiamen drove onto the Indian reservation with intentions to intimidate and parked their vehicles in front of the welcome center. They exited the vehicles quickly as if they had someone in mind to capture.

The Indian chief stepped out of the building, unafraid, and said, “Sheriff, we don’t have Jews here.”

“Who said I was looking for Jews?”

“You wouldn’t be here with the militia if you weren’t.”

“That’s what I don’t like about you savages. You think you’re smarter than the white man.”

The chief kept his mouth closed and stared at him with passive eyes.

“We need to search the reservation.”

“This is sovereign land. You can’t arrest anyone here without a warrant.”

“I can arrest whoever I want, whenever I want, warrant or no warrant. If you try to prevent me from searching, I will arrest you and every savage here. *Comprende?*”

“Go ahead and search, so I can enjoy watching your frustration when you finish.”

“One way or another, it won’t be a waste of time.” The sheriff turned to the caravan and said, “Do a thorough search.” He took out his gun and pointed it at the chief. “Let’s see who enjoys the search more.”

Screams and cries were in the background as the chief stood with eyes on the sheriff's smirk.

“Your children are calling you,” the sheriff mockingly said. “If you turn your head, I will shoot you. I want you to hear and smell what the white man is doing to your reservation and the people on it. You and your people better not be here when we come back. If you are, your bodies will lie to feed the vultures and wild animals that you are.”

After nearly an hour, the militia leader said to the sheriff, “There aren’t any Jews here.”

“But there are Indians,” the sheriff said. “So, we didn’t waste our time.”

As the caravan prepared to leave, the sheriff stared at the chief and said, “Don’t wait to be told by the president to leave the country. He has already told you.”

The chief kept a closed mouth and used his eyes to speak the sulky discontent.

The sheriff said, "I see more than three hundred years of hate for the white man in your eyes—but we hate you more. Remember that!" The sheriff and the caravan of militia drove away as fire circled the reservation and painful groans the voice of many.

As soon as the sheriff and caravan headed off the reservation, the people sped to put out the fires, but the chief yelled, "Let it burn. I want them to think they have won. Tend to those who are hurt, and bring me the dead."

With scars from a physical and sexual assault, Aponi ran into the chief's arms and cried. He tightened the embrace and kissed the top of her head. "The spirits of those they have harmed will pursue them," the chief said. "Be strong. They took what they cannot have. Boha will make you fresher than you were. Gather the people for prayer. Your strength will give them strength."

After gathering the people above the tunnel, Aponi crawled into the tunnel and said in her native tongue, "Come and pray." The elders caring for the Jews immediately stopped the things they were doing and followed her.

Rhoda concerningly said, "Aponi, what happened to you?"

"The men hit me."

"My God! You have a black eye."

"I'm okay. The Great Spirit will haunt them."

"Are the people okay?"

"Some hurt but none die. We strong."

Rhoda and the other Jews had tears in their eyes. "Wh-where are you going?" Rhoda asked.

"The men gone. We pray. You safe here."

Drumbeats and a rhythmic song in the native language greeted Aponi and the elders as they exited the tunnel and joined the circle lit by fire. Minutes later, every Jew in the tunnel came out and joined the prayer.

When the chief passed the pipe around, every adult Jew took a puff. After, everyone danced around the fire to the beat of drums and rhythmic songs. Under the stars, the Jews and Indians were one that night.

* * *

The decision to lift the curfew and the facade to hold special elections seemed to weaken the resistance. There were fewer protesters in the streets, and the citizens had returned to their daily routines. American society looked normal again. But the hunt for Jews and illegals continued.

* * *

DAY 55

Inside the daily Situation Room meeting, the president said, "As of today, we are no longer members of NATO and the United Nations."

The room fell silent with hidden thoughts.

The president continued: "In five days I will announce the New World Order."

Mr. Reaves said, "Sir, what is the New World Order?"

"The New World Order is the Fourth Reich, which is America first. In the New World Order, we hand Poland, Ukraine, the rest of Eastern Europe, and the Baltic states to the Russians. We allow China to control all of Asia except for the Philippines, because the Philippines will be our territory to protect us from any invasion from the west. Russia will control North Africa. China will control Central Africa. South Africa and Cuba will be added to our territories. Canada, Mexico, Central America, South America, Australia, England, France, Spain, and Germany are allies of the Fourth Reich. We have laid claim to Greece and others and will invade those countries to remove their democracy."

The chair of the Joint Chiefs said, "That means a war that won't end quickly."

The president replied, "If we bomb indiscriminately, the war will end quickly."

"But that is a war crime."

The president sneered and said, "There are no rules in war!"

Mouths stayed closed with their eyes on the president who said, "We are the Fourth Reich, and our laws will send every homosexual back into the closet for fear of death. The LGBT community will cease to exist in this country. The disabled and retarded are cut off from government funding—even veterans. I am declaring Social Security bankrupt and Medicare voided. We are purging the country of the disabled, retarded, elderly, poor, and all non-Aryans. Are we in agreement?"

Everyone in the room said, "Yes."

The secretary of defense said, "I was told the blacks, Hispanics, and Asians in the military are exempt."

The president said, "They are. But when they leave the military or become disabled, they can no longer stay in the country. The same goes for professional athletes. They are exempt, but when they are no longer on a team or a champion, they must go."

Mr. Rudolph said, "What about the Arab-born Americans?"

"They are exempt for now. We don't want the Arab world angry at us. We need them to help us exterminate the Jews."

Mr. Reaves said, "Mr. President, we have society under control. There are fewer people protesting. Folks are preparing for the special elections. If you make that announcement, it will strengthen the resistance. The streets will fill again with protesters."

"So what! I'm tired of waiting. I never liked that ninety-day plan. Let them take to the streets. I won't impose a curfew. I want them in the streets. It'll be easier to purge."

* * *

DAY 57

The eyes and ears of the world were on the president as he addressed the nation from an undisclosed location. Inside the twenty-thousand-seat venue was a capacity-filled audience of enthusiasts. A popular male singer sang the National Anthem, and a popular female singer sang "America the Beautiful."

The president received a standing ovation that exceeded a minute when he stepped onto the stage. He turned and faced the row of American flags behind him, and in unison with the audience recited the Pledge of Allegiance with the Bellamy salute.

He faced the audience with a smile and gestured them to be seated. Then he said, "My fellow American patriots of the Fourth Reich, in preparing the new Declaration of Independence, we will not repeat the failures of the past that allowed our blood to be poisoned and our purity stained. I am therefore voiding the citizenship of all non-Aryans. Blacks, Latinos, Asians, Indians, and the biracial have thirty days to leave the country or face arrest and deportation." The audience stood, cheered, and applauded.

The president continued. "The exempt includes active military, militia, law enforcement, professional athletes, and others that will be notified. But there is no exemption for biracial couples and children. All are forbidden. There is no exemption for singers, rappers, actors, musicians, and other artists and entertainers, but Arab Americans are among the exempt.

"Homosexuals, the handicapped, and the retarded are not allowed in the states or territories of the Fourth Reich. Jews are not allowed on the face of the earth!" The audience again stood, applauded, and cheered.

The president continued. "This is the new America, the Fourth Reich, the pilgrim's pride, the puritan religion, white power!" Applause and cheers were loud and rambunctious.

The president continued, "Hear this: Blacks, go back to Africa. Latinos, go where your language is spoken. Asians, go back to Asia. Indians, go to India. America is a country where only Aryans are citizens. All other races need an invitation to visit." The standing ovation lasted nearly two minutes.

As teens dressed like Hitler's youth moved the American flags to the side, the president summoned the chief of staff, secretary of defense, attorney general, FBI director, and the Joint Chiefs of Staff to the stage.

They stood with their backs to the audience as an immense portrait of George Washington standing in the middle of American flags, with a swastika next to each flag, was lowered. The audience exploded in applause.

One of the president's aides gestured to the audience to stand and they did. The teens who had moved the flags to the side lifted the flags from the holders and pointed the flags forward in front of the thirty-foot portrait. And the president led the audience in the Pledge of Allegiance with the Bellamy salute.

He turned and stood at the podium. "Hold your applause until I'm finished speaking," he said. "George Washington, our first president, was the first American fascist.

"My fellow Americans, we are the Fourth Reich, and we shall be first for a thousand years. I am not bringing something new to this country. This is who our founding fathers were. 'All men are created equal,' was written in the Declaration of Independence. And when was the Declaration of Independence written? Was it not July 4, 1776? And didn't this country have slaves in 1776? And wasn't Thomas Jefferson, the leader of the document, a slave owner, and George Washington, our first president, the same? Hence, our founding fathers didn't see blacks as men. Men in their eyes were white men—Aryans.

"And is it not written in the Declaration of Independence, I quote, 'merciless Indian savages'? Our founding fathers did not see Indians as men, but as savages."

He lifted a document. "This is the new Declaration of Independence that had to be written because the liberals and radical left were allowed to institute laws that wouldn't have the support of our founding fathers if they were alive today. If we allow the liberals and radical left to grow, a black man will become president in this country one day."

The angry voices from men and women in the audience yelled, "Over our dead bodies! It's time to take our country back!"

The president continued. "This new Declaration of Independence is the New World Order, which makes America great again, to stand a thousand years as the Fourth Reich! The New World Order is America first, and in the New World Order, we are no longer members of NATO or the United Nations.

"In the New World Order, Russia is given Poland, Ukraine, and the rest of Eastern Europe.

"China is given Taiwan and all of Asia except the Philippines, which is our territory for strategic reasons. Cuba and South Africa are added to our territories.

"I will speak more about this at a later date. Goodnight, my fellow American patriots, and God bless America."

As the president left the stage, a famous country star sang "God Bless America."

* * *

The leaders of the aforementioned countries were blindsided and scrambled in preparation to defend themselves against the invasion from Russia, China, or America.

The world was in chaos as democracies fell within days across the globe, and dictators rose in unexpected places.

Pandemonium was the norm in every country as many filled the streets to oppose totalitarianism. But death was the order for all protesters against the New World Order in the aligned countries of the Fourth Reich.

* * *

At the end of the president's address, Mr. Jeffries answered the phone, "Good evening."

Shawn said, "Mekhi, I'm calling to let you know that you and the staff are exempt from having to leave the country. I have special identification cards for the staff. Please share that information with them."

"Sir, what about their families?"

"Their spouse and children only. No brothers, sisters, grandparents, aunts, uncles, nieces, nephews, cousins, and friends. Maybe you should get married before the thirty days."

After a few seconds of silence, Shawn said, "Mekhi, are you still there?"

"I am, sir. I'm just grateful that we are exempt. I will inform the staff."

"Goodnight."

"Goodnight, sir."

Mr. Jeffries sighed when the call ended. *Fucking bastard! We ain't leaving.*

* * *

Prior to the president's address, William had turned his investigative reporting to Shawn Smith. Beth had become a dead end for information. Steve wasn't in the know, and Valarie had resigned.

In William's investigation, he learned about the murder of Summer's fiancé. *He was a Jew, and they haven't solved the case. I wonder if her Nazi brother had something to do with the murder. I need to talk to her.* He searched for her address and discovered her residence and private practice was in Gillette, Wyoming, and that Shawn's residence, and corporate headquarters, was listed in Cheyenne. *I'm going to Gillette when I leave Cheyenne.*

William hired a freelance camera man and walked the streets of Cheyenne, asking residents about their political views. One man said, "I'm a Republican, and I will always support the Republican nominee."

"Even if he is a convicted criminal?"

"Yes."

William asked another man, "Will you vote for the president if he runs for reelection?"

"I will," the man said.

"So you agree that Jews should be evicted from the country?"

"Yes."

"Why?"

"Because they killed Jesus Christ. All non-Christians should be evicted. America is a Christian nation."

William asked a woman, "Are you a Democrat or Republican?"

"Republican."

"Have you ever voted for a Democrat?"

"No."

"Are you going to vote in the special elections for the Republican nominee endorsed by the president?"

"I am."

"Why?"

"Because he's a Republican."

"Do you agree with the president's decree to remove Jews from the country?"

"I don't."

"The Republican nominee agrees with the president that Jews should be banned from the country. If you disagree, why will you vote for him?"

"Because he's a Republican."

"Help me understand. Banning Jews from the country is a mindset like Hitler. You said you disagree with the banishment of Jews, yet you will vote for that mindset anyway—just because he is a Republican? Banning Jews or any citizens is against the Constitution."

"I agree with the president that the Constitution should be revised because it's old."

"What about voting for someone just because they are a member of your political party?"

"Aren't you a Democrat?"

"I am."

"Don't you vote for Democrats because they're Democrats?"

"I don't if I disagree with their position. But I will vote for the lesser of two evils. Tell me, what should happen if a Democrat president tries to terminate the Constitution?"

"He should be impeached and thrown in jail."

"Isn't that what the current president is doing?"

"What?"

"Trying to terminate the Constitution."

She paused as if she wasn't sure, then said, "He's trying to keep the country from removing Christianity. That's different."

"How?"

"Anyone who tries to remove Jesus Christ as Lord and Savior is against the Constitution. You can't be against the Constitution if you believe Christianity should be the national religion."

"So, you believe Christianity should be the only religion allowed in America?"

"Christianity should be the national religion, and any religion that tries to change that should be removed from the country."

"You believe the Jews are trying to change that?"

"I don't know. The president said they are, so I have to believe him."

"You don't have to believe him just because he said it."

"He said he has evidence."

"Why hasn't he shown the evidence?"

"I don't know, and I don't care. Have a nice day. Goodbye."

She walked away.

William approached an elderly couple. "Sir, are you a Republican?"

His wife said, "We are."

"Are you on Social Security?"

She said, "Yes, we are."

"What about Medicare?"

"Yes."

"There is talk that the president will cut spending by removing Social Security and Medicare."

"I don't believe that. He's talking about the illegals and undocumented."

"They don't receive Social Security and Medicare."

"He's not talking about us."

"Who is he talking about?"

"Not us. Have a nice day."

William went searching for a black person on the street but couldn't find one, so he asked another woman, "Are you a Republican or a Democrat?"

"Republican."

"Do you support the president?"

"No."

"Will you vote for him if he run for reelection?"

"If he's the Republican nominee."

"Why?"

"Because I'm not voting for a Democrat."

"Why?"

"Because I'm a Republican and will always be a Republican. I don't like the Democrat policies."

"What if the president says all non-whites have to leave the country. Do you support that?"

"I do not, and he won't say that."

"Are you sure?"

"I don't believe he will. He's a Christian, and Christians love all races and languages."

"But hypothetically, if he says all non-Christians and non-whites must leave the country, will you still vote for him?"

"I will because he knows best."

* * *

That evening, William was searching for a black hangout to watch the president's address and entered a place called Cowboys R Us. He was intrigued by a man at the far end of the bar dressed in a black, high-crowned wide-brimmed hat, tight black-leather vest, and black gator cowboy boots with red tassels, and approached him.

William extended his hand. "Hi, I like your outfit."

The man didn't shake his hand, and suspiciously said, "What's your name?"

"William."

"Where you from?"

"Harrisburg, PA."

"You're a long way from home. What brings you to Cheyenne?"

"I'm a reporter working on a story."

"Then you should be interviewing me. The history of black cowboys is the only good story around here."

"Black cowboys? I know about Deadwood Dick."

"You don't know about George Washington, George Robinson, and Zebrien Bates?"

"Who are they?"

"They rode with Billy the Kid. I know you heard of him."

"I have. But I didn't know black cowboys rode with him."

"Yeah man. We were the first and baddest cowboys. Who you think taught those white boys how to rodeo?"

With his lips puckered and brows lifted, William nodded, and said, "Who?"

"Bill Pickett! Report on that!"

"You sound excited but look angry. Which one is it?"

"Both. I'm excited because the first cowboy was the black cowboy. I'm angry because people like you don't report it."

"Now that I know, I will."

The music stopped and the television was unmuted. William said, "Looks like the president is getting ready to address the nation."

"What the fuck does that Mussolini wannabee have to say now?"

"Maybe he's reinstating the curfew."

"Fuck his curfew. We don't obey curfews."

When the president appeared on the screen, everyone inside the venue had their eyes and ears on one of the four televisions. In the first twenty seconds of his speech, the bar erupted with obscene language. "Who the fuck he think he's talking to?" the cowboy said. "We ain't going nowhere. He better kiss my ass before I bust a cap in his. We ain't Jews muthafucker. You can't pull that shit on us and get away with it. We ain't going back to Africa. We weren't born there."

William said, "I knew that shit was coming."

One of the cowboys at the bar fired a shot into the television and shouted, "That dumb muthafucker think the fight won't start for thirty days! It's on now, and we got guns too!"

The cowboy that was speaking to William stood, raised his gun, and said to the folks, "We knew this shit was coming but thought they were smart enough to come when we were asleep. They then fucked up now. We now know when they're coming. We'll be ready. Nothing is scarier to a redneck than a nigga with a gun. Deadwood Dick ain't got nothing on me!"

Everyone except William stood and raised their guns, men and women cheering. When the cowboy sat, William said, "How are you going fight them? They got tanks, planes, and rockets."

The cowboy curved his closed mouth upward. "I'm not gonna tell you. You might be one of those house Negroes."

"I'm not a snitch. I'm down with the cause."

"I don't know that. Tell you what, you can report this: tell your president he better not send the militia this way. We're not taking prisoners." He chuckled. "If you're still around here in thirty days, you can report how we kicked the militia's ass."

"I won't be around. I'll be kicking their asses in Harrisburg."

The cowboy smiled with eyes of acceptance and shook William's hand. "My name is John Clark." He wrote down his number and said, "Call me if you come this way again." He left the establishment, and the other patrons followed as if he was their leader.

With only the bartender visible, William finished his drink, went to the pay phone, and dialed Devin's home. "I know you heard the president."

Devin said, "My people in Cleveland are lined up to California. And from California to New York. Let them bring it. We ready."

"I met a lot of black cowboys out here. These bruthas are ready to fight. But they think I'm a house nigga. They're not sharing any information."

"Can't blame them. We can't trust a person because their skin is black, like we can't distrust a person because they're white. This war isn't black against white, but the righteous against the unrighteous."

"Are you headed to the streets?"

"Nah. The word is out to stay off the streets."

"The president didn't announce a curfew."

"That's because he wants us to run out into the streets so the militia can easily take us out. We're not falling for that. If they want us, they gonna have to come and get us. The militia don't know our neighborhoods. The National Guard doesn't know our neighborhoods. We can easily ambush them here. We're gonna fight them in the hood."

"You know what they did to Black Wall Street? They gonna drop bombs on the neighborhoods."

"They won't because this war won't be fought only in black neighborhoods. It's gonna be fought in every neighborhood. Whites, Latinos, Asians, and others will be fighting with us."

"The National Guard aren't aggressive, but what will happen when they give their tanks to the militia?"

"Man, those tanks are just there to scare us. This war will be fought in their cities. They're not going to blow up their cities—tanks and planes are null and void."

"But they will use chemical weapons if they have to."

"Yes, they will. That will be a big problem for us and their last resort. We have to convince the majority of the Army to join us before that happens. When the soldiers realize their families are fighting with us, what do you think they will do? Remember, this is a war of righteousness against unrighteousness. There are always a great many more people on the side of righteousness. If we stay disciplined, they will be confused because they are expecting us to come to them, but we're going to make them come to us.

"What do you think they are thinking right now? They're wondering why we aren't on the streets protesting, rioting, and looting. We're not doing what they expected, so we are winning right now because we're in their heads. We know what their plans are, but they don't know ours."

"When did you have time to plan all this?"

"While you were searching for stories, we were organizing."

"Y'all got people up here in Wyoming too?"

"For sure. We're nationwide. But I only know the names of the Pennsylvania contacts."

"Word. I'll be back home in a few days. I gotta finish this lead."

"Stay smart and you will stay safe."

With a new reality at hand, William drove back to the motel, surprised to see the streets empty and the neighborhoods quiet. *Everybody's on the same page. How did that happen?*

When he arrived at the motel, he hurried into his room and phoned Sandra.

"Hi."

"Hi."

"You okay."

"I'm okay."

"Did you hear the president tonight?"

"I heard him."

"What you think about it?"

"I ain't going back to Africa. I ain't going nowhere I don't wanna go."

"I love you, Sandra. I miss you. I wanna be where you wanna be."

He couldn't see her expression but could feel it, and said, "I should've told you why I left. I was wrong when I said it wouldn't bother me if you were with another dude. It bothers me a lot. I love you like that. In all my dreams and thoughts, I haven't seen you coming back to me, and that hurts. I love you, Sandra, and I want you back because I will always love you."

In her silence he could feel her tears.

"Can I have another chance?" he said.

She murmured, "Where are you?"

"I'm in Wyoming working on a story. I'll be home in a couple of days. Can I see you?"

He could feel her answer before she said, "Okay."

"When?"

"Call me when you get back."

"You sound sleepy."

"I am. I'm very tired. I have a lot on my mind. Call me when you get back."

"Okay. Goodnight."

"Goodnight."

The sound of hearing her say "Goodnight" stuck in his mind as he climbed under the sheets and turned off the light.

In the quiet of the room's darkness, the vision of his conversation with Sandra was replayed until he fell asleep.

* * *

The morning after the president's address, blacks, Hispanics, Asians, and other non-whites tried to join the militia.

At one militia post, the militia leader was interviewing a group of black men. "Why do you want to join us?" he said.

One of the black men said, "To defend the country?"

"You didn't want to defend the country last week. Why now?"

"I was conflicted."

"Oh, conflicted huh? But now that the president is removing all blacks from the country except those in the militia, you want to join us. That's the real reason why you're here, isn't it?"

The man lowered his head with guilt on his face. Then lifted and said, "Yes. But I'm going to fight with you."

"Are you? Can you kill an unarmed black man, or woman, or child?"

"If I have to."

"Well, you have to, if you want to join us." He led the man into the back of the compound, and ordered a black man, black woman, and nine-year-old black boy removed the overcrowded cage. He handed the man a gun and said, "Shoot one of them."

The man turned his eyes to the militia leader and said, "Are you serious?"

"You need to ask yourself that question. Are you serious about joining us?"

"I can't do this," the man said. "This isn't for me."

The militia leader took the gun, pointed it at the man's head, and fired.

The sound of an empty gun brought the man back from the thought of death.

The militia leader said, "You failed."

"I'm sorry. Thank you for giving me the opportunity."

The militia leader took out his gun and shot the man in the head. Then looked at his men and said, "If I didn't kill him now, I would've had to kill him later, and that might've been after he had killed one of us.

"Anyone not with us is against us. Anyone who doesn't pass the interview doesn't leave here alive. Remove this body and send me the next candidate."

Forty-six black men suffered the fate for not passing the test. The last candidate for the day was a twenty-one-year-old styling a Jheri curl, and when given the choice between an elderly black man, black woman, or black child, he chose the child.

Instead of staying on the spot that was twenty feet away, he walked up to the boy, planted the barrel on the forehead and fired. Then kept firing until he realized the gun was empty. The militia leader said, "What's your name?"

"Travis."

"Welcome to the militia, Travis."

"Can I bring my sister?"

"Is she anything like you?"

"Better."

"What's her name?"

"Roxanne."

* * *

With MapQuest in hand, William drove to Summer's listed residence/office. As he approached the gateless estate, he was startled by the sight of the militia camp across the road and thought to turn back but continued and followed the signs on the estate to her office, marveling at the size and beauty of the property.

He saw the parking spaces outside the residence/office empty. *Doesn't look like anyone is there.* He parked in one of the six spaces, stepped out of the car, walked to the door, and rang the doorbell. After waiting a few seconds, he knocked. *No one is here.* He was headed back to the car when he saw a burly black man approaching.

"How can I be of assistance?" the man said.

"Hi. I'm a reporter looking for Ms. Summer Smith."

"Only State TV has sanctioned reporters. I know you don't work for them."

"No, I don't. I'm an independent reporter working on a story to publish when this coup is over. My name is William by the way." He extended his hand.

The man shook his hand and said, "My name is Mekhi Jeffries. I work for the owner of this estate. Do you really believe this will be over soon? You only have thirty days to leave the country."

"I only have thirty days. What about you?"

"The staff here are exempt."

"Huh. Exempt. You remind me of house Negros in modern times. I hope you don't believe black people are going to leave the country or be forcibly removed without a fight."

Mr. Jeffries said, "Are you in the resistance?"

"Are you going to call the militia across the road if I am?"

Mr. Jeffries grinned. "Do I look like a house Negro?"

"You're dressed like one."

"You're wet behind the ears."

"Wet behind the ears? You remind me of the black cowboy I met yesterday. He's a militant in cowboy boots."

"Was his name John Clark?"

"Yeah," William excitedly said. "You know him?"

"Every black person in Wyoming knows him."

"Can you tell me where I can find Ms. Summer?"

"What do you want with her?"

"I'm investigating her brother, Shawn. I believe he's a Neo-Nazi and might have something to do with the death of her fiancé."

"I don't know where she is. She's been gone for weeks."

"Shawn is your boss, right?"

"He is."

"I guess you wouldn't tell me anything about him?"

Mr. Jeffries' smile turned upside down.

"I didn't mean to offend you," William said.

"What did you mean to do?"

"I only meant because he's your boss you wouldn't want to say anything that might get you fired."

"I'm not afraid to lose a job for telling the truth. That's how the white man has suppressed us. Too many are afraid to speak the truth for fear of losing their job or life. I'm not of them. But I have the wisdom to know what to say, when and when not."

"The revolution is coming. Are you ready for it, Mekhi?"

"Haven't you heard? The revolution will not be televised."

This is no ordinary black man. Who is he? "Who are you?" William asked.

"I am one listening for cries in the wilderness."

"What cries?"

"The cries for salvation. Are you crying for salvation?"

"I'm crying for the salvation of all righteous people—black, white, brown, and yellow."

"Follow me," Mr. Jeffries said.

As they stepped side by side toward the mansion, Mr. Jeffries said, "Where are you from?"

"Harrisburg."

"Pennsylvania?"

"Yes. And you?"

"Do you want the truth?"

"Of course."

"I'm from every place where unjust pain and suffering exist."

William said within, "This brutha is weird, but he makes sense."

When they entered the house, they sat in the living room, and William said, "How long have you worked here?"

"Thirty-five years."

"You are obviously a very intelligent man. Why are you working as a servant?"

"Because God put me here for a purpose."

"What's the purpose?"

"I told you. I'm listening in the wilderness for salvation cries."

"Not to offend, but how can you help those crying for salvation? You're only a servant."

Mr. Jeffries paused in a focused expression and said, "I have saved your life and you don't realize it. If someone else was in my place like the house Negroes during slavery, you would be in the hands of the militia right now. It's not the job that you have but the purpose for having the job. The time at hand has revealed my purpose."

William stared with an understanding mingled with incomprehension.

"I can see you're very ambitious," Mr. Jeffries said. "That's a good thing—but a bad thing when you are only thinking about yourself. I can see that you care more for yourself than others."

"I care about others."

"Do you really? Do you put the feelings of others before your own feelings?"

"My feelings should come first, but I care about the feelings of others."

"As a servant of God, your feelings don't come first. Your concern for others comes first, and with it you are rewarded. Do you know James Baldwin?"

"The writer?"

Mr. Jeffries nodded.

"Of course, I know him."

"Have you read any of his works?"

"No."

"Then you don't know him. I've never met him, but I know him from his works. He's a servant like me. He doesn't write for himself but for others that they might learn about themselves and their environment to understand and better their life. That is the true meaning of a servant. Are you a servant?"

In William's eyes were thoughts circling for an answer.

Mr. Jeffries said, "Why are you investigating Mr. Smith?"

William didn't answer as if he didn't know.

"I'll tell you why. Because you want to write a sensational story that will earn you a lot of money. Isn't that right?"

"What's wrong with that? I'm exposing people for who they are and making money for it."

"But what is the purpose for the story? Is it to uncover the truth for the sake of exposing the truth, or is it to find a story that will earn you a lot of money and expose the truth too?"

"You are trying to make it sound like I'm wrong for trying to write a story that will earn a lot of money. James Baldwin writes to earn money."

"That's where you're wrong. His purpose for writing isn't to earn money but to enlighten and make people aware. If he doesn't earn a dime for his works, he won't stop writing, because earning money isn't his purpose for writing. Most reporters are looking for stories to make them famous, not stories to educate and prevent ill from happening."

The phone rang. "Hello, Smith estate."

"Hi, Mr. Jeffries, it's Summer."

A broad smile covered his face. "Summer! How are you!"

William perked up.

"I'm fine. I miss you. I'm calling because of the president's address last night. I want you and the staff to know that I'm here to help in any way needed."

"Your brother called last night and informed me the staff will receive a special ID to stay in the country."

Mr. Jeffries could feel her dislike for Shawn and said, "I saw the room. You left it open."

With the thought of him knowing the family secret, she turned silent.

Mr. Jeffries said, "There is a reporter here looking for you."

"For me? What does he want?"

"Would you like to speak to him?"

"Is he from State TV?"

"No. He's independent, working on a story about your brother."

"Shawn?"

"Yes."

"I'll speak to him."

Mr. Jeffries handed William the phone. "Ms. Smith, my name is William Walker. I work for the local newspaper in Harrisburg, Pennsylvania. I'm working on a story about your brother, and in my investigation I learned your fiancé was killed and the murder unsolved.

"I don't want to anger you, but I believe your brother is a Neo-Nazi and a major financier of this coup. I also think he might've had something to do with the murder of your fiancé. I spoke to the woman attacked that night and her story contradicts. I did some research and learned the woman worked for a small company in Syracuse that was purchased by your brother Shawn about a month before the murder."

Summer interjected, "You said she worked for the company. She's no longer there?"

"No, she's not. She didn't go back to the job after the murder. She's currently working for a shipping company that your other brother oversees."

"Theodore?"

"Yes."

"How come you know all this and the police don't?"

"Maybe because they aren't looking hard enough. Can we meet somewhere to discuss?"

"How long will you be in Gillette?"

"Depends."

"I'll be there tomorrow."

"Okay, I'll wait for you. What time?"

"Let's try three."

"Three it is. Thank you. Look forward to meeting you in person."

"Me too. Let me speak to Mr. Jeffries."

"Yes, Ms. Summer?"

"Notify the cook to prepare dinner in my residence."

"I will."

"Thank you. See you tomorrow."

Mr. Jeffries hung up the phone and faced William. "If she decides to confirm what you already know, you will have the sensational story you're seeking. I hope your purpose is for the right thing."

William paused, seemingly in thought about the words that were spoken, then said, "The right thing is to stop this coup. That is the most important thing we need to do. If I don't earn a penny from this story but it contributes to stopping the coup, then no amount of money can replace that accomplishment."

"Amen. I just heard one crying in the wilderness for salvation."

* * *

Summer immediately phoned Leigh. "I'm meeting with a reporter tomorrow."

"Who?"

"I forgot his name. He's from Pennsylvania. Sounds like a black guy. He's writing a story about Shawn. He believes Shawn is a Neo-Nazi and involved in the coup."

"We know he's a Nazi, and I'm sure he's involved, but he's still our brother. Are you going to tell him about the family secret?"

"I don't know. But something drastic has to happen to stop this coup."

"How will telling the family secret to him stop the coup? He's black, so who's gonna believe him. I mean, his newspaper isn't sanctioned. The story will fall into the hands of only a few, and that's not enough to stop the coup."

"The truth must come out. It's eating me up inside. My fiancé is dead, probably killed because I was going to marry him. My best friend is in hiding because she is a Jew. People are going to be exiled from the country because they're not white. This is crazy! We're living Nazi Germany in America—and our brother is one of them. Should we cover up the family secret because of him, or because of us?"

Leigh's thoughts kept her silent.

Summer held silence too.

"I think you should tell him what you know," Leigh said. "Show him the room. But first we need to tell April and my husband what we know."

"Are you going to tell them both? I can tell April if you want."

Leigh sighed. "I'll tell both of them."

"The reporter told me that he has information about the woman who Saul was trying to help that night. She was working for one of the companies that Shawn had recently purchased and then transferred to a company managed by Theodore."

"What? What the hell is going on? Do you think Theodore is involved?"

"I think he's naive. He's just following Shawn like a puppy."

"How come this reporter has learned things the police haven't?"

"Maybe the police know but are keeping it under wraps, or maybe they are involved in the coup."

"How could a country change so quickly?"

"Our father couldn't've started this unless the people who wanted it were already close to power."

"Summer, we've got to stop this somehow. I don't want to live in Nazi Germany."

"We can only do our part, and if others do theirs, we will stop it."

Chapter 16

"You should stay here tonight. It's not safe to drive at night with the militia across the road," Mr. Jeffries said.

"I appreciate it," William said. "Where will I sleep?"

"There are four rooms in the staff bungalow. Keisha is the only one staying there when we aren't fully staffed."

"Who's Keisha?"

"She's one of the staff."

"Okay. Thanks. What about my car? Is it okay out front?"

"No. Give me the key. I'll move it. There's a dirt road behind the bungalow. That's the entrance and exit for staff."

William handed him the key, and Mr. Jeffries led him to the bungalow located out of sight at the back of the mansion.

Keisha was sitting on the verandah and said, "Hello."

"Hi," William said and followed Mr. Jeffries inside.

He led William to the room at the far end from Keisha's room.

William looked around at the room's tight space and said, "Are all the rooms small like this with two bunk beds?"

"They are."

"Where's your room?"

"In the mansion's basement."

"You really do live like a house Negro."

Mr. Jeffries smirked. "Keisha will fix breakfast for you in the morning. See you in the morning." He left the room.

William sat and leaned back on the bottom bunk with hands inside his pockets and thoughts across his face. Bored, he left the room and went outside.

Keisha was singing on the verandah.

"What is the name of that song?"

"I haven't given it a title yet?"

"You write songs?"

"Yes."

"That's awesome. Why do you work here? You should be in Hollywood, writing songs for the superstars."

"Maybe one day."

"How old are you?"

"Twenty-three."

"How long have you been working here?"

"Since I was seventeen. Mr. Jeffries got me this job after I was released from juvenile detention."

"Where are your parents?"

"I don't know."

"You don't know?"

"I ran away from home when I was thirteen."

"Where was home?"

"Dearfield, Colorado. Have you heard of it?"

"I hadn't until now. Tell me about it?"

"My mommy told me that my grandparents were among the first residents. She said in 1910 the town was a hundred and sixty acres of desert when a black man named Oliver Toussaint Jackson established the land as a colony for black families. She said the land was worth $25,000 at the time, but in 1921, the value was over $750,000."

"What?"

"That's right, over $750,000. She said God blessed the town with a lot of rain so the farming would be plenty. She said sometimes the only place it would rain in the state was Dearfield."

"Wow. What did they harvest?"

"Things like corn, vegetables, potatoes, barley, oats, strawberries and cantaloupes. She said they shipped the harvest to Denver, about seventy miles away. She said Dearfield became wealthier because the prices of agricultural products soared during the Great War. But she said God got mad at the people and turned the land into a desert again, so the people started leaving for Denver."

"When did you leave?"

"I left with my mommy in 1971. I was thirteen. I didn't like the man my mommy married. He would come into my room at night. When I told her, she believed him, so I ran away and got into trouble. I don't know what my life would've become if I hadn't met Mr. Jeffries."

"Where did you meet him?"

"In the youth detention center. He came one Sunday and spoke to us. I was the only one giving him my undivided attention. I guess he noticed that and approached me after he spoke. He gave me his phone number and said to call him if I needed anything, so I called him every time I could. He wrote to me, and I wrote to him. He became the mother and father I didn't have."

"Does he know that you write songs?"

"Of course. I tell him everything. He told me to keep writing because I love it, and that's why I write. I don't write to make money. But if I do make money from my songs, it won't be the purpose for writing the songs."

"I hear you. You sound like one of his protégés.

* * *

Shawn arrived at the estate unexpectedly two hours before the scheduled meeting between Summer and William, and with him were four militia. They followed Shawn into the mansion, and after looking around on the first floor, Shawn yelled downstairs, "Mekhi, are you here?" He looked at the militiamen. "I think I heard something. Wait here." And he went into the basement.

Neri's heart was pounding as she hid in the hamper.

Shawn entered the unlocked door to Mr. Jeffries' residence and loudly said, "Mekhi." He looked around the studio-like space and saw two plates, two forks, and two glasses in the sink. *Somebody has been down here. Maybe they are still here.* He lifted his gun and pointed it as he checked the bathroom, closets, and under the bed. He opened the hamper with the intention to search it, but the thought left as quickly as it came, and he closed it. He turned on the television and a soap opera appeared. *A woman was here.* He stood and scanned the surroundings with suspicious thoughts before he went back upstairs.

"Follow me," he said to the militiamen and led them to the bungalow.

The sound of footsteps alerted Mr. Jeffries, and he quickly hid William in Keisha's room.

Shawn yelled, "Mekhi!"

Mr. Jeffries came out from Keisha's room. "Yes, Mr. Smith."

Shawn looked at him with suspicious eyes and said, "Why is the cook at the guesthouse?"

"Ms. Summer called and asked me to have the cook prepare dinner for her. She said she will be here later today."

"Why is she coming here?"

"I don't know. She didn't tell me."

"Who did you have in your room?"

He hesitantly said, "In my room?"

"Yes, in your room. I saw two plates, two forks, and two glasses in the sink. I turned on the television and someone had been watching a soap opera. Who did you have down there?"

Mr. Jeffries didn't flinch though nerves had taken over his body. And as if someone was speaking for him, he said, "You told me that I should get married, so I invited a friend over."

A relaxed grin replaced Shawn's suspicion.

Mr. Jeffries saw the threat removed and said, "What can I do for you, sir?"

"Nothing, Mekhi. I'll wait for my sister at the guesthouse."

When Shawn and the militiamen left the bungalow, Mr. Jeffries hurried back into Keisha's room and told William that he had to leave. He gave him directions to the highway from the back road then sped to his residence.

"Neri, it's safe to come out."

When she stepped out, her face had turned red.

"What's your job?" he said in an angry tone.

"Wash the dishes after we eat and keep the basement clean," she shamefully said.

"You didn't wash the dishes, and that's not the first time. You're getting careless. We could've been caught. I told you someone could come at any time. You can't relax because days go by without any visitors. Our life is on the line here."

She cried, "I'm sorry."

"Sorry is not going to save us. What are you supposed to do when I'm not here?"

Childlike she replied, "Don't cook, stay quiet, keep the blinds closed and doors locked, keep the television on closed caption, and hide when I hear voices or footsteps."

"And when do you come out from hiding?"

"Not until you tell me."

"Do that every time, and we might survive this."

He hugged her to build back up what he had torn down.

* * *

Via private plane, Summer arrived at the Northeast Wyoming Regional Airport with Senator Elizabeth Rainey. A private vehicle driven by the senator's security officer took them to the Indian reservation.

Summer cried when she saw the ravaged land. "Is everyone dead?" she whimpered.

The senator had never been on the reservation but was stunned by the sight. She followed Summer out of the vehicle as they looked around for signs of life. The security officer followed closely behind.

"Maybe they're in the tunnel," Summer said.

"There's a tunnel?"

"Yes. Follow me."

She led the senator to the tunnel entrance, and the senator said, "That's the entrance? No one will look here for a tunnel."

"You can see we have to crawl to get inside. You can wait here."

"No, I'm crawling with you. I've crawled in the mud before, and this is only dirt," the senator said. "I'm glad I wore jeans."

The security officer said, "If you are crawling, I'm crawling too."

"You're wearing a suit," Summer said.

"I go where the senator goes."

"You sure you want to do this?" the senator said. "It's okay if you stay here."

"I'm going."

They slithered through the opening for several feet before dropping down into a spacious area about six feet high.

Summer yelled, "Is anybody here?"

The chief and others stepped out from hiding and embraced her.

Summer screeched, "Who destroyed your homes?"

"The sheriff and militia," the chief replied, seemingly unconcerned.

"Was anyone hurt?"

"We have some with bruises, but none were killed."

"When did it happen?"

"A few days have passed," the chief said. "We are staying down here to make them think that we have run away."

The senator said, "Where are the Jews?"

"Chief, this is Senator Rainey of Wyoming. She is here to help."

The chief greeted her and said, "The Jews are at the end of the tunnel. Come, I will take you to them."

After they had walked a seemingly long distance, the senator said, "How long is this tunnel?"

The chief said, "A thousand paces."

"How long is that?"

"About a mile," Summer said.

At the end of the tunnel, Rhoda joyously screamed, "Summer!" and ran into the loving embrace like sisters who hadn't seen each other in years.

"Aponi!" Summer yelled and entered into her embrace.

Summer hugged each of the Jews like members of her family and introduced them to the senator, of which a few were her constituents.

The senator said, "We will defeat the coup very soon. But there will be a war, and everyone has a role." Her eyes shifted to the chief. "We are going to need you and your people in this fight. I'm hoping you can mobilize the other tribes to join in."

"The tribes are ready to fight. We're waiting to be led."

"Thank you," the senator said. "I'll be in touch."

Summer said to the chief, "Do you have enough food and water?"

"We have enough for one hundred and eighty-three days."

"I'll send more before I leave the state."

Aponi interjected, "If you can't bring it yourself, you should wait until we need it."

"I agree," the senator said.

Summer seemed to be in thought before she said, "Okay. I'll wait until I can bring it. What do you need that you don't have?"

"Medicine," the chief said. "And medical supplies."

"I have a meeting at the estate. I'll bring some tonight before I go back home."

* * *

When Summer arrived at the estate with the senator, they were greeted outside the mansion by Mr. Jeffries. "What happened?" he said. "How did you get so dirty?"

"We went to the Indian reservation," Summer said. "It was burned to the ground by the sheriff and militia."

"Is Aponi and the chief alright?"

"Yes, they are."

He turned his eyes to the security officer whose dark suit was filthy and torn in spots. "I'm sure I can find something for you to wear."

"No need. I'm good. Thanks."

Mr. Jeffries shifted his eyes back to Summer. "Your brother Shawn is waiting for you at your residence."

"Shawn! How did he know I was coming?"

"I don't know. He showed up a couple of hours ago with four militiamen."

"Where's the reporter?"

"I had to send him away as a precaution."

She faced the senator. "Now he knows you are against the coup. I'm sorry for asking you to come."

"Don't be sorry. It doesn't matter if he knows. We're in this together."

Summer looked at Mr. Jeffries. "Do you know where the reporter is staying?"

"I told him to call me at four."

The senator looked at her watch. "We have forty-three minutes. I can wait."

"Shawn is probably watching us right now," Summer said. "We better go there and have dinner as planned." She turned to Mr. Jeffries. "When the reporter calls, tell him to leave a number. We can still meet tonight." Her eyes shifted back to the senator. "I need to make a call before we go to the house. Wait here."

Summer went into the mansion and phoned Leigh. "Did you tell April about the meeting with the reporter?"

"You told me to tell her. But she doesn't believe Father was a Nazi."

"Shawn is here. She must've told him."

"Most likely she told Theodore, and he told Shawn."

"Well, they know now that I know. I can't pretend like I don't."

"Are you alone?"

"No, I have the senator with me."

"Who?"

"One of the senators from Wyoming."

"I know it's not Hoffman."

"You're right. It's Mrs. Rainey."

"She's the one that was just elected?"

"Yes, I donated to her campaign. She's a true Republican."

"But Shawn knows you are meeting a reporter that's investigating him, and the senator is with you. Her life is in danger now."

"She knows that. My life is in danger too."

"Shawn wouldn't kill his sister."

"Shawn is capable of killing his own mother. He won't hesitate to kill me."

"Oh my God! This has gotten out of hand! You need to tell Shawn that you won't tell anyone about the family secret."

"I can't do that."

"Why?" she pleaded.

"Because I would be lying."

"So what! Lie! Your life is more important."

"No it's not. Stopping this coup is more important. I won't enjoy living if the coup isn't stopped."

"What are you going to say to Shawn?"

"I don't know. I'm going to pray on it. Talk to you later."

Summer hung up the phone and quickly went back outside.

The senator seemed to know her thoughts and said, "I'm not the only Republican senator willing to die to save our republic. There are others waiting for people like us to give them the nerve."

Summer's grim expression turned into a smile. "Let's go."

With the security officer close behind, they boldly walked to Summer's residence. When they entered, the four militiamen were sitting in the office reception area.

"Can you kindly move to the residence side," Summer irked.

They didn't move, and she continued to the residence side where she saw Shawn sitting at the dining table. Annoyed, she said, "Why are you here?"

He stood like a king and said, "You know why I'm here. Why is the senator with you?"

"This is between you and me, Shawn. Let's go into the study."

He followed her into the study but didn't close the door. "Why is there dirt on your clothes? Looks like you, the senator, and her bodyguard were crawling in dirt. Is there a secret tunnel around here where you are hiding Jews?"

Summer ignored the comment and said, "Close the door please."

Without removing his eyes of evil from her, he slammed the door closed.

"I know the family secret. I was inside the room. I know who you are. I know who Father was. I'm not like you and will never be like you. I'm going to do everything in my power to stop you. I'm not afraid to die. You already killed my fiancé. If you want to stop me, you will have to kill me too."

Shawn's eyes narrowed in a deep-thought expression with his chin lifted. His left fingers were gently massaging the Adam's apple before he said, "While I would love to take the credit for having that Jew killed, it was actually Theodore's plan."

With the upper lip raised and lower dropped, Summer's mouth froze. Her eyes cried without tears. She stood that way in the room's silence for several seconds.

"Why are you shocked? Father raised his sons to be like him. Mother should've raised all her daughters to be like her. Thankfully April isn't like you and Leigh. If she was, I wouldn't be here right now, and you and that Rino would be talking to that trivial nigger reporter."

Summer's expression turned contemptuous. She stepped toward Shawn and said, "Mrs. Rainey is the most conservative member in Congress, and you call her a Rino. That means you're not a true Republican but are using the party name to deceive Republicans."

"There is only one party, and that is the America First party. We didn't bring white supremacy here. The pilgrims did. We are here because our blood founded this country. God has made America our promised land. It doesn't matter if you tell the world about the family secret. The Fourth Reich has risen and can't be stopped because God has ordained it."

"My God hasn't ordained it and never will."

He snorted, "Your God? Your God's arms are too short to reach us."

"How ignorant can a man so intelligent be? You have just told me how much he can."

Shawn sarcastically laughed. "The militia will set up a camp on the estate tonight and will stay until the final solution is complete. Goodbye. You are no longer my sister but an enemy of the Reich. If I were you, I would leave the country. I'm giving you and that Rino senator the same time as the niggers."

Shawn left the room, and as he walked to leave the house with the militiamen, he stared at the senator with death in his eyes and said, "You are not deserving of your Aryan beauty."

* * *

Summer waited until Shawn's chauffeured vehicle headed toward the estate's private airstrip before she came out of the study. She told the cook to take the dinner home, and she and the senator, with the security officer, walked back to the mansion. During the walk, she told the senator the details of the conversation with Shawn.

When they entered the mansion, Mr. Jeffries was waiting and handed Summer the number to call William. She called him and agreed to meet at Cowboys R Us.

After the call, Summer arranged for a vehicle to be available at the Cheyenne airport. Before she and the senator left, she said to Mr. Jeffries, "Shawn has told the militia to set up a camp on the estate."

Mr. Jeffries concerningly asked, "When?"

"Tonight. Be careful."

"I will."

"I need a favor."

"What is it, madam?"

"Jews are hiding with the chief on the Indian reservation. They need medicine and medical supplies taken to them tonight. Can you take them the supplies in my office?"

"Yes, madam."

"They're hiding underground in the tunnel."

"I know where it is."

"You do? How do you know?"

"Me and the chief used to hang out like the Lone Ranger and Tonto."

Summer and the senator smiled. "You continue to amaze me," Summer said. "And stop calling me madam. Call me Summer."

"Yes, Summer. And call me Mekhi."

"I will. Thank you."

When Summer and the senator left, Mr. Jeffries scooted into his residence and anxiously said, "Neri, come out."

Nervous by the sound of his voice, she lifted herself from the hamper.

"The militia is setting up a camp on the estate. You need to be extra careful not to be seen or heard. I'm sure they won't be coming inside the house, but they will be walking around with nosey ears and eyes."

He could see the uneasiness that fell across her face and said, "Just follow the rules and we will survive this."

"I'm scared. The bounty is ten thousand now. You might need that money."

Mr. Jeffries seemed taken aback by her words. In the silence of his thoughts, he turned his back, then turned and faced her. "Don't ever say that again! I am risking my life every second of every day that you are here."

With tears leaking, she whimpered, "That's why I said that. You might be tired of risking your life for me now that the militia will live here."

"I told you before to stop using the one-track mind. If I turn you in, I will be turning myself in because you will tell them that I was hiding you. The one-track mind doesn't realize that."

"I'm sorry. I-I l-love you."

Mr. Jeffries didn't show a reaction and said, "What do you want for dinner?"

* * *

When the senator's security officer drove into the Cowboys R Us parking lot, the senator said, "Doesn't look like there is a space available."

The driver said, "I'll look for one on the street." He tried but didn't find one in reasonable walking distance.

"Pull up to the front of the place and wait in the car," the senator said.

"Senator, I can't let you go in there without me."

"Who do you work for?"

"You, senator."

"Wait in the car like I told you."

"Yes, senator."

When the driver pulled up to the entrance, Summer and the senator quickly exited the vehicle and stepped into the venue. As they began to look around, they saw a hand at one of the back tables waving to come forward.

"Is that William?" the senator asked.

"I don't know. It must be."

They squeezed themselves past the crowded tables, and when they were two feet away, William stood with his hand extended. "Hi, I'm William."

Summer shook his hand and said, "I'm Summer."

He extended his hand to the senator. She shook it and said, "I'm Senator Rainey."

He pointed at the man sitting next to him and said, "This is John Clark."

With a smile, the senator and Summer nodded and sat with their backs facing the front door.

Summer said, "You waved at me like you had seen me before. Have you?"

"No."

"How did you know I was the one you agreed to meet?"

"Take a look around. Do you see any white people? John told me that white people only come here if a brutha is with them." He cracked a closed-mouth smile and said, "You didn't have a brutha with you."

Summer smiled and nodded.

"I want to thank you for meeting with me. Do you mind if I record the conversation?"

"I do not."

He pressed the record button on the hand cassette player.

Summer said, "I'd like to know more about the woman my fiancé was trying to help when he was murdered."

"I was hoping you could tell me more about your brother."

"What do you want to know?"

"Is he a Nazi?"

"He is."

"How did he become one?"

"My father was a Nazi. We were born in Germany and moved to America after the war. The CIA brought us here in a deal that my father would spy for them."

"Spying on who?"

"The Russians. My father had a close business connection with Stalin. And, from what I was told, provided the CIA with valuable information over the years."

"How many years was he a spy?"

"I don't know; I didn't ask. But he found some powerful members in the Republican party who shared the Nazi ideology. My father was very close to Himmler and Hitler. He was guilty of war crimes but was pardoned. That's the family secret."

William leaned back, seemingly absorbing the knowledge received. *Wow. This is golden information.*

He was about to speak, but the senator said, "I'm here because Summer told me that she was meeting with a black reporter. I need a reliable black contact."

"Why?"

"Because there are people working on the inside against the coup. We will bring down the president soon. The problem then will be the militia. The country will be in a civil war. It won't be blue states against red states because the militia is in every state. Some members of the National Guard will fight with the militia and some of the U.S. troops will also fight with the militia. We are going to need an army of black people fighting with us."

John interjected, "Why do you need an army of black people? Don't you have enough white people?"

The senator shifted her eyes to John and said, "Mr. Clark, I'm a historian who doesn't hide the truth. We haven't won any of our wars without blacks fighting with us. We need you to help us win this one."

Her eyes shifted back to William. "To gather the information that you have about Shawn tells me that you are a very smart man and well connected in the black communities."

"I am smart, but what makes you think I'm well connected in the black communities? I'm sure you never heard of me until Summer mentioned my name."

"You're sitting here with John Clark."

Surprised, John looked at the senator. "You know me like that?"

"I do. I'm a member of the Senate Intelligence Committee. Your name is very prominent among the blacks in Wyoming, and you are well connected with black leaders nationwide. By the way, Congressman Jefferson and Senator Schumacher are alive and well and are active in the resistance."

"Where are they?" William asked.

"I don't know."

"You don't know, or you're not willing to tell us?" John said.

"I honestly don't know. I just know they are safe and working with the resistance."

With his eyes shifting between the senator and Summer, John said, "Don't ever sit with your back to the door or window."

"Why?" the senator asked.

"Because you can't see the assassin. Do you have a gun?"

Summer interjected, "My late fiancé taught me how to shoot."

"But do you have a gun?"

"He has a few at the house."

The senator said, "Who in Wyoming doesn't have a gun?" She pointed to the concealed gun on her belt and said, "At home I have one for hunting and one for assault."

Silence held the table a few seconds before William eyed Summer and said, "There is one more thing that I learned about the woman your fiancé tried to help."

Summer's eyes became very attentive and she eagerly said, "What is it?"

"The woman left work that day to meet someone named April."

Summer's eyes seemed to stretch to the limit. "Who told you that?"

"One of the black co-workers. She and the woman talked often. The woman told her that she was going to meet her friend, April, for happy hour. I don't know if that April is your sister."

Summer held the dazed expression.

The senator laid her arm on Summer's shoulder. "Are you alright?"

"I'm okay."

"She might be a different April," the senator said.

"Maybe." Summer's eyes swung to the senator. "I have to leave. Can you take me to the airport?"

"Where are you going?" the senator asked.

"I have to go to my sister's house."

"Do you want me to go with you?"

"Just take me to the airport. You can take the plane back to Washington. I'll fly domestic."

* * *

With medical supplies in the trunk, Mr. Jeffries drove toward the Indian reservation and was stopped by the militia roadblock. The man that approached said, "Nigger, where are you headed? You should be leaving the country. This isn't the road to Canada or Mexico."

Mr. Jeffries meekly said, "I'm going to the Indian reservation."

"What are you going there for? The place is burned, and the Indians are gone."

"I know. I'm looking for a souvenir."

"In the dark of night?"

"I have my flashlight."

"Souvenir? What kind of souvenir?"

"Anything that I can find."

"Nigger, this is your unlucky day."

"Why?"

"'Cause I feel like killing a nigger. Get out of the car!"

Mr. Jeffries hesitated before he stepped out.

The militiaman yelled to the others, "How do you want to kill this nigger?"

A few suggested to lynch him, and one said, "Tie him to the back of the truck and drag his ass a few miles on the highway."

"Yeah, I like that," the militiaman said and used his rifle to push Mr. Jeffries toward the truck.

Another militiaman grabbed the rope and tied it to the back of the truck. Smiling, he said, "It's ready for him."

Mr. Jeffries tried to resist, but a blow to the back of his head from the butt of the militiaman's rifle knocked him to the ground. And like a swarm of degenerates, the militiamen were kicking and punching him while another tied his hands to the end of the rope.

"It's my kill," the militiaman boasted. "I'm gonna drag his ass a hundred miles an hour." He jumped into the driver's seat. "Where is the key?"

The rowdy noise interrupted the militia leader and he came out of the tent. "What the hell is going on out here?" he barked.

A half-naked woman yelled from the tent entrance, "C'mon back here! Let them have some fun with that nigger!"

With a liquor bottle in hand, the shirtless leader said, "Who you boys got there?"

The militiaman in the driver's seat answered, "Some nigger said he wants to go to the Indian reservation to find a souvenir."

The leader walked closer and saw a face that he recognized. "That's Shawn's nigger. Untie him."

The joyous mood among his men was dampened and one of them reluctantly untied him.

The leader helped Mr. Jeffries to his feet and said, "I apologize for my boys. They thought you were one of the bad niggers. Get in your car and find your souvenir." He turned to the men and women and said, "Remember his face. Don't stop him again. He's a good nigger."

Bruised and bloody, Mr. Jeffries proceeded to the reservation, delivered the medical supplies, and had a long reunion conversation with the chief.

When he drove back to the roadblock, the militiamen didn't stop the vehicle but stared with hate-filled eyes.

"Only envy with jealousy can cause them to hate us so much," Mr. Jeffries said within.

And when he returned to his room, Neri nursed him and fell asleep beside him.

* * *

"Who is that this time of night?" was April's reaction to the doorbell. She grudgingly got out of bed and went to the door. "Who is it?" she furiously said.

"It's me. Summer."

Summer. She opened the door and Summer entered.

April closed the door and faced her. "It's after midnight. What's so important that you couldn't wait until the morning.

I already told Leigh that I don't believe what you said about Father."

"I'm not here to talk about him. I want to know why you were in Syracuse the day Saul was murdered?"

"What? I wasn't in Syracuse. Who told you that?"

"Why did you tell Shawn that I was meeting with a reporter?"

"I didn't. I told Theodore."

"Why?"

"Because we talk every day. We don't keep secrets from each other."

"What about your husband? Do you talk to him every day? Are you keeping secrets from him?"

April didn't answer.

"I'd like to talk privately."

"Go ahead. Brian isn't here. He's on a business trip."

"Shawn told me that Theodore was the one who planned Saul's murder. And the reporter you tried to keep me from meeting told me the woman Saul tried to help that night worked for a company that Theodore oversaw and that she left work that day to meet you."

April looked away, seemingly to avoid eye contact.

"Why, April? Why did you help Theodore murder Saul?"

April couldn't hold the tears and screeched, "I'm sorry. Theodore told me that he was using you to spy on the family."

"And you believed that?"

"I do. He said Saul was a member of the Mossad, trying to spy on our family. That's why he came to celebrate Christmas with us and didn't want to leave when you wanted to leave. He was pretending to be in love with you so he could learn the family history. He wanted to expose our family as children of a Nazi war criminal. That would've ruined our family name and put our lives in danger."

"Danger from who?"

"The Russians."

"The Russians?"

"Yes. If the Russians learned that Father spied on them, they would kill us."

Summer snickered. "How can the Russians kill us in America?"

"They killed President Fitzgerald."

"I don't believe that, and you shouldn't either."

"Why not? It's true. The Jews are friends with the Communists. They killed the president and kidnapped the vice president and speaker. They are trying to take over the country. Can't you see that?"

Summer stared in a unilateral expression. "What I see are lies and people who believe the lies. Saul loved me. He wasn't spying on the family. He wasn't a member of the Mossad. His heart would've been broken if he knew the family secret.

"I know I should forgive you, but I don't. I don't want to see you or Theodore again. I hate you and everything you believe in. But you are my sister, so I'm going to leave you with this advice: Tell your husband the family secret before he reads it in the newspaper."

"That story won't make the newspaper. Everything is controlled by the Fourth Reich."

"I guess you haven't heard. The Fourth Reich will fall before the country becomes all Aryan. Tell your husband the truth before that happens."

Summer stormed from the house and entered the waiting cab.

When the cab drove away, April phoned Theodore.

"Summer was here. She just left here. She knows I helped you in the planning of Saul's murder."

"How does she know you were involved?"

"That black reporter. Now she hates me, you, and Shawn."

"It won't last. She will eventually accept the truth about Saul."

"She also said the Fourth Reich will fall before the country becomes all Aryan."

"She's living in a pipe dream. Where is your husband?"

"He's on a business trip."

"You sure about that?"

"Yeah, I took him to the airport. Do you know something I don't?"

"He's having an affair."

Her jaw dropped with vengeful eyes.

Theodore continued, "I learned about it tonight. I was going to tell you tomorrow when I got the pictures."

"How did you find out?"

"You know I love you, and I don't want anyone to hurt you, physically or emotionally. I suspected Brian was having an affair, so I hired a private investigator. He called me earlier and told me that he has pictures and will bring the pictures to me tomorrow. I was going to show you the pictures when I got them."

April was crying and said, "I don't want to see those pictures. I want to see him dead."

"Are you sure?"

"Yes."

"You should sleep on it. You might feel different in the morning."

"No, I won't. I don't want him to come back into this house. I don't want him to see his kids again. Kill him!"

"You won't see him alive again. Get some sleep. The police will be coming to your office tomorrow. Goodnight."

April hung up the phone as if she didn't hear her brother say goodnight and went to bed.

After she dropped off the kids at school, she went into the office and waited for the police. Before noon, two detectives came to her office.

"Mrs. Holloway, I'm detective Crowder, and this is detective Feldman. We are sorry to inform you that your husband was discovered dead this morning in his hotel room."

She cried, "Dead? How? I just talked to him last night."

"Why was your husband in Dallas?"

"He was on a business trip. I took him to the airport yesterday. You haven't told me how he died."

"The authorities in Dallas haven't released the cause of death."

"Are you sure it's my husband?"

"They are sure it's him. His ID was in the room, and his face wasn't damaged. When we receive more information on his death, we will share it with you. Can you tell me who he was meeting?"

“I don’t know.”

“What was his profession?”

“An actuary.”

“Thank you. That’s all the questions we have for now. The authorities in Dallas would like you to come there and identify the body.”

She laid face down on her desk and cried.

Chapter 17

All publicly known homosexuals, including celebrities and athletes, were arrested or listed as fugitives. Those that were suspected and stayed in the open were brutally beaten or murdered. Those who weren't suspected ran back into the closet.

Biracial couples and their children were savagely assaulted and killed. The culprits were the militia, who had grown to nearly eight million, from every state and city, men and women. The youngest was fourteen and the oldest was eighty-three. Every one of them believed the president was sent by God to save America.

Under the pretense of needing to reduce spending to save the country from bankruptcy, the president removed funding for the disabled, even disabled veterans.

Social Security was taken away, leaving millions of seniors without the income to pay their bills and buy food.

Food stamps were no more.

Hospitals and private doctors turned away everyone that had Medicare because the insurance was invalid.

All those things were done to purge the country of the queer, disabled, elderly, and poor.

* * *

William phoned Sandra from the airport when he returned to Harrisburg. "I'm back. I'm glad you're not at work."

"Work? Ain't none of us going to work. You should know that."

"Some are working. I'm glad you're not. Can I come see you?"

"If you want."

He jumped in a cab.

The driver was an Arab American.

William said, "I guess it feels good to be exempt from being kicked out of the country." He could see in the rearview mirror that the driver didn't like the comment and said, "I didn't mean to offend you."

The driver said, "Yes you did. I don't appreciate the sarcasm. If all you got is snide remarks, keep your mouth shut, or get out."

"I apologize. I'm sorry."

The driver sighed.

William saw the eyes of a man that wanted to say something but didn't.

"Can we start over?" William said.

The driver replied, "If you want."

"My name is William."

"Jamal."

"Jamal, we're not leaving this country. We're ready to fight. I was just wondering whose side you were on?"

"Do you think the Muslims in this country are dumb? We're exempt for now because the president wants the Arab world to kill the Jews for him. Then he will kick us out of the country too. We know we're next. I'm tired of smart-ass people like you thinking we don't know we're next."

William held the expression of being put in his place and thought to keep quiet but said, "Jamal, ten months ago, I went to DC, thinking I knew it all. First, I lost my girlfriend because I took her love for granted. Second, I learned that I wasn't ready for the things I was preaching about. Third, I learned the work I was doing wasn't to enlighten others but to make me famous. I didn't give a damn if anyone was enlightened. That wasn't my purpose. Now I realize how selfish that was and how less of a man it made me to be. And lastly, so far, you made me realize how narrow-minded I still am. For that, I thank you."

Jamal nodded lightly as he approached the red light. He looked into the rearview mirror and said, "Allah is humility. You cannot worship God without humility. You have humbled yourself. You cannot know God without learning yourself. You have learned yourself. Don't forget what you have learned and you will be the man that God made you to be."

Closed mouths were the remainder of the ride, but each man heard the thoughts of the other—and each man felt the feelings of the other. Those were moments in the spiritual world, which is the understanding of things that are spiritually discerned.

* * *

William arrived at Sandra's apartment without the arrogance he had when he last saw her and said, "I'm sorry for not telling you why I had to leave."

"You still haven't told me."

"I told you Nazis hijacked the Elephant party. I saw this coming. I just wasn't expecting it so soon."

"But why did you leave? What was up with that?"

"I moved to DC because I went undercover to get an inside story on the Nazis in the White House."

Sandra angrily said, "Why couldn't you just tell me that?"

"Because it was dangerous. I didn't want you involved, and I didn't want my cover blown. I could've been killed if they found out I wasn't who I said I was."

"You just threw our relationship away to get a story? And you say you love me? You don't love me. You love yourself."

"I thought I was doing the right thing, but I was wrong. I should've told you."

"Nigga, please, be straight up. You were trying to hook up with one of those white girls to get inside information. Ain't that right?"

William didn't say a word, but the truth was clearly written on his face.

Sandra said, "I moved on. I wasn't going to wait for you."

"I know. You still seeing that nigga?"

"I dumped his punk ass."

"Why?"

"Because he was afraid to violate the curfew."

"I'm sorry, Sandra. I was stupid. I learned a lot about myself, and now I realize how much I love you. I want to fight this battle ahead of us with you at my side. I need you, baby. I need you with me, day and night."

William felt that she was ready for him to kiss her, and he did, and it felt like the first time.

* * *

DAY 63

"I'm going stir crazy," Senator Schumacher said. "We can't watch C-SPAN because both aisles of Congress are gone. What are we doing here? We can't just sit here!"

Congressman Jefferson angrily whispered, "I told you before to keep your voice down. Somebody's going to hear you, and they will know you don't belong here because there aren't any white people living in this complex. There's a bounty on our heads. You think someone who doesn't live in this apartment isn't interested in collecting that money?"

The senator lowered his voice, "I'm sorry. I'm just frustrated."

"I'm frustrated too, but this is where we need to be for now. At least you're sending and receiving mail to and from your wife."

"I'm grateful for the postal contact, but I need to see her, at least talk to her."

"You can't call her."

"I'll only talk for a minute. They won't be able to trace it that quickly."

"Listen, if you get caught, I will get caught. Don't fuck with my life. They can trace the call the moment it rings."

"I can't stay locked up here any longer. It's been two months."

"Do you want to live, or do you want to die? The coup will end soon. You know what's in the works."

"The coup should've been over by now. What's taking so long? Time is running out. The president is removing all non-whites from the country. What are you going to do about that?"

"That's not going to happen without a fight that we will win. Like I told you when he made that announcement, that was his biggest mistake. Black people aren't leaving, Hispanics aren't leaving, and Asians aren't leaving. And the Jews that are hiding will join us when the fighting starts. Stay patient. You been here for two months, you can wait another week or two."

"No, I can't!"

Congressman Jefferson grabbed the top of his shirt and whispered, "I told you to keep your voice down!"

* * *

Through the apartment's attenuated front door, Senator Schumacher's raised voice entered the ear of a neighbor. "That's the voice of a white man," he said to his wife. "That's the third time I heard that voice. Somebody is hiding a Jew in their apartment."

The wife said, "Maybe he's a visitor."

"White people don't come here, especially at night."

"Maybe he's the maintenance man?"

"The maintenance man is black. That's a Jew. I know it."

"It's none of our business. We got our own problems with the government."

"But if we call the police and they find a Jew, they might give us an exemption to stay in the country, plus the $10,000 reward. We might get more because it's probably more than one."

"Randy, we aren't snitches. If someone is hiding a Jew, the police will arrest everyone in that apartment."

"So what! It's every man for himself right now! Someone is hiding a Jew in their apartment, and we need to tell it to save our family."

"I trust the resistance."

"The resistance? Where is the resistance? People aren't even protesting anymore. You know why? Because they're afraid of being shot."

"That's not why. You read the mail."

"Fuck that mail. We don't even know who is sending those letters and flyers. Probably coming from the government to keep us fat for the kill. It's time for us to start thinking about what's best for us. This is an opportunity given by God. God has provided a way for us to stay in this country, and we would be fools not to take advantage of it."

His wife was silent as if she was considering he was right.

Her husband picked up the phone and dialed 911.

"What's your emergency?"

"I think someone is hiding a Jew in our building."

"What's the location?"

"3529 Half Street, Southwest. I'm in apartment forty-one. One of the neighbors on this side of the floor is hiding a Jew."

"Have you seen the Jew?"

"No. I heard a white man's voice come from one of the apartments. This is the third time I heard that voice."

"What makes you think the person is a Jew?"

"I live in the projects. There aren't any white people living or coming inside these apartments. They drive into the complex to buy drugs, then leave. If somebody's got a white person in their apartment, it's a Jew with money."

"Okay, thank you. I will notify the militia."

"Will I get the reward?"

"If they find a Jew, you will."

"Do you need my name?"

"What's your name?"

"Randy Caldwell."

"Thank you, Mr. Caldwell."

"One last question."

"What is it?"

"Will the arrest be discreet?"

"What do you mean?"

"I mean they won't say that I'm the one who told."

"I will make sure they don't."

"Thanks."

He hung up the phone with a smile and turned to his wife.

Sadness had filled her eyes.

"Cheer up," he said. "I just saved our family from being evicted from the country."

His wife looked him in the eye and said, "You haven't saved us. You cursed us."

* * *

At 4:17 a.m., every east-side front apartment door on the fourth floor except number forty-one was breached.

A shootout occurred in one of the apartments when the residents tried to defend their home from intruders. The militia killed nine in that apartment, ages three to forty-nine, without one survivor.

Inside the apartment at the end of the hall, the militia were surprised to discover Senator Schumacher and Congressman Jefferson. Like one holds a championship trophy on the day it is won, they paraded the senator and congressman out of the building and into the paddy wagon. Ruby and her two sons were also put into the wagon.

The other residents on that side of the floor stepped out into the hallway and noticed every apartment door breached except for number forty-one.

"They the ones that snitched," one of them said.

Another yelled, "You're a dead man, Randy! We know it was your family!"

Others shouted, "Y'all ain't shit! Fucking snitches!"

Three militiamen were inside Ruby's home and two were standing outside in the hall. One of the female teens in the hallway was crying and said, "Y'all muthafuckers killed my cousins." With her hands balled, she tried to approach the two militiamen but was grabbed by her weeping mother. "Let me go! I ain't scared of them."

"Chill shawty," one of the male teens said and stepped in front of her. "Y'all muthafuckers were too scared to come up in here during the day! You gonna have to come back 'cause we're not leaving! And when you come back, we gonna be ready for your asses! Day and night!"

A young shirtless man stepped forward with a gritty expression at the two militiamen. "We got chopsticks too! You feel me?"

The two militiamen kept their mouths shut and rifles pointed while the three inside continued the search.

Moments later, the militia leader entered the building with six men and walked up to the east side of the fourth floor. He scowled at the residents in the hallway as he went to apartment forty-one and knocked on the door.

Mr. Caldwell begrudgingly said, “Who is it?”

The voice outside the door said, “I have your money.”

Mr. Caldwell paused stressfully.

His wife was crying.

Bewildered, his fourteen-year-old daughter said, “What money?”

The knock on the door was louder. “Open up, now!”

“Yeah, open up the door, you muthafucker!” yelled one of the residents. Others added their anger and profanity.

Mr. Caldwell opened the door, and the militia leader and two of his men entered without closing the door.

“I was promised the tip would be anonymous. Now everyone knows it’s me.”

“So what? You think I care. Here’s your money.”

“That doesn’t look like ten million dollars. I heard them say they arrested the senator and congressman. That’s five million each.”

“You called in a Jew, and that’s the reward for a Jew.”

“Yeah, but it was the senator and congressman. I found them. You couldn’t find them. I need that ten million dollars to start a new life. We can’t stay here with everyone knowing we snitched.”

His daughter shouted, “I didn’t snitch! I’m not going!”

Mr. Caldwell kept his eyes on the militia leader. “I helped you. Give me my money.”

The militia leader turned and headed toward the open door.

Mr. Caldwell grabbed his arm. “You can’t leave us here. They will kill us.”

The militia leader faced him and said, “If you don’t let go of my arm, I’m going to kill you.”

Mr. Caldwell removed his hand and whimpered, “P-please, don’t do this.”

The militia leader turned again to leave.

“If you take us with you, I won’t tell anybody, and we can split the money.”

The militia leader paused, seemingly in thought before he turned and shot Mr. Caldwell.

His wife and daughter screamed as they rushed to his aide. They were crying on their knees, trying to resuscitate him when the militia leader shot both.

With cold-blooded eyes he stood over the three bodies, opened the pouch and spilled the money then left the building with his men.

The residents in the hallway went to the open door and looked at the dead family without sympathy. One of them said, "Karma is real," and walked away. The others were racing to grab the money, even looting the home.

* * *

At the morning Situation Room meeting, the president said, "I know you heard the militia captured Senator Schumacher and Congressman Jefferson. God bless the militia! They are doing what others cannot."

"Sir, where do we go from here?" the attorney general said. "We don't have any evidence to support the accusations against them."

"We don't need any evidence because none of the political prisoners will go to trial. I am their judge and jury. I know some of you believe the Fourth Reich has risen too soon. But now that it's risen, the duty of everyone in this room is to ensure it doesn't fall."

The vice-chair said, "If the Reich falls, the world will end. No one here wants the world to end."

"Amen," the president said. He led the Bellamy salute and adjourned the meeting.

* * *

The news of the congressman and senator's arrest filled William's eyes with sadness and dissolved his energy. That mood seemed to spread among the ground resistance nationwide.

The news of Ruby's arrest led the DC, Maryland, and Virginia postal workers in the resistance to take their families underground. When the wife of one asked, "Why do we have to go into hiding?" the husband replied, "Ruby will be tortured for information. She probably won't talk, but we need to assume she will. That way we won't get caught with our pants down."

* * *

DAY 66

Inside his mistress's secluded Virginia home, the chairman of the Joint Chiefs was drinking a glass of brandy and smoking a cigar while she massaged his shoulders. Classical music was the only sound in the dimly lit room when a former member of joint special operations entered the room like a ninja and executed the chairman. He quickly fastened the mistress's mouth, blindfolded her, and tied her hands and feet behind her. There she lay until the chairman's security officer entered hours later.

The president was asleep in the middle of two women when informed of the assassination. "It was the Mossad!" he shouted. And in the darkness of the early morning he summoned his team to the Situation Room.

"Effective immediately, I want every non-Aryan that's not on the exempt list imprisoned or killed. That includes the Rinos!" He swung angry eyes to the vice-chair. "You are the new chairman. I want our troops, National Guard, and militia in control of every city by midnight."

The new chairman said, "It shall be done, Mr. President. But before I can begin, I need you to inform the nation that I am the new chairman of the Joint Chiefs. Everyone in this room heard it, but I need a formal announcement from you to the nation so the troops will follow my orders without questions."

The president said to the press secretary, "Notify State TV that I will make a major announcement this afternoon in the press room." His eyes shifted back to the chairman. "I want you at my side when I make the announcement."

"Yes, Mr. President. And might I suggest we open it to the banned outlets for them to broadcast the announcement as well."

"Why?"

"For maximum effect. When I announce my immediate steps to crush the resistance, some of them who only watch the underground news will hear it and lay down their arms, and others will become informers."

The president said, "I like the way you think."

"Mr. President, I believe it will be a good idea to have Congressman Reaves with us."

"I'm skeptical of him. He wasn't at my last speech."

"Sir, you know why he wasn't there."

"Remind me?"

"We agreed to keep him away so it would appear that he wasn't a supporter of the Reich."

"Where is he now?"

"Identifying the traitors among us before they can betray. We need him at this announcement to address the crimes of Congressman Jefferson and Senator Schumacher. It's important for the troops to know the reason why they are killing Americans."

The president screeched, "But they aren't Americans!"

"In our eyes they aren't, but in the eyes of the troops, they are until we show them that they're not. Congressman Reaves can say they confessed to treason."

"Wouldn't the attorney general be a better person to make that announcement?"

The new chair swung his eyes to the attorney general, then shifted his eyes back to the president. "With all respect, no, he wouldn't, because the troops and the American people trust Congressman Reaves even more now because he wasn't present at the speech."

The president nodded. "Any other suggestions?"

"Yes. I would like all the Joint Chiefs to be in the backdrop because it will show unity to the troops. I will wear my combat uniform, and I suggest we have marines in combat gear stationed in the room, and four marines with combat gear behind you when you enter the room. That will show the world that we are at war with everyone that stands against the Fourth Reich."

The president said, "I love it!" and shifted his eyes to the press secretary. "The press room will be too small. Schedule the east room at one p.m." He stood with the Bellamy salute and walked out of the room.

* * *

The news of the chairman's assassination on the heels of the senator and congressman's arrest reenergized the ground resistance. And the news that the president would allow the banned news outlets to be present for his address had the nation in high anticipation.

William was waiting for the president's address with Sandra at his mother's house. Devin and his family were there too.

Summer was waiting for the address with the Jewish family in her home.

With the Senate buildings and Capitol doors locked, Senator Rainey was waiting for the address at the home of Mr. Rosenberg.

Mr. Jeffries, Neri, and Keisha were in Mr. Jeffries' residence, waiting for the address.

All eyes were locked on the television screen. Those without televisions had their ears locked on the radio.

The president said, "The chairman of the Joints Chiefs was assassinated by a killer hired by the Jews and big donors of the jackass party. All who stand against this government are threats to our national security.

"The new chairman of the Joint Chiefs is the man who sat as the vice-chair. He has my full confidence. He will give some orders that might make some in the military hesitant, but know this: every order he gives has my full endorsement, and I am ordering every member of the military personnel to follow his orders to the letter. I now introduce the new chairman of the Joint Chiefs of Staff."

The president stepped to the side, in front of Congressman Reaves, and the new chair of the Joint Chiefs stepped forward and stood at the podium.

"As the new chair of the Joint Chiefs of Staff, we, the military, and all in government authority took a vow to serve the Constitution and not a man."

The president swung irate eyes at the chairman. *What the fuck is he doing.*

The chairman continued, "In keeping my vow, I am ordering all military personnel to cease from participating in martial law."

The president shouted, "That is not my order!" and grabbed the chairman by the throat.

Congressman Reaves quickly stepped forward and pulled the president's hands away.

The secret service agents went to the president's defense and took hold of Congressman Reaves.

The commotion didn't stop the chairman from finishing his words. He said, "I am ordering the arrest of the president under the Insurrection Act."

"You son of a bitch!" the president shouted. "Arrest him!"

But the marines intervened and took the president into custody, and the secret service backed away.

Sandra blissfully hugged William.

With joyous tears, William's mother was praising the Lord.

Devin was in the elation of his wife's embrace and said to everyone, "This isn't over. The militia is coming."

William said, "But most of them have only shot at things that don't shoot back."

"Don't sell them short," Devin said. "Enough of them are ex-military, ex-rangers, ex-special ops, and ex-seals. But we're ready for them. We have those too. We knew it would come to this."

* * *

Jubilation lit every face in Summer's home. And after kissing his wife and hugging his child, the husband turned to embrace Summer. "What's wrong? It's over," he said.

"It's not over. You can move freely about in the house right now, but it's only the beginning of something else."

Dumfounded, he said, "The beginning of what?"

"Civil war."

"Civil war?"

“There will be a civil war. The militia is ten million fighters by now. We need to stay out of sight. Do you know how to use a gun?”

“Yes.”

“Good.”

Her eyes shifted to his wife. “Have you used a gun before?”

“No, but I’m not afraid to use one.”

“Good. I have a gun for you and your husband.”

With her eyes shifting, she said, “The war can start at any time. We need to make the safe room our permanent place until the war is over. We cannot trust the neighbors.”

She faced Deborah. “I need you to fill the safe room’s refrigerator, freezer, and cabinets.”

Her eyes shifted to the husband. “Alan, I need you to help me bring in supplies from the garage.”

With a sense of urgency, they proceeded.

* * *

Senator Rainey and Mr. Rosenberg knew the president’s arrest would occur, and after celebrating in a manner reminiscent of the New Year, they turned their eyes back to the television and heard the chairman say, “Congressman Reaves is the new Speaker of the House, and by the line of succession the president of the United States of America.”

The Chief Justice of the disbanded Supreme Court entered the room in his robe and swore in Congressman Reaves, who said, “I hereby free all political prisoners and order the militia to lay down their weapons or face arrest. All enablers of the coup, both in Congress and the cabinet, are under arrest.” He turned and pointed at two of the Joint Chiefs and said, “You are under arrest.” He scanned the room for the chief of staff, secretary of defense, attorney general, and others, but they had disappeared. He called out their names and the names of those in Congress who enabled the coup and listed them as “fugitives from justice.”

He closed with these words: "America is back! We are returning to NATO. We will defend every inch of NATO soil, and Israel's!"

Senator Rainey said, "Now the war starts."

Mr. Rosenberg said, "We have hired twelve thousand of the best mercenaries to join the fight. They are waiting instructions from the new chair of the Joint Chiefs."

"He's already contacted them. I'm confident we will win at home. But Israel is extremely vulnerable because they're surrounded by those waiting to take advantage of our war at home."

Mr. Rosenberg's enthusiasm seemed to lower, and he said, "Is there a plan?"

"There is. Hopefully Saudi Arabia and Egypt will keep their word."

"The war here won't end quickly. At last count, there are approximately ten million militia under General Weiskopf's command. That is a formidable army. We only have a million active-duty troops and some of them are on the side of the militia."

"But most in the militia are weekend hunters. What are they going to do when they are the ones being hunted twenty-four seven? I'm betting a lot of them will surrender or desert. We have millions of citizens, at least fifty million that are ready to fight with our troops."

Mr. Rosenberg's smile disappeared when Breaking News announced the militia had attacked military bases in Texas, Maryland, North Carolina, Minnesota, Pennsylvania, and Ohio. Videos of the attacks released by the militia showed them waving American, Confederate, and Nazi flags.

Active-duty members of the military in support of the militia were also included in the propaganda that blanketed the airwaves from State media.

Chapter 18

Russia seized the moment of America's turmoil and invaded Ukraine. In that same hour, China invaded Taiwan, and the Arab nations that surrounded Israel were unleashed. But the dictators that had risen in Great Britain and France were removed by their military in the same hour the American president was arrested.

With the world at war, President Reaves gathered his newly assembled team into the Situation Room with the heads of every NATO member on the phone.

President Reaves said, "You all know there is a civil war in my country. The enemies of NATO are trying to take advantage by forcing us to fight on multiple fronts. Russia hasn't attacked a NATO country, but if they capture Ukraine, Poland is next, then the Balkan states. We cannot let Russia capture Ukraine. The Ukrainians are tough and will fight to the death. They don't need us to fight for them. They only need us to supply the weapons. We must give them weapons, tanks, and fighter jets. That means every one of you must send them extra arms because we cannot carry the load while fighting at home. If America falls, your country will fall."

The newly appointed head of France said, "How long will we have to carry the load without America? It's 1981. The last civil war went four years and that was North versus South. This one is in every state. We cannot provide Ukraine with the weapons of war for more than a year without America's help. We have to worry about our own defense."

"We will help monetarily," the president said. "But we cannot be the vanguard for weapons and troops. We need our weapons and troops at home. I'm not sure how long this war will last. But I'm confident we will be victorious."

The newly appointed British Prime Minister asked, "What about Taiwan?"

"You all know how important Taiwan is to America strategically. The country is certainly a major non-NATO ally, but we cannot commit troops there, and we cannot fight from the air and sea to defend them and Japan at the same time.

With that, Taiwan will be sacrificed. We can retake Taiwan after the civil war.

"As for Israel, we are positioned in the sea and air to help defend the country from their attackers. But we do not have the available manpower to put boots on the ground. We need our troops at home to protect our northern border because of that demagogue in Canada. Thankfully, the only threat at the southern border is the crossing of illegal immigrants. If they fight with us against the militia, we will grant them citizenship.

"I have met with each of you personally at some stage in your life. You know me to be a man of my word. I will not turn my back on you. I will not forget you. The demagogue in Germany is under threat from the citizens, so he won't try to attack your countries, especially since you turned back the attempt to replace your governments. I am with you. America is with you. Together we will defeat this movement of Neo-Nazism."

* * *

With inside help, the militia overran four of the six military bases. Those who surrendered were killed because the militia didn't take prisoners. The females were raped before they were killed. Some of the males were sodomized before they were killed.

With chaos and bedlam running rampant across the country, President Reaves addressed the nation: "Our country is under attack by domestic enemies. I am asking all Americans to put aside their political differences and come together as Americans who believe no one person is above the law.

"As a proud member of the Republican party, I am appalled by those who call themselves Americans yet stand against the foundation of America, the Constitution, the three branches of government. The radicals aren't on the left but the far-right, and now they are showing their true colors, which isn't the Stars and Stripes but the red, white, and blue of the Russian flag.

"We are in a civil war that is not the North against the South, or Democrats against Republicans, but those who want an autocratic government instead of the freedoms given by a democracy. I choose democracy. Why? Because in a democracy, I have freedom of speech. In a democracy, I can change the channel if I don't want to listen to the president. But in an autocratic government, I will be arrested. In a democracy, the power is in the hands of the people, but in an autocratic government the power is in the hands of one, the leader, who can rape your wife and daughter as often as he likes because there is no power in your hand to stop him.

"I refuse to live in a country without the freedoms of democracy. To quote Patrick Henry, 'Give me liberty or give me death!' Put aside your party affiliation. If one side is wrong, cross over and do what is right. We are Americans. We can disagree, but we shouldn't be fighting each other. I took an oath to defend the Constitution against all enemies, foreign and domestic. If you are an enemy of mine, then you are an enemy of the Constitution. And if you are an enemy of the Constitution, which is the three branches of government, then you are an enemy of America even if you call yourself a patriot because your patriotism is not on the foundation that is the Declaration of Independence.

"America was built on three basic ideas: First, God created all men equal with the rights of life, liberty, and the pursuit of happiness; second, a government whose purpose is to protect those rights; third, and most important, if the government tries to remove those rights, the people are free to revolt and set up a government that will restore those rights. We are in that moment now when a government rose up to withhold those rights; therefore, our duty was to revolt and restore the rightful government, which we have done. But though the rightful government is back in place, the enemies that backed the unlawful government are trying to bring it back.

"The enemy is within our gates. They are known as the militia. They call themselves patriots but are traitors like the confederacy were traitors. Their strongholds are in the rural and mountain areas. I am calling for all true Americans to fight against these domestic enemies seeking to take away the freedoms given to us by the Founding Fathers. Rest assured, we will win this war with or without you. Those not among us in battle are against us and will face the consequences. We will prevail.

"Despite this civil war, I'm urging the Americans who are not fighting with the Army to report to work. Our stores will be open, and our transportation services will operate. We will try to live our normal lives despite the interruption by these insurrectionists, who will be crushed soon. Social Security, Medicaid, food stamps, funding for the disabled, and other programs our citizens depend on are restored with compensation for any missed payments. All government workers who didn't report to work during the coup will receive back pay for the days they didn't report. We are restoring all federal lifeline programs."

The president lifted a reversible armband. "This armband is to be worn by civilians willing to fight with us. Use the white side during the day, and the black side at night. This armband is available at every police station, state capital, and federal government building under our control. If you reside in the rural part of the state and want to join us but cannot because the militia is in control of your area, be ready when the opportunity comes. And it will come because we're bringing the fight there."

The president stepped aside.

Congressman Jefferson stood front and center. "With the release of the political prisoners and arrest of the coup enablers in Congress, I have been elected Speaker of the House. All floor discussions have returned to C-SPAN in collaboration with the Senate, led by the Republican leadership of Senator Elizabeth Rainey, because Democrats and Republicans are one in the fight to keep the democracy of our republic alive."

The speaker stepped aside.

Senator Rainey stood front and center. "There isn't a more conservative member of the Senate or House than me. If your values are conservative values, then you will stand with me. But if you are hiding behind the name of the Republican party to excuse your bigotry and extreme ideology, then you will not stand beside me because of your ignorance and foolishness. Those fighting against democracy are not Americans but infiltrators bent on returning the country to the days of Jefferson Davis and Andrew Johnson. I am here today to say that I am fighting to my last breath to keep democracy alive in America, the beacon of the world. We will prevail!"

* * *

The militia went to every home in the rural parts of America that didn't have an active member in the militia. At one of the homes, an eighty-three-year-old woman answered the door, and the militiaman said, "If you're not fighting with us, you're fighting against us, and if you're fighting against us, we have to kill you."

"Kill me then," the woman boldly said. "I'm too old to fight."

The militiaman pointed his rifle, but the team leader said, "Don't. She can't help us or hurt us." He looked at the woman and said, "What is your name?"

She spitefully said, "Abagail Tolson."

"Abagail, are you a Republican?"

"All my life."

"Why is your anger directed at us? We're Republicans."

"You're not Republicans. You're insurrectionists."

"Insurrectionists? We're fighting to save our country."

"From who?"

"From those who killed our Lord and Savior, from those committing crimes in our cities, and from those trying to make us say, Feliz Navidad instead of Merry Christmas."

Her brows puckered in a frown. "That's bullshit."

He stared at her for a few seconds. "Where's your husband?"

"He's with Jesus, waiting for me to join him."

The leader seemed to be at a loss for words before he said, "God bless you."

He and his team went to the house across the narrow road. An obese man in blue overalls with a long red beard answered the knock.

"I'm looking for Ralph Davidson," the militia team leader said.

The man tightened his expression. "I'm Ralph Davidson."

"Mr. Davidson, our records show that you left the militia. Why?"

"I resigned when the president removed Social Security, Medicare, and funding for the disabled. I felt betrayed."

"Betrayed? You still feel betrayed?"

"I do."

"As a member of the militia, your household was exempt from the removal of Social Security and Medicare, and I don't see a record of anyone in your household that's disabled, so why did you leave?"

"Because I have friends that are not members of the militia and their Social Security and Medicare was taken away. Some of them are disabled veterans. All of them are America First Republicans, and the party abandoned them. That's not right."

"Uh-huh, so you've decided to join the other side?"

"I'm not on any side."

"If you're not on our side, you're on the other side."

"I'm definitely not on the side that takes away funding for the disabled and Social Security and Medicare for those who need it."

The team leader lifted his 9mm and shot him. He went inside the home, shot Ralph's wife and dog, and set the house on fire.

The next home on the list was a mile away.

On the front porch was a middle-aged couple slowly swinging in a wooden love seat when three pickup trucks that flew American flags upside down rolled onto their property.

The man said, "They're probably coming to coax us back."

"We ain't going back," the woman huffed. "They are wasting their time coming here."

The man said, "They sure are."

The team leader jumped out of the lead vehicle and approached the couple with the group closely behind.

"Mr. and Mrs. Randolph?"

"That's us," the man said, slowly rocking in the love seat.

The team leader stood with one foot on the bottom step and opened his handbook. "I see here Mr. and Mrs. Randolph that you were members of the militia. Why did you leave?"

Mr. Randolph said, "We left because it wasn't what we signed up for."

"What did you sign up for?"

"We thought the country was under attack by Communists, but that's a lie."

"Why do you say that? We are under attack by the Communists and Socialists funded by the Jews."

His wife interjected, "That's not true."

"Not true? Ahem, are you Democrats or Republicans?"

"We're Democrats but we aren't beholden to a party. We voted for President Ronald and believed he was assassinated by the Communists to take over the country. That's why we joined the militia. But now we know the truth."

"What is the truth?"

Her husband interjected, "The truth is the assassination was an inside job. We haven't seen any proof that the Jews were involved. They lied to get us to help the coup. Don't believe what they're telling you. Look at our country? We are in another civil war over the same thing—opposition to the laws of the federal government. Back then it was slavery, now it's democracy. I wouldn't've fought for slavery, and I'm not fighting against democracy."

"Uh-huh. Then you and your wife are enemies of the people."

"What people? Your people? Those who are traitors to the Constitution!"

The leader stepped closer and struck him with the butt of his rifle. A man and woman in his group dragged the man onto the front lawn. Another woman grabbed the arm of his wife and threw her down next to him.

The team leader stood behind them and said, "Stand up and don't face me."

They stood with their eyes in search of heaven.

The team leader said, "Can democracy save you now?"

The wife said, "Jesus has already saved us. Nothing you do can change that."

"On your knees!"

They dropped to their knees with imminent death written across their faces that turned into a smile as if Jesus was welcoming them.

The team leader pointed his rifle and shot the wife in the back of the head, followed by a shot into the back of the husband's head.

A sign was placed on each body that read: "TRAITOR," and the house was set on fire.

* * *

William and Devin were on the midnight shift of their mother's neighborhood watch. With their backs against diagonally parked cars used as barricades, William said, "It's been over a week and not one militia has come this way. They aren't even trying to attack the state capital."

"That's because they have to go through the watch groups to reach the capital. For now, it looks like they're staying in the rural areas."

"Yeah, they want to fight on their turf."

"The Army will eventually force them this way. All we need to do is stay patient and keep watch."

"Yeah, but it's boring."

"The militia wants us to feel bored. They want us to let our guards down. Don't think someone in this group isn't a spy for them."

"There aren't any whites in our group."

"None that you can see, but there are some Oreos."

"Who?"

"Mr. Harper is one."

"Really? How do you know that?"

"I had a conversation with him once. It wasn't what he said, but what he didn't say."

"What was that?"

"He didn't say President Milhouse was a criminal."

"You think he's an Oreo just because he didn't say that?"

"If I had a conversation with you about Milhouse, what would say?"

"He was a criminal."

"Exactly. Not saying that means you're like the house Negro that tells the massa what the slaves are planning."

"Ah, I feel you."

"Word. We have to be careful. We can't trust everyone because they're black."

"Soo, what we gonna do about him?"

"Nothing right now. But when the time comes, we will use him to our benefit."

"What do you mean?"

"We'll feed him some false information, he'll share it with the militia, and then we will kill them and him."

William held an unsure expression and said, "Do we have to kill him?"

"If we don't, he's gonna get someone killed. Maybe our mother."

That thought took hold of William's face and he said, "We need to bounce him now."

"Nah, it's not time yet. Stay patient."

"What happens when this is all over?"

"The same that was: politicians who lie for a living and the people that continue to vote for them will make the laws. Those who led and participated in the coup, that mindset isn't going away but will try again because there is an appetite in the country for it.

"This country has been divided since it was founded. The first civil war didn't change it, and this one won't either. As long as there are two or more political parties, there will be a divided country."

"Wait, you believe there should only be one political party? Isn't that what we're fighting against?"

"No. We're fighting against dictatorship. I'm talking about one party that's the people's party. One person, one vote. Throw away the electoral college. That's some bullshit. No one who loses the popular vote should be elected president. The electoral college takes away the power of the people. It's like a backdoor to the presidency."

"I don't think the electoral college is going to change anytime soon."

"That's why the country will stay divided and the mindset we're fighting against will live on."

"But even if the majority rule, the country will still be divided."

"But the majority won't have a threat because there are more righteous people than unrighteous, more smart people than foolish. But if you divide the states into districts, you can get unrighteous and foolish people into office. One rotten apple will contaminate the whole barrel, so don't include the rotten apple."

"How can you prevent the apple from turning rotten in the barrel?"

"If the apple isn't rotten before it gets into the barrel, it won't become rotten. We have to be patient and inspect every apple before we put it in the barrel. Laziness doesn't take the time to inspect every apple. If we want a clean society, we can't be lazy. We have to inspect every apple and throw every rotten one away before it gets into the barrel."

"But lawmakers become corrupt after they get into office."

"No, they don't. They are already corrupt. That's why the people should make the laws. Get rid of Congress and the state and city legislators. Elect a president, and the policy of that president is the law of the country. Get rid of city and state laws. That's just a way to circumvent federal law."

"Should he or she have a term?"

"Absolutely. One term is long enough. And if the president turns out to be a wolf in sheep's clothing, the people and not the politicians should be the final decision for impeachment. A perfect union is when the people make the final decisions. The people make the laws. The presidents, governors, and mayors enforce the laws made by the people."

"What about the Third World countries where the most votes win and politicians buy votes because the people are poor and succumb to the temptation?"

"That's why they will remain a Third World country, because despite those who sell their soul, the majority of eligible voters are lazy and don't vote, which allows corruption to continue. How can a country be poor when the person who rules is rich? Greed is the reason Third World countries exist, and that corruption is allowed to continue because of the people's laziness to vote."

"But the richest person in those countries will win every time because he or she has more money to advertise and travel."

"Again, if the people make the laws that the leader of the country has to follow, then it doesn't matter who the president is because law enforcement that includes the military follow the orders of the people and not a man or woman."

William nodded. "I see you've been thinking about this for a while."

"I have. I want to live in the perfect union. I believe in we the people."

* * *

The blinds and drapes in Summer's home were kept closed, and the lights were kept off.

Inside the hidden room, Deborah said, "When will this end?"

Summer smiled to cover the worry. "I don't know, Deborah. But when it does, we will end on top."

"I pray so."

"With prayer and togetherness, we will be safe."

Alan said, "I'm seeing neighborhood watch groups on the news. Do you think there is one in this neighborhood?"

"Maybe. But I don't trust people I don't know. They weren't friendly to me before this happened. Why would they be friendly to me now?"

"Maybe they need you now."

"That's the problem. If you don't want to be my friend when things are good in your life, then any friendship now is not sincere. They will only use me to save their life."

Aaron interjected, "Ms. Summer, can you play Atari with me?"

She smiled, "Of course. Which game?"

"Star Raiders," he excitingly said.

"I'm going to beat you again."

"No, you won't. I've been practicing."

"Okay, show me what you got."

While Summer and Aaron were playing the video game in laughter, and Alan and Deborah were cheering for their son, the warning light interrupted.

Summer quickly stopped the game and whispered, "Stay quiet. Someone is in the house." She grabbed her gun and pointed it at the hidden room's entrance.

Deborah and Alan stood with their guns pointed at the entrance and Aaron standing in between them.

Inside the house were five armed neighborhood teens that had broken in through the back door. One of them said, "She's around here somewhere. Her car is in the garage."

One of the two girls said, "She gotta be here. The alarm isn't on."

One of the five said, "Maybe she left without taking the car."

"Why would she leave and not take her car?"

"Maybe she's hiding out at a neighbor's house," another one said.

The oldest said, "Who gives a shit! Let's find the money."

The other girl said, "Maybe she took the money with her."

One of the guys said, "Maybe she don't have any money."

The oldest scolded, "This is the house of a Jew! Have you ever seen a poor Jew? Every Jew has a safe in their house. Let's find the safe. If it's empty, she took the money with her."

They ransacked the house, deliberately destroying everything in view.

"There's no safe," the second girl said.

The oldest shouted, "There is a safe somewhere in here! Jews have secret rooms. Let's check the master bedroom again."

They searched but didn't find it. "Fuck it! Burn this bitch down!" the oldest said.

The first girl said, “You can’t do that! My house is next door. The fire might spread.”

“Your house is ten yards away and separated by concrete. It won’t spread.”

“There might be a bomb hidden in this house. I told you the militia came to this house before. Maybe she booby-trapped it in case they came back. She isn’t here, she left her car, and the alarm is off. That’s a hundred-thousand-dollar car in the garage. She’s begging someone to try and steal it.”

One of the three guys said, “That it! There’s a bomb in the car. She left it thinking someone would try to steal it and blow the fucking neighborhood up. Fuck this, let’s get out of here!”

They hurried out of the house and spray-painted on the garage, “THERE IS A BOMB IN THAT CAR! DON’T TOUCH IT! IT WILL BLOW UP THE NEIGHBORHOOD! NO JOKE!!!

* * *

Apprehensiveness was in the minds and on the faces every second of every minute as the hours passed in the hidden room.

Alan concerningly eyed Summer and whispered, “Do you think they’re gone?”

She whispered, “Maybe. But they might be downstairs.”

Deborah whispered, “It’s been two hours since we heard them. When are we going to check?”

Summer murmured, “It’ll be dark soon. We can’t walk around in the dark, and we can’t use flashlights. We’ll wait until it’s daylight. We heard them ransacking the house, so they aren’t planning to squat here. They most likely have already left or will before morning.”

Deborah softly said, “What are they looking for?”

Alan eyed his wife and murmured, “Maybe you and me.”

“How would they know you’re here?” Summer whispered. “They were probably looking for valuables. I’m sure they took my car. Keep the television on with closed captions, stay quiet, and don’t cook anything. We’ll check the house in the morning.”

Summer used her watch to know the midmorning and said, "Let's go now."

"I'm ready," Alan said and grabbed the gun and flashlight.

With a flashlight in her left hand and the gun in her right, Summer slowly led Alan out of the hidden room that led into the master bedroom. The broken glass from the full-length wall mirror that covered the hidden room door crackled beneath their feet. The sunlight that came through the naked windows removed their need for a flashlight, and they turned it off.

Tears rose in Summer's eyes at the sight of her bedroom torn apart as if starving animals were searching for a morsel of food.

WHITE POWER, and DEATH 4 ALL JEWS & JEW LOVERS was spray-painted on the walls.

With guns pointed, Alan walked behind Summer as she slowly stepped into the upstairs hallway and peeked into rooms that were also ransacked.

"I know what downstairs looks like," she said, "but we need to check if the car is still here. I doubt it, but we need to check."

Alan followed her timid steps down the stairs with eyes and ears on the alert for sights and sounds. They found the damage downstairs worse than upstairs and entered the garage.

"The car is still here," Summer excitedly said. "We need to leave."

Alan said, "Something is spray-painted on the front of the garage."

"Whatever it says is not important. We're leaving in the morning darkness."

"Where are we going?"

"I know a place not far from here. A congressman owns land where he was hiding Jews. I'll call him."

"How? They ripped out the phones. You know how to repair one?"

"No. But there's a phone in the safe room."

"You didn't tell us there was a phone. Where is it?"

"It's hidden. I didn't tell you because I didn't want you to be tempted to use it when I wasn't in the room with you. I couldn't take the chance that you wouldn't try to contact someone."

Alan seemed disappointed.

"I'm sorry I didn't trust you. When we get back to the room, you can make your calls after I contact the congressman. C'mon, let's go back to the room."

He followed her steps back to the room as they both resisted the temptation to peek out the windows.

Relief replaced Deborah's worried expression when they returned, and with her son beside her, she sped into her husband's embrace.

Summer uncovered the phone and dialed.

"Congressman Buck speaking."

"It's me, Summer."

"Summer, I'm glad you called. Are you safe?"

"I'm safe for now. My home was ransacked, but they didn't find us."

"Are you able to get to the farm?"

"If the roads are clear."

"We control the interstates, but some of the routes to the interstates are blocked by the militia. The route off the interstate to the farm is clear if you can make it to the interstate."

"I don't know if I can."

"Maybe it's best if you stay put until the Army get control of all the highways."

"I can't. Something was written on my garage door. Don't know what it says because I can't go out. But my house might be marked for burning. I saw the reports of houses being burned in the suburbs."

"How far are you from the interstate?"

"About four miles."

"Better to walk. I can arrange a unit of the guards to meet you on the I-81."

"Good. We will leave at two in the morning. We should be there by three. If we're not there by four, we're either dead or captured."

“I’m confident you will make it.”

When she ended the call, Alan made a few calls that went unanswered.

Summer felt his sadness and said, “They’re probably in a safe place. When we get to where we’re going, try again.”

With her eyes shifting between Alan and Deborah, she said, “Wear dark clothing. We can only carry a gun and flashlight. Anything else has to fit in the pockets. The walk is four miles. At least two of the four are through the woods. Make sure you put a bottle of water in your pocket.”

Aaron said, “Can I take my backpack?”

“Oh yeah. I forgot about that,” Summer said. “We can put some extra bottles of water and other things we might need. But it can’t be too heavy. You need to be able to keep up with us. We’re going to try to cover a mile every fifteen minutes. It’s not as easy as it sounds. Let’s eat and get some rest. Our minds and bodies need to be sharp for the journey. We don’t know who or how many are out there.”

* * *

Summer’s watch alarm was set for 1:30 a.m. At 1:45 a.m., she said, “Are we ready?”

“We’re ready,” Alan replied and led his wife and son behind Summer’s cautious footsteps.

They left the house through the broken back door and quietly headed toward the pavement lit by streetlights.

Alan whispered, “Why don’t we follow the backyards? That way is darker.”

“Some of the neighbors have dogs. The barks will draw attention to us. I rather walk in the light and flee into darkness than walk in darkness and flee into the light. When we cross the street, we’ll stay on the sidewalks.”

The streets were empty, and every house was dark.

Alan whispered, “Where is everybody?”

“They either left for the city or are hiding like we were. The shortage of cars tells me that most fled to the city.”

About a half a mile into the walk, headlights from a speeding vehicle lit the path ahead.

They quickly laid in the grass beside one of the few parked cars on the street.

The vehicle stopped in the middle of the street about a hundred feet from where they lay, and voices were heard.

Summer peeked from the edge of the front tire and saw familiar boots stepping toward her. *Those are Saul's boots.* She pointed her gun.

Alan and Deborah did the same.

Tension was written across their faces.

Seconds later, a vehicle from the opposite direction stopped in the middle of the street.

The boots that were in Summer's direction stopped and turned when the female voice shouted, "We own this fuckin' neighborhood! Let's party!"

Alan whispered, "That's the voice I heard inside the house."

Summer swung her face toward him, with the index finger on her lips and eyes that said, "Shut up!"

An assembly of celebratory voices and gunshots went into the air. "Hell yeah! Let's party!" was another familiar voice.

The boots stepping in Summer's direction were heard fading away.

After several seconds, Summer lifted eyes over the car's hood and saw the backs of bodies entering a house on the other side of the street. She waited until the door closed and whispered, "C'mon, let's go."

They scooted down the street, lowering their bodies behind the parked vehicles. Empty liquor and beer bottles lay in front as they entered the woods that housed possums, red foxes, deer, and rabbits. Flashlights lit the way as mingled sweat from nerves and fatigue ran down their faces.

In the bed of a pickup truck, two of the four men saw lights in the woods and yelled, "Stop!" One of them smacked the back window.

The driver pulled over, shifted the gear to park, and he and the woman in the passenger seat jumped out. "What happened?" the driver asked.

"I saw lights in the woods back there headed toward the interstate."

The driver and passenger hurried back inside the truck and made a quick U-turn. The truck sped down the road and parked at the edge of the woods about a mile from the interstate. "They have to come this way to get to the interstate," the driver said and led the dash of six that strategically positioned themselves and patiently waited in the woods.

Alan grabbed Summer's arm and said, "I got a bad feeling."

"What is it?"

"I believe there's trouble ahead."

Summer maneuvered the flashlight left to right, up and down, and back again. "I don't see anything."

Alan nervously said, "How far are we from the interstate?"

"Another mile at least."

"There's trouble ahead. I can feel it."

Summer was contemplating and pondering next steps. "We can't turn back."

Alan said, "Let's walk along the road. I can feel harm in the woods."

"We'll be exposed if we walk along the road. I don't want to take that chance."

"We're taking a bigger chance if we keep straight. God is my witness. Evil is waiting on this path."

"If we go your way, we will lose at least forty minutes."

"We can still make it by four."

Summer was thinking with her eyes locked on his. "Okay, let's go your way," she said. "Turn off the flashlights. We're gonna hold hands until we get to the road."

In a straight line, they followed Summer, holding hands through the dense woodland. When they reached the road, Summer said, "Let's cross here. If anyone is down there waiting for us, we'll be on the other side of the road."

They crossed over, and Summer said, "We need to speed it up. Run until you get tired, then we'll walk again."

A half hour or so later, they spotted the pickup truck.

"Is anyone in it?" Deborah asked.

"No," Alan said. "I'm sure they're in the woods, waiting for us. I told you evil was waiting for us."

Summer eyed the area and said, “We have to go in there. It’s the only way we can get to the interstate from here.”

Alan said, “How many do you think are in there?”

Summer sighed. “At least two, and as many as ten.” She sighed again and eyed Alan. “I’ll go. If they are in there, they will take me prisoner and bring me to their camp. When they leave, you and your family run to the interstate.”

“Nooo!” Alan said. “They will rape you first and might kill you. I’ll go. They won’t kill me because they want me alive to collect the bounty. When they bring me out, they won’t be expecting anyone to be at their back or in front. Since you are a better shot, you should hide there.” He pointed to the spot and said, “Their backs will be to you.”

“What if they don’t want the bounty? What’s going to keep them from killing you in the woods?”

“I’ll think of something.” He turned to his wife. “You and Aaron hide behind the truck. When I yell, Alohim, that’s your signal to stand and shoot once, then duck. Your shot is the signal for Summer to shoot. Hopefully, there are less than ten.”

Deborah was crying and tearfully said, “I might shoot you.”

He embraced her. “This is the only chance we have. Just aim and shoot. Trust God to guide the bullet.” He kissed her on the lips then his son on the forehead.

He faced Summer. “If you hear a gunshot, they killed me.” His eyes shifted between his wife and Summer. “Stick to the same plan if you hear a gunshot. May God be with us.” And Alan ran into the woods with tears rolling down his wife’s cheeks.

Summer said, “God is with us, get ready.”

About a hundred yards inside the woods, Alan raised his hands as one of the militiamen pointed the rifle at him. “Where are you going?” the militiaman said.

With the appearance of being startled, Alan stammered, “We were headed to the interstate.”

The other five came out from hiding, and the driver of the truck said, “We? Where are the others?”

“They got scared and ran back?”

"Where?"

"About a mile up the road."

"How many?"

"Three women."

"Old or young?"

He hesitated.

The militiaman pressed the rifle on Alan's forehead. "Old or young?"

"Young."

"Show us."

"Leave them be. You got me. They're still virgins."

"Show us, or I will kill you right now."

Alan beggingly said, "P-please, don't kill me. Promise me that you won't kill me, and I will show you."

He shoved Alan in the direction of the truck and said, "Show us."

All six were walking with Alan in front. About ten yards from the truck, Alan screamed, "Alohim!" and fell flat on the ground.

Deborah rose and fired one shot, then ducked.

After Deborah's first shot, Summer stood and put a bullet into the backs of the five that were still standing.

After a few seconds of silence, Alan stood and ran to his wife and son.

With her gun pointed, Summer walked up to the fallen bodies, and one was still alive. He pleaded, "Don't kill me."

Alan and his family walked up to Summer.

"What are we going to do with him?" Alan asked.

"Leave him," Summer said. "We have to get to the interstate."

They dashed into the woods and continued their trek to the interstate. At 3:51 a.m., they boarded the National Guard truck that carried them to the safety of the congressman's farm.

* * *

At the Gillette estate, Shawn, Theodore, Mr. Rudolph, the former chief of staff, and General Weiskopf were in the mansion's bunker. Encamped on the grounds were more than a hundred thousand militiamen in infantry and manning surface-to-air missiles and anti-aircraft guns. A hundred tanks were camouflaged, and a stolen nuclear weapon was hidden.

Inside the bunker's war room, in-person or on the phone, were the militia leaders from every state.

General Weiskopf said, "My travel is restricted because the government knows my face. I cannot leave Wyoming, and you cannot call me freely because the government is intercepting most of the calls. That makes this meeting the most important of my leadership. While I'm restricted, you're not. Therefore, send your lieutenants across the state with the information given here to keep every squad on the same page, which will ensure our victory.

"Listen carefully: The military bases under our control cannot surrender. Our camps in the rural areas will soon be under bombing. We are going to lose some good men and women when the bombing begins, but stay strong in the bunkers and be ready for the ground attack. Their strength is in the air, and they will use it—but some of those pilots are on our side and some of their ground troops also.

"In the rural areas where there aren't any bunkers or mountains, the air and ground attack will drive us into the inner cities, which according to reports are heavily armed and well organized, particularly in the black neighborhoods, which I find hard to believe."

His eyes shifted to the team leader in Georgia. "It's my understanding that we are on the brink of losing Georgia because of the black army."

The team leader shamefully lowered his head.

The general said, "If we don't get control of the inner cities, we will lose this war. So, this is our strategy to win against the inner cities. Send black members on your team to infiltrate the black groups protecting those cities."

One of the team leaders said, "There are whites, Spanish, Asians, and Indians fighting with them too. We have those among us. Shouldn't we send them to those neighborhoods?"

The general replied, "In Texas, Arizona, New Mexico, Nevada, et cetera, send the Spanish. Send the Asians and Indians into the communities where they are prevalent. But the blacks are the most dangerous even when they are the few. Look at what those black cowboys and Indians are doing here in Wyoming? They are mocking us in Cheyenne, Caspar, even Laramie. They are in control of those cities without the help of the Army and riding on horseback with bows and arrows."

The general opened a bag and pulled out armbands worn by the government neighborhood watch groups. With his eyes shifting, he said, "While infiltrating every inner city watch group is our target, the most important are the ones led by blacks. We need to get to Site R in Blue Ridge Summit, which is fifty-something miles outside Harrisburg, Pennsylvania. I need three to five blacks to infiltrate the black groups in the 6th and 7th Street corridors in Harrisburg. They cannot be from that city or state because they might be recognized as patrolling the streets during the curfew. Talk to your comrades and see who's a good fit to transfer into Harrisburg, Atlanta, Chicago, Cleveland, Milwaukee, Detroit, Minneapolis, Washington, DC, and New York.

"Have them ditch the camouflage gear and put on some urban clothes with one of these armbands. Give them an address to remember and the name of an elementary, junior high, and high school they attended in that city. Use affluent addresses where mostly whites reside. For example, in Harrisburg, most of the whites are in the northwest part of the city. Blacks are mostly in the central places. Stay away from those addresses and schools.

"When your men get inside the group, kill the leader immediately. Blacks aren't that bright. They usually only have one capable leader in each group. We discovered that when Captain Kingsberry took out the leader in Salisbury. They ran like antelopes from a hungry lion. It's critical for us to conquer the inner cities, or we will not win this war."

Chapter 19

Two men and a woman entered the 6th Street Corridor with their hands raised and shouted, "Don't shoot! We're on your side!"

The watchers at the entrance saw the armbands and allowed them to enter. They were given food and water and they promptly told how they had escaped from the militia.

One of the neighborhood watchers went to inform Devin, and when he and William arrived, the three were sitting on the ground with their backs pressed against a car.

Devin said, "Have they been checked for weapons?"

Mr. Harper said, "I checked them at the entrance."

"You're not assigned to the entrance."

"I know. I was there talking to Charlie when they showed up."

Devin slowly nodded with the blank expression.

"Did you find a weapon?"

"No, they're clean."

"William, check them again."

With an offended tone, Mr. Harper said, "You don't trust me?"

"If I didn't trust you, you wouldn't be here. Lesson number twelve, always have two people check for weapons."

"They're clean," William said.

"I told you they were clean."

"You did a good job, Mr. Harper."

The eyes of the three slid toward Mr. Harper and then quickly back to Devin.

Why did they react to his name? Devin's eyes narrowed in thought and he said, "Mr. Harper, I need you to go to the Hall Manor and tell Rick I have three people to send him tomorrow."

"You want me to go now?"

"Yes, and come right back. I'm going to need you in the morning to take them."

Mr. Harper seemed reluctant to leave and made excuses to stay.

Devin said, "Go now. That's an order."

"Paul, go with him."

Devin waited until the car drove off then said to the three, "Where are you coming from?"

The one with the Jheri curl said, "We were trying to form a watch in our neighborhood when the militia captured us."

"Where is your neighborhood?"

"Nottingham Place."

"How long have you been living there?"

"All my life."

"What school did you attend?"

"I graduated from Central Dauphin."

"Your elementary school?"

"Linglestown."

Devin glanced at William then quickly shifted his eyes back to the three. "Are all of you from the same neighborhood?"

The young woman in a zip-up shoulder pad jacket with an Afro said, "We are, but I graduated from Susquehanna Township."

"All three of you were raised in Harrisburg?"

"Yeah," the three said.

"What's your names?"

The one with the Jheri curl said, "Travis."

The girl said, "Roxanne."

The other guy said, "Larry."

With a thought in his eyes, Devin looked at William, who seemingly had the same thought. And William eyed the three and said, "I don't hear the Harrisburg accent. Do you have an ID?"

Travis said, "The militia took our IDs."

"Hmm. What county is Harrisburg?" William asked.

For a moment, not knowing covered their faces. Then Travis said, "Franklin."

Devin and William lifted their guns and pointed at them.

"Who the fuck are you? You're not from here," Devin said.

William said, "This isn't Franklin County. That is where the underground Pentagon is located. You're militia."

Devin's expression turned sour. "What's your mission?"

They kept their mouths closed.

Devin turned to one of the watchers and said, "Get the word out nationwide that militia are wearing armbands, pretending to be residents of the city." He faced the three and said, "You're gonna tell me now, or tell me later. It'll be pain free if you tell me now. There is nothing I hate more than a nigger. Do you know the original meaning of the word?"

Their mouths stayed closed with eyes wide open.

"The original meaning is 'an ignorant person.' You and every black, white, Asian, Latino, and others that stand with the militia are niggers. None more than you!

"Do you know how many black people, including women and children, were killed by the hand of white supremacists? And here you are, blacker than me, aligning yourselves with those who hate you. They are only using you until they don't need you anymore, and then they will kill you. Do you know how many black people suffered for you to be able to shit in the same toilet as whitey? Niggers like you are the scum of the earth. You are one of them that will help kill my mother, wife, and children. Do you think I will have mercy on you if you don't answer my questions?

"Tell me your mission? If I have to ask again, it will be after severe pain is inflicted. Think about an eye for an eye, a tooth for a tooth, and a tongue for a tongue." He turned to William and said, "Go get my tools."

William ran toward the house as if he was excited to witness a torture.

Pointed guns and thoughts of torture surrounded the three, and Larry said, "I'll talk."

Devin crouched in front of him. "I'm listening."

"We were sent to clear the way for the militia to get to Site R."

"Site R? What is Site R?"

"It's the underground Pentagon."

"How were you going to clear the way?"

"By killing the leader of each neighborhood watch group."

"You thought killing the leader would clear the way?"

"We know blacks are the leaders in the neighborhoods we have to pass. The belief is that there is only one leader among the blacks in each neighborhood watch group, and if you kill the leader, everyone else will scatter."

"You see how much of a nigger you and your friends are. This is not Salisbury, where they were less than twenty and without ammunition when the leader was killed. We are more than ten thousand strong, stretching over two miles. Every one of us has an Army-issued M16 and extra ammo. Every street gang is among us. And when one leader of a group goes down, the next person steps up into the role because we're all leaders. No one will scatter. They will just fight harder."

Larry was whimpering and said, "I'm sorry. I thought I was fighting on the right side."

"What made you think that?"

"I believed the Jews and Communists were trying to take over the country."

"What made you stop believing that?"

"In Ohio there were Jews fighting against us, and I assumed Communists too because white men and women were fighting with the Jews."

"You still haven't told me why you stopped believing you were on the right side?"

"Because my party is called the right-wing, and I thought this mission was a black leader with an army of Jews and Communists, but all I see are black people. The way your group accepted us told me they weren't fighting to take over the country but to unite it. One of your men told me that he and his family are Republicans and were against the Democrats because of abortion and gay rights but left their neighborhood to join this group. He said, 'The Constitution is more important than a political party.' When you think about it, we're attacking you. It would be the other way if you were trying to take over the country."

William returned with a heavy book bag.

Devin said to Larry, "Why did you look at Mr. Harper when I mentioned his name?"

"He's the name given as our point of contact, the person that would provide the weapons for us to kill you and the other leaders."

Devin allowed those words to sink in to him and the other watchers among them then said, “Where’s the camp?”

“In Wildwood Park.”

“How many are there?”

“I don’t know exactly. A few thousand.”

“How were you going to communicate with them?”

“When we had killed the leader in this section of the corridors, Mr. Harper would inform the Park that this section was clear for them to march through.”

“What was the next move of you three?”

“We would split up and blend in with the watchers in the other corridors and kill their leaders.”

“You’ve been very cooperative. I appreciate it.”

“What’s going to happen to me and my cousins?”

“You and your cousins will remain our prisoners. We will speak favorably on your behalf at trial. As for them, they haven’t been cooperative but will get a fair trial. I can promise that we will request leniency because of you.”

* * *

Mr. Harper was incarcerated when he returned. He claimed someone else named Mr. Harper was their point of contact, but there wasn’t another Mr. Harper among the 6th and 7th Street corridor watchers.

The next day, Devin put Mr. Harper on trial. The people in their section of the corridors were the judge and jury.

“Mr. Harper, I only have two questions,” Devin said. “And the answer will prove your innocence or guilt. You told me in front of witnesses that you searched the three at the entrance. Charlie said they weren’t searched at the entrance. When did you search them, and who saw you?”

“Charlie is mistaken!” Mr. Harper shouted. “I patted them down at the entrance. Your brother searched them too and didn’t find a weapon.”

“Second question: Who saw you check them for a weapon?”

“I don’t know. I wasn’t looking around before I searched them.”

"No one has come forward and said they saw you search them. Charlie was the only person with you at the entrance but not the only witness. The snipers said you didn't search them at the entrance. Somebody or somebodies are lying. The people are your judge and jury."

Every person except one, which was his wife, voted Mr. Harper guilty.

Devin said, "Mr. Harper, this a chance for you to confess. Why are you assisting the militia?"

"I'm not. I'm innocent. I'm being framed because you never liked me. You never trusted me."

"I confess I never liked you and I never trusted you. Should I believe you over the witnesses? Everyone here asked themselves that same question before they voted, and only one person has taken your word over the witnesses. That concerns me. Maybe you're not the only traitor among us." Devin's eyes shifted to Mrs. Harper.

"I'm not a traitor," she shrieked. "I voted for him because he's my husband."

"Is your husband more important than any of us here? Is my wife more important than anyone here? We cannot win this war with that mindset. Wisdom is always greater than love. When you choose love over wisdom, you will accept the unrighteous thing. You will become an accessory after the fact.

"Those three were sent to kill me and every section leader in these corridors. They came unarmed in case they were searched. Mr. Harper wasn't supposed to be at the entrance but just coincidently happened to be there when they arrived. They didn't know his face but had the name. He was the person that would give them the weapons to assassinate me. And they wouldn't've stopped with me. They would've killed my wife, children, brother, and mother. And with Mr. Harper's help they would've moved on to the other leaders in these corridors because once you get inside this entrance there aren't any more checkpoints. You can easily blend in and take out the leader. That's why I have secret watchers at the entrance and snipers that most of you don't know about. That exists in every entry point into the corridors.

"Mr. Harper, your wife has proven that she loves you. How much do you love your wife?"

He didn't answer.

"Here is your opportunity to prove your love for her. Your fate is sealed. If you want to save her life, call your contact at the militia and tell him this corridor is clear for them to come through. Will you do that?"

He looked at his wife as if he didn't care if she died.

She cried, realizing he didn't share the same love.

"I can't do that because I don't have a contact with the militia. You have the wrong man."

His wife screamed, "You bastard!" and swung her teary eyes at Devin. "He has a contact. I heard him talking to him. I know where the phone number is hidden."

Devin's eyes shifted from the wife to the husband. "Mr. Harper, may God have mercy on your soul, because I won't." Devin shot him multiple times.

* * *

The next day, Mrs. Harper phoned the militia contact.

"This is Mr. Harper's wife."

"Where is he?"

"He was killed in the melee after the leader of the watchers and his family were killed."

"Who killed Mr. Harper?"

"The leader's brother killed him, then I killed the brother."

"Where are the three men we sent?"

"They have gone to the kill the leaders in the other sections of the 6th and 7th Street corridors. This corridor is clear. The people think all the leaders are dead and have abandoned their posts."

"I knew that would happen. No offense, but most niggers are cowards. They fought their own side more than the Viet Cong. But you and your husband are among the good ones. We will be there before nightfall. We will bury your husband in the morning."

She said, "Thank you," and hung up the phone.

Devin said, "Good job."

When Devin's wife escorted Mrs. Harper out of the house, William said, "Can we trust her to be alone? She might call back and tell them it's a trap."

"She won't be alone. Candace is watching her. Trust me, if she makes one false move, Candace will shoot her."

* * *

Three thousand militiamen entered the corridor that seemed abandoned. The leader repeatedly yelled, "Mrs. Harper!" as he led his soldiers through the corridor with cautious steps.

About a quarter of a mile inside the corridor section, the militia leader saw Mr. Harper's dead body on the bottom steps of a house and yelled again, "Mrs. Harper!" *That bitch got scared and ran away too.*

They continued another thirty yards or so with rifles pointed without a person in sight. Then suddenly, gunshots came from the east and west and north and south of them. They scattered in search of cover but only found bullets waiting for their arrival.

In less than twenty minutes, three thousand militiamen had surrendered or were killed. Their leader was the first to surrender and said to the others, "My gut told me not to trust a nigger."

The national guardsmen that participated in the ambush took those that surrendered into custody.

Larry and his cousins were taken to the state capital and handed over to the US Army.

Mrs. Harper was pardoned by the people and remained among the neighborhood watchers.

At the state capital, one of the black civilians who had escaped from the militia in Ohio was fighting with the US Army and recognized Travis and his sister as the killers of black people in Ohio.

He waited for the opportunity, and when it came, he didn't hesitate to execute them, sparing Larry's life because he saw him trying to stop the senseless killings.

The civilian deserted his post before the bodies were discovered and was never seen again.

* * *

Inside a white suburban Alabama neighborhood, the residents had organized a heavily armed five-mile radius perimeter to block the militia's aggression and spurn their multiple attacks. This neighborhood watch group was led by former Rangers and Navy SEALs. And in less than a week, they expanded their perimeter another five miles to protect the city of Montgomery from an invasion. The heroics and battle savvy from this group was duplicated in the suburbs of Birmingham, Huntsville, Mobile, and Tuscaloosa.

* * *

In Oklahoma, suburban, multicultural neighborhood groups prevented the militia's onslaught from entering Oklahoma City. The militiamen who were already inside the city were either killed or arrested by the residents and National Guard.

Wounded in a gun battle with the US army, the militia leader fled into the unlocked front door of a house and was stunned at the sight of Abagail Tolson sitting in a rocking chair, holding a shotgun.

"Remember me?" she said. "I told you that I was too old to fight, but I'm not too old to pull this trigger."

With his hand pressed against the blood that covered the side of his camouflage shirt, he feebly said, "I need your help."

"Why should I help you?"

"Because you're a God-fearing woman."

"That I am, but you're not a God-fearing man. You killed my husband's best friend."

"Who was that?"

"Ralph Davidson."

"I don't know him. I didn't kill him."

"Let me remind you. He has a long red beard. You shot him, his wife, and his dog. Now God has delivered you into my hand for justice."

"You're a Christian woman. You have to forgive."

"I don't want to, but I forgive you for killing Ralph and his wife. But I don't forgive you for shooting his dog." She fired one shotgun blast into his chest and waited for the US Army to remove his body.

* * *

In Texas, the militia seized the capital, the city halls in every major city, and part of the largest fort.

President Reaves sent fighter jets and a massive army with hundreds of tanks into the state, but the militia didn't surrender.

Inside the Texas state capital, the militia leader held a conference call with his captains and said, "They won't use their tanks because they don't want to destroy the cities. They won't bomb our area of the fort because we have hostages. Their only recourse is to wait us out. But in keeping food and water supplies from entering the cities, the residents will also suffer. So, let's wait them out. As long as we keep the residents confined, the Army will allow food and water to enter. We have the upper hand. Texas is our state now. The first state of the new Reich.

"I want every Jew, nigger, spic, and slant eye in this state dead! Begin with the employees we captured. We don't need them any longer."

The militia led thirty-nine of the seventy-four employees captured at the capital onto the grounds to dig a mass grave. And when it was done, the employees were executed and tossed into the grave.

With the ethnicity and addresses of the residents, militia death squads in the state forced their way inside the targeted homes. Some were met with gunfire; others entered without resistance. Everyone inside the homes they entered was killed—from the youngest to the oldest.

With little resistance from the residents, the militia in Austin held the city and kept the US Army on the outskirts. But in Houston, Dallas, El Paso, and San Antonio, the militia were met with stiff resistance and were forced to retreat when they entered the Hispanic and black neighborhoods.

Pissed, the militia state leader replaced the leadership in those cities, but the new leaders suffered the same fate and were pushed into a corner by the US Army, who opened safe zones in every ward of those cities.

To lift morale, the militia state leader spoke to his soldiers on their radios. "We control five miles on each side of this capital. That means the Army cannot set up a safe zone within five miles, which means we are in control of those neighborhoods, which have more than 150,000 homes. If we average only two persons to a household, we have at least 300,000 hostages.

"The Army cannot roll in their tanks or drop any bombs without destroying homes and killing civilians. We are in control here. Unfortunately, it will take a while before we can get reinforcements from Louisiana, so we must hold on until then."

One of the team leaders said over the same frequency, "It's a good thing there are a lot of guns in Texas. We have confiscated enough to give every man and woman four extra assault rifles. We can fight twenty hours a day for three months before we run out of ammo."

Another team leader added over the radio, "There are still a lot of homes with non-Aryans in our perimeter. What are we going to do about them?"

The militia state leader said, "We can dangle some of them as hostages if need be, so don't kill them all yet. Enter two or three homes a day—and use a bullet as the last option to kill."

* * *

Inside the Austin home of a devout evangelical family, the father said, "We have to get to a safe zone."

"How? That's two miles with militia in every direction," the mother worryingly said.

The fourteen-year-old son said, "Dad is right. We can't stay here."

The seventeen-year-old daughter said, "We should stay here and wait for the Army. We'll get killed if we try to leave. They aren't harming white people who stay in the house."

Her brother said, "Brooke, we live in a wealthy neighborhood. It's only a matter of time before those men come here to pillage. What do you think they will do when they see you?"

"Nothing, because I look Aryan."

"They don't care about that. Most of them are criminals, released from prison to serve in the militia. They will rape you and probably Mom too. Dad is right. We need to get to a safe zone or die trying. We aren't safe here."

"Where are we going to go if the militia see us on the street? I don't want to die in the street," the mother said.

Her son said, "Better to die trying to escape than to sit and wait to die."

The father eyed his son. "Winston, your mother has a good point. Where are we going to go when we're out there and the militia are chasing us?"

"What happened to the faith that you and Mom were always preaching? I haven't lost my faith. I know Jesus will provide. He's already told me what to do."

His father curiously asked, "And what is that?"

"We can follow what the black people did."

"What did they do?"

"During the curfew, there were houses that only had the porch lights on. That meant the house was a hiding place if you were chased for violating the curfew. I'm sure they are still using that signal because black families need to get to a safe zone more than us."

"But we're not black," his mother said. "They won't accept us."

"Yes, they will. Black people aren't racist."

"How do you know?" Brooke questioned.

"I play basketball with them. I've been to their houses. I hadn't invited them here because I know you and our parents don't like black people."

"It's not that we don't like them," his mother said. "I know some are good, but most of them are delinquents. We don't want you to get mixed up with the wrong ones. It's best to stay away from them."

"Ma, are you listening to yourself? Do you realize what you are saying? That's a racist mentality and you don't even realize it."

His mother slapped him. "Don't raise your voice at me! And don't tell me what I don't realize!"

The father stood in-between. "Both of you stop! You're dividing the house, and a divided house cannot stand. Don't let the devil loose in this house!"

The son walked away and sat on the sofa.

Teary-eyed, his mother sat beside him and said, "I'm sorry," and hugged him.

"Let's go to bed," the father said. "We can talk about this in the morning."

* * *

Inside the Austin home of a Korean American couple, the wife said, "It's only a matter of time before they come to kill us. We need to try to escape."

"How are we going to get past them? They're covering all the streets."

"It's not enough of them to cover all the streets."

"It's enough of them to keep the Army from getting into the city. That means it's enough of them to keep us from getting out of the city."

"We are just going to sit here and wait for them to come and kill us?"

"They won't kill us. They need hostages."

"They need hostages, but they might not need us. You want to take that chance?"

"Yes, because it's the best chance we got."

The wife lifted her two-year-old child and carried her upstairs.

Two days later, in the middle of the night, the militiamen stormed the house, raped the wife, sodomized the husband, and murdered all three.

* * *

Inside the Austin home of two Chinese American senior citizens, the man yelled, "Hua, the news said government workers should report to work, and the grocery stores are open."

From the kitchen, Hua excitingly said, "Oh, good!"

"I'm going to Safeway."

"Qiang, bring back some tofu."

"Okay."

With pep in his step, Qiang was walking to his car parked on the street in front of his house when the neighbor across the street yelled, "Mister, where are you going?"

"To the grocery store," Qiang replied. "You want me to bring you something back?"

"Wait!" The neighbor sped down his porch steps and hustled across the street. "You can't go to Safeway or any store. They are still closed."

"No. The stores are open. I heard it on the news. The stores are open and government workers are to report to work."

"You heard it on RM News?"

"Yes."

"That's why you don't know what's truly happening. I used to watch that news religiously until I learned it was fake news. The stores are still closed. Schools are still closed. The only people working are those who work at the hospital and the police officers who patrol for the militia. You see all these parked cars. You think they don't need groceries? Most of the people in this neighborhood work for the local or federal government. None of them are going to work."

Seemingly confused, Qiang said, "Why is the news telling people the stores are open and to report to work?"

"Again, you're watching fake news. That station are pundits for the militia. They're telling government workers to report because they need them to do the administrative work. The militia has all of their hands on deck trying to keep the Army from advancing. They don't have the manpower to check all the files and send correspondence. They 're telling people the grocery stores are open so people like you, non-white, will come out in the open so they can kill you. They were going to the houses of Jews, blacks, Latinos, and Asians to kill them but don't have the manpower now because they need every man on the front line twenty-four seven. They are trying to make you come to them by saying the grocery stores are open and government workers should report to work."

"How do you know all this?"

"Because I was a member of the militia. I am a retired Marine and joined them because I thought Russia was trying to take over our country. But when they started shooting peaceful protesters, I left because that's not American. You and your wife should come and stay with me because the militia will come for you."

"Who are you?"

The neighbor extended his hand and said, "Carlson Holcomb. I've been living in this neighborhood for nineteen years."

"I see you many times, but you never speak. Why should I trust you now?"

"I'm telling you the truth. Turn on another news station and see for yourself. You know where I live. The invitation is open. But don't come running to my house when the militia is chasing you. I can't help you then."

"Why do I have to leave my house?"

"Because the militia is killing all non-white people, and they know your race and address because they have the city hall records."

"Why do you want to help me? I could tell you never liked me."

"True. I didn't like it when you and your wife moved into the neighborhood. But I don't hate you. You are a human being. Only God has the right to take your life. My duty is to stop others from trying."

Qiang's eyes reflected the confusion and indecision in his mind. "How did this happen? This is America."

"One of the human weaknesses is to take things for granted. This is what happens when you take democracy for granted. You don't realize what you have until you've lost it."

Qiang said, "I have to talk to my wife."

"Sure." Carlson pointed. "My house is right there. The door is open."

Qiang shook his hand, went back inside, and shouted, "Hua!"

"You're back already."

"Come here."

She stepped out of the kitchen and stood at the edge of the living room. "Yes, dear?"

"We've been lied to."

"What?"

"We've been lied to."

"Who lied to us?"

"The news."

He turned on a cable news station that he and his wife had never watched, and the anchor said, "Austin is the only major city in Texas where the militia hasn't been cornered. Schools and stores remain closed. The city is completely shut down. There are reports of death squads entering the homes of non-Aryans and killing even the infants.

"The militia leader in Austin is demanding food and water to be sent daily into the city, and then he will open the grocery stores. He is also ordering all local and federal government workers to report to work, but most are refusing.

"The Army has agreed to allow food, water, and medical supplies to enter the city in exchange for the release of hostages. But the militia leader's position is without conditions. More on that story later."

Qiang turned off the television and looked at his wife's watered eyes. "There isn't a Communist attack. They are trying to kill us. We have to get out of here."

"Where are we going to go?" his wife cried.

"The neighbor across the street has invited us to stay with him. Empty the fridge and freezer. I will empty the cabinets. We need to take all the supplies we can and leave as quick as we can."

Qiang and Hua carried all they could, which wasn't much, and went to Carlsons' home.

“Let me help you with that,” Carlson said and set the suitcases in the hallway and carried the bags of food into the kitchen.

Qiang said, “That’s all we could carry. We’re going back to get more.”

“I’ll go with you,” Carlson said. He looked at Qiang’s wife and said, “You stay here.”

They hurried across the street and returned with the remaining items.

“Thanks for bringing some extra supplies,” Carlson said, and introduced himself to Qiang’s wife.

When the sun went down, they had bonded in the friendship of longtime neighbors, a friendship that was tested two nights later.

* * *

Rapid knuckles in the midnight hour rattled Carlson’s door.

He whispered, “That’s the militia. Hide where I told you.”

Louder knocks followed.

Carlson shouted, “Who is it?”

“Militia, open up!”

He opened the door.

The team leader said, “We’re looking for the Asian couple across the street.”

Carlson sarcastically said, “Why aren’t you across the street?”

The team leader sneered. “Because we know they came here. Where are they?”

“They’re not here. You were given false information.”

“Can we come inside and check? Maybe you didn’t see them come inside.”

“Nothing is inside this house that I haven’t seen.”

“We’re coming in, move out of the way!”

Carlson yanked out his automatic pistol and pointed it at the team leader’s face. “Your team might get in here, but you won’t. If I were you, I would go back to where I came from and take your team with you. Nothing but death is waiting for you here. Are the persons you're looking for worth dying for?"

Carlson could see in the eyes of the team leader that he was considering, and whispered, "Walk away now. You won't lose honor with your men."

The team leader turned and led his men away.

Carlson watched until their vehicle drove off then closed the door. "Qiang and Hua, you can come out."

They stepped out from the back room and said, "Thank you!"

"We need to leave," Carlson said.

"Where will we go?" Qiang asked.

"The only place that's safe. We have to leave the city."

"But they left."

"They left but will be back. Most likely in the early morning. Grab some food and water. We leave in five minutes."

* * *

In the Austin home of El Salvadorian Americans, the family decided to try to get out of the city. With the moon as their guide, the mother, her adult son, and the grandmother were ducking behind cars and in-between houses to avoid detection by the militia and police patrols.

"How much further?" the grandmother asked in the nervous state of mind.

"Less than two miles," the son said. "Shhh." He whispered, "I hear voices. Get under a car."

Each one crawled under a car in the hope of not being seen. With their ears attuned to the slightest sound, they heard the voices turned in another direction. Seconds later, the son crawled out onto the sidewalk grass and said, "You can come out."

He helped pull his grandmother from under the car. She was trembling.

His mother lifted herself up on scared knees and tried to calm her mother.

After a few seconds, they continued down the dark and empty streets, paranoid of every sound, when they saw a slow-moving vehicle in the distance shining a spotlight and heading toward them.

"We got to go another way," the son frantically said and led them on a blind detour. Moving at a pace that his mother and grandmother could maintain, he said, "We need to find a house with the porch light on."

A few blocks later, his mother pointed and tiredly said in Spanish, "There's a house with the porch light on," and ran toward it.

"Nooo! Don't go there. We need a house with the porch light the only light on," he said in Spanish.

"Why?"

"Because those are the safe houses. That house is a trick to call the militia."

His grandmother was bent over and said in Spanish, "I can't go any further."

He looked around for a dark place to rest and led them behind a construction site dumpster. "We'll rest here," he said in Spanish.

In Spanish, his mother said, "I haven't seen a house that only has the porch light on."

"It's gotta be one around here somewhere," her son said in the same language. "This looks like a black neighborhood."

His mother said, "We want to be in a black neighborhood?"

"*Sí.*"

In her native language, his mother said, "We need to find our way back to our route."

"No, we need to find a safe house and try again tomorrow night."

After ten minutes of rest, they continued, with the son ignoring the complaints from his mother and grandmother about walking in a black neighborhood.

Their anxiety was enhanced by the sound of sirens in the distance, and their desperation to find a safe house grew.

"There's one," the son said in Spanish. "C'mon, run as fast as you can." He led the dash to the bottom steps of the house and waited for his mother and grandmother to catch up. Then led them up the steps onto the porch and impatiently knocked on the door.

The porch light was turned off, and the door opened with a teen voice that said, "Hurry!"

They sprinted inside, and the door seemed to close as quickly as it opened.

The son, mother, and grandmother stood in the darkness lit by white faces. "You look surprised to see us," the man said.

"We thought this was a black neighborhood," the son said.

"It is. This isn't our house. We were running from the patrols and saw the only light from this house was on the porch. My son told us this was a safe house, so I knocked but no one answered, then I tried the door and it opened. We looked around but no one was here. The house hasn't been ransacked. God must've put it in the heart of the person who lives here to provide this place for those in need. My name is Tolliver. This is my wife Lydia, my son Winston, and daughter Brooke."

The son said, "My name is Jose."

The mother said, "My name is Marie."

The grandmother said, "My name is Rosa."

Tolliver said, "Nice to meet you."

Lydia said, "Are you hungry or need water?"

They nodded, and said, "Thank you."

They sat in the house darkness, and Jose said, "Do you think the militia will become suspicious of houses that only have the porch light on?"

Tolliver said, "Maybe."

Winston interjected, "They think it's a sign for those in search of a safe place not to come."

"Why would they think that?" Jose asked.

"Because when they asked those arrested during the curfew what it meant, they told them that lie."

"How do you know that?" his father said.

"I told you my best friends are black. They not only made me a better basketball player, they also educated me about the streets." Winston shifted his eyes to Jose. "The best time to travel is between two a.m. and five a.m. The best route is through black neighborhoods because there are safe houses along the way." He shifted his eyes among the group and said, "I'm sure most of the blacks in this neighborhood have made it to the safe zone. It isn't that far away."

Tolliver faced Jose and said, "We're leaving at two. You are welcome to join us."

He looked at his mother and grandmother. "Do you want to go with them?"

"*Sí.*" Marie shifted her eyes to Tolliver. "We want to go with you."

"Good," he said. "You should get some rest. God willing, we'll be in the safe zone by sunrise."

* * *

Conrad, Qiang, and Hua were trekking toward leaving the city when they saw patrols ahead.

"Damn," Conrad said. "The way is blocked. We can't turn to Congress Avenue or 6th Street. We have to detour to the Negro district."

Qiang's brows furrowed. "We have to go there? They have criminals. They will kill us. Isn't there another way?"

"Not if we want to make it out before sunrise. I can protect us."

Qiang nervously said, "Why can't we go the way of Congress Avenue or 6th Street? It shorter and safer."

"Shorter, yes. Safer, no. Those are our main roads. The militia has a heavy presence there. We have to take Six Square if we want to make it to I-35 before sunrise."

Hua locked arms with her husband and said, "It'll be okay. I feel safe with him."

They followed Conrad into the black neighborhood, and along the way Qiang said, "Why some houses have porch lights and others don't?"

Conrad said, "If a house has a porch light on, it means if you go there, they will call the police."

Hua said, "I'm tired. Can we rest?"

"Not here! This black people neighborhood," Qiang said. "We need to get out first."

Conrad agreed but said, "We have another mile. We can rest then."

A mile and a quarter later, they found a wooded area and rested in the darkness of it with a distant view of I-35. Conrad pointed and said, "Three miles on that highway will take us to the safe zone."

"Let's go," Qiang enthusiastically said.

"No. We have to scout the area ahead to see if the way is clear. If it's blocked, we need to know how many are on patrol. You wait here. I'm going to scout the area. It's 3:13. If I'm not back in thirty minutes, I'm dead. Here, take this gun. You will need it if I don't come back."

"Don't come back? You have to come back."

"Take the gun."

Qiang took the automatic pistol.

"If I don't come back, stay here until you think the road is clear. You have enough supplies to last a few days."

Teary-eyed, Hua said, "You come back."

"I'm planning on it," and he darted under the cover of trees.

With an assault rifle in hand and a Poshland RAM-211 strapped on the side of his leg, Conrad stopped where the cover of trees ended. He looked around before he ran across the streetlight into another wooded area. He continued about thirty yards when he heard voices outside the wooded area. He ducked behind a bulky tree that held the recent odor of human feces and urine and saw seven people sitting detained on the sidewalk. Standing in front of them were three militiamen.

He said within, "Shit. I have to help them."

The night air carried the voice of a militiaman that said, "Let's shoot them. We don't need more hostages."

One of the other two said, "Wait." He stepped up to the auburn-haired girl who was crying, and said, "How old are you?"

With her head lowered, she muttered, "Seventeen."

"Mmmm, I love that age. What's your name?"

She didn't answer.

"Look at me!"

She lifted her head. Her eyes were red with tears rolling down her cheeks.

"What's your name!"

She reluctantly said, "Brooke," and lowered her head again.

He pointed. "Is that your mother, Brooke?"

Her head stayed lowered, and her mouth stayed closed.

"Bitch, look at me!"

She lifted her head.

He pointed again. "Is that your mother?"

"Y-yes."

"She's almost as pretty as you. Get up!"

Brooke stood with a trembling body.

Her brother yelled, "Leave her alone! I'll kill you if you touch her!"

The militiaman's eyes swung to the voice. "I take it that you're her brother."

"That's right! And I'm not scared of you!"

"I like that. You got more balls than your father." His eyes shifted. "He is your son, right?"

"He is."

"You should be proud of him." He looked at the mother and said, "Your son is a man, but your husband is a pussy. I'm gonna fuck you after I fuck your daughter."

"Leave me one," the third militiamen said.

"You can have that señorita over there. She's got a lot of miles on her but she's still running."

His eyes swung to the militiaman who wanted to shoot the prisoners. "Don't shoot anyone until I come back." His eyes shifted to Brooke. "If you make me happy, I won't fuck your mother, and I won't kill your family. Are you going to make me happy?"

She sniveled and nodded slowly.

Her brother shouted, "Don't do it, Brooke! You can't trust him! He will kill us anyway!"

"Shut that boy up!"

The third militiaman gagged him.

The second militiaman dragged Brooke into the woods a few feet away from where Conrad was hiding.

"Take off your clothes and get on your knees."

Sobbing heavier, Brooke slowly removed her blouse.

"Take off your bra."

She was unhooking her bra when Conrad came into her sight with his index finger pressed against his lips with eyes that said I'm here to help you.

The militiaman noticed her looking at something behind him, but before he could turn, Conrad had slit his throat.

Brooke was about to scream but Conrad quickly covered her mouth and whispered, "Shhh, be quiet. I didn't kill him to replace him. I'm here to help you and your family."

Brooke nodded with grateful eyes in a body mingled with shock and fear.

"I saw two more," Conrad whispered. "Are there any others?"

She shook her head.

"Good. Listen carefully, I need your help. If I use my gun or they use theirs, others will come. I have to get close enough to use my knife. I need you to lure them here."

She confusingly whispered, "How?"

He spoke in her ear, and she nodded.

With his mouth to her ear, he said, "I need to hear you say it. Can you do that?"

She nodded again and whispered, "Yes."

He whispered, "Good. Be strong. This will be over soon."

Dressed in only her panties, Brooke went to where she was dragged into the woods and made herself visible to the other militiamen. She yelled, "Your friend told me to tell you to tie the prisoners' feet and hands, and for you to come in here. He said if I have sex with all three of you, he will let my family go."

"Where is Trey?" the first militiaman shouted.

"He's taking a shit. He said you can go first."

The third militiaman said, "Damn! She looks like a doll. C'mon, let's hurry up."

The first militiaman said, "Tie their feet and hands. I'm going to see what's up with Trey."

Brooke waited until he got within five yards, turned, and walked a few feet past where Conrad was hiding.

With his gun pointed, the militiaman said, "Hold up, bitch! Where's Trey?"

Brooke stopped and turned. "Don't you want me to suck your cock before he comes back?"

"Bitch, where did he go?"

Those were the militiaman's last words.

Conrad slit his throat and dragged the body out of sight next to Trey.

A couple of minutes later, the third militiaman hurried into the woods and saw Brooke standing alone. With his rifle hung on his shoulder, he said, "Where are the others?"

The voice behind him said, "I'm gonna take you to them."

The militiaman reached for his rifle and turned into a knife that twisted in his belly.

"Put on your clothes. We got to move fast," Conrad said.

Brooke quickly put on her clothes and followed Conrad to the sidewalk.

The prisoners were bound and gagged, but their eyes reflected tears of joy.

When they were freed, the moment was filled with hugs and thanks to God and Conrad.

After introductions, Conrad said, "I have two people less than a mile back waiting for me. Get in the truck. I'll pick them up, and then we will ride to the interstate."

They hopped in the militia pickup truck and sped back to Qiang and Hua, and all ten headed for I-35.

When Conrad saw the city line checkpoint in the distance, he pulled over. Conrad said, "Tolliver, take the wheel. Winston, sit up front with your father." Conrad took the gun from Qiang and gave it to Jose. "Do you know how to use it?"

"Yes."

"Tolliver, when I say go, push the pedal to the floor and keep it there." He turned to Jose, who was with him in the bed of the truck. "I will cover the front," Conrad said. "You cover the back, and don't stop firing until you are out of bullets. Everyone else, pray and stay low."

Tolliver was driving ten miles above the speed limit when Conrad said, "Go!"

He opened fire on the militiaman standing at the front of the barricade.

Jose opened fire on the militiamen that pointed their weapons at the back of the truck.

What seemed like minutes ended in seconds, and the pickup truck was on the interstate with all passengers unharmed.

They sped down the highway, and when the safe zone came into view, Conrad said, "Pull over."

Tolliver said, "Why?"

"Pull over!"

He pulled over. "Why are we stopping?"

"Because we don't want to get accidentally killed. This is a marked militia vehicle. We'll walk the rest of the way."

They walked the quarter mile to the safe zone, entered, and found rest.

Chapter 20

In rural Mississippi, the mayor of the black town assembled an emergency meeting. "I called this meeting because I received notification that a band of militia fleeing Alabama is headed this way en route to Louisiana," the mayor said. "I'm sure they are looking for soft targets and will see us as one on their way to Baton Rouge. We need to prepare ourselves for an invasion. Is there anyone without a gun?"

One of the men in the meeting interjected, "Why wasn't this meeting called when the civil war started?"

The mayor looked at him with irritated eyes and said, "Who are you? I haven't seen you before."

"My name is Ezekiel. I'm from Mound Bayou in Bolivar County."

"You need to go back to Bolivar County. This is Jefferson County and a meeting for the residents in this town."

"I'm speaking for my grandmother who can't attend the meeting because she is confined to her bed with a stroke. That's why I'm here in Fayette, to be with my grandmother in her last days. You all know Ruth Williams."

Voices lifted with acknowledgment.

"She is famous throughout Mississippi for her cakes, pies, and cobblers. Folks in Mound Bayou would drive a hundred and sixty miles just to buy her cakes, pies, cobblers, and rice pudding.

"Since I been here, I asked a few people why there isn't a neighborhood watch group and was told it wasn't necessary because the local militia wouldn't attack this town. When I asked why, I was told that you made an agreement with them that made everyone in this town exempt from having to leave the country. When I asked about the agreement, no one knew. They were content because the militia hadn't attacked.

"I've been trying to meet with you to learn about the agreement made with the militia, but your office kept saying you weren't available. You're available now, so I'm sure everyone here would like to know the details of the agreement."

"This meeting isn't about the agreement. That's not important. What's important is we have a group of militiamen from another state headed this way with bad intentions."

"So where is the local militia? If they are protective of this town, they should be able to divert that group elsewhere. Why is the town under the threat of an invasion?"

"Mister, you are an outsider. You need to sit down and keep quiet. We have serious business to conduct here."

A woman interjected, "Mayor, the young man has a point. Why are we preparing for an invasion if the local militia is protecting this town?"

Others joined in and raised the same question.

The mayor said, "Calm down. Y'all letting this outsider get you all riled up. Haven't I kept us safe during this civil war? Aren't you able to go about your daily lives while other places in the country are under siege? We are safe because I made us safe. I'm telling you we need a plan to prepare for what might be an invasion. This group of militiamen are from another state. They might make war on the local militia. They might be more than the local militia. We need to be ready for whatever comes our way."

One of the longtime residents raised her hand.

"Yes, Althea, what is it?" the mayor said.

"Who told you the militia is headed this way?"

"The mayor of Prichard."

"That's outside Mobile."

"Yes," the mayor said. "His community and the residents in Africatown helped turn the militia away from Mobile."

Althea said, "Have you asked yourself why the militia on the run from Mobile is traveling north to go west?"

"Maybe they are hooking up with another group."

"Have you considered that group might be the militia from this county?"

The mayor held an expression that said he hadn't considered that.

Althea held stern eyes on the mayor and said, "What was your agreement with the militia?"

The others in the meeting echoed the question.

The mayor said, "I told the sheriff that Fayette and the other black dwellings wouldn't organize a neighborhood watch group if the local militia agreed not to bother us and make every black person in this county exempt from having to leave the country. He promised me that would happen."

Ezekiel interjected, "Of all the county sheriffs in Mississippi, you trusted the most racist. He won't honor his word. He only agreed to keep you from forming a neighborhood watch like in the other counties. He fears blacks with guns. You see what happened in Pritchard and Africatown. Now that you're vulnerable, they're coming to kill everyone here. If the sheriff was so protective of this town, why didn't he inform you the militia is coming this way? But now we have the upper hand because they don't know we know they're coming. So what's the plan?"

The mayor said, "That's why we're here—to make a plan. Any ideas?"

A hand raised and the mayor said, "Mr. Sykes, the floor is yours."

"How many in here have a gun?"

About three-fourths of the meeting raised their hands.

Mr. Sykes said, "How many have used a gun? By that I mean gone hunting or target practice."

Less than half raised their hands.

"How many have an extra gun that someone who doesn't have one can borrow?"

A few hands raised. A man that didn't raise his hand said, "I have a few extra guns, but I'm not willing to let someone who doesn't know how to shoot borrow it. That's wasting a gun and ammunition that I can use."

Mr. Sykes said, "Emery, a five-year-old knows how to pull the trigger. Those without experience need to be strategically placed where the enemy will be close enough that they can't miss. We need every person with a gun if we have enough guns. If not, those without guns can throw Molotov cocktails."

There were a few chuckles, and one of the chucklers said, "That's funny. They can get them drunk."

Mr. Sykes eyed that man and said, "A Molotov cocktail is an incendiary weapon. There are other weapons that can be used if you don't have a gun. Of course a knife is one, but also pepper spray, tactical flashlights, and a kubotan, to name a few. I was in the military for thirty years and learned a few things. How to make a bomb is one of them."

The chucklers were silent, with egg on their faces.

Mr. Sykes continued, "Like the brother said earlier, most likely the militia from Alabama is planning to meet the local militia and attack us. I'm expecting them to be the first wave of the invasion, because if the local militia was strong enough, they wouldn't need the Alabama militia.

"Even if they outnumber us significantly, we still have the advantage because they don't know the neighborhoods. There are several places where we can set-up ambushes. This is the hard part. We can expect children as young as twelve and seniors as old as ninety among the militia. You cannot hesitate to shoot, stab, or bomb them. If you do, you and others among us will die, because they will not hesitate to shoot you. They will not hesitate to kill your babies.

"Here is the easy part. Because this neighborhood was built to keep us confined, there is only one way in and out of town. We can expect them to come when they think we are asleep, so we need a few night watchers camping out unseen on the side of the road, about five miles outside of town. This job is perfect for those without a gun or feel they would freeze if they had to shoot.

"I have a set of walkie-talkies that I took when I left the Army. The range is ten miles. When the watchers see the militia, they will notify us on the walkie-talkie and let us know how fast they are moving. We will have at least five minutes to man the ambushes."

One person interjected, "Why not push the watchers back further than five miles since the range is ten. That will give us more time to get ready."

"We can't afford to take that chance. There might be something that will cause interference if it is more than five miles. We can test it after this meeting, but five miles is enough time. We need to sleep during the day so we can be awake all night."

The mayor said, "What are the ambushes?"

Mr. Sykes replied, "When the watchers inform us the militia is on the way, the person assigned to the rec center will turn on all the lights and blast the music with the blinds closed."

"What is the purpose of that?" the mayor asked.

"The road into the town leads directly to the rec center about a mile ahead downhill, which is a dead end. All the town lights will be out except for the center. They will see the rec lights and hear the music and think we are having a party. They will go directly there to catch us by surprise, but we will catch them by surprise because no one will be in the rec center. We will surround them in front of the center and open fire. And when they retreat, we will have a blockade in place to prevent their vehicles from leaving the way they came in. I'm not sure what we will use, but we will find something.

"The bottom line is that when they retreat, they will run into bullets because we will fire guns from behind the blockade. They will scatter, looking for a way out, but we have several dead-end streets. We need to remove the signs, so they won't know the street is a dead end and enter another ambush. Those with little or no gun experience will be at those dead ends because the militia will be close enough to shoot them without missing.

"A quarter mile out of town will be another group of watchers on both sides of the road, who will throw Molotov cocktails if any of the vehicles get through the blockade. We cannot take any prisoners. We have to kill every one of them—young and old, man and woman.

"The local militia will know what we have done and will not come this way. All we will have to do is wait for the National Guard and US Army to arrive."

Mr. Sykes pointed at the young man and said, "What's your name again?"

"Ezekiel."

He said, "I need Ezekiel and Althea to help me put this plan in motion."

* * *

Two days later, at 12:34 a.m., a voice over the walkie-talkie said, "They're on the way, moving slowly."

Mr. Sykes signaled the get-ready, and said over the walkie-talkie, "How many?"

"Looks like several hundred. The trucks are flying freedom flags and banners with a portrait of George Washington."

"Copy."

The caravan was moving about twenty-five miles an hour. When they came within a quarter mile of the town, they sped their vehicles into town at ninety miles an hour.

In the lead truck was the militia leader. He stopped the caravan when he heard the music and saw the lights from the building down the hill. "Let's crash the party!" he yelled. The vehicles sped to the rec center, emptied, and when they headed toward the building, bullets were unloaded in front and at the sides of them.

The militia fired back and scrambled for cover. The trucks in the back made a U-turn and headed back the way they entered, but the road was blocked by vehicles, furniture, and overturned grocery carts. Gunshots from behind the blockade scattered most of them from out of the trucks, and in a frenzy, they ran aimlessly in the unfamiliar town and entered dead ends that led to their actual deaths.

A kid ran into a pointed gun held by the mayor, who hesitated to shoot. *He's a child.* The mayor said, "How old are you?"

With a terrified expression, the boy said, "Nine."

The mayor lowered his gun, and the boy raised his and shot the mayor in the face.

Althea saw the boy shoot the mayor and shot the boy.

On the main street, a few of the trucks had barged through the barricade and sped out of town but were torched by the Molotov cocktails from the watchmen at the side of the road.

Every one of the militiamen that entered the town was killed—even those who surrendered.

The local militia heard about the slaughter and didn't go anywhere near the town.

And after the burial of the residents killed, Althea was elected the new mayor, Ezekiel had a girlfriend in town, and Mr. Sykes went back into seclusion.

The town had peace and waited for the arrival of the US troops, who had retaken every militia stronghold except for the city of Austin, a fourth of Fort Hood, and Gillette, Wyoming.

* * *

Inside Fort Hood, the general of the US troops said, "We can't wait any longer. We have to retake the Clear Creek Gate before tomorrow night."

The Colonel in the room said, "The hostages will not survive."

"They're soldiers. A good soldier dies for his country. They will be remembered as heroes."

"What about the civilian hostages?"

"Casualties of war. When we retake that section, we will crush the militia's morale in Austin and retake the state."

The general gave the order to bomb that section of Fort Hood and sent in the troops to complete the mission, which they did before the sun had set.

* * *

In Austin, the militia leader tried to keep up the morale of his men and said over their radios, "The Fourth Reich hasn't fallen. Fort Hood was a defeat, but what war has been won without a defeat? We control the capital of Texas, so Texas is still our land, and General Weiskopf is still alive.

"Don't believe the reports from this government. They are telling lies to keep up the morale of their troops. We are winning! If we weren't, we wouldn't be holding the state capital in our hand."

Those words seemed to uplift his men until a missile struck the state capital with the militia leader in it. The building was in complete ruin, and the militiamen that weren't killed in the explosion surrendered as US troops stormed the city behind tanks and armored vehicles.

That evening, President Reaves addressed the nation. "My fellow Americans, we are continuing to return our country back to its foundation of democracy. Yesterday, our troops regained complete control of Fort Hood, and today the city of Austin has been liberated. None of this could've been done without the patriotism of the American people, who fought back against the insurrectionists that defiled the great name of George Washington.

"I am calling on General Weiskopf and the remaining militia holdouts to surrender. The Fourth Reich has fallen and will never rise again in America. Lay down your arms. There is no need for any more bloodshed. It's time to atone for your treasonous actions. I am giving you forty-eight hours from midnight to surrender or face the might of the US Army and its citizens. Please do the right thing and lay down your weapons.

"God bless America, our troops, and our citizens."

Chapter 21

The news of the militia's defeats across the country, combined with the account of Fort Hood and Austin, had dwindled the militia to less than two hundred on the estate. Thirty of the remaining men and women were mercenaries hired by Shawn, and their quarters were inside the mansion.

Inside the bunker's meeting room were Shawn, Mr. Rudolph, General Weiskopf and his right-hand captain, the former chief of staff, former secretary of defense, former FBI director, and two of Shawn's mercenaries.

General Weiskopf said, "We are depleted. The only reason the Army hasn't come within five hundred miles of us is because of our threat to use the nuclear weapon. We can use that threat as the bargaining chip for safe transportation out of the country."

"They're not going to allow us to leave the country," Mr. Rudolph said. "They can just wait us out."

Shawn said, "We need an alternative. We can't use the nuke because it will destroy our future, and that is all we have left."

"Out of a hundred thousand militiamen that landed on this estate, we now have less than two hundred, including your mercenaries," the general said. "There is nothing standing in the way of the Army bombing or using a ground attack against us except for that nuclear weapon. If we are going to survive, we need to use that threat. That is the purpose of having the weapon—not to use it, but to have the threat of using it."

"How far will that threat get us before they call our bluff," Shawn said. "Rudy is right. They won't let us leave the country. They want us dead. Alive, we are a bigger threat than that nuke. The nuke can only change the look of a city. We can change the look of a country."

The former chief of staff said, "We have the private plane and airstrip. Let's go to Canada."

The former secretary of defense said, "The Army will blow the plane out of the sky."

Shawn said, "That's right. They will. But what if we're not on the plane but make them think we are. By the time they are able to identify the bodies, we'll be gone."

"Gone where?" Mr. Rudolph said.

"Most of the general's men are unknown faces. We can use the armbands to make it look like the citizens attacked us and we fled from them on the plane. In the chaos, the mercenaries can smuggle us off the estate grounds and take us to the CIA safe house. It's only fifteen miles away."

Mr. Rudolph said, "Two questions. How are we going to make it look like the citizens attacked us when the only citizens in this state with enough nerve are led by black cowboys? And how are we going to make the Army believe we are on the plane?"

"The general has at least ten blacks among his men. There are enough cowboy hats and boots in this house between my father, me, and Theodore to make them look like followers of John Clark. The citizens don't know we have a nuclear weapon. The Army will think that John Clark in his brashness attacked us.

"For the other question, the Army is monitoring our communication lines and spying on this place from the air. The general will communicate over the radio to his men that we are under attack and headed for the plane. There are enough men here to use as doubles if we put them in the right clothing. They will be on the plane instead of us. The pilot will radio to Canada that we are on board, and the Army will shoot the plane down. While the Army is busy watching the right hand, the left hand will smuggle us out."

The general said, "You want me to order my men to kill each other? I won't do that."

Shawn angrily said, "You won't do that?"

"No, I won't! Those men are patriots. I will not order them to kill each other so we can escape."

Shawn eyed one of the two mercenaries, and as if verbally told, the mercenary executed the general.

With his eyes shifted to the general's right-hand man, Shawn said, "Are there any more not willing to follow orders?"

The man held a blank expression.

Shawn told the two mercenaries to leave the soundproof room. When the door closed, his eyes shifted back to the general's right-hand man. "The general was due twenty million dollars in cash. It's yours if you follow my orders."

The man nodded.

Shawn said, "Make my plan happen tomorrow night around nine p.m."

The man nodded.

Mr. Rudolph said, "With the general dead, how will we make the Army believe the ground communication?"

"He will say the general was killed in the attack and that we are fleeing to Canada on the plane. They know he's the general's next in command. We have twenty-four hours to relax. Let's leave this bunker and get some fresh air."

* * *

In the basement residence, Mr. Jeffries whispered to Neri and Keisha, "I have to kill them. If I don't kill them, they will kill us. The coup is over and they know it, but out of spite they won't let us live."

Keisha whispered, "How can you kill all of them?"

Neri whispered, "I will help you kill them."

"No. I need you and Keisha to escape. I don't know how, but I will think of something."

The buzzer sounded. "That's probably April. I'll be right back. Keep the door locked."

Mr. Jeffries went upstairs, and April wasn't there. He went to her room on the next floor. The door was open, and he said, "Yes, Ms. April?"

She rudely said, "I need you to feed my children."

"Yes, Ms. April. But I advise you and the children to leave."

Her expression changed from rude to vile. "Whose side are you on?"

"I'm on the side of freedom and justice for all."

She looked at him as if he had offended her. "You're a smart aleck?"

"No, Ms. April, I'm not. I just told you whose side I'm on. You should be on the same side."

"Get out of here before I tell Theodore you tried to rape me."

Mr. Jeffries turned and left. *She's going to tell him that lie.* He went to his residence, got his gun, and said to Keisha and Neri, "If you hear a gunshot, hide and don't come out."

Keisha frantically said, "What's going on?"

Neri was crying, and Mr. Jeffries hugged her. "Everything will be alright. Just do what I said."

He went upstairs and made dinner for the children. And when he took the food to April's room, she and the children weren't there. He went back to the kitchen and waited with his hand on the concealed gun. *She must've gone into the bunker.*

While waiting, he played the cassette *Pharoah Sanders live in Paris 1975*, and the song "Farrell Tune" mellowed his thoughts. It no longer mattered if April told Theodore the lie. Mr. Jeffries was going to shoot Shawn and Theodore as soon as he saw them. He was ready to die to save Keisha and Neri.

Five minutes into the song there was an outburst of gunfire that didn't cease. Mr. Jeffries ducked under the table as the sound of bullets shattering glass and penetrating walls covered his ears.

A wounded mercenary fell on the kitchen floor with blood leaking down the corner of his mouth. His eyes told the story his mouth couldn't.

As the gunfire continued, one of the mercenaries shouted, "The militia is attacking!"

"They have turned on each other," Mr. Jeffries said within as rapid gunfire from inside and outside the mansion continued.

He crawled into a space that was free from stray bullets and heard the footsteps of mercenaries running up from the bunker. *I'm sure Shawn is down there. If not, he will be soon. I need to get inside that bunker. The door is probably open.*

Mr. Jeffries waited until there was a lapse in the gunfire and ran downstairs to the bunker. The door was open, and he entered the surprisingly large area. "Wow. I didn't think it was this big." He kept straight, not knowing if anyone was down there, and didn't open the closed doors on each side.

The first open door had the stuff he had seen in the secret room. *Ah, they moved it here.* In the next open room were April's kids sleeping on a queen size bed in a furnished room that had a television and bathroom.

The last door was straight ahead about fifty feet from where the kids were sleeping. *That room is Shawn's. I can feel it.* He leaned his ear against the door and heard nothing. His indecisiveness ended when he heard voices outside the bunker. He quickly entered, scanned for a place to hide, and stepped into a closet space where coats were hung. Peeking through the cracks between coats, he saw Shawn and Mr. Rudolph enter the room.

Shawn was distraught with tears in his eyes, and wailed, "My brother and sister are dead!"

Mr. Rudolph tried to console him, but Shawn was in a frenzy and said, "I'm going to kill him! I want that motherfucker captured alive! You hear me! Tell them to bring him to me alive!"

"They know you want him alive," Mr. Rudolph said. "Your chief of staff, secretary of defense, and FBI director were also killed. You shouldn't've killed the general in front of him. His loyalty to the general is worth more than twenty million dollars."

"You speak like you knew that before we left the room. If you did, why didn't you say something?"

"I didn't know it then, but I wouldn't've trusted him."

"I didn't trust him. I was going to kill him after he made the communication. Now my brother and sister are dead, and I can't bury them. We have to leave tonight. Is the pilot still alive?"

"There are five mercenaries guarding the plane. I'm sure he's still alive."

"I'm sure the Army's spy planes and satellites have detected the shootout. The plane will be empty, but they don't know that. They will believe we are on it when the pilot radios Canada that we are on board. Tell Keith we need to be smuggled out tonight."

"What are you going to do with Mr. Jeffries and that black girl?"

"Shoot them, and put cowboy boots and a cowboy hat on them and any militia that were killed out of the sight of the spy plane. We need to be ready to move when the plane takes off."

Mr. Jeffries watched Mr. Rudolph leave the room. He stared at Shawn with death in his eyes until he felt Mr. Rudolph had left the bunker, then revealed himself.

"How did you get in here?" Shawn bossily said. "What are you going to do with that gun? You're not man enough to shoot me?"

Mr. Jeffries pointed the gun and cocked it.

"You think killing me will end this? It won't. You can kill me, but you can't kill the ideology. It will live on—and with it I will live on. It will give birth to me in a new body and a new face. It might take forty years, but I will come back." He scornfully laughed.

With hate-filled eyes, Mr. Jeffries said, "If I'm alive in forty years, I will kill you again." He fired two shots into Shawn's chest and quickly turned with the gun pointed at the door.

He waited for the door to open. The seconds became minutes, but he kept his eyes on the door.

Mr. Rudolph rushed in with a mouth that was saying, "I can't find Mr. Jeffries and that girl," when an unpleasant surprise took hold of his face. Shawn lay in a puddle of blood, and Mr. Jeffries was pointing the gun at him.

"Wait!" Mr. Rudolph said with raised hands.

"Wait for what?" Mr. Jeffries said. "The time is now." He fired two shots into Mr. Rudolph's chest and sat on the bed, anticipating the mercenaries to enter and kill him.

After a few minutes, two of them entered with guns pointed after seeing Mr. Rudolph dead in front of the door.

Mr. Jeffries no longer had the gun in hand. He looked at the mercenaries and said, "I killed them. And if I'm alive in forty years, I'll kill them again."

The two mercenaries lowered their weapons and left the room.

Mr. Jeffries sat there, thinking about the journey that had brought him to this moment, when a thought surfaced. *There's money in this room. You don't live in a bunker without bringing money with you.*

He started to search but stopped. *I need to get Keisha and Neri.* He put the gun in his pocket and moved Mr. Rudolph's body from in front of the door. When he left the room, he saw April's kids awake, seemingly wondering where their mother was, and led them out of the bunker to his residence.

Sporadic gunfire was heard in the distance. *That sounds like it's coming from the airstrip.*

When he reached his residence, the door was hanging off the hinges, and he shouted, "Keisha, Neri!"

They quickly came out from hiding under the clothes in the hamper with relief written across their faces. They hugged him. Keisha said, "They came looking for us. We thought you were dead."

"I know. We'll talk about it later. We need to get inside the bunker."

Keisha and Neri took hold of the kids and followed the hurried footsteps that led them into the bunker.

Mr. Jeffries quickly locked the bunker's entrance. And with his gun pointed, opened the doors he hadn't touched and saw the rooms were empty.

Mr. Jeffries pointed with his nose, "Neri, babysit the kids in that room. Me and Keisha need to search for something." He closed the door when Neri and the kids entered.

Keisha said, "What are we looking for?"

"We're going into Shawn's room. Don't be alarmed. He's dead—I killed him. There's another man in there that I also killed. We're looking for money. I believe a lot of money is somewhere in that room."

He opened the door and Keisha gasped at the sight of Shawn then the other man.

"I don't think it's hidden in a secret compartment," Mr. Jeffries said. "It's probably in one of these closets."

Keisha found a stack of duffel bags in the closet of coats and opened one, "I found it!" she screamed and opened the others as Mr. Jeffries joined.

"How much is here?" she excitedly asked.

"Maybe twenty million."

"T-twenty m-million d-dollars?"

"Maybe more. We don't have time to count it."

"What are we going to do with it?"

"We're going to keep it. But we can't keep it here."

"What are we going to do? I haven't opened all of them, but I counted fifty bags."

"I'm pretty sure the Army is on their way here. This money can't be here when they arrive."

"What are we going to do?"

"The mercenaries and the militia were fighting. I'm sure there are plenty of dead bodies on the grounds."

"Are they still outside?" Keisha worryingly asked.

"I heard the last gunshots at the airstrip. I don't think they are coming back this way. We need to get these bags outside and into one of those trucks and take it to the Indian reservation. Time is of the essence, so let's hurry. I'll get the supply wagon. You and Neri tell the kids they are playing a game and blindfold them before you take them upstairs and outside to find a truck that has the keys in it. Tell Neri to stay with the kids, and you come back and help me load the bags on the wagon. It's probably gonna take about six or seven trips."

Keisha and Neri had stunned faces as they led the blindfolded children around the dead bodies that lay in the mansion and past the dead outside that included the children's mother and Theodore.

Neri was singing to the kids while Keisha searched for a truck that had the key. When she found the truck and drove to the front of the mansion, she said to Neri, "I didn't know you could sing. You have a beautiful voice."

"Thank you."

"Take the kids into the truck. I have to go back and help Mekhi."

It took an hour for Mr. Jeffries and Keisha to transport all the bags from the bunker, out of the house, and onto the M35 military truck.

Neri curiously asked, "What's in those bags?"

"Money," Keisha said. "Lots of money."

"Our money?" Neri excitedly asked.

Mr. Jeffries replied, "Ours and those who need it, if we keep it secret."

* * *

Mr. Jeffries was driving past the airstrip when General Weiskopf's right-hand man and several of his men opened fire on the truck.

Keisha was hollering. One of the bullets had struck her.

Neri was in a panic, and the blindfolded kids were crying.

Mr. Jeffries was dividing his attention between the road and Keisha and continued to speed, with periodic glances in the rear-view mirror, relieved each time there was nothing seen.

With anxiety spilling from his eyes he said, "Neri, keep pressure on the wound! We can't stop."

When they arrived at the Indian reservation, Mr. Jeffries looked at Keisha's wound and said within "It's really bad." With hope in his eyes he looked into Keisha's frightened eyes and said, "Stay calm. It's not that bad." When his eyes lifted to Neri, she felt his true feelings and her watered eyes leaked. "Stay here and keep her and the kids calm. I'll be right back."

He scampered into the secret tunnel and came back with the chief, Aponi, and one of the Jews who was a doctor. At the tunnel entrance, Neri removed the kids' blindfolds and Aponi led them into the tunnel.

While the doctor was tending to Keisha inside the truck, Mr. Jeffries led the chief about twenty yards away and said, "I killed Shawn. His brother and the kids' mother are dead. Those bags in the back of the truck are filled with money. I need to hide that money before the Army arrives."

"You can hide it in the tunnel."

"No. Too many eyes will see it. Also, the tunnel will no longer be a secret when the Army arrives."

"I have a place in the burial grounds. We can put it in the ground there."

"We have to dig a grave?" Mr. Jeffries uncomfortably asked.

"No, there is a vacant grave where we hide our valuables to keep the white man from stealing it."

"Perfect."

* * *

When the doctor had temporarily bandaged Keisha, Mr. Jeffries and the chief slowly dragged her into the tunnel where unlicensed Indian doctors assisted with the care.

Then Mr. Jeffries and the chief returned to the truck and drove the quarter mile to the Indian burial ground, where they stashed the bags.

The next day, the Army swarmed the Gillette estate, securing the nuclear and chemical weapons, removing the tanks and artillery and the dead.

Senator Rainey came to the Indian reservation with a Colonel and his troops to help the Jews return to normalcy and promised the chief that the state would rebuild the reservation.

The Colonel confiscated the M35 truck. His medical vehicle transported Keisha to the hospital, and Senator Rainey took April's kids to Summer's location.

When they left, Neri sauntered up to Mr. Jeffries, her head tilted in a smile. "You told me to tell you when this was over if I still feel the same. I still feel the same."

He looked at her straight-faced, then smiled.

* * *

On New Year's Eve, 1984, more than three years after the fall of the Fourth Reich, Summer had adopted April's children.

The Indian reservation was rebuilt, and two duffel bags were in the grave.

Keisha had won a Grammy for song of the year and still had four of her five bags untouched.

Neri had won a Grammy for record and album of the year and hadn't spent a penny of the five bags in her possession.

Speaker of the House Mr. Jefferson was elected president, and Senator Rainey was the vice president.

Ruby Thomas had anonymously received three duffel bags.

The postal workers received the promise from Mr. Rosenberg.

Mr. Jeffries was a philanthropist who had opened trade schools for teens in the inner cities and provided start-up grants for small black businesses. He anonymously sent tens of thousands to hundreds of charitable foundations that worked with at-risk youth, family strengthening, financial literacy, and the black college fund, among others. He had two of his five duffel bags untouched.

Devin was the CEO of a charitable foundation established by his brother.

William had turned his investigation into a book of fiction to protect Summer's remaining family name. The book was number one on the bestseller list for two-hundred weeks. The movie based on the book set a box-office record. He was also married to Sandra and the father of two boys.

His mother didn't leave Harrisburg but moved to the southwest part of the city. She hosted the New Year's Eve party that her son Devin and his wife, William and his wife, Summer and her fiancé, Keisha and her boyfriend, Mekhi and Neri attended.

www.ingramcontent.com/pod-product-compliance
Lightning Source LLC
Chambersburg PA
CBHW070552310726
48982CB00011B/1561/J